THE LITTLE OLD LADY
STRIKES BACK

Catharina Ingelman-Sundberg is the Swedish author
of the internationally bestselling *The Little Old Lady
Who Broke All the Rules*, *The Little Old Lady Who Struck
Lucky Again!* and *The Little Old Lady Behaving Badly.*
After pursuing a career in journalism and a stint as a marine
archaeologist, Catharina turned her hand to writing fiction.
Her books have been translated into thirty languages and
have sold over two million copies internationally. Catharina
lives outside Stockholm, in Sweden, and writes from a
log cabin in her garden.

To find about more visit her website,
www.catharinaingelman-sundberg.com

Also by Catharina Ingelman-Sundberg

The Little Old Lady Who Broke All the Rules
The Little Old Lady Who Struck Lucky Again!
The Little Old Lady Behaving Badly

THE LITTLE OLD LADY STRIKES BACK

CATHARINA INGELMAN-SUNDBERG

Translated from the Swedish by Rod Bradbury

PAN BOOKS

First published in 2020 under the title *Goda rån är dyra* by
Bokförlaget Forum, Stockholm, Sweden

First published 2023 by Pan Books
an imprint of Pan Macmillan
The Smithson, 6 Briset Street, London EC1M 5NR
EU representative: Macmillan Publishers Ireland Limited, 1st Floor,
The Liffey Trust Centre, 117–126 Sheriff Street Upper,
Dublin 1, D01 YC43
Associated companies throughout the world
www.panmacmillan.com

ISBN 978-1-0350-0556-7

1 3 5 7 9 8 6 4 2

A CIP catalogue record for this book is available from the British Library.

Typeset by Palimpsest Book Production Ltd, Falkirk, Stirlingshire
Printed and bound by CPI Group (UK) Ltd, Croydon, CR0 4YY

Visit **www.panmacmillan.com** to read more about all our books
and to buy them. You will also find features, author interviews and
news of any author events, and you can sign up for e-newsletters
so that you're always first to hear about our new releases.

To my brother, Henrik Ingelman-Sundberg,
who has read, encouraged and supported me.
My warmest thanks!

Prologue

It was a perfectly ordinary afternoon. But perhaps not entirely so . . .

Martha Andersson turned into Nybrogatan and inhaled deeply. Here, at the Stockholm Auktionsverk, they would be auctioning jewellery to a value of seventy million kronor, a sum of money that ought to be enough for many poor pensioners. She looked around. The wind was cold, and she shivered. Elderly well-dressed ladies with little dogs on a lead and men wearing hats walked past, while youths with earbuds and mobile phones rushed by and looked as if they were being chased. She checked her wig and nodded discreetly to her friends. It was now time to strike.

Nobody noticed the five pensioners who approached the auction house in a slow and dignified manner. Three elderly ladies in fashionable furs, and two gentlemen of similarly mature years wearing elegant camel-hair overcoats, went up to the windows and looked in. Some workmen were busy drilling, while stressed auction-house employees were running between opened cartons and the exhibition halls. The staff were occupied with setting up objects and hanging paintings to be ready for the imminent classic auction, and they were totally engrossed in their work.

The last-minute rush before a viewing was the same as it always was, and Martha was ready. She had a hat with a hatpin and was disguised, as were her friends. Brains was almost unrecognizable and his big overcoat had wide pockets. Inside them were a bag of gypsum, two plastic bags and a Thermos flask filled with water. He was walking with a slight limp, since unfortunately he had one leg in plaster right up to his hip – with an extra-large space at the top. Because how else could he hide his battery-driven drill? Martha, for her part, had her plastered arm in a sling. The members of the League of Pensioners quickly glanced through the windows and crossed over to the other side of the street. From here they had a clear view of the outer door. Now all they had to do was wait.

The gang kept a discreet watch on the entrance, and it wasn't long before one of the auction-house company vans drove up, parked outside the premises and the driver got out. When he opened the back doors and lifted out two boxes, Martha gave the signal. This was what they had been waiting for.

'OK, time to get going!' she told them, whereupon Brains pulled out the bag of gypsum, uncrewed the top of the Thermos and emptied the white powder into the water. He shook the flask and poured out the porridge-like plaster mix into the two plastic bags. Martha took one of them and put it inside her arm sling, while he put the other one in the wide space beside his hip. The countdown had begun. Now they only had five to ten minutes before the plaster set. Martha glanced up at the auction-house door and couldn't help smiling. Just as they had expected, the driver had left the door open so that he could carry in the boxes. When he turned his back, the gang hurried across the street. Martha and Brains crept into the auction house, while the others stayed out on the pavement to keep watch.

As soon as Martha and Brains had got inside, they went directly to the jewellery department where the display cabinet with the Russian earrings was situated. The building workers were drilling holes for the electric wiring in the adjacent room, and the spotlight above the display cabinet hadn't yet been installed – but that didn't matter. The famous blue-and-pink diamond earrings were already lying on their black velvet cloth ready for the weekend viewing. Martha gave Brains a nudge in his side.

'Now!'

'Yeah, damn it, one drill more or less . . .' muttered Brains, and drew his power drill from his hip as fast as if it had been a pistol. And while the building workers were busy with their drilling, he used a hole-saw attachment to make an opening in the side of the cabinet, with Martha acting as cover as best she could. Then, when he had got through the wall, he pried out the plug and made room for Martha.

With the speed of a weasel, she stuck her fingers into the hole, got hold of the earrings and carefully slipped them out, after which she let them drop into her plastered arm in which lay the plastic bag with the ready-mixed plaster. With her sharp hatpin, she punctured the bag and let the white mixture ooze over the jewels until these were no longer visible. Meanwhile, Brains put the plug back in the hole in the cabinet, rubbed some dark-brown pigment powder around the edges and put his drill back in its place by his hip. Then he punctured

3

his own plastic bag and the loose, ready-mixed plaster slowly spread over his power drill until it was completely covered. Brains and Martha looked at one another. A few more minutes and the plaster would have set. Then nobody should be able to find anything.

'Stop there! You're not allowed in here!' a stern voice behind them suddenly proclaimed, and Martha twisted round. An employee in a white coat was waving her arms in irritation.

'Oh, goodness me,' said Martha, giving the woman her most ingratiating smile while fishing out the auction house's autumn programme from her pocket. She read aloud: '"*Classic auction opens on Saturday the third of December . . .*" That's right, isn't it?'

'Yes, but today is Friday, so if you would be so kind as to –' The woman lifted her hand to direct them towards the exit.

'Oh, I'm so sorry! Tut, tut, I'm always getting the day wrong! It isn't always so easy to see that it's closed when you can walk straight in. But no problem, we'll come back tomorrow,' said Martha courteously, linking arms with Brains and walking towards the door. But just as they were about to step out onto the pavement, police sirens could be heard and a police car came to a sudden halt right in front of them. Two police officers with protective helmets and batons jumped out.

'Bloody hell, they must have had a silent alarm . . .' Brains muttered, as he felt a snare being pulled around his neck. Martha saw how scared he had become, and squeezed his hand.

'Prevention is better than a cure, we'll manage this,' she said, and walked up to the uniformed police with a smile on her face.

'We just came out of the exhibition halls, so perhaps you'd like to search me and my bag before I move on?' said Martha, waving her arm in its sling and opening the front of her mink coat to show her belt bag. At the same time, Brains held his hands up over his head as if he had been threatened with a gun. But the police officer just waved them away.

'Get out of the way! We must get in. The alarm has gone off!'

In the Kungsholmen residential district in the centre of Stockholm, spirits were high in the five-room flat where the League of Pensioners lived. There was plenty of jolly giggling while Martha and Brains relieved themselves of the plaster casts. But before they did that, everybody had to sign their name in different colours on the white surface and they also added happy emojis, hearts and other fun things. And while Rake, the gang's oldest member at eighty-two years old, busied himself chipping away with his hammer and chisel, applauded by the gang after each blow, they simultaneously sang, 'Happy Birthday to us . . .' in harmony. Then they switched to 'You broke my heart' – but they changed 'heart' to 'cast'. So, while they sang 'You broke my cast' and clapped their hands, Rake chipped away until the diamonds fell onto the floor. Then the singing stopped abruptly and they all bent down to inspect the booty.

'Woooow,' could be heard from the hardened criminals because they had never before seen anything so beautiful. The diamonds glistened and glowed in the light from the lamp, and when they held up the riches, cascades of light like fireworks danced on the cut facets.

'To think that these earrings have ended up in Sweden. In New York they would have sold for at least eighty or ninety million kronor,' said Anna-Greta, their bank man and the one who always counted money. 'It would be best if we sell them there.'

'Yes, for sure, but first we must hide them,' Martha – the hearty leader of The League of Pensioners – said as she stroked the rare stones with her forefinger. 'Or what do you think, Christina?'

Christina, approaching eighty, was the great humanist as well as being artistically gifted. Besides her literary knowledge, her watercolours were of the highest standard. She could paint in oils too, and now and then had tried her hand at making sculptures. While the others waited, she went into the wardrobe and fetched her latest work of art, *David and Venus*, a piece of sculpture that depicted the two figures standing holding hands on a pedestal. David was a table copy of Michelangelo's well-known statue in Florence, and Venus a reproduction of the plump, world-famous 25,000-year-old Venus sculpture from Willendorf in Austria.

'Here's our hiding place,' she said, greatly satisfied with herself. 'But where shall we insert the earrings?'

'We can hide them in David's hair,' Anna-Greta suggested. 'No – what about – yes, I know,' she corrected herself and looked sly. 'Why not insert the millions in that hair a bit further down. Surely nobody looks there.'

'Anna-Greta, you should be ashamed of yourself!' protested Christina, who was brought up in Jönköping in the Swedish bible belt and now looked absolutely horrified.

'But couldn't we drill through the plinth from below, put

the earrings there and then fill the hole with plaster?' Martha proposed.

'Far too simple. Venus is a goddess of fertility, isn't she? Well, then, let me fix this,' said Rake. And since he had had such a minor role in the actual theft, Martha thought it best that he got to decide. Pleased as punch, he now borrowed Brains's power drill and drilled two holes in Christina's sculpture, mixed some new plaster and inserted the earrings where he thought they fitted best. One in each breast. With this, not only was Christina's Venus a plump goddess of fertility, but she also had a precious bosom.

When Rake had finished the plastering, they all toasted with champagne, and Christina composed some poetry about precious bosoms and bosom friends. Then they all realized that they had become far too silly and that it was time for bed. With that, the League of Pensioners' coup was complete and the booty hidden. Now all they had to do was keep out of the way of the police.

1

It was snowing and drifts were building up on the road in front of them. Damnation, they simply mustn't end up in the ditch now. Why hadn't the road been ploughed? You could hardly make any headway. Martha changed to a lower gear and peered through the windscreen. Abandoned farmhouses, dilapidated barns and endless forest. They ought to get there soon. The property that they had just purchased was supposed to be close to the main road going through the little village, a two-storey timber building with transomed and mullioned windows, a veranda, a workshop and three outhouses in the yard. It was the sort of graceful building that nowadays you only found out in the countryside. And what was best of all: it had once been a local bank branch and that gave familiar vibes for a gang of bank-robber pensioners. Martha had already decided on a name for the house: The Vault.

The house and all the outhouses and the large plot of land had been purchased by the League of Pensioners for a sum that wouldn't even have bought a tiny one-room flat in the centre of Stockholm. But nowhere else would you find such beauty and such calm as in this sort of Swedish rural district.

People must be crazy nowadays. Why were they all moving into the big cities?

'Are we really safe here? What if the police find us?' Christina's piteous voice could be heard from the back seat. She was the member of the gang who worried most, and since she had once dreamed of becoming a librarian, she read lots of books – unfortunately, far too many of them were crime novels. And they made her so dreadfully frightened. She wiped the mist from the window and looked out. Forest and more forest. What was she doing out here among all the trees? Was it just because they had to keep out of the way of the police? She, who wanted to buy beautiful clothes, put on make-up and feel attractive. What was the point of looking your best for an old gnarled pine tree?

'Out here in the sticks there aren't any cops at all, Christina dear. The only ones who pretend to be here are those police we see on TV,' Rake, Christina's partner, consoled her. 'And don't worry. It is unlikely that there will be more police in the next few years.'

'Exactly, everything's all right!' Martha agreed.

'But the police are after us. If only you hadn't said they were welcome to search you. Why did you do that?' Anna-Greta wondered.

'Somebody who voluntarily helps the police isn't a criminal, is what I thought. And the police fell for it,' Martha mumbled with her hands firmly gripping the steering wheel.

'But they saw the belt bag!'

'Pah, there must be lots of fashion-conscious elderly ladies in Östermalm who go around with those nowadays. It is modern again.'

'But the belt bag was included in the description issued by the police, and now we've ended up here.'

Anna-Greta grunted her dissatisfaction, upset because the gang had been forced to move house yet again. It had been so nice where they lived in Stockholm, and what were they going to do now out in the countryside? But some pensioners and an elderly lady with a belt bag had been seen in the vicinity of the auction house, and the police were looking for them. They had had no choice but to move out of the city.

'We'll keep a low profile for a while. Everything will sort itself out,' Martha reassured them. 'By the way, how's it going with the sculpture, Christina?'

'David and Venus are doing fine. I think it is one of my best pieces.'

'Yes, but I was thinking about the earrings . . .'

'I reckon they're hanging nicely where they are,' said Rake.

And then they all giggled and it was calm in the minibus again.

Martha and her friends were thus obliged to hide away for a while, because they didn't have time to sit behind bars. When society no longer provided adequate health care, schools and decent social services, the gang had to finance this themselves, by stealing and giving money to the poor. And nowadays, too, there were lots of people who had worked all their lives but couldn't survive on their pension; in such a situation the League of Pensioners couldn't sit back and relax. So, in recent years, Martha and her gang had been carrying out robberies as a sort of older – but slightly less mobile – variant of Robin Hood and they had done their best to hand out the booty to people in need. But now they needed to get hold of more money and it was irritating to be forced into passivity. Besides, all of them ought to have something sensible to occupy themselves with so as not to age prematurely.

Martha had thought about this. Perhaps they could do good works in different ways? She had noticed the abandoned farmhouses and several deserted villages. Surely one could do something about that? But while driving up to the village of Hemmavid she had had a new idea – even though she hadn't yet dared to tell the others about it . . .

'We've arrived!' she exclaimed with relief when finally she caught sight of the Hemmavid sign. The snow had eased up a bit, and they had been able to see where they were going. She looked at her watch: it was almost five in the afternoon. That was perfect, they'd have time to fill the minibus with petrol and buy some food. Then they could enjoy their first meal in their new home. To be on the safe side, they had bought the property furnished. At their age you didn't have the energy to run around and buy bargains at IKEA, let alone assemble the bits of furniture with those tiny hex keys and fiddly screws. No, Martha and her friends had come to an agreement with the former owner to take over the property, and all its contents, in its existing condition.

'There's the petrol station!' Brains, Martha's fellow villain at the auction house, pointed at some petrol pumps a bit further on.

'That's perfect,' proclaimed Christina, who had learned a lot from all the crime fiction she had read. 'If you're a crook, you must always have a full tank of fuel in your car.'

'Talking about a full tank, I'm running out of fuel myself so

I think we ought to eat first,' said Anna-Greta, who was tired as well as hungry. For the time being she was also suffering from a broken heart, and she consoled herself by eating too much. Her relationship with the retired detective Ernst Blomberg had come to an end, and she still hadn't got over that. First, he hadn't let on that he was a private detective and a former police detective, then he had embezzled some of the proceeds of the robberies that the League of Pensioners had worked so hard to carry out, then he had done a runner. He had quite simply been a con-man. Anna-Greta felt heartbroken and stuffed herself with sweets. In the last months she had put on seven kilos.

'We can buy some sweets and cakes and other tasty things, make a lovely dinner when we arrive, and then we'll have a nice tart for dessert. Oh look, there's a shop,' she said, pointing towards a sun-bleached *FOOD – OPEN* sign that was visible next to the petrol station. Her tummy was rumbling.

'Lovely!' the others exclaimed, and since they hadn't eaten since lunch, they suggested everything from hamburgers and something ready-roasted to shellfish and salads. They talked loudly and made such an intense noise that even Martha began to feel hungry. She drove up to the Q8 station, skidded in the slushy snow, but managed to come to a halt. Then she got out of the minibus to fill the tank. And that was when she saw it. The petrol station was closed. But perhaps they had another pump that you could use a bank card with? She walked round the back of the building – but there was nothing. The station wasn't just closed, it had shut down for good! That must have happened fairly recently because there were still posters and messages on the noticeboard outside the station. Cursing to herself, she returned to the others.

'The whole place has shut down! So where shall we go now?'

'Pah, let's eat first; we can get some petrol tomorrow,' Anna-Greta insisted with such a loud voice that they all gave a start. She always talked too loudly when she wasn't using her hearing aid – but she didn't want to have it on in the car, so there wasn't much they could do about that.

The *FOOD – OPEN* shop was a bit further along the road, so Martha started the minibus and drove up to the parking space in front of it. While the others took their time in the back, she got out of the minibus again, opened the big back door and pulled out her wheelie shopping bag. It struck her how quiet and deserted it was around them. Next to the shop lay an old bicycle and a Volvo estate car covered in snow, but there was nobody in sight. And when she came closer, she suddenly realized: the shop was closed. But goodness gracious! What were they going to do now? The opening hours would certainly be displayed on the door, so Martha bent down and discovered a handwritten note:

Our village shop has closed down. We would like to thank all our customers over the years. Malin and Lilian.

Martha felt the door handle. Yes, it was closed, definitely extremely closed. She remained standing there. What had she gone and done? Taken the entire League of Pensioners to a place where you couldn't buy food or petrol. It hadn't been like that in the countryside just a few years ago. What had happened? Worried, she returned to the others and got into the minibus.

'It's shut. The shop has closed down,' she said.

'Didn't I say that we shouldn't do any more robberies?' Brains muttered. 'Then we could have stayed at Diamond House and wouldn't have ended up here.'

'And I didn't want to commit any more crimes either. We were having such a nice time with our courses, jazz evenings and all the activities there. Diamond House is the best sheltered housing for seniors in Stockholm, and we created it ourselves too! And now we're stuck here in the middle of nowhere,' Rake sighed.

A murmur of agreement was heard from the others. They, too, had liked living in Diamond House. A wave of despondency went through Martha's tired head. She felt it in the air. She didn't really have the support of the others.

2

When the gang of pensioners found their way to their house, had parked the minibus and taken off their coats, they had a quick look around the building before settling down. The seller had informed them that the building was from around 1900 and that it had been turned into a bank branch in the 1950s. The bank manager had his bedroom, sitting room, dining room and private office on the upper floor, but when the branch office closed a few years ago, the premises had been turned into two large flats and one smaller flat. The ground floor, where bank customers used to come, had been converted into a kitchen, library and a large sitting room with a fireplace. Now the friends drew lots to decide who would live where, took their suitcases to their rooms and mumbled something about how nice it would be to relax after their meal.

Martha hoped that everybody would feel better after they had seen how lovely the house was, but an hour or so later, when the League of Pensioners sat down to eat, the mood was rather depressed. Since Martha had said that they would shop for food when they reached Hemmavid village, they didn't have much to eat. Thankfully, she had packed a few tins of mackerel in tomato sauce, and Brains, who liked his porridge in the mornings, had taken along a packet of oats. So the gang made some porridge and put bits of mackerel into it.

'Aah, what an aroma. Such delicious gourmet food. This is really something special,' said Anna-Greta, rolling her eyes.

'Yes, what a wonderful meal; which five-star restaurant did this come from?' said Rake, studying the sticky mass.

'Never mind, tomorrow we'll drive to the nearest village and stock up,' Martha promised.

'Lucky for us that the fridge and freezer work. Now we can at least have cold champagne to console ourselves with,' noted Brains.

'When people from Stockholm end up in sparsely populated rural areas without mod cons, they are at a loss as to what to do. We do at least have something to eat,' Christina maintained.

'It isn't so easy for country folk to manage in the big city either,' mumbled Brains. 'Incidentally, aren't you going to phone your kids and tell them that we have arrived?'

'Not that they tend to worry, but you're right,' said Christina, and she picked up her mobile phone and dialled the number of her beloved son, Anders. Nothing happened. Then she got up, went upstairs, and tried to phone from the balcony. But she couldn't get any signal there either. When she came down again, she looked irritated.

'Seems to be poor mobile coverage here. How on earth . . .?'

'Like they say, when Stockholm folk end up in the middle of nowhere, they become totally confused. Try using morse code,' Rake teased her. 'When I sailed the oceans, we didn't have telephone contact for weeks.'

17

'Now listen to me, we'll deal with the practicalities tomorrow, but now I think we should treat ourselves to some champagne. We've driven a long way today,' said Martha, and she went into the kitchen. There she fetched a tray with champagne glasses and a bottle of champagne and handed it over to Rake. As a young man, he had been a waiter on several cruise ships and he could still handle a tray of drinks with style. He took the tray, opened the bottle of champagne without spilling a drop, and filled the glasses with professional elegance.

'Well, cheers, then, everybody, and thanks for a lovely day!' Martha exclaimed heartily.

'Lovely day? There isn't even a hamburger kiosk in this remote spot. Surely you don't think we're going to live here?' muttered Rake as he put down the tray.

'And here you have to stay healthy. Did you see that they've shut down the local health clinic too?' Christina sighed. They all looked accusingly at Martha.

'Would you rather end up in prison?' she retorted and adopted a sharper tone. 'No, we're going to lie low from the police for a while and make the best of the situation. Cheers to you all!'

They toasted, but Martha didn't feel any enthusiasm in the room. They must all be tired, she thought. Still, as long as we can buy some good food, get settled in and find something sensible to occupy ourselves with, then everything will be all right, she consoled herself. But they had, of course, been obliged to leave in a hurry. The day after the robbery at the Stockholm auction house, the police had distributed the description of two elderly people who had visited the exhibition. Apart from the workmen and auction house staff, they were the only people who had been inside the room where the earrings were displayed. Three pensioners, who had been caught on CCTV, had been in the vicinity on the pavement. This gave the police reason to believe that the notorious League of Pensioners might have been involved. And since Martha and her friends were not only suspected of stealing the diamonds, but also of quite a lot of other crimes, they had had no choice but to immediately leave the city. Martha put her glass down. What had she gone and done now?

When all the others had gone to bed, she went to have a bath. She liked the bathroom with its large washbasin, mirror in a gilded frame, blue-and-white tiles on the walls and an old-fashioned bathtub with lion feet. She filled the tub and sank down into the deep water so that her thin, white hair got wet.

The bubble bath was lovely and hot and she slowly started to relax. Now she could be alone with her thoughts, and make plans for the future. The hot water engulfed her in a cosy embrace and she shut her eyes.

In Stockholm she and her friends had succeeded in creating Diamond House Residence for Seniors with gymnastics and courses in choir-singing, ceramics and watercolour painting. In addition, Christina had organized book circles, while Rake had arranged music evenings when they ate good food and danced to rock music and big-band jazz.

And they would probably have gone on living there, if it hadn't been for the irritating police description after the jewellery coup. Her own fault . . . but seventy million kronor! So much money, and so many poor people that they could help now! Martha blew on the bubbles so that they made a fluffy white cloud formation on her tummy. It reminded her of the plump 25,000-year-old Venus figure. She had had quite a tummy too, but in those days, they worshipped generous, feminine forms. Nowadays, it was those half-starved sinister-looking figures in high heels that counted, skeletons invented by the fashion industry! Christina's combined *David and Venus* statue was something quite different and they couldn't have found a better hiding place. The booty would be safe there until they could put the jewels up for sale. Unfortunately, they would have to wait a while until everything had calmed down! Meanwhile, she and her friends must think of something else to do. Lying low in a little village in between nowhere and nothing would not suffice for long; they would have to find something with which to occupy themselves. But what?

They had once had a vision of creating a model village where all the inhabitants would be happy and contented. Why not take up that idea again? Hemmavid was a little community which already had all the buildings necessary . . . all that remained was to try to get things moving . . . Martha could see before her how one could open a village shop, a library, a hairdresser's, a health clinic, a dispensing chemist's and all the other things that one would have found in a village once upon a time. And how the village would become a meeting place for the people in the district. Wouldn't that be really nice!

Previously, she and her friends had gathered together their stolen millions in their Robbery Fund, and from that had handed out money to needy people. But one ought to invest in the future too, and that required innovative thinking – why not concentrate on the sparsely populated countryside? Martha pulled the plug out, emptied the bath and got out. She dried herself and put on her thick, warm dressing gown. Nothing is impossible, she thought. Some projects are just a bit bigger and take a bit longer.

3

After breakfast the next morning they all did a round of the house and the surrounding grounds to see where they had ended up. They inspected the property and discovered, to their delight, that the main building was actually in better condition than they had expected. There were proper wooden floors with thick, wide planks, old windows with hand-blown glass, tiled stoves, panelled doors and an open fireplace. It smelt of wood and linseed oil and the blue-and-white English wallpaper gave a cosy feel to their new home.

'Just look at this!' said Christina and she pointed. 'They really have retained the character of the building. And the windows are at least a hundred years old.'

The residential building faced the village road and the steps that the bank customers had once used were still there. They had black iron railings and some of the mortar had loosened from one of the steps. At the back, which was dominated by a large gravelled yard, there were two outhouses painted with red ochre, some old stables with a workshop and garage, and a large greenhouse. Right next to the main building was a kitchen garden with a lot of rhubarb, some redcurrant bushes and flower borders. We ought to be able to make it really nice here, Martha thought.

After having looked around a bit, the whole gang set off for the closest country town, Skogsås, to do some shopping and to get things they needed. They bought some rag mats, curtains, bed linen and household equipment at a hypermarket at the edge of the town, and at the same time ordered a new, more modern, freezer and a large microwave oven. Then they bought food items to last them a while. After a good lunch they went back to the minibus to drive to the closest DIY store. But just as they were about to drive off, Martha caught sight of a placard for the evening paper, *Expressen*, which proclaimed: *DIAMOND ROBBERY IN STOCKHOLM ABOUT TO BE SOLVED.*

She felt a lump in her tummy, turned off the engine and went in to buy the newspaper. She quickly put it under her arm, paid and went back to the others. The robbery was front-page news and the paper also showed a copy of the newspaper article that had described the crime a few weeks earlier.

'I wonder whether they really do have anything new about us,' she muttered to herself (her voice definitely seeming to fade). She opened the paper and started to read:

'The audacious robbery at Stockholm Auktionsverk, when jewels worth seventy million kronor were stolen, is about to be solved. CCTV recordings from the premises have been of great help and the police have secured tracks from the thieves.

'The valuable jewels disappeared when the staff were busy preparing the viewing display for this year's classic auction. They were engaged in unpacking and building up the display cabinets when the thieves in an unguarded moment managed to steal two rare diamond earrings. Some workmen in the vicinity didn't notice anything unusual, but a female member of staff observed two elderly people on the premises. The objects were connected to an alarm, but although the police immediately came to the scene, the perpetrators could not be apprehended.

'One police officer noticed a group of pensioners outside the auction house and searched an elderly lady with a belt bag, without, however, finding anything. Now police experts have examined the CCTV images and found similarities between this robbery and earlier crimes committed by the League of Pensioners, who are still at large. The police believe they are on their trail, and that the case will soon be solved. The jewels were owned by the wife of the Russian oligarch, Yuri Ivankov.'

Martha's voice wavered even more as she read the last sentence, but then she looked up and nonchalantly slapped the newspaper with her hand.

'Pah, those are just standard phrases. It doesn't say anything actually new. And even if the police think the League of Pensioners lie behind it, they won't catch us. There isn't a soul who knows where we are.'

'And besides, you've stopped wearing a belt bag,' Christina tried to console herself. She was terrified of ending up in prison again, so Martha had solemnly given her word that she would use another bag, even if it was an unpractical one that you had to hang over your shoulder.

'The police aren't so efficient out here in the countryside

and if we lie low a while, then everything will sort itself out,'
Martha went on and her voice sounded more even now.

'The League of Pensioners lie low? And how many days
would that last?' mumbled Rake.

On their way out of Skogsås, Brains bought some timber and
tools for his future workshop. Rake bought some garden tools,
seeds and plants for the greenhouse, which he planned to do
up. They drove home, and once they were inside the house
they breathed a sigh of relief, drank tea with an unusually
large dollop of cloudberry liqueur and ate an awful lot of
cinnamon buns as well. It had given them a bit of a fright.
Why had it said, *DIAMOND ROBBERY IN STOCKHOLM ABOUT
TO BE SOLVED?*

4

Freelance journalist Ingmar Sjöberg gobbled down the last mouthful of his hamburger and emptied the beer can. He had already eaten the chips and the bread too; now only the sticky paper was left. He pushed the plate away and looked at his watch. There was still an hour to go before the removal van was due to arrive. He might just as well plan how he was going to furnish the place. His new office (really a one-room flat) was forty-two square metres with a kitchen and a little balcony, and was centrally situated. He was lucky to have found such a place here in the middle of Stockholm. Evidently the man who had rented it before him had left in a great hurry and the landlord had wanted to get a new tenant immediately. Ingmar had made a quick decision. He had long been looking for an office for his freelance work and now he had chanced upon one. He had probably been given the contract because he had said he was willing to pay three months' rent in advance. The things you do when you've stumbled across something you really want! He brushed away some crumbs from his beard and looked around. He could have shared a freelance office in the southern part of the city centre, but as an investigative journalist, he really preferred to be on his own.

He got up and started to walk around the flat while he thought about how he would furnish it. It would be better to think that through before the removal van arrived. The man who had lived here before had evidently been a guy who was over sixty-five and who had worked at Kungsholmen police station in another part of Stockholm; a certain Ernst Blomberg, who had opened his own detective agency after retiring from the police. The landlord had told him about the former chief inspector and had given vent to his fury about him. He had, admittedly, paid the rent, but he hadn't bothered giving the statutory three months' notice and had just left without even taking his furniture. He gave his notice on a Monday, and he was gone on Tuesday.

'He must have had a debt to the taxman or perhaps some criminals were chasing him,' the landlord explained. 'If you hadn't taken over the flat directly, I would have lost several months' rent money. Dreadful having tenants you can't trust. And he had been a policeman too. Anyhow, now you can rent the flat furnished.'

I've been bloody lucky, Ingmar thought. The rent was exceptionally low and there was a garage space included too. And the furniture? A sofa, chairs and a bookcase could remain, but he had his own kitchen table and corner cupboard. While he waited, he might just as well take the stuff he didn't want down to the storeroom. He resolutely filled the lift with furniture, pressed the button for the cellar and then walked down the stairs.

Once he was in the cellar, he opened the lift door and fixed it in that position, then he unlocked the storeroom. He dragged out the table and the corner cupboard. The table wasn't a problem, but the cupboard turned out to be terribly heavy. Just as he managed to get it over the threshold, it tipped to one side and banged into the doorframe. Something fell out. He kicked it aside, flexed his muscles and, with a grunt, succeeded in standing the cupboard against the wall. On his way out, he picked up what had fallen onto the floor. He raised his eyebrows; a flash drive . . . what the dickens was this? Presumably, it had fallen out of the cupboard. He fingered the stick and started thinking. The former tenant had been a detective. The flash drive might well contain crime cases, investigations, evidence in cold cases and much more besides. He ought to check it out. With a bit of luck, he could perhaps have material for many articles here. And he needed it.

He was considered to be one of the newspaper's best investigative journalists and one of his scoops was that he had revealed that the police suspected the League of Pensioners of being behind the robbery at the auction house. The article had been highlighted on newspaper placards in heavy type all over Sweden, but then he hadn't had much more to show. Nothing seemed to be happening at all, and he had no new information. But the flash drive could be a gold mine for him, indeed, and provide material for more scoops and front-page stories. Unless, of course, Blomberg had deleted all the content . . .

5

When the League of Pensioners finally managed to get online, they scrolled around to see if there was any more information about the auction house robbery. But they couldn't find anything new. Things became calm and they tried to make themselves at home as best they could. Brains, an octogenarian, whose name was actually Oscar Krupp, once had his own workshop in Sundbyberg, a Stockholm suburb, and now he improved his new workshop with benches for woodworking, shelving and a lathe. He also managed to get the building's old electric truck and MIG welding equipment back into working order. He already had tools.

Meanwhile, Rake tidied up the greenhouse and put in benches, tables and chairs. Here, his sweetheart, Christina, could sit with a book and keep him company while he kept himself busy, he thought, or the whole gang could have their afternoon coffee there. Now they'd see that Martha wasn't the only one who could arrange this and that; it was going to be really good!

Martha thought that the gravelled yard looked boring and she didn't like to see their parked minibus – a not particularly attractive utility vehicle that had once been a taxi specially fitted for transporting passengers with wheelchairs, hence the back ramp which it also boasted – and all the junk out in the yard. So she parked The Red Menace (their nickname for the minibus) out of sight and removed the worst of the junk that was lying around. Later, when Christina and Rake offered to dig over the borders and plant some pretty flowers in front of the outhouses, she thawed out. They would probably get to feel at home here in Hemmavid, but to do so they must, of course, get to know the village.

They put on their everyday outer clothes (the furs and camel-hair overcoats were stowed away in a box in the attic) and went out onto the potholed road that ran through Hemmavid. It was narrow and curved like a half-moon in the middle of the village, with houses on either side. Some had white rendering or were painted yellow and white, but most of them were painted with Falu red, the traditional Swedish red ochre. It all looked nice and pleasant. Martha experienced the cosy feeling of living in the countryside. She had moved from Österlen in southern Sweden to Stockholm to study at what is now called the Stockholm University College of Physical Education and Sports but which, in her day, was called the Royal Gymnastics Central Institute, and she'd stayed on in the city . . . it had just turned out like that, but more often than not she missed being close to nature.

They walked past the village hall and the old cruciform church built in timber, and when they came to a stone building with hardboard covering the windows, they stopped. This was evidently the closed-down health clinic. A bit further on lay the car park, the closed-down village shop and petrol station. The village wasn't large, but when they went down a little

30

side street, they were surprised to discover a café. It was a little cottage painted in Falu red with white trimmings and two large windows on the ground floor. Martha became curious.

'What about going in for a coffee?'

'Good idea,' agreed Anna-Greta, who had a sweet tooth.

They went inside and looked around. The café was cosily furnished with furniture from the 1940s. The walls were green and the dark mahogany tables went well with the stuffed grey chairs. Several of the tables were decorated with flowers and embroidered tablecloths, and at the far end of the room there was a pinball machine where some men were standing. In one corner there was an old jukebox and a one-armed bandit. The League of Pensioners stepped up to the counter and chose between ready-made sandwiches, fancy cream cakes and various sorts of biscuits. Everybody except Anna-Greta had a cup of coffee with a hot cheese sandwich, while she asked for a piece of cream cake and three smaller sweetbread biscuits. They went and sat down, and a little while later the café assistant came with the trays.

'I haven't seen you before. Are you local?' she asked, after putting their orders on the table. The woman was in her forties and had dark hair and beautiful brown eyes.

'No, we're from Stockholm,' Martha answered.

'Oh right, you are from the big city, then? Do you boast about being climate-friendly and travel by bus instead of car too?'

'No, we have our own minibus.' Martha looked in astonishment at her. She had sounded almost aggressive.

'We used to run the village shop, but now we must make

31

sandwiches and serve coffee instead. If we hadn't owned the building, we wouldn't even have been able to do that. Now at least we have something to occupy ourselves with.'

Ah, so evidently Malin and Lilian had opened a café after being forced to close down the village shop. Then you would hardly be in a jolly mood, Martha thought. She was just about to say something consoling when a clatter could be heard from the kitchen and a woman came out. They were very similar, perhaps they were twin sisters.

'Ah, right, you must be the new people in the old bank building. Welcome! Malin, let's treat them to something tasty, don't you think?'

Malin nodded, and put another plate of sweetbread biscuits on the table.

'This is to welcome you to Hemmavid!'

'Thank you very much,' said Martha, and she noted that the only other guests in the café were the pinball players. So she and her friends could hardly vanish in the crowd. But now it was too late. The five of them had already been seen together. On the other hand, which police officer would look for them here?

They sat down and Martha glanced at the sisters. Malin had thin, plucked eyebrows, a straight nose and a well-shaped mouth, and she had put her long hair up in a ponytail. The sister, who must be Lilian, had dark hair too, but she had cut it in a short, boyish style. She smiled at them.

'Do you like it here with us deep in the countryside?'

'Indeed! It is so beautiful and it is nice and quiet,' Martha answered. 'In contrast to Stockholm.'

'Yes, that's why we've stayed here,' said Lilian.

Malin straightened her ponytail with her hand. 'I don't understand how people can live in Stockholm. In the big cities it costs a fortune to buy a flat, and you don't have forests or hydro-electric power. You don't have cows or fields which give you food either, for that matter. You wouldn't survive without us.'

'You're talking about Stockholm folk. But I am from Göteborg,' Rake protested in a loud voice.

'And I'm from Jönköping,' Christina pointed out.

'Admittedly I've lived in Stockholm for many years, but I grew up in the south, in Österlen,' said Martha.

Brains was just about to say that he came from the Sundbyberg suburb outside Stockholm and that Anna-Greta had grown up in an upper-class home in the posh Djursholm, but he stopped himself. They mustn't reveal too much about themselves. They were meant to lie low. Instead, he quickly changed the subject.

'What lovely shortbread biscuits you bake!'

'Yepp, we use Granny's recipe. We are reduced to doing this now. And our family had run the village shop for fifty years,' Malin sighed.

'Why did you close down?' Martha wondered.

'The shop was losing money, it was no longer viable. People buy everything they need from the hypermarkets. In fact, it's these big articulated lorries which ruin everything. Foreign hauliers bring in cheap food from abroad and that lowers the prices so that we haven't a chance to compete.'

'That doesn't sound good.'

'If only the lorry drivers could take another route and drive directly to Stockholm. Then we wouldn't have to compete with that cheap milk from Germany and old, unchecked meat from Poland.'

Martha gave Malin a tired look. She did nothing but complain! On the other hand, it was, of course, not easy to try to survive in a rural district which was losing its population. They ought to visit the café for a snack often so that the sisters increased their takings. But a nearby farmer ought to be supported too. She had seen a sign about farm produce being sold directly from the farm. They drank up their coffee, and on their way home decided to look in at the farm.

The bell sounded when they entered Roland's Farm Shop, and the first thing they noticed was all the shelves lining the walls. On them were flour, herbs, crispbread, biscuits and chocolate, and, in the corner, a fridge where you could buy dairy products and meat. There was also a big freezer, next to which were some crates of beer and baskets with veggies. The shop smelt of freshly baked bread and herbs. The gang picked out what they needed, and then went up to the cash desk. Nobody was there, but when they called out, they heard a glad voice.

'New people in the village, I see. Welcome!' a man in a green overall and with dark curly hair greeted them. He had a broad smile and his blue eyes were bright and alert. He sat down at the cash desk. 'Roland Svensson at your service!'

Martha and the gang mumbled their names so quickly and quietly that they couldn't be heard, but that didn't bother the farmer. He kept on talking while he packed their purchases and managed to tell them that the old school was about to be closed down, that the church from the late nineteenth century had become an artist's studio and that the post office and bank had long since gone. And he grumbled about the fact that many villagers had left too. But what really irked him was that it took more than an hour before the police and fire brigade arrived after an alarm.

'Yes, it must be dreadful not to have any police constables here,' Martha lied and she thought about the newspaper placard. The others nodded amicably and they too politely agreed.

'But what if a bunch of dubious types come to the village? There'd be nothing to stop them. The police don't have any resources.' Roland Svensson looked worried.

'Really shocking,' Martha lied through her teeth again, looking down at the floor. 'But I don't think we need be afraid. Those sorts of criminal types mainly stick to the big cities.'

'Yes, you're probably right,' said Svensson and the wrinkle between his eyebrows vanished. Martha and Christina exchanged glances and hid a little smile. Christina was the one who quickly changed the subject.

'What you were saying earlier, about it being so difficult out here in this sparsely populated area – why do you stay on?' she wondered.

'I was born and brought up in Hemmavid, and my family have lived here for generations. We don't want to move to the big city with its stress and exhaust fumes. Or end up amidst the gang violence and concrete. No, we want to have nature around us and look after ourselves!'

'So you live here on the farm with your family?' Martha wondered.

'Yes, my wife and I have a large farm with cows and sheep,

and we run this farm shop together. Sometimes my two children help, but they are still at school – as long as that is kept open.'

'But surely you can save the school? There must be something you can do about it?' Martha asked.

Roland gave her a tired look. 'Yes, sure, you can travel to the moon too . . .'

When they had reached home again, Brains settled down in the old worn armchair in the living room. Then he caught sight of *David and Venus* on the bookshelf. He looked at Christina's sculpture for a while, raised his eyebrows and suddenly got up. After a while he came back carrying tools and a spotlight. Without asking anybody to help him, he screwed the spotlight into position above, and directed it so that it lit up the plaster sculpture.

'There you are, now it looks like a genuine work of art,' he said contentedly, then he returned to the armchair and joined his hands together on his lap. A murmur of agreement could be heard from the others.

'When you're sitting on seventy stolen million, it feels rather nice that the closest police are at least an hour away if not more,' he noted. 'Then we're safe here. We can relax and become real pensioners.'

'Safe in a manner of speaking,' said Martha. 'Or put it like this: then we can bring a bit of life to this village without being disturbed by the authorities.'

'But as newcomers in a district, you shouldn't start deciding how everything should be done,' Brains protested.

'Exactly. People in the countryside should be treated with

respect,' Christina added. 'We Stockholmers are not going to come and turn everything upside down.'

Brains glanced at Martha. Why did she have to be so on the ball, so energetic? Bring a bit of life into the village? He took her hand and stroked it somewhat clumsily with his thumb.

'Can't we just take it easy? You stir up things around you, darling.'

'Pah, we don't want to die of boredom!'

Brains got up and shook his head. They had just robbed an auction house, broken away from their residence for seniors and moved up here. And now she was going to think up some new scheme again. He took some firm steps to the medicine cupboard and took a paracetamol.

Later in the afternoon, he took Martha out onto the balcony from where they had a good view of the surrounding district. It was getting dark and in front of them they could see fields, some farmhouses and the dark forest. There was no wind and the full moon rose slowly over the hills on the other side of the valley. It was large and honey-yellow and was reflected in the lake far away.

'Martha, you are right. It is beautiful in the countryside, but then one should also take it easy and allow oneself to enjoy it.'

'We've time for that too.'

'But don't you understand? We are a bit older now and shouldn't have too much stress. And you and I are engaged. Have you forgotten that? There isn't room for our love in your full calendar. We ought to have got married long ago.'

'Yes, of course, but we simply haven't had time,' said Martha.

'*Not had time!* Can't you hear what that sounds like? Emotions demand presence. Our relationship risks going to pot just because you have so much else going on. Think about it!'

Brains turned his back on Martha, and went back inside the house without waiting for an answer. The last he heard her say was: 'But darling, a day only has twenty-four hours . . .'

6

A guerrilla campaign, yes, that was the only thing that could save the countryside, Martha thought, having woken up early and gone done to the kitchen to make breakfast. She had repressed what Brains had said out on the balcony and hoped that everything would sort itself out once they had made themselves at home in the village and found something sensible to do. That's how it always was. People want something meaningful to busy themselves with.

After a cup of coffee, she felt a bit perkier and started to hum, which could even be heard by the others from upstairs. That gave them cause to worry. Because when Martha sang or hummed at this early hour of the day, she usually had great plans in mind.

'You know what, last night I lay in bed thinking . . .' she started when they were all sitting at the kitchen table. 'The thing is, Hemmavid village can't manage without a petrol station, a health clinic and all the rest. Can't we try to get the village back on its feet?'

'You mean our new occupation instead of robbing banks?' Brains wondered.

'Yes indeed, my dear!' said Martha, who couldn't hide her

enthusiasm. 'Let's become guerrilla activists who save the countryside.'

'Hmm, guerrilla activists, that sounds dangerous. You could at least call us rebels,' Rake said before mumbling, 'And what do you mean by save? People who live here might not want to be saved.'

'All right, but can't you see? The village is going downhill. We must attract tourists, create new jobs and get people to move here,' Martha went on, with excruciating energy. 'You need to think like this: we have always wanted to support the elderly to give them the opportunity to have a good life. I want everybody to have a good life. And now we have the chance to create a real model village.'

'Oh really, and nothing else?' Rake immediately looked tired.

'The countryside has been populated for many thousands of years, it simply can't be abandoned, you must realize that!'

'You've never thought about governing all of Sweden, becoming prime minister or something like that?' was the quick response from Rake, irony dripping in his voice.

Martha checked herself. Now she had gone too fast again, but who could live in the countryside if there was no service, no village shop and no mobile coverage? And in times of crisis a country must be able to support itself, yes, produce its own food. And there was no way you could have cows and wheat fields on the balconies in the cities. No, there must be a living countryside. Nowadays, Martha and her friends knew a great deal about crime. Saving the countryside was, of course, a bit more complicated. But why not? It wasn't impossible. She was thinking about Norway.

'Now listen –' she went on, making a theatrical pause to

make sure that everybody was listening – 'in Norway they still have village schools, swimming baths, libraries and police stations in their sparsely populated countryside. There the politicians want the entire country to live, and not just Oslo. So why couldn't we manage to do that in Sweden too? Together, I'm sure we can think of something good.'

'Now Martha's going to set us to work again,' Brains said, smiling.

'But have you thought about it?' Rake said in a low voice and with a knowing look. 'Why is it us who have to save everything and everybody all the time? Even if she is right, we don't need to obey her, do we?'

Freelance journalist Ingmar Sjöberg pushed his office chair back and stared at the computer screen. He swore to himself and twisted some strands of his beard between his thumb and index finger. He had thought he would stumble across something exciting in private detective Ernst Blomberg's flash drive, but he hadn't managed to access the contents. Nevertheless, he couldn't bring himself to throw it away. There ought to be something interesting there. And to get at that information, he needed some help. Why not go to Kungsholmen Police Station, where Blomberg had worked earlier? There they could surely hack their way in. And if the police IT department found something exciting, he would demand the sole right to all the interesting revelations. It would make difficulties for himself, he realized that, but he couldn't help it. He was always on the lookout for a scoop. He wanted to be the best. Perhaps it was because he had been teased at school because he was little and feeble and developed late. And the fact that he had found it easy to cry and had often clung on to his mum hadn't made it any better. They had called him mother's darling.

But as an adult he had gone to the gym twice a week and built up his muscles. Determination, muscles and a winning social manner had made him popular with the ladies and the people he interviewed had opened themselves up for him. Nobody worked as hard as he did, or had so many front-page articles as he had. But if he took this flash drive to the police, they would of course have to promise him that he would get all the information before anybody else . . . that ought to be possible. The police trusted him. He had never leaked anything or revealed his sources.

Ingmar Sjöberg turned off his computer, got up and tied his long hair in a Zlatan-style top knot. Then he opened the fridge and took out a cold beer. After having drunk a few large gulps, he made his decision, fetched the stick and wrapped it in a piece of cloth. He stood there for a while holding it. Ernst Blomberg might have left it in the cupboard because it was worthless, but it was more likely that it had stuck between two shelves so that he hadn't seen it. Ingmar himself hadn't noticed it when he opened the cupboard, and it wasn't until he pulled it over the threshold that the flash drive had fallen out.

He looked at his watch. He would just make it to the police station before it was time to start on the day's work. He reached the door in two steps and pulled his jacket on. The decision to hand the flash drive over to the police felt good. Now, at last, he would find out what was on it. . . .

7

An ambush, yes, that was what they must plan! For more than a week, Martha had gone to the trouble of listening to her friends and had given them her word that they would get to know the district first. But she hadn't mentioned the ambush yet. She must proceed with caution. Besides, she had reassured the others that it would all just be an experiment, and that she wasn't going to try to save the entire Swedish countryside (at least not yet, but she didn't say that out loud). On the other hand, if they were successful, they could always spread their ideas, couldn't they?

The gang had rested, filled their cellar, fridge and freezer with food, played bridge and canasta, sung their choir songs and enjoyed coffee and snacks now and then in the little café, which was called The Danish Pastry. But they hadn't achieved anything sensible. This pained Martha, but she didn't say anything; instead, she tried to adapt. She and her friends often sat at one of the tables and had a cup of coffee with a Danish pastry, while the men played on the pinball machine. And sometimes the menfolk would sit at the coffee table while the women played on the one-armed bandit, or went for a walk.

'Weird,' Malin observed. 'They live in the same house, but hardly ever sit together here at the café.'

'Perhaps they're tired of each other,' her sister suggested.

'But then why buy a house here, where they don't know a soul? Why come here at all? They don't have any connections to Hemmavid, do they? You know what, when people move, I'm always a bit suspicious. You never know . . .'

Martha and her friends visited the Danish Pastry café to enjoy a snack and coffee, but also to find out as much as possible about the district. This was where Martha had heard about how, in the old days, they had mined iron ore in the forests, and there were traces of old foundries and mines in the district. The Swedish National Heritage Board's archaeologists had even found ancient dwelling places, and Martha wanted to see them. So she took the others with her out into the forest to investigate the surrounding area. In the dark forest of fir trees and bushy pines, they discovered several old mine shafts, traces of old foundries and slag heaps, and they even found an old trapping pit from the Stone Age. But they didn't see any people.

'A pity that nobody sees this. We ought to arrange a fascinating forest safari for tourists,' Martha said when, a few days later, they were sitting in Rake's greenhouse with a cup of tea. On the table was a teapot decorated with a design of large flowers and there was a plate of wafers. But there were only two left. Anna-Greta had eaten all the rest.

'Forest safari? What's wrong with an ordinary walk?' Anna-Greta wondered.

'We must make it sound exciting. So that it can be marketed in a modern way.'

44

'What about the lake, then? We could arrange fishing expeditions and teach people to sail,' Christina suggested. 'That would mean activities with visitors spending the night here too . . .'

'And more money in the till,' Anna-Greta added. 'But people go for walks and go fishing anyway. We must think of something new. Make the whole thing more hip-hop – isn't that what they call it?'

'Well, then, I know. Why not hold courses in how to rob a bank? We could have web courses on the Internet; that's modern, right?' smirked Rake and he looked at Brains. They exchanged looks in agreement.

'Now listen, this is serious. Let's arrange something nice that nobody here in the district has ever come across before,' Martha said.

And when Martha said this, everyone realized that she was cooking up something special, but that she wasn't going to tell them everything. Because they knew that she had discovered that it was much easier to get her own way if she only revealed a bit at a time. Otherwise, it was too much at once. For everybody.

They had gone to the café to relax one day when Martha struck. The three ladies sat at a separate table in the café while Brains and Rake stood beside the one-armed bandit and the pinball table. She went up to them.

'Now come and sit with us at the table over there where nobody can hear us.' She nodded towards the corner table where Christina and Anna-Greta were drinking coffee. 'We're going to plan an ambush,' she added in a whisper.

45

'An ambush!' Rake exclaimed in horror, and missed the flipper so that the pinball fell down into the hole with a plop.

'Sssh, not so loud,' said Martha, and put her index finger over her lips.

'We'd better go and sit down,' Brains sighed. 'It sounds as if she's serious.'

'Yes, I can understand if you're mystified,' said Martha when the men had taken some coffee and a croissant and she had everyone's attention. 'But I've had an idea.'

'How come I'm not surprised?' Rake sighed.

Martha didn't pay any attention to him. 'The long-haul lorries that pass here must be prevented.'

'Oh right, is that all?' Rake put his index finger on his forehead, looked at Brains and nodded knowingly in Martha's direction.

'We haven't been able to buy fresh food for a long time. Neither chicken nor meat, and if it hadn't been for Roland's cows, we wouldn't have been able to get any milk either,' Martha spelled out. 'Malin said that when they had the shop they sold meat, cheese and milk from the farms round about. Now all those products are transported in long-haul lorries from other countries and are sold so cheaply that no local producer in the area can compete against those prices.'

'And now you want to get rid of those monster lorries with an ambush,' Brains added, knowing so well how Martha's mind worked.

'Precisely,' Martha made it even clearer.

'So exciting,' said Anna-Greta and she clapped her hands with delight. 'So, are we going to hide behind a bush and jump out with a raised gun?'

46

'No, no – no weapons!' Martha protested. 'We are going to do this in style.'

'Guerrilla activists, but elegant ones; shall we wear a tie?' Rake wondered.

'But seriously, Martha, what *are* we going to do?' Brains asked.

'It's simple. We'll frighten off the long-haul lorries. It's just a matter of thinking up how to do it.' Martha waved her hands enthusiastically.

'How to do it? So, there's just one little detail missing,' Rake murmured.

'Just go for them!' Anna-Greta called out. 'Why not make them pay road tax or something like that?'

'That's a good idea. We'll set up a roadblock,' said Martha and her eyes came to life. Brains looked at her with scepticism. Now his Martha had started up again. Her eyes glowed and she waved her arms. Why could she never just take things easy?

'If we set up roadblocks, demanded a toll fee and that sort of thing, then the long-haul lorry drivers will hopefully choose another route – and then we'll save Hemmavid . . . and Roland Svensson's little farm shop can become the new village shop,' she went on.

'Five old pensioners stopping a forty-ton long-haul lorry. Don't you have any limits, Martha, my dear?' Brains wondered.

'No, none at all. Not now, and I never will have. And I'd like you to know that nobody is too old to make a difference.'

8

It was dark out on the big main road which bypassed the village, and the headlights of the long-haul lorries swept in wide cascades of light across the deserted landscape. The ground shook now and then, and a roaring blanket of noise blocked your ears every time one of the juggernauts went past. Martha lowered her binoculars and handed them over to Brains.

'What monsters! Look at that foreign whopper, it's like three lorries joined together.'

Brains looked through the binoculars at the vehicle which disappeared southwards. 'Yes, dear, there are long-haul lorries that weigh eighty tons and are more than thirty metres long. So it isn't simply a matter of stepping out into the road, holding up your hand and saying "Stop".'

'I'm sure it will work. We're not talking about oil tankers. I bet you that this sort of modern lorry can be steered with your little finger. They can probably be braked just as easily too.'

Brains took a step back, turned up his collar and glanced at Martha. How on earth could he stop the woman? Her plans were always so risky . . .

'So you still think we should set up roadblocks?' he asked in a pathetic voice.

'Absolutely. If you want to be a rebel and a countryside activist, then you've got to do what it takes.'

Brains squirmed and didn't really know what to say. Just because the Government didn't take care of the countryside, it was hardly the job of the League of Pensioners to try to solve the problem. Five old pensioners couldn't be a parallel power to the state; it sounded crazy. But Martha had already decided on her vision.

'Without farms, dairies and village shops, the villages will die. But now we'll frighten the giant lorries away. Hurrah!'

What could you say in answer to that? Martha always sounded so certain, and now she had adopted the role of social reformer. She had previously got involved in the care of the aged, and made life difficult for billionaires who dodged paying tax. And now it was about the sparsely populated countryside. Two long-haul lorries roared past, and the ground shook.

'Martha, you can see for yourself. Huge, dangerous monsters,' he said pointing to the road. His hand was shaky. 'They can run us over, or before we know it, we can be facing mafia drivers from Eastern Europe. And besides, don't you need permission to put up roadblocks?'

'And since when have we followed the law?' Martha retorted looking at him in surprise. 'You must know what happens if one does that, you don't get anything done!'

Hearing those words, Brains felt so tired that he hadn't the energy to answer. He had tried to tell her that they ought to go easy, hadn't he? Love demands mental presence, not ambushes, he wanted to shout out, but what did you say if your darling partner was a law-breaker? He kept quiet.

'Now we know what it looks like here, let's go home and plan our strategy,' Martha continued. 'I promise you, this can lead to really great things.'

It was getting darker and Brains longed to be home in his armchair. He couldn't face having an argument. And with that, Martha turned round, turned on her head torch and took the lead in the walk back to the village – with Brains a few feet behind.

She walked with fast, hearty steps because she had been so inspired and after a cup of coffee and some cloudberry liqueur, she would be bound to get everybody to agree with her. The district would be saved and a necessary roadblock – or road toll, it didn't matter what you called it – would work wonders. She might be naive, but you had to put up a struggle!

When they reached the The Vault, the others were waiting in the kitchen and Anna-Greta, who saw the stressed look on Brains's face, asked him to sit down.

'Well, did you have a nice time?' she asked, serving him a cup of steaming hot coffee and a slice of lemon sponge cake.

'Well, at least we didn't get run over,' Brains mumbled.

'You should have been there. It was terribly exciting,' said Martha joyfully and she sat down too. In high spirits, she took a slice of lemon sponge and raised her glass with cloudberry liqueur high over her head to give a toast, but the glass bumped into something. The head torch! Somewhat embarrassed, she put it down on the table.

'Our project is feasible,' she went on. 'We can buy police uniforms on the Internet. Then, wearing uniforms and holding a police stop sign, we can stop the long-haul lorries and ask to see their driving licences. Then we can look at their recorders and check whether the drivers have had their statutory rest periods. And after that, they would have to do a breathalyser test. This is going to work.'

'But hang on a moment, Brains, I thought you said that you had her under control?' Rake teased his friend and looked him in the eye.

Brains grunted something inaudible in response, and looked glum.

'Now we mustn't forget a toast,' Anna-Greta broke in, feeling the tension in the air. 'I believe in this. Police checks scare most people off,' she exclaimed, then she threw her head back and emptied her glass. 'I read about a long-haul lorry driver who reversed a whole kilometre on the motorway when he caught sight of a checkpoint. Getting caught can be extremely expensive.'

'So now we are going to be the terror of the roads,' Brains moaned.

'Yes, indeed! This will be just as exciting as a bank robbery,' said Martha.

9

Inside Kungsholmen Police Station, Detective Chief Inspector Gert Aronsson was sitting with his feet on the desk and his laptop on his knees when the door was suddenly pulled open.

'Boss, you'd never have thought this about Blomberg!' His colleague Brynolf Jönson stormed in with his hair on end.

'You what – Blomberg? You mean Ernst Blomberg? What's he gone and done now?' Aronsson patted his bald head and yawned.

'We managed to get into that flash drive the journalist gave us. Blomberg hadn't encrypted it particularly well.'

'He thought, of course, that nobody would find it.'

'Look at this, I must show you.' Jönson logged in on the desk computer and clicked on the icon. After a while, several files were listed.

'He was working on a number of cases in parallel, and I haven't had time to check them all yet. But what did catch my eye was this: A gang of pensioners outside the National-museum.'

Aronsson leaned forward. A few indistinct figures were visible walking back and forth outside the pompous nineteenth-century building.

'Mmm, the pictures are not very sharp . . .'

'But it is the same gang that can be seen outside Handelsbanken and the Grand Hotel, where we had those robberies, you remember? Blomberg seems to have been checking up on them, but then not continued with it.'

'The robberies at the hotel and Handelsbanken have never been solved either. And some oldies were seen inside the auction house too. That was quite a robbery, seventy million vanished without trace! What if we're on to something here?'

The men sat down in front of the computer and studied the images. Most of them were fuzzy CCTV images and you couldn't see any detail, but there was no doubt that they showed five old people moving about in the immediate vicinity. And Blomberg had talked about that shady gang of pensioners who always got away with it. Oldies who had committed several serious crimes. Brynolf Jönson leaned closer to the screen. His face glistened with sweat.

'What if it is them?' he almost whispered.

'If it is the gang of pensioners, then we might be able to place them at the scene of the crime. Although we need more information. How could Blomberg have just left this behind?'

'He was in a hell of a hurry, I've heard; he'd been engaged in illegal transactions with Russia and the police were after him. He probably had a whole load of disks and flash drives and simply lost this one.'

The men continued to examine the CCTV images for a long while; finally Chief Inspector Aronsson pushed his chair back, put his hands behind his neck and nodded.

'With a bit of everyday, patient detective work, we can probably lay our hands on that gang. And then, bingo!'

'Quite right. Sooner or later they'll make a mistake and then we'll arrest them,' said Jönson. 'Then the whole bunch will end up in prison. Like I said, it's high time we put them behind bars. I think we should put them on the wanted list!'

'The question is why Blomberg didn't arrest them himself . . .'

'Perhaps he was going to do just that, but then all the Russian business got in the way.' Brynolf Jönson poked his ear with a paper clip. He ought to have had a cotton bud but they weren't environmentally friendly any longer. He threw the paper clip into the waste bin. 'And now we've got CCTV images from the auction house. Admittedly, there were only two elderly people inside the jewellery display area, but there were three more oldies not far away out on the pavement. That was no coincidence. Two plus three makes five, the League of Pensioners!'

'The article in *Expressen* could be read throughout the country. And if we now say we are looking for those pensioners, surely the public will notice a gang of five oldies.'

The men nodded in agreement and got up. Ingmar Sjöberg, who had handed over the flash drive, had already written about the robbery at the auction house and had mentioned the League of Pensioners. They thought that he had jumped the gun. But perhaps not. Perhaps he had been right after all!

10

The snow was melting, they didn't need their kicksled any longer and they could go out walking without using ice cleats. You could feel it in the air. The light and spring were on their way. And now it was irrevocable, their first 'guerrilla attack'. The gang of pensioners stood in front of their big dining table and, with a mixture of horror and delight, looked at the opened packages in front of them. The police uniforms had arrived.

'Lucky that there isn't anybody inside them!' said Brains, picking up one of the uniforms and sniffing it.

'Police uniforms like this frighten me,' said Christina in a rather pathetic voice. 'What if we end up in prison again?'

'Don't you worry, Christina, police uniforms don't usually put people in prison,' Rake tried to console her while looking through the pile of clothes. On the table lay five complete dark police uniforms with stylish buttons and the familiar police emblem which commanded respect. There were five matching caps too. They had also ordered yellow high-visibility jackets and black, orthopaedic boots which they put on the adjacent chairs. Martha had a good look at the hi-vis jackets and handed them out.

'Now there isn't a soul who can miss the fact that we are police officers,' she declared with satisfaction.

'You might have thought about different sizes,' Anna-Greta complained, being so tall that the jacket looked more like a large, yellow brassiere with POLICE stamped across the front.

'But it's good that the jackets are high up,' Martha tried to calm her. 'Then they will be seen easily from the lorry cab.'

'Incidentally, I don't understand that it can be legal to buy this sort of stuff,' Anna-Greta went on, before putting a police cap on her head with a credible emblem highly visible. 'People might think I'm a real police officer.'

'No, no chance of that. Police officers don't usually have white hair or go around with a stick,' said Rake glancing at Anna-Greta's bent oak walking stick which she always had with her – despite the fact that she didn't really need it. It was a gimmick and she used it mainly for reasons of nostalgia. The walking stick, which Brains had repaired many a time, had been on so many adventures during her criminal life that she found it hard to be without it.

Each of them chose a uniform of the right size, and then went to their room to try it on. Martha put on her uniform and thought that it looked really credible. Christina, for her part, eyed herself from several angles in a mirror and considered the uniform to be a very good fit. Brains and Rake suddenly found themselves feeling very masculine, while Anna-Greta shouted out 'Stop! Police!' and was amused to see her own image in the mirror. When they had all put their uniforms on, they went into the kitchen and were close to falling over backwards in fright. The police uniforms looked so realistic that, for a few seconds, they felt they were being arrested there and then – before realizing that the police officers were their own friends.

'Help! I thought I was going to get ten years behind bars when I saw you,' Martha said, looking at Anna-Greta. She did indeed look like a real police officer, and besides the uniform she had decked herself out with a baton and some handcuffs. The baton would be her replacement for the walking stick.

'Don't get too immersed in your role as a police officer, Anna-Greta,' Rake commented. 'We're not going to arrest any law-breakers, just so that you know. Like other police officers in this country, we don't have sufficient resources.'

The League of Pensioners giggled and after discussing the problem of the shortage of police officers and the current reorganization of the police force, they returned to their traffic-control mission.

'But we must have a warning triangle which says *POLICE* on it,' said Rake, 'and a hand-held police sign, of course.'

'I've already constructed two triangles and two hand-held police signs and Christina has painted them,' said Brains, and he hurried out to the workshop. 'Just look at these!' he said when he returned, and he held up a sign and a triangle.

'That's great, Brains!' said Martha. 'And painted too, that's perfect, Christina.'

'Yes, I tried to make them as realistic as possible,' she said, flattered by the praise. 'If we're going to wave down a long-haul lorry, then everything must look genuine, of course.'

'But how are we going to explain that we are so old?' Anna-Greta wondered.

There was some embarrassed mumbling in the kitchen and a lot of humming and hawing before Martha spoke out.

'There's a shortage of police officers at the moment and they haven't been able to train a sufficient number of new ones to replace those who have retired. So, we say that we have been called in as reinforcements. We simply have to lie. It's as easy as that.'

'All right, then,' said Christina. 'And I can put some make-up on you. What about a look which is ten years younger?'

'Excellent,' Martha settled it. 'And when you have made us look like sixty plus, then we'll go out and set up a police checkpoint.'

After which, Christina took command and hid each person's face behind a thick layer of skin-coloured make-up. None of them looked like a Mr or Miss Universe exactly, but quite a lot of wrinkles disappeared. Finally, Christina put on her own make-up, and knocked ten years off her age just like that. The job was done, and the kitchen smelt a bit like a beauty parlour. Christina had used a whole can of hair spray on her own hair.

'It's a fact, when you look at film stars without any make-up on, that they actually look just like we did before. So, actually, we are just as beautiful as they are,' she summarized as she gathered up all her make-up items. And then they all smiled and thought it sounded very sympathetic.

'But you know what, your inner beauty lasts the whole of your life,' said Martha. 'And if you could only turn yourself inside out, then the beauty industry would be superfluous.'

'My dear, as this is about a police checkpoint where we need to be credible, I don't think your idea is so smart,' said Brains.

*

When the friends had finished, they gathered up their note-books, smartphones and breathalysers, and put everything in their backpacks before going out and getting into the minibus. Now it was suddenly for real. Martha turned the ignition key and drove out into the road. From bank robber to police officer, that was a big step . . . but this would probably work too.

11

When they got close to the spot where they were going to set up the checkpoint for the long-haul lorries, Martha pulled into the side of the road a few hundred metres before it, so that their minibus wouldn't be visible from the lay-by. 'Because police officers in a minibus with a wheelchair ramp,' as Martha said, 'wouldn't exactly make it look more credible.' Then she parked the minibus, turned off the engine and looked at the others.

'Now we'll carry out our traffic control and terrify them. Are you ready?'

'Absolutely! I've never felt so much like a police officer in all my life,' said Anna-Greta enthusiastically.

As soon as they stepped onto the asphalt, they could feel the shock waves from the heavy vehicles. Thankfully, there wasn't very much traffic but, nevertheless, a surprising number of long-haul lorries drove past. For a while they stood, still and indecisive, looking over towards the entrance to the lay-by.

'I've just thought of something,' said Christina suddenly. 'How do we know what's inside the long-haul lorries? Perhaps they aren't transporting food at all. And not all freight transport is illegal either.'

There was an embarrassing silence while Martha blushed and desperately tried to think up a good answer. She had believed that you'd be able to gain an impression of what type of goods were being transported, but if the lorries weren't marked with logos and were driving very fast too, then it would be difficult.

'You're right, Christina. But if we stop enough lorries, then we're bound to find several shady lorries. It'll sort itself out, you'll see.'

And then they all understood that no objections would put Martha off, and they would simply have get on and do the job.

'Right, then, let's go!' said Martha heartily, but in a voice that revealed a certain degree of nervousness. At that moment, she felt a hand in hers.

'You will be careful, won't you, Martha dear. Lorry drivers can be tough types,' said Brains.

'I promise,' she said, leaning forward to give him a hug. Because she was, of course, a bit worried about him too.

In silence, and somewhat hesitantly, they started to walk towards the lay-by. Martha, Christina and Anna-Greta took the lead with their fully-loaded backpacks, and they were followed by the others carrying a camera on a tripod and two heavy yellow wheel clamps. But that was mostly for appearances, because they hadn't a clue as to how to lock a clamp on to a lorry wheel. But if a lorry driver got a bit stroppy, then they could at any rate threaten to clamp a back wheel.

The camera that Rake was carrying on his shoulder looked professional and could be used with a remote control. If

61

anything happened, it would be good to have it recorded, Martha had said, mainly to reassure Christina.

'Besides,' she went on, 'the police usually connect cameras to an automatic weighing device and check that the lorries are not carrying an excess load. So you can imagine how our camera is going to scare them.'

And then Brains smiled and gave Martha's hand a warm, appreciative little squeeze. She really did think of everything!

When they reached the entrance to the lay-by, they opened their backpacks and quickly pulled out their yellow high-vis safety vests, equipped themselves with their smartphones and breathalysers, then set up the two triangular signs with *POLICE* written on them. Then they cleared their throats lots of times and repeated their mantras for each other: *Your driving licence, please; can we see your tachographs. And please blow into this.* Finally, they all looked at Christina when she pretended to walk round a lorry and check the tyre tread while somewhat nonchalantly kicking the tyre. Her kick was very stylish, and looked highly credible.

'Excellent, then we're ready, aren't we?' said Martha.

'When we robbed banks, we had a stationary object to outmanoeuvre. But these are moving objects. It's going to be tough,' said Brains watching a giant articulated lorry roar past.

'Come along, no problem, it'll sort itself out, just as long as we deal with one long-haul lorry at a time,' Martha reassured them.

Then they divided the various work tasks between them. Rake, who looked both determined and masculine, was given the task of halting the vehicles and waving them into the lay-by, while the others were going to carry out the checks. Rake looked around, stretched himself, and walked authoritatively out to the edge of the road. But then he let several long-haul lorries pass before plucking up courage and finally waving one in. It was a Volvo that seemed to have been driven ten years past its best-before date. The others were standing in readiness.

Martha took some firm steps up to the driver's cab, signalled to the driver to lower the side window and adopted her most authoritative voice.

'*Körkort tack!*' But then she was answered with something totally incomprehensible and she realized that the driver was from some distant foreign country. So she tried afresh: 'Driving licence, please!'

At that point, she realized that she couldn't judge whether a driving licence was genuine or not, but that didn't stop her. Nonchalantly, she examined the card that the driver showed her and noted something down – it did, at least, look serious and professional.

'Now you *blås* here!' she went on, and held out the breathalyser. The man gave it a funny look. 'Ah, yes, you need the *munstycke* as well.' Martha went on and pretended that she was joking when, in actual fact, she had completely forgotten that detail. She attached the mouthpiece, made the guy blow into it, and then checked the scale. Dearie, dearie me, the marker had gone right into the red. And she ought to have thought about that before . . . what did the police do now, ask the driver to follow along to the police station?

While she wondered about this, Christina walked round the vehicle and kicked the tyres as professionally as she could, and Brains leaned down under the chassis and fastened a GPS there. At their last meeting, they had decided that they would keep a check on where the long-haul lorries ended up to see whether their scare project actually worked. Would the long-haul lorries return or not?

'You look very old,' said the driver, peering at Martha.

'Me? Oh no, just tired – and some love problems,' she said as she nonchalantly tapped her hand-sized computer. She pointed at the breathalyser.

'Bad, bad. You are not allowed to drive any more. You are drunk. You are absolutely *dyngrak*. You should have your *dygnsvila*. The driver looked dejectedly at her, pulled out a hundred-kronor banknote and dropped it on the ground. Bribes, Martha thought; she had read about how things were done down on the continent. So she bent down, but at the same moment heard the engine rev up. Before she could stand up again, the driver had accelerated and driven off. And even though a long-haul lorry takes time to pick up speed, there was no way Martha could run after it.

'The bastard, he almost ran me down,' Brains shouted out, and shook his fist after the lorry. While Christina, who had just kicked the tyre when the lorry set off, came limping towards them with one boot missing.

'The wheels started rolling and almost took my boot with it,' she exclaimed angrily. Martha searched with her torch and caught sight of the boot. She bent down.

'Here it is,' she said, and handed it over to Christina. 'Lucky you weren't injured. 'That devil is a danger to traffic! But thankfully we caught that idiot on film!' she said and nodded towards the camera.

'We'd better be careful. Those drivers from Eastern Europe, they can be very nasty,' said Anna-Greta, and Christina nodded.

'Yes, right, perhaps I shouldn't kick so hard.'

The League of Pensioners took a bit of a breather and several lorries roared past before Rake again plucked up courage and waved another one into the lay-by. Christina, having reacquired the missing boot, began again to kick the lorry tyres while Brains checked the tachographs. In one of the lorries, he discovered that something wasn't quite right.

'The driver has manipulated the tachograph with a magnet,' he whispered to Martha.

'Then the wretched fellow won't get his stipulated rest,' she said and felt sorry for him. 'But it's a rotten way to take jobs from Swedish lorries.'

'Sure, but now we'll frighten him off,' exclaimed Brains, bending down to attach a GPS to the chassis. 'Guess what a fright he'll get when he realizes that Swedish authorities can follow him.'

'Authorities, well, I'm not sure about that . . .' Martha muttered and pulled out the hand-held computer to print some fines.

'And the tyres are totally worn, no tread at all. That vehicle was a bloody danger in traffic,' said Christina, who had walked around kicking a bit.

'Then there'll be fines for the tyres too,' said Martha, printing a report on her little computer and handing a copy over to the driver.

'This is a dangerous place for *fuskande* cheat drivers like you!' she hissed. 'Don't come here again!'

The driver accepted the print-out of the fine, and after that the whole gang became more self-confident. Then they waved in one long-haul lorry after the other, and every driver who was found to be doing something illegal was given an enormous fine – which actually became higher and higher as the evening wore on.

Finally, the League of Pensioners changed tasks with each other so they would have something different to do, with Anna-Greta waving in the lorries while Christina, Martha and Brains checked that everything was in order, and Rake walked round the vehicles and kicked at the tyres. Everything went well until it started raining. Then it became hard to see what sort of vehicles were on the road, and the increasingly wet road surface started to cause problems too. The heavy long-haul lorries that passed sprayed up dirt and mud into their faces and Anna-Greta's spectacles in particular were doused several times. She tried to dry them as best she could, but after a while they were just as dirty again.

When she waved in a fire engine and shortly after that a post van, they all realized that it was time to call it a day, pack up their stuff and get away from there as quickly as possible. Because the firemen had thought there was a fire somewhere and the driver of the blue Postnord van swore at them because he had been delayed.

'Just like letters nowadays, then,' Rake had happened to comment, causing the driver to get angry, rev the engine and shoot off, spraying them with even more dirt.

But before they had had time to stop Anna-Greta, it was already too late. Just at that very moment, she had mistakenly waved in a large police van. The tyres squealed and the blue light shone out in the night when the frightening-looking van with *POLICE* written on the bonnet and side doors came to a halt. The door quickly slid open and out poured five police officers wearing *real* uniforms.

12

'Oh dearie me, goodness gracious . . . I never thought of that,' said Martha, her earlobes turning bright red when she saw the police officers approaching them. 'I mean, that the police might come along just now.'

'Perhaps they are going to set up a traffic control point,' said Rake in an unusually weak voice. They all looked at Martha. She was the one who had thought up all this, so it was up to her to solve it too. But before they had time to say anything else or decide on a strategy, a well-built policeman with a moustache came up to them holding a notebook.

'And what's going on here, then?' he asked, looking first at Martha and then at Anna-Greta.

'We're doing very nicely, thank you, and you yourselves?' Martha replied.

'I can see that you're wearing police uniforms.' He thumbed through his book until he found a clean page. Weird that a police officer had to use a notebook; couldn't the police authorities afford smartphones? Martha reflected, and was just about to offer him her own, before she managed to restrain herself.

'Ah, yes, the uniforms, aren't they absolutely stylish?'

'Mind you,' Anna-Greta added to be on the safe side, 'your uniform is even smarter.'

'And for what reason are two old ladies going around disguised as police officers, if I might ask?'

'The profession of our dreams, constable,' Martha lied.

'Oh, is it indeed . . .' The policeman stopped there because he suddenly caught sight of Rake and Brains in their yellow hi-vis vests. 'What the hell, are there more of you?'

'Yes, in times like these you can't be too careful. We've caught three illegal long-haul lorries with manipulated tachographs. What about that!'

'But heavens above, what do you think you're doing? Playing at being police?'

Martha, who realized that this could go totally wrong if she couldn't think up a suitable apology, straightened her uniform cap and leaned forward.

'Would you like to be in our film?' she asked with her sweetest and friendliest smile. 'I mean, so that we can have some real police officers too. We're making a short film for the pensioners' club. It's about difficult and tough professions in Sweden, and we immediately thought of the police. Men like you, yes, professions that are in the front line and ought to have a pay rise.'

The constable was lost for words.

'What are you saying, are you making a film?'

'Oh, yes. We have already filmed you,' Martha chirped and nodded at the camera tripod next to them. 'But if you don't want to be in the film, just say so, and we'll cut you out.'

The policeman thumbed his block and wrinkled his forehead. 'But do you have permission to do this?'

'For goodness' sake, don't you see? You police officers have so much bureaucratic work anyway, so we thought we'd save you a bit of paperwork. It is much more important that you catch villains, isn't it?'

The police constable muttered something and his colleagues started to become restless. He straightened his back.

'We're going to have a traffic checkpoint here this evening, so you had better be on your way.'

'A police checkpoint?' Martha quickly adapted. 'Oh well, in that case. Then perhaps we can help you. Because we were filming, as you know, and it was very realistic. You see, we checked driving licences, tyres, tachographs and even did some breathalyser tests. We have studied how the police work, so if you want, you can use our results.'

'Well, thank you for the offer, but we'll manage on our own.'

'But there were lots of threadbare tyres and the breathalyser tests often reacted,' said Martha, and she held out the breathalyser they had bought on the Internet.

'Oh, I see, those. They're only toys, but thanks anyway.' The constable saw how his colleagues in the background were growing impatient and felt he must come to a decision. A gang of pensioners who were playing at being police officers, there was nothing in the law books about that. The only solution was to try to get rid of them. He straightened his uniform cap, drew a breath and said, 'Well, good luck with your film, but don't do this again. It isn't permitted and you can get into difficulties. So, if you would be so kind as to be on your way . . .'

'You know what, one of the lorry drivers was really brazen. We were almost run over.'

'Exactly. This is not for pensioners. So, if you would please be on your way.'

'Of course, no more filming of the police force, OK, and we shall pack up everything right this minute. But you know what? We've got another film in the pipeline too. We are thinking of dressing up as Vikings, role-play they call it. What do you think? Would you like to be in that? We need some strong and muscular menfolk.'

'Sure, sure, but will you please leave this lay-by now, so we can start working.'

'Naturally, Constable. You have a very important job to carry out and what would we citizens do without you?' Martha held up her thumb, so she could press thumbs with the constable. Helpless, he looked at his smirking colleagues, took a deep breath and pressed his thumb against Martha's.

'There you are, then. No more filming today. Now we'll leave,' Martha decided, and she pretended to break off the filming. The League of Pensioners had never before packed things away so fast, and never before had their minibus got off to such a flying start.

Behind them in the lay-by they left two long-haul lorries with threadbare tyres on wheels which Rake had clamped. Unfortunately, he hadn't yet worked out how to take them off . . .

13

'It was my spectacles, yes that was the problem. They were so mucky that I couldn't see anything,' Anna-Greta moaned, looking crestfallen. 'And when I tried to clean them, it only got worse.'

The tall, former bank virtuoso stood by the sink at home in their kitchen and tried to clean her horn-framed spectacles, while time after time apologizing for mistakenly waving down the police van. She was still in shock, and well aware of the fact that the police check could have ended up disastrously for all of them.

'No, thank God that Martha sorted it out and nobody suspected us. But from now on we must be a bit more careful,' said Brains.

'Yes, and just how many traffic checks are we actually going to carry out to save the village? Those milk and food lorries will probably continue regardless,' Rake said.

'Not to mention the fact that we can get into trouble. The police might start checking up on us,' Christina sighed.

'No, I think we've made a good start with our plan. Next time, the haulage companies will be wary of letting their drivers use the route near Hemmavid. Believe me,' said Martha.

'But what about the police?' Rake insisted.

There was silence for a while and Christina picked at her ear lobes. It looked as if she wanted to say something but not until she had devoured a carrot and drunk a glass of apple juice did she pluck up the courage.

'Perhaps we shouldn't have asked the drivers to pay the fines to us directly,' she reflected. 'I fined them twenty thousand kronor each time a long-haul lorry had too heavy a load, and ten thousand for threadbare tyres. The haulage companies pay. I think we should rake in quite a lot, actually.'

'But goodness me, whatever are you saying, Christina? We hadn't agreed that,' Martha groaned.

'Pah, no problem. The police can't keep track of Swish payments to mobile phones. Besides, I let the money for our Robbery Fund go via the Dark Web – you know, where you encrypt IP-addresses so it's difficult for anybody to trace you. Anna-Greta instructed me. After all, she has worked in a bank all of her life,' Christina answered, proud of herself.

Anna-Greta dried her spectacles and put them on again. As usual, they slipped down a little. Nevertheless she managed to see the horrified looks in the eyes of the others.

'You don't need to worry, I arranged a false digital bank ID. No way will the police be able to trace us,' she said quickly. 'We aren't beginners any longer, Martha. We have learned how to do things. A few more police road checks and we'll have plenty of capital to get things going in the whole district.'

This was unbelievable. What were the girls doing? Martha was accustomed to deciding everything herself, and felt rather lost when the others suddenly made decisions on their own without letting anyone know. Of course, it was fine to use your own initiative, but if you didn't tell anyone, then it could go dreadfully wrong. She would have to raise that issue very diplomatically and at the right moment. Now she took a deep breath – in fact, several very deep breaths – and tried to think positively.

'As long as the fines go to those who need support out here in the countryside, then everything's all right. And you seem to have thought of that,' she said with a forced smile.

'Oh indeed, of course they are earmarked,' said Christina, but she turned red in a disquieting manner.

'But listen, the most important thing at the moment is how we should deal with the police, isn't it?' Anna-Greta broke in. 'Because even if we always donate our robbery money to the needy, we are still guilty of the crimes.'

The others looked thoughtful. The police had every reason to catch them. At the auction house, they had been recorded on CCTV, and before Blomberg disappeared out of their lives, he had revealed to them that they had also been recorded on CCTV during their previous robberies. He had images of them outside Handelsbanken shortly before it was robbed, and outside the Nationalmuseum in connection with the major art theft. His love for Anna-Greta had prevented him from using those images in the investigations, but had anyone other than Blomberg seen them? And what if he had saved the images on his computer or on a disk or stick? Then they really would be in a dreadful pickle.

Martha cleared her throat. 'The police, yes, it was unlucky to meet them at the traffic checkpoint. But I'm sure that it was an exception, their being here,' she said. 'Regardless, we need to do more for Hemmavid.'

'But we can't save an entire rural district on our own. We must get some people from the village to help us,' Anna-Greta put in. 'Why not join forces with Roland Svensson and his wife in the farm shop, the head teacher from the school and other important people? It's not until we do that, that we'll become really strong.'

They all nodded and praised Anna-Greta for her foresight. They could, of course, lead the way themselves, but they would need more people to build a strong countryside movement. They all agreed on this in complete harmony, and, satisfied with themselves, Martha and the gang called it an evening and went up to bed.

Before she went to sleep, Martha thought for a long time about what they had achieved so far. The long-haul lorry drivers would certainly think twice before using the route close to Hemmavid again. And if the drivers from abroad did try it on and do pick-up and deliveries on domestic Swedish routes, then Brains could report them to the police. His GPS thingamajigs on the lorries' chassis were very firmly attached. Yes, with a few more police traffic checks, Hemmavid would certainly become a living village again. That evening Martha fell asleep without any worry wrinkles between her eyebrows; instead, she was smiling. Because she had no idea that Ernst Blomberg's flash drive was at Kungsholmen Police Station. Or that talk of their remarkable police operation would reach all the way to Stockholm.

14

Chief Inspector Kurt Löwander, who had been obliged to take part in a traffic checkpoint because of the shortage of traffic police, returned to the station both tired and hungry. His uniform was splashed with salt and mud, his boots soaking wet. He washed his face and moustache, hung up his outer clothes, put his boots by the radiator and changed into civilian clothes. What an evening! All those threadbare tyres and manipulated tachographs, overloaded long-haul lorries and bothersome drivers who had found it difficult to answer questions. Some of them tried to speak English but they were almost impossible to understand. Others gesticulated and explained something in their own language while waving their foreign documents. He knew from experience that they were often false. And the worst drivers he had had to deal with had been aggressive too. Real mafia types.

No, it had been so very much nicer with the pensioners. They had been a crazy bunch. Playing at being police officers for a film for the pensioners' club. He would love to see that film; it would make for brilliant entertainment at the police Christmas party.

But what a thing to do! Did you lose all sense of proportion when you were elderly? One of those old ladies had even gone around kicking the tyres of the lorries while her bloke – or whoever he was – had clamped two big juggernauts. He couldn't help but smile! Amidst all the grey everyday police work this was something that cheered him up, but of course that gang of pensioners couldn't go on doing that, they were ruining the reputation of the police force.

He looked at the clock. Time to go home, he was done for the day and had finished his shift. He gathered together some papers on the desk and was just about to leave when he changed his mind. He hadn't eaten all evening and was so hungry. He went into the kitchen, took a pizza out of the freezer and shoved it into the microwave. It was best to get something in his stomach before he went home. His wife refused to cook anything for him if he came home after eight in the evening, and he certainly didn't want to have to start messing around in the kitchen as soon as he got home. A delicious pizza aroma filled the room and the microwave gave a ping. He took his plate out, and put two more Capricciosa in. The others in the station would definitely want something to eat too.

It wasn't long before his colleague Hammarström sauntered in through the door.

'Pizza! Uhm, lovely. I'm famished.'

Others, too, must have noticed the pizza aroma because Löwander hadn't even put the pizzas on the plate when their boss came into the room.

'Been busy working all evening . . .'

'There's enough pizza for you too.' Löwander took some cans of beer and a cola out of the fridge and put them on the table. The men sat down. At first, all you could hear was the munching sound as they took their first bites, but then the conversation started up. Löwander and Hammarström described the evening's traffic checkpoint and pulled out their notes. Finally, they sighed over the frightening increase in the number of drivers and lorries breaking the law.

'Those shady haulage companies are responsible for most of the traffic accidents in this country. How the hell are we going to deal with them?' said Hammarström.

'It was more fun with those pensioners,' Löwander said.

'Pensioners?' the boss asked.

Löwander described their meeting with the five oldies and their film project.

'They were evidently going to show the film at some pensioners' get-together,' Hammarström added.

'Stopping long-haul lorries to make a pensioners' film? Err, that sounds pretty weird. Were the whole lot of them senile?' the boss wondered.

'No, no, there was nothing wrong with them, they were jolly types. They had done lots of work too, and said that they had revealed lots of illegal lorry transports. And they had even clamped two long-haul lorries.' Löwander smiled.

'Bloody hell!'

'Yes, they had waved in two vehicles with threadbare tyres which they thought were a danger in traffic and could lead to accidents. But I don't know how they managed to clamp them.'

'Did they issue fines too?' The boss suddenly looked serious.

Kurt Löwander gave a start and fingered his moustache nervously. He hadn't thought of that.

'That lot? Issue fines? No way, not a chance. They were just lovely old folk who were enjoying themselves. I don't think we should begrudge them that.'

'Well, I'm not sure. Because there was a grumpy driver who phoned the police station and complained. He admitted that he had done wrong, but he couldn't understand why he had to Swish in the fine straight away. He needed his money while he was in Sweden. The haulage company that he was driving for could pay the fine later, he said.'

Löwander and Hammarström looked at each other. Was the driver telling a lie or had those crazy pensioners quite simply tried to increase their pensions? Löwander started to laugh.

'I know that pensioners have a tough time today, but surely they're not that cunning?'

'Don't say that. Don't underestimate elderly people. Perhaps we ought to keep an eye on them.'

'As if we don't have enough to do already,' Löwander sighed and took a large slice of pizza. 'No, now let's forget about it.'

'Hang on, I'm not so sure. How many of them were there?'

'Three women and two men. All over sixty I'd say, perhaps a few years older.'

The boss gave a whistle. 'Do you remember that art robbery at the Nationalmuseum in Stockholm?'

'Ah yes, that notorious coup, you don't forget that in a hurry,' Löwander recalled.

'The museum hung paintings by Renoir and Monet on ordinary wires, just there for the picking. But now there are guards everywhere and all the paintings are securely fastened.'

'My goodness, you do seem well informed,' Löwander cut in. 'But what has it got to do with this?'

'Well, I used to work with Chief Inspector Ernst Blomberg, he was at Kungsholmen station. When he retired, he opened a private detective agency and then he told me about these oldies. He suspected them of having committed several crimes, the robberies at the Grand Hotel, and other stuff too. But then it all went quiet. I don't know what happened later.'

There was silence around the table. The step from a pensioners' film and waving in long-haul lorries to the art robbery at the Nationalmuseum was a bit too big, Löwander and Hammarström thought, and they cleared their throats in discomfort. They exchanged a look of mutual understanding. This was typical of the boss. There wasn't a crime that he didn't think he could solve. That must be what happened when you were transferred to the countryside, when you had expected to make a brilliant career in Stockholm. But the two police officers were tired after their long shift and hadn't the energy to deal with yet another of the boss's theories. They quickly led the conversation on to cars and women instead, before getting up, throwing away the remains of the pizzas in the waste bin and putting their plates in the sink. Then Löwander's wife, Bettan, phoned.

'When are you coming home? I've been waiting all evening.'

'I'm on my way,' he mumbled briefly and closed his phone. His wife was so difficult nowadays. Ever since she had lost her job at the health clinic a few years ago, she hadn't given him a moment's peace and quiet. She was always phoning, and when he came home later than usual, she thought he had been unfaithful. But he was a police officer and had irregular working hours. Besides, his job wore him out, and he had neither the time nor the energy for much else. Yet she didn't believe him. He could, of course, have gone home earlier, but he had actually preferred to relax with the other guys after work. Once upon a time he had been deeply in love and proud of having captured the school's most desirable girl. And they had had some happy years. But now . . . when he came home, she would ask him where he had been and be suspicious of his answer. It was almost always like that nowadays. More and more often, he thought of leaving her. Starting afresh with somebody else . . . He was interrupted in his musings by Hammarström.

'Have you finished?'

Löwander nodded. On his way out of the door he said to the boss, 'Don't sit up too long working. Time to go home.'

But his boss wasn't listening. 'You know what, those pensioners – what if it's the same gang that stole the paintings at the Nationalmuseum and the diamonds at the Stockholm auction house . . .' he thought out loud. 'It's such a damned cunning idea, to get the people who have broken the traffic laws to send in money by Swish. In a way, it's the same style of crime.'

'But if the money ends up with us, then it doesn't matter. We could do with it to top up our wages,' Löwander replied.

'But that's just the point. I checked. No money bloody well came in here. It vanished without trace. I bet you there is something fishy about this.'

15

From long-haul lorries to gambling? Well, actually, that wasn't such a big step. Because, before the friends had gone after the lorries, Martha had been thinking that their ambushes ought to be alternated with some pleasant attraction which would tempt people to come to the area. And what she had finally thought up wasn't just any ordinary lark, it was cow bingo. She herself had seen how people had found it so amusing when it had been arranged down in the south of the country, and in her childhood village the betting as well as the activities organized around it had provided a large addition to the village funds.

So, when she heard that Roland Svensson on the nearby farm was going to let his cows out into the fields after they had spent the winter in the cowshed, her brain started working straight away. That very same day, she walked over to him and suggested that his cow release should be combined with cow bingo.

'Cow bingo?' he repeated and put his hands into the pockets of his green overalls.

'You can't imagine what fun it is,' Martha answered, and then explained that cow bingo had attracted a large public down in the south, so why couldn't they arrange something similar in Hemmavid too? The farmer looked at Martha and raised his eyebrows.

'Cow release and cow bingo?'

'Yes, indeed,' said Martha, putting on the loveliest smile she could. And then Roland said that he wanted to think about it for a while first, and see whether it was feasible. But, certainly, it sounded exciting.

So Martha visited him once, twice and several more times. And showed him a video clip of cow bingo on her laptop.

Brains noted her growing interest in the talkative farmer, and for each day that passed felt all the more ignored. He was getting fed up with the sight of the man who was sooo nice and had sooo many interesting things to say. Smelling of manure, Martha enthusiastically described his organic farming methods where so much on the farm was environmentally friendly and adapted to climate change, and the cows had lots of space in the cowshed.

But Brains was terrified of cows. If the farmer had at least had a car workshop, then they would have had a shared interest to talk about. He could put up with the smell of diesel and motor oil, but manure! No, Brains was feeling really sorry for himself. What could he do to make Martha take things easy? Thousands of cookery books were published every year, but nobody had written a sensible handbook on how to deal with energetic women. Although Martha wouldn't, of course, have fitted into that category either. You would have needed an instruction book just for her alone.

A few days later, when the members of the League of Pensioners were drinking their evening tea in the living room,

Martha started her major persuasion campaign. Roland Svensson was beginning to come round to the idea, and she was feeling hopeful. Now she only had to get her friends on board too. So, after a bit of small talk, and once they had drunk their tea and eaten their usual wafer biscuits, she sat down, putting her laptop on the table.

'Now this, everybody, is something that could attract people,' she said, clicking on a YouTube video. 'Just look at this; it's about cow bingo. An event like this would bring money to the village, I promise you,' she said, gesticulating so enthusiastically that her cup fell onto the floor.

'Are you going to bring cows to the village? I thought you wanted to populate it,' said Rake.

'So you think we should save the village using cows? Have you really thought this through properly?' Brains asked and sighed.

'Oh yes, this is as easy as pie. Now just listen. First you mark out large squares on a grassy meadow, then we give each square a number, for example from one to twenty, and then we let the cows out. Depending on where they leave their visiting cards –'

'Visiting cards? That's rather an idealized description,' said Rake. 'Cow shit!'

'All right. Then the cows walk around the meadow and eat grass and leave their pats. They do so on different numbers, and finally someone gets bingo.'

'They shit!' Rake repeated.

Anna-Greta, who always thought in economic terms, came to life. 'Now listen, there could actually be money in this,' she said. 'All we need are Svensson's cows and some white

84

marking paint. Then we mark out the squares on the grass and number them. No printed material or expensive investments. Smart!'

'Usch, bank robberies are more lucrative,' Brains protested.

'Exactly! God knows how many cowpats we'd need to get in a million,' Rake agreed.

They all spoke at once, and Martha was beginning to find it unpleasant. 'Now, everybody, I think we should sleep on it. And if you can't think up anything better at our meeting tomorrow morning, then I propose that we organize our first cow bingo.'

Her friends looked helplessly at one another because now they realized that whatever they said, Martha would put them to work. Again!

Brains and the others had found it hard to sleep, so the gang of pensioners didn't wake up the following day at their usual time. Thus they missed their morning meeting. So, when the big grandfather clock in the living room struck ten and nobody showed up, Martha confidently went across to farmer Svensson to talk him round. Because, as she said, the takings from the cow bingo would go directly to Hemmavid.

Then she gathered her friends together and asked them to help paint the newly cut common meadow with white squares and then number them. It wasn't easy to convince the others, but after she had shown them the YouTube video again, and pointed out how happy the people looked, her friends began to thaw. Besides, she claimed that even if the cows were a bit slow, they could earn money selling knick-knacks, hamburgers and ice cream while they were waiting.

'But cow bingo! Our robberies were at least an intellectual challenge,' Rake sighed.

'Bank robberies and cow bingo are admittedly not the same thing, but –'

'Certainly not. When did you last hear a bank moo?'

The members of the league grumbled a while longer, but finally agreed to paint the meadow and do their bit for the stunt. It wasn't bullfighting, thank God, and ordinary cows ought to be docile.

16

It was a lovely sunny day and over by Roland Svensson's cowshed, you could hear a clattering and mooing here and there. Some sunburnt farmers in checked shirts and wide shorts stood there, each with a can of beer in his hand, and the women in flowery dresses and worn jeans were chatting away or trying to keep their kids under control. A bunch of children chased each other around the fenced-off area and a large Labrador rolled in a pool of water outside the cowshed. Beside the large grassed area there were lots of people, and Anna-Greta beamed. She had counted 280 paying visitors to this simple event, a happening with four-legged artistes who didn't want paying! Could it be better?

Brains blinked away a drop of sweat and rubbed his face. With Roland Svensson's help, Martha had arranged Hemmavid's first cow bingo, and as if that wasn't enough, the farmer seemed to have fallen for her. Sometimes life was difficult.

Brains was nervous for Martha's sake. Because naturally he wanted her to be successful. He looked over to the cowshed. Just so long as the animals behaved themselves. Shortly after Martha had agreed with Roland to do this, he had heard a rumour that the cows were not perhaps as docile as one might think.

But then they had already gone too far to stop things. The local press had written about the cow release and cow bingo, and Roland Svensson had promised fantastic entertainment. Brains shook his head. How was it all going to work out?

Martha stood by the fence wearing a dress with a pattern of large flowers, and with a blue handbag over her shoulder. He went up to her.

'It's going to go well, Martha darling,' he said and squeezed her hand. But really it was he himself he was consoling. He was terrified by those mooing animals.

'Of course it's going to work well, my dear. Now we're going to enjoy ourselves!' she answered and gave him a jolly smile without a hint of worry. At that particular moment, he envied her.

Suddenly, there was a loud mooing when Rake led out the first cow through the gate. Farmer Svensson had entrusted him with the task of handling the animals, and he nonchalantly let the cow loose onto the numbered bingo field.

The brown-spotted cow Rosa gave a long moo and stumbled tiredly out onto the grass. Rake raised his eyebrows. What was this? Svensson had promised that his cows would be in top shape, but now the miserable creature could hardly wave its tail. She moved arduously further across the grass and listlessly trampled the numbered squares. But then she stopped and started ruminating. Now Christina and Anna-Greta came up to them.

'Martha, what did you give the cows to eat? It's embarrassing that nothing is happening,' said Anna-Greta, glancing at the animal. The brown-spotted cow strolled lazily among the marked squares and ignored everything and everybody. Now and then she looked about her with an empty gaze, wobbled, and said moo. But she didn't manage to produce even the smallest of cowpats. The spectators waited and time passed.

'Now something must damned well happen,' Brains muttered. 'Did you give that bloody cow some blueberries or something similarly constipating?'

'No, dear, it was Roland who fed the animals,' Martha defended herself, and Brains noted that she now called farmer Svensson by his first name.

'Asch, cow bingo takes time. This is a sort of mindfulness for cows. It's good that they are taking it easy,' Christina pointed out.

'Yes, and if it takes time, then the tension grows,' Anna-Greta added. 'And while everybody waits, we can sell more ice cream.' She had opened an ice-cream stand with home-made ice cream and she was keen on the idea. She had heard that you could make lots of money selling ice cream.

'Now listen to me! This is not about ice cream but about where the cows are going to shit,' Rake muttered and again looked out across the common meadow.

But nothing happened and Rosa wandered around slowly, filled with her own thoughts.

'How much will the winner get?' Christina wondered after a while.

'Two thousand Swedish kronor and I'm talking proper money and not bitcoins or that sort of stuff,' Anna-Greta answered.

'Only two thousand? I don't think I'd be bothered to make an effort either if I was a cow,' Rake said.

'But, Rake, it isn't the cow who gets the money,' Brains pointed out.

'But why not make the prize bigger, Anna-Greta? Let's say twenty thousand for the winner,' Martha suggested.

'As if that would speed up that joke of a cow,' Rake sighed.

But at that moment, Rosa yawned, lifted her tail and emptied her bladder. The spectators applauded and exchanged expectant looks. Any second now! But Rosa satisfied herself with that, and continued on her way at her leisurely pace.

'Now that goddammed cow must perform! Eat some grass, damn it, do something!' an impatient gentleman shouted out and he clenched his fist.

'Now then, cow bingo isn't a hundred-metre sprint in nine seconds,' said Rake in a loud voice as he observed how Rosa did a few more sluggish turns. But then she stopped, shook her head and seemed to be concentrating.

'Hurrah, whoopee, now it's going to happen!' exclaimed Christina with a joyful howl, but so loudly that Rosa was frightened and forgot what she was about to do. Instead, she set off at full speed, and as Rake unfortunately had not closed the gate properly, the scared animal managed to get out of the fenced-in area and up onto the slope outside the cowshed. And there she farted very loudly before dropping two cowpats.

'Bingo!' Anna-Greta shouted out in delight. 'In this sort of situation, we keep the prize ourselves.'

'No, no, no, that doesn't count. The game must go on,' shouted the man with the clenched fist. But Rake had the presence of mind to react, stepping forward and letting out cow number two, the black-and-white three-year-old called Saga. But, as before, he forgot to close the gate, which unfortunately resulted in two more cows, Rosöga and Katja, rushing into the bingo site too. And they had eaten lots of grass the previous day so they had hardly got onto the grass before they dropped one cowpat after the other – without anyone really seeing which cowpat belonged to which cow. And they landed on three different squares, too.

'Bingo, bingo, bingo,' Christina roared.

'Oh my God,' murmured Brains. 'What do we do now?'

'Don't worry,' Martha reassured him. 'We'll have three winners and then everybody will be happy.'

'If we carry on like this, we'll go bankrupt,' Anna-Greta complained.

'Yes, but it is important to have a good reputation,' Martha said, upon which she climbed up on the stand, took the microphone and pronounced that all those who had bet on the three numbers would be winners.

The mood improved, people bought more ice cream and when all the new bets had been placed, they started the bingo again. Now it was the turn of Maj-Ros, but she was a cow with a mind of her own. She went straight across the playing field to square number 28, where she stopped, mooed a few times and . . . just flopped down onto the grass. A disappointed murmur could be heard from the crowd, followed by shouts and the stamping of feet. Yes, the spectators shouted and called out, but Maj-Ros was having a little snooze and had no intention of getting up. No, Maj-Ros didn't budge an inch.

At this point, Rake had had enough and went to fetch Hugo,

without reflecting upon the fact that this colossal cow was a bull. Hugo rolled his eyes, lowered his head, and aimed for Maj-Ros. And then a great deal took place, but it wasn't what is called cow bingo.

A lot of the members of the local ladies' sewing circle demurely lowered their gaze, and the vicar from the neighbouring village looked the other way, while a granny and her husband immediately started pointing at all sorts of other things so that their grandchildren would look at them instead. Brains put his hand on his forehead. Bulls were not allowed in cow bingo, but Rake hadn't listened and now there was one great big hullabaloo. And as if that hadn't sufficed, Rake had also left the gate wide open so that Blenda, too, rushed out. Hugo caught sight of her and bellowed in delight. The spectators backed away and Blenda mooed with what was, for her, rare enthusiasm.

In the end, things got so lively that farmer Svensson – who was enjoying a hot dog and a strong beer behind the outhouse – realized that it was high time to do something. He quickly rushed out onto the common, gathered together all the cows and, with some effort, managed to get them back where they belonged.

Then all the spectators booed and wanted their money back, and Brains looked at Martha in despair. But she took his hand and stroked it reassuringly.

'Darling, we'll arrange a few other fun things instead of cow bingo in future,' she said. 'And now we'll give the spectators a bonus in anticipation of the next event and hand out some lottery tickets. We want them to be satisfied before they leave.'

And how she managed that, he didn't know, but when they had tidied up after the public and all the cows, farmer Svensson and all the others were in a good mood. Anna-Greta counted the money and could tell them that they had taken 132,570 kronor during the day, money that Martha and the gang donated to Hemmavid's fund for culture and entertainment. And, by so doing, Martha and the League of Pensioners had gained the confidence not only of the farmer but also of the villagers. Or so they believed.

In the village café, the villagers talked about the cow event over steaming cups of coffee, while simultaneously expressing surprise over the fact that the newcomers hadn't shown any inhibitions at all, but had set up such a large event right away. Malin was grumpy because they hadn't been able to sell ice cream in the café during the event, while Lilian was pleased about all the extra customers they had received in the café during the day.

'We'd best keep an eye on those pensioners,' Malin muttered when she had served coffee and Danish pastries to the guests and had sat down beside Lilian with a cup. 'You can't trust Stockholm folk.'

'Hmm, if they think they can kick-start Hemmavid with various spectacles, then they haven't a clue, of course,' Lilian agreed.

'Newcomers always think they can change things. But here? No, it won't work. If we got a railway back again, people would simply use the train to get away from here more easily.'

'But it'll be difficult to keep Hemmavid alive regardless. If that Allan Petterson becomes the new mayor in Skogsås, then that will be the end of us. He wants to centralize everything, and move all services to the town. If he's given a free rein, the result would be that there'll be nobody left here at all.'

'Don't be so pessimistic. I'm sure Allan Petterson knows what he's doing,' Malin objected, blushing slightly. Because she hadn't told her sister that she had started seeing Allan in secret. You kept some things to yourself.

'What, that man? A confidence-trickster type! Pleasant, looks all right and knows how to behave in public, but not a person you can trust. But I do, however, like the oldies. Don't get annoyed with them. They have brought some fresh air to the village.'

'Fresh air? But, heavens above, they get up to so much, it makes me feel quite exhausted. No, what are they doing here? There is something fishy about them.'

'Why should you think that? Malin, there's a burning smell. Don't forget the buns in the oven.'

Malin swore and got up. When she and Lilian had run the village shop, they had been the calm, secure centre point for the village, and they had got on well. But now it felt as if things were getting out of control. Because of those Stockholmers who were thinking up all sorts of things to liven up the village – was there no way to stop them?

94

17

The newly appointed mayor in Skogsås, Allan Petterson, sank down behind his desk and lit his pipe. He was happy. Overjoyed. A unanimous district council had chosen him to be mayor of all of Skogsås, so now he was the boss and controlled everything himself. There were, admittedly, only ten thousand inhabitants in the town, but he wasn't going to sit back and accept that. He would let the municipality grow and become a place people talked about. And if you could incorporate the village of Hemmavid with Skogsås and make them one municipality, you could save lots of money and he would have a bigger domain. So now it was a matter of moving all activities to Skogsås.

Hemmavid was where the asphalt roads turned into gravel roads, and was a godforsaken hole filled with farmers and oldies. The trains no longer stopped at the railway station and the school would soon be closed down. Not to mention that dump of a building that used to be the vicarage. That building was becoming derelict and it could just as well be demolished. No, the only thing of value over there was the land. And, of course, his beloved Malin. She was still living there, even though she and her sister had been forced to close down the village shop. He had hoped that it would mean she would move to Skogsås and live closer to him, but instead the sisters had opened a café, The Danish Pastry. Anyhow, that wouldn't survive much longer, and then . . . She was single and had no children, so it shouldn't be a problem for her to move. Besides, he could certainly fix things so that she could rent a flat in town. And then at long last she would be closer to him.

It gave him butterflies. To think that an out-of-the-way village could produce a beautiful woman like her. He longed for their moments together and wished they could have more. But he must be careful. His wife had become suspicious. More than twice last week he hadn't dared to drive off to his secret meetings.

His thoughts wandered hither and thither and he found it hard to concentrate. When all the more municipal activities were moved to Skogsås, he must use the taxpayers' money properly. And how could he best do that? Above all, he must rationalize the schools. The one in Hemmavid ought to be closed down and then you could bus the children to Skogsås instead. He leaned back in the grey office chair while he thought about it. There were more things he ought to deal with too, like that dreadful recycling centre and rubbish dump outside Skogsås. Once the two municipalities were amalgamated, he could make sure that it was moved to outside Hemmavid instead. It was a question of taking over activities that ran at a profit, and getting rid of those that you didn't want. He straightened his necktie and the creases of his trousers. That was how things were done in the big wide world – he knew that after studying in the US. He was good at Social Studies, and he had inherited his father's nose for

96

business. And now things would damn well start moving in his Skogsås. And the few people still living in Hemmavid? There was no need to consider them. No need at all.

In the period after their police traffic control and the cow bingo, Martha was in an exceptionally good mood. In secret she was already pondering new plans. It ought to be feasible, because the others had now perked up. Christina painted her watercolours and Anna-Greta played her vinyl records and happily joined in when Frank Sinatra sang 'My Way'. During the cow bingo she had also managed to sell all of her home-made ice cream and she was over the moon about that – ice cream that she had concocted herself.

'How much did we make today?' Christina wondered when she stood beside the hall mirror putting on a bit of new mascara. She had decided to wear her bright yellow coat instead of the blue one, and she wanted her make-up to be the right colour too. Then she stopped, and quickly ran her fingers through her hair. Oh my God, it was tinted blue nowadays and wouldn't at all match the yellow coat. No way could she look like a Swedish flag. She had better put the blue coat back on again.

'How much did we make today? Well, the police traffic control was bingo for us; we raked in all of 128,550 kronor. You seem to have fined the drivers for everything, payments have come in for excess weight, threadbare tyres and manipulated tachographs. Neat work! The ice cream sales didn't bring in as much, but that, too, resulted in a profit of several thousands. But to bring in more money there, we need to sell even more ice cream.' Anna-Greta looked thoughtful.

'Why not buy professional Italian ice cream machines so that you can make more ice cream and create your own flavours?'

'Yes, sure, but I will need lots of milk.'

'Easy as pie,' Christina said, her self-confidence now having been given a real boost. 'I know what to do,' she exclaimed so strongly that her lipstick slipped and she ended up with a red line on her cheek. 'Those dairy tank-lorries we saw during our police traffic control, they come from Finland, Denmark, Germany and certainly other countries too. We can stop them and syphon off a bit of milk and that will suffice for your ice cream.'

'What?' Anna-Greta was astounded. What had happened to Christina? She had become full of ideas since they had moved out into the countryside.

'The perfect crime,' Christina went on. 'The drivers won't discover the missing milk until they arrive at their destination. Too late to do anything about it. Good idea, don't you think?'

Anna-Greta looked at her friend admiringly. She herself was the sort of person who could count and administrate, but she wasn't as good at thinking up new ideas as Christina was.

'Brilliant idea. Where do they all come from?' said Anna-Greta, a happy expression in her eyes. She was thrifty by nature and here she could immediately see the potential to earn a bit extra. And it wasn't only that; they would certainly have a bit of fun doing it. 'But,' she added a little hesitatingly, 'do you think Martha will go along with it?'

'Martha this, Martha that – does she need to know everything? She is always bossing us around. If we syphon off milk from the occasional tanker, it isn't such a big deal, is it? And besides, we'd have a little adventure all on our own.'

And Anna-Greta, who had been very lonely since she had been obliged to end her relationship with Blomberg, perked up enormously. She immediately felt needed again. Ever since the League of Pensioners had stopped carrying out their bank robberies, she had been bored and had felt depressed, but now she could feel a flutter of expectation in her body again. She and Christina would do something rather bold and dangerous together. That would be really nice.

'But, Anna-Greta, let's keep this idea to ourselves. OK? Otherwise, Martha will just interfere.' Christina suddenly looked serious.

'Agreed!' Anna-Greta answered, and she made the sign of the cross to be on the safe side – even though she was an atheist. 'This is going to be our little adventure, just you and me, nobody else's, a secret project for the good of the League of Pensioners and Hemmavid village, right?' She looked up at the ceiling and quickly calculated how much she thought they could earn from the ice cream – yes, when foreign milk tankers were going to provide 80 per cent of the ingredients completely free . . .

'Although – I don't know, wouldn't it be theft?' she wondered, lowering her gaze in a becoming manner.

'Pah, if a tanker contains twenty thousand litres of milk and we syphon off a few drops, it won't really make a difference. That's written off as wastage. And fifty litres of milk is enough for three hundred and fifty portions of ice cream, what about that!'

'You're a genius.' Anna-Greta smiled. No more was needed

99

to silence her guilty conscience. 'And if they should nevertheless discover what's happened, then perhaps they'll decide to avoid Hemmavid. No more foreign milk transports here. A double whammy!'

'A double victory,' Christina corrected her.

The boring old town hall in Skogsås would hardly be noticeable in all its greyness, if it hadn't been for several windows which were lit up. The town council had just had a meeting and the mayor, Allan Petterson, flung open the door in majestic style. With a satisfied demeanour and a wad of papers under his arm, he left the council chamber and went off down the corridor. The school in Hemmavid would be moved to Skogsås next year, and, in the long term, would be closed down. The year eight pupils would finish their schooling, and then that would be it. He had expected angry reactions and firm resistance at the meeting, but Hemmavid's finances were so bad that the councillors realized the seriousness. The decision could soon be pushed through. The local municipal tax level was already much higher than in Stockholm, and nobody imagined that they could raise the taxes even more. All that remained was to close down and to centralize.

He whistled in satisfaction while hurrying down the corridor with long steps. Most things had gone as he wished, and before long Skogsås would grow and his own home district become the leading town in the county. And then ever more people would move to his municipality.

But there were still things to do; he had to sort out rubbish collection and recycling too, because when the wind was blowing in the wrong direction, there was a dreadful stench in Skogsås. He had already worked out his plan. Behind the school in Hemmavid there was an old mineshaft. That was just perfect to use for rubbish and hazardous waste. All they needed to do was move everything there, and that problem would soon be solved too. Yes, it was looking really good, and everything had gone better than he had expected.

18

The morning sun shone in through the open bedroom window – because Brains had forgotten to draw the curtains – and woke Martha up. A week had passed since the district's first cow bingo, and Martha knew it herself: they had arranged a gimmicky event that had attracted the public, but saving the countryside was a much harder task. She glanced at Brains, who was still snoring, and carefully got out of bed. She tiptoed silently down the stairs and started to prepare breakfast without waking the others. She put the coffee on, boiled some eggs and made some porridge. She had nothing against being on her own of a morning. The kitchen in Hemmavid reminded her of her old childhood kitchen in Österlen, in the south of Sweden. There they also had wooden floors and panelled walls. Here, too, were traditional wooden cupboards with glass doors so you could see what was kept inside. Below the wall cupboards stood a majestic work table with shelves underneath for pots and pans. The kitchen furniture stood beside the window on the short side.

She looked at the large pine gateleg table, the comfortable, blue-painted chairs with proper back support and the old-fashioned rib-backed settee where Brains and Rake liked to sit. The kitchen didn't boast a kitchen island or a fancy modern cooker which made all sorts of funny noises, but here was an honourable old kitchen range with a big oven and slow hotplates. Above the range were some cookbooks on a little shelf under which hung some spatulas, ladles and whisks. Next to that was a genuine wood-fired stove which they lit almost every day. Brains liked to chop wood, and a fire in the stove meant that he felt he was being useful. The only luxury in the kitchen was a newly installed dishwasher, which they had hidden behind a panelled door, but Martha often preferred to wash the dishes in the sink. This was her way of relaxing when she needed to think. Like she did now.

Roland Svensson, their farmer neighbour, was so nice, always in a good mood and ever ready to have something amusing to talk about. She liked people who cheered you up and weren't forever sucking energy out of you and in need of support. And thank God he had gone along with the idea of the district's first cow event. He had a sense of humour. He understood. She actually really rather liked him. She loved Brains, of course, but he had become more and more difficult when it came to agreeing on various things, and he preferred to get on with his own stuff.

When breakfast was ready, she put on a record of Handel's trumpet concerto – a nice way to get her friends out of bed and a great deal better than an alarm clock or a military reveille. No, people were fragile in the morning and must be treated with respect. She opened the door to the upper floor and the music flowed up the stairs.

Soon, steps could be heard from the rooms above, and shortly afterwards one after the other they made an appearance

103

in the doorway, rubbing their eyes and anxiously looking at her. Why had she woken them? There was something suspicious about it. She either wanted to dispatch them on a mission or to convince them to do something.

During the night all of them – with the exception of Christina, who had taken a sleeping pill by mistake – had been awake a long time before getting to sleep, and getting them into action in the morning was no easy matter. They drank their coffee and ate their breakfast, but didn't say very much as they were fully occupied with waking up properly. When they finally started to perk up a little, Martha reached out towards Brains's hand, stroked it gently a few times and then said:

'Darling, now I think we should have a morning meeting again.'

'Mooo . . .' said Brains, who was tired, demonstratively folding his hands on his stomach. Then he woke up. 'Yes, indeed, Martha!'

'We ought to divide ourselves up into groups,' Martha went on, and looked around at them.

'You mean one person in charge of tourism and events, some creating new jobs and others leading guerrilla attacks – is that how you want it?' Anna-Greta wondered.

'Yes, exactly.'

'But Martha! Have you thought about this? We can't be doing things all the time; we must rest too.'

Martha looked at them and sensed opposition. Then there was only one thing to do. She put on some more coffee and when that was ready, she fetched the cloudberry liqueur. Then she changed her mind and fetched a little bottle of vodka instead. And splashed a little into each cup.

'Well, it's like this,' she said when they had all drunk up their unusually good coffee. 'Nowadays the big companies take electricity, timber and minerals from the countryside, but don't pay any tax there. That simply isn't viable. Hemmavid and other places must receive tax revenues or otherwise they'll die out.'

'Now Martha's preaching again,' Rake muttered, poking Brains in the ribs.

'Shhh, perhaps it's important,' his friend broke in.

'We must change that. Besides, we ought to arrange more pleasant events so that people will discover the village. So what do you say, Christina, can you think of something?'

'I know, a wife-carrying contest, have you heard of that?'

'Who the hell wants to go around carrying their wife?' Rake muttered.

'Wife-carrying is a sport in Finland,' Christina protested. 'The men carry a woman on their back while negotiating an obstacle course as fast as they can. The one who comes first, wins the wife's weight in beer. It's hugely popular.'

'I think there are more enjoyable things you can do with women than carry them around,' Rake emphasized.

'You and your dirty imagination!' Anna-Greta sighed.

'Wife-carrying? Couldn't we have hubby-carrying too?' Christina went on.

'So not only do you have to look after your hubby, but you also have to carry him too,' Anna-Greta objected.

'Yes, you do your carrying. That would be a real tourist attraction,' Rake added with a smirk.

They all burst out laughing and it took a while before Martha could go on.

105

'The entertainment is to pull in money for the village. But we must do something for the school and arrange job opportunities too.'

'I could open a workshop and employ somebody,' Brains suggested, trying to sound positive.

'And what if we could get a library bus organized?' Christina wondered.

There was silence for a few moments while they all racked their brains. Rake hummed a long time before finally speaking out.

'I'm thinking about the idea of jobs,' he began. 'As you know, I went to sea when I was young.'

'We haven't missed that, no,' Christina chipped in.

'My parents said that, uhm, that I was something of a delinquent and ought to learn to behave better. So it was the sea for me.' Rake ran his fingers through his beard. 'I must have had one of those letter-combinations that are so modern nowadays, but I learned a great deal out at sea.' He paused a while and made sure everybody was listening. 'So, we could open a school for teenagers who need a bit of extra support in life. They want to close down the school here, but if we widen the curriculum and apply for special grants, perhaps the school can survive. And then there would be more jobs.'

'You're a genius, Rake. What a good idea!' Martha said, and she made some notes.

'I think we should work with especially gifted teenagers with ADHD and Asperger's and then we'll arrange jobs for them after they finish school', Christina joined the discussion. She had a lot of respect for people who were seen as 'different' and had thought a great deal about that. She loved reading about eminent people and, currently, was deeply fascinated by Albert Einstein, Stephen Hawking and Steve Jobs, people who had gone their own way in life. She raised her voice. 'Many great personalities who have helped mankind to advance have been rather special. Now we can help a new generation of geniuses.'

'We might even find a new Leonardo da Vinci,' said Brains, enthusiastically. 'After school hours I can have courses on carpentry, lathe work and other practical skills in the work-shop. It could be really great.'

'And why not let them go to sea?' Rake chipped in. 'You can't imagine how tough it is when the hurricanes are raging, the waves are high and you must lower the sail. Then you jolly well learn to –'

'Great, Rake. We'll buy some dinghies and you can teach them seamanship over by the bathing place. That would work well,' Christina added.

'I can tell you that MS *Kungsholm* and a sailing dinghy are not the same,' Rake corrected her and looked offended.

But now the gang of pensioners had got up speed and they all threw in various suggestions. In the end, they agreed that they would try to get the school idea up and running for the autumn term and even arrange boarding.

'They could live in the old vicarage. It hasn't been sold yet. I can talk to the parish committee,' said Christina, who was well informed about most things concerning the Church. Since the vicar had moved, and the old church had been converted into an artists' studio, the vicarage had fallen into disrepair. It needed attention.

'Live there? Help! Don't you know that there is a rumour

107

that the vicar's wife was murdered in the cellar?' said Anna-Greta.

'Well, that's perfect!' Rake exclaimed. 'Then we can buy the place and have ghost trails there.'

Now they were all talking at the same time. Countryside activities inspired by guerrilla tactics, teaching and how to bring up children were also debated in good spirits, as was dance-band music and wife-carrying. Martha looked at the others. Now suddenly they all seemed to want to go in the same direction again. Or had they just babbled on to keep her in a good mood?

19

The sun was shining and they were now well into a lovely, hot summer. Some cows were grazing out in the meadow; daisies, cornflowers and buttercups brightened the roadside ditches. A butterfly danced around between the flowers and was lifted up into the air by a summer breeze, and there was a lovely scent. Martha slowed her pace. The head teacher at Hemmavid co-ed secondary school, Irma Höglund, lived along here. She lived on her own; she was a widow and had no children. I just hope she hasn't become a bitter, grumpy type who just turns you away, Martha thought. That can happen with unhappy people. She felt uncertain, but gained fresh courage when she saw the sign outside the head teacher's house.

'Without farms, we would be hungry, naked and sober,' was written on a beautifully painted sign next to the entrance to the big corner plot. Yes, the sign quite clearly related to education and admonition, whilst being funny at the same time. Nowadays, many youngsters from the big cities hardly knew where their food came from, let alone how you made cloth or brewed beer. Now Martha began to feel hopeful that the almost fifty-year-old head teacher was a creative woman who saw the crazy things in life and perhaps would even be prepared to do something about them. Otherwise, you wouldn't put up a sign like that.

At this time of year, school teachers would, of course, be on their summer holiday, but it was still worth knocking on the door. Perhaps she would be pottering in the garden or sitting reading in a sofa swing. That was a holiday too. She wouldn't necessarily have gone away.

Martha opened the gate and walked along a neat gravel path between fruit trees and berry bushes up to the house. She stopped when she came to the steps and looked around. On both sides you could see fields, stables, outhouses and pasture meadows, and a bit further away lay the forest. Dark swallows hovered above the red timbered farmhouse and you could smell the meadow and honeysuckle. An idyll like so many homes in Hemmavid, and a place where most people would feel comfortable. Yet there were so few people in the village and there would be even fewer if that new mayor in Skogsås got his way. Martha had heard the rumours. Close down the local school indeed! No, that power-hungry Allan Petterson would have to fight her over this.

Nobody answered when Martha pressed the doorbell, so she went round to the back to see if Irma was there. And indeed, as soon as she reached the back garden, she saw a broad-shouldered woman in jeans and short-sleeved blouse weeding over in the borders. Her upper arms were tanned by the sun and her blond hair was tucked under a red headscarf. She was determinedly pulling up dandelions and thistles and throwing them onto an old wheelbarrow. Her big black earphones were evidently playing a nice song because she was humming in time with the music. It was not until Martha was very close, that she reacted. Irma straightened her back and took off her work gloves.

'Look who's coming. I recognize you; you must be one of those newcomers.'

She held out her hand and said hello. Her handshake was firm and so hard that instinctively Martha pulled her hand back. The arthritis in her fingers had its limits.

'It's about the school. I've got an idea,' Martha began, while rubbing her tender fingers. Irma looked at her, interested.

'Let's sit in the arbour. Do you like coffee?'

Martha nodded.

'Would you like something to go with it?'

Martha smiled and wondered whether she meant biscuits or perhaps a drop of something strong. Irma was of Danish extraction and you never knew with Danes.

'I eat and drink everything.'

'Excellent. I had thought coffee and cakes or biscuits, but perhaps you'd like to taste my home-made liqueur too? A blackthorn liqueur.'

Martha raised her eyebrows. 'Sounds delicious!'

'Right, then, take a seat on the sofa swing meanwhile,' said Irma and she went into the house.

While Irma was busy in the kitchen, Martha rocked slowly back and forth on the swing seat. Some hens were picking on the ground over by the hen shed, and a cat slept on a warm rock in the shade. A bit further away from the house were rows of redcurrant bushes and neatly pruned apple trees, and beyond those the rolling fields spread out. A warm summer breeze rustled the treetops, fanning her pleasantly. Martha brushed a fly away and closed her eyes. It was so nice and peaceful. Here was the calm that she had so rarely experienced in Stockholm, a tranquillity that you could only find in the countryside. Yet people were moving away from here – not because they wanted to, but because they had to. To earn a living. So sad!

Martha felt like tasting the redcurrants and she got up off the swing seat, but that very same moment Irma came out of the house. She was carrying a tray with a coffee Thermos, cups and a plate of cinnamon buns. There was a lovely aroma.

'Freshly baked,' she said, putting the tray down.

'Ahh, and I love cinnamon buns, especially when they have a lot of sugar on them,' said Martha, taking the top bun.

'I'm curious now, you mentioned something about the school,' Irma got straight to the point after she had poured the coffee.

'Yes, that's right. The school in Hemmavid must be retained. Without it, the village will die.'

'I know, but aren't you from Stockholm? I thought you people from the big cities didn't care about the countryside.' Irma looked sceptically at Martha.

'I grew up in the countryside and know that lots of people feel uncomfortable in their tiny flats in the city suburbs. They could live here instead. Perhaps we can cooperate and try to get people to want to settle here.'

'How can that happen when the politicians are busy moving all our facilities to Skogsås? Next year it might be the turn of the school.'

'Exactly. And that's what we must put a stop to. Now listen to me –'

Martha opened her handbag and pulled out her notebook with the points she had jotted down.

'Today your school has about thirty pupils. I suggest that you increase that to fifty by broadening the intake.'

'Broadening the intake?'

'Hemmavid can create a profile for itself by looking after especially gifted young people with Asperger's and ADHD. They are children who can achieve great things. They need schools where they can receive good, specially adapted teaching. Where they can flourish and be themselves. Employ competent teachers who will look after them, and offer places here, then you could increase the number of pupils already this autumn.'

Irma beamed. 'A bit late now, but it might work . . . a dozen or so new families in the village would be marvellous.'

'Absolutely! They could start their own business, perhaps arranging courses in handicrafts, tourist activities, web companies or the like. In that way, they can create jobs for themselves as well as for others, to my mind.'

Irma looked at Martha with new respect. A newcomer who was also a positive person who tried to solve problems. That was exactly what they needed just now. She had been worried about the school for a long time. Without it, the village would slowly die and she would lose her job too. Irma stirred her coffee.

'But we must look after the people who move here too. The banks won't lend money to people who want to build a house way out here in the villages. Where would people live?'

'There are always some people who want to sell their summer house. And we have the former old people's home.

113

With a bit of renovation, that building could be used for boarding the youngsters.'

'Well, now, you've really thought a great deal about this!' said Irma, with something like admiration in her voice. 'You are right! We can't remain passive any longer!'

Martha nodded, held out her notebook and pointed at two pages full of jottings.

'I have sketched out a plan here. You could look at this.'

Irma took the black, worn notebook and looked quickly through the first few pages. The wrinkles in her face smoothed out, and her lips widened into a happy smile.

'Wow, this is a revolution indeed. Now I'll go and fetch the blackthorn liqueur.'

20

The rain had stopped and it was still a bit overcast although not cold – which is a good thing when we are out on surveillance duty, Christina thought, keeping her eyes on the big road. She and Anna-Greta had taken up position close to the lay-by where the lorry drivers sometimes used to stop. The traffic was heavy and the long-haul lorries roared past. She sharpened her attention. Among all those big lorries she hoped to catch sight of a shiny tanker full of milk. She and Anna-Greta – who had said they were going for a little walk to get some fresh air – stood close to the edge of the road and made notes as to how often a dairy tanker turned into the lay-by just a bit further on. During the summer, the two friends had observed many dairy tankers parked there so that the drivers could have a rest. And that, of course, was when they would make their attack. Without involving Martha . . .

It felt both weird and exciting. But Christina and Anna-Greta wanted to show that they had learned something and that they could make a contribution too. Besides, they had grown tired of how Martha was always bossing them. When they had planned the bank robbery, that was fair enough; for that they needed focus and a strong leader who kept track of everything. But now that she was going to save the Swedish countryside – an enormous political project – it all just felt too much.

'But Christina, you've always been such a worrier. Are you going to manage this?' Anna-Greta suddenly asked, giving her friend a searching look.

'But don't you understand? I've been working on self-development, and this is a way for me to mature.'

'So syphoning milk from dairy tankers is a way to gain a stronger ego?'

'Yes, I mean, everybody works on their self-development in their own way,' said Christina, trying to sound brazen. But she picked at her cuticles for a very long time and wondered what she would have said to a psychologist – perhaps something like: 'I strengthened my ego by stealing milk'?

Christina and Anna-Greta decided to do the deed on Thursday night, the following week – they chose Thursday because then the drivers would have been driving four days in a row and would be very tired. As soon as they had parked, they would be snoring deeply and wouldn't notice the theft at all.

And when eventually the two ladies had decided on the day, they started exercising more intensively than usual. They did their usual gymnastics with Martha, but Anna-Greta also took part in Christina's yoga to get into even better shape. During the next few days, they especially concentrated on balance exercises and weightlifting, and they put a great deal of effort into this, even though it was tough going. On the Wednesday morning, they felt a lot of muscle soreness, but were otherwise in excellent spirits. They had sweated profusely, showered, and were now sitting outside the newly equipped gym in their house, The Vault, relaxing in two reclining chairs, each holding a glass of vegetable juice.

'Now we've eaten our health foods, done our yoga and so many gymnastic exercises, I think our biological age must be ten to twenty years lower than usual,' Christina chirped.

'Well, fifteen at least,' Anna-Greta said.

'Indeed. You can't imagine how strong I feel now. Just look!' Christina rolled up the sleeves of her bathrobe and flexed her muscles – which were a bit less flabby than the week before.

'Yes, fancy bulges you've got there,' Anna-Greta laughed, pointing at the two little lumps that Christina had achieved, after which she knocked back her vegetable juice with a noisy slurp. 'And for that matter, my biological age has also certainly become lower too. I do as much gymnastics as you, and I take those hormone pills too,' said Anna-Greta, getting up and crossing to the balance board over by the wall. She resolutely stepped up onto the board, smiled at Christina and happily lifted her left leg up into the air.

'Now look, fancy being able to do this. And even more, here we go!' she called out, waving a bit extra with her foot – an exciting circular movement she had spotted on the Internet. The balance board wobbled, Anna-Greta wobbled in turn, wildly waving both arms hither and thither before the law of gravity took over and she fell onto the ground. Christina rushed up to her.

'Oops – Anna-Greta, are you all right?'

Her friend got back onto her feet. 'Pah, no problem. My skeleton is like Swedish steel. But that's a funny balance board.'

'Uhm, I'm not sure there's anything wrong with that in

particular – but be careful, because tomorrow we'll be going into action. Think guerrilla ice cream!'

'Guerrilla ice cream is the slogan for the day!' Anna-Greta giggled.

The Thursday for their secret guerrilla operation started just like all other days, but as the hours went by, Christina became increasingly nervous. Now she was going to be in charge, not Martha. And besides, it would all be done without anybody knowing. After lunch – when both she and Anna-Greta ate surprisingly little and pushed the food around on their plates to an unusual degree – the two conspirators started to prepare the night's exercises.

First, Christina went out to the garden shed where she fetched a light aluminium ladder that they had purchased in the ironmonger's in Skogsås on the grounds that it might on occasion be 'useful to have' (and now was most definitely such an occasion). She unfolded the newly purchased climbing tool and leaned it against the shed wall, after which she tested going up and down a few steps to see if she could manage it. And when she had tested that ten times in a row, she became, if anything, even more cocky. It worked perfectly and at that moment she praised the yoga and gymnastic exercises. She wouldn't have managed ten times up and down a ladder without Martha's morning gymnastic routine.

After her climbing test, Christina and Anna-Greta drove into Skogsås to rent a trailer and acquire some tools, tubing, head torches and a siphon pump for the evening's mission. They unhitched the fully loaded trailer in a forest glade and hoped that nobody would steal it. Then they returned home

118

and parked the minibus in the yard. The next task was to practise the illicit syphoning or 'Operation suck up milk'. Anna-Greta somehow associated the whole process with a breast pump for nursing mothers, and the idea of somebody doing that illicitly made her laugh, a loud laugh which sounded like a neighing horse, before Christina could silence her. They practised by sticking the plastic syphon pump into the water barrel and sucking up the water, which they then emptied onto the ground, but they stopped immediately when Martha walked past and gave them a questioning look.

In the evening, they ate their dinner as usual with the others, but now and then exchanged glances in secret mutual under-standing. They felt mischievous and expectant at the same time. Then they played cards, drank their evening tea and talked with the rest of the gang until it was time to go to bed. Christina gave a wide yawn and told Rake that she was tired and must go to bed, and when he came into the room an hour or so later, she pretended to be asleep. He was soon snoring like an old Bauer compressor, which was a good sign, because then it would take a lot to wake him. After he had fallen asleep, she had set the silent alarm on her iPhone, put it inside her bra under her nightdress and allowed herself two hours' sleep before it was time. Her phone vibrated just as she was in the middle of an erotic and very lovely dream, so at first – before she had woken up properly – she thought that Rake was behaving very seductively. Indeed, for a brief moment, she was fully prepared to abandon the entire plan for his sake. But then she heard his compressor snores, now more like an imminent volcanic eruption, and she realized that the man in her life was sleeping deeply.

Silently she crept out of their bedroom, fetched the spare key for the minibus and, while doing so, shook some life into Anna-Greta. Half an hour later (being elderly, they were not super quick at getting dressed), the two women crept out into the yard and across to the minibus. It was now 11.30 and that meant time for action!

To be on the safe side, Christina looked a final time up towards Martha's window to make sure that the lights were turned off up there, and then breathed more calmly. The coast was clear. She quickly climbed into the minibus and turned the ignition key. When Anna-Greta had also climbed in and fastened her seat belt, she pressed lightly on the accelerator and drove off in low gear out of the yard. Not until they were out of hearing range did she speed up and drive off into the darkness. They hitched on the trailer – which thankfully nobody had touched – and drove on towards the lay-by. It wouldn't be long before it would get light again.

Just outside Hemmavid they drove into the lay-by and discovered that it was empty. No long-haul lorries, no dairy tankers. Not a vehicle to be seen.

'We get a bad mark here; this was not something I had expected. Yesterday, there were two tankers here,' Anna-Greta sighed. 'I saw those big Arla lorries. To think that there must be thousands of litres of milk inside those!'

'Perhaps we're a bit early. A tanker might come along later,' said Christina, blowing her nose. She found it terribly cold and she felt a bit out of sorts.

'Why not play cards so it won't be boring,' Anna-Greta suggested. Besides being very good at figures she was also very clever when it came to card games.

Christina nodded, drove up to some trees further along the lay-by and turned off the engine.

'Right you are. Out with the pack of cards!'

The two ladies played one round after another and yawned more and more often, but there was no sign of any lorries. Finally, when Christina could hardly keep her eyes open, and Anna-Greta had spilled a whole pack of cards onto the floor after Christina had cheated, it happened. Suddenly they saw large, dazzling headlights in the dark and heard a tanker drive into the lay-by. The driver parked and turned off all the lights. The two elderly ladies looked expectantly at one another. Over there, barely twenty metres distant, stood a large tanker. The driver was evidently going to take his mandatory rest period. They waited patiently until they thought that he must have fallen asleep.

'We'll wait another fifteen minutes, then we'll board her,' Anna-Greta said. To board a vessel was a maritime term that she had borrowed from Rake, and it fitted in so well now that they had become road pirates.

'OK,' said Christina, smothering a cough as she looked out. It was still dark and not even the moon was visible. But that hardly mattered as they had their head torches.

'Does it say "Arla" on the lorry?' Anna-Greta asked after having stared into the darkness without being able to see any fancy logo.

'I don't know. Arla's tankers are usually all shiny metal and they have a green logo right at the back. If it's a shady milk transport, then it won't have any logos at all.'

'But we can't syphon off just any old milk; it must be approved and quality controlled. My ice cream customers

121

mustn't end up with tummy troubles,' Anna-Greta exclaimed, horrified.

'Asch, we'll notice what sort of lorry it is when we get closer!' said Christina, who then climbed out of the minibus and opened the trailer. With Anna-Greta's help, she lifted the gear out, put the large, empty, plastic barrel on the trailer and then the retractable ladder on top. Then they moved towards the tanker as quietly as they could. Anna-Greta directed her head torch along the long side of the tank and saw that it was all shiny.

'This must be an Arla tanker,' she whispered.

'All right, then, what are we waiting for?' said Christina and she tried to stop herself from coughing.

The two friends parked their trailer and crept silently round the tanker to reconnoitre. The enormous vehicle was in the dark and there wasn't a sound to be heard. It seemed as if the driver was asleep.

'We only need to unscrew the top lid and start up the syphon pump, then?' Anna-Greta whispered tensely.

Christina nodded and, with a joint effort, they managed to extend the ladder and lean it against the tanker. Christina climbed up.

When she reached the upper part of the tank, she saw the big hatch which had to be unscrewed before you could push in the syphon pump tube. That was where they usually poured in the milk. But now, when she lit it up with her head torch, she realized that you couldn't possibly walk right along the top to the hatch, let alone open it. She would need help here. Frustrated, she climbed down again. Damnation, she ought to have thought about this: a shiny, slippery surface and a hatch that couldn't possibly be screwed open by an old lady. It would hardly go much better if there were two of them.

'It's going to be difficult to suck up milk with the syphon,' she sighed, disappointed.

'But we could have a look at the back door. Perhaps you can syphon off the milk in tubes there,' said Anna-Greta and she fished out an old Visa card from her back pocket. 'It's difficult to withdraw money at a bank nowadays, but the plastic cards are good for locks.'

Just as professionally as a villain, she slid her Visa Gold into the lock and tried several times before it clicked and the door opened. She was just about to get hold of the handle, when the door flew open with a bang and something fell out. Christina and Anna-Greta stumbled backwards.

'Jeepers!' Anna-Greta exclaimed. 'A good job that we trained our balance with the yoga!'

'That driver can't have hung up the hose properly. So careless of him!' Christina said.

They stood in silence for a few moments and waited for a reaction from the driver's cab, but nothing happened. Anna-Greta squeezed the rubber hose.

'But it's thick and it feels extremely sticky.'

'Asch, that happens,' said Christina. She fetched the trailer and unscrewed the cap on the empty fifty-litre container. 'Right, where is the hose? Just stick it in!'

'But doesn't it smell a bit strange?' Anna-Greta wondered, hesitating just as she was about to push the hose into the container.

'No, let's get on with it,' Christina replied. She signalled and opened the tap so that it flowed.

'Stop! Stop! Bloody hell!' Anna-Greta whimpered and gesticulated wildly.

'Wow, what a flow!' Christina said happily. She sneezed a few times and turned the tap to maximum so that it squirted out.

'Oh my goodness,' Anna-Greta moaned, and then so much liquid came out of the hose that even somebody with the heaviest of colds could smell what the tanker contained.

'Oh dear, oh dear, this must be manure for the fields. We've got the wrong tanker,' Christina muttered, embarrassed.

'We? You . . .' Anna-Greta pursed her lips and took a huge step to one side.

'Help, it's squirting out,' Christina despaired and tried to close the tap. Anna-Greta did her best to help, but despite using all their strength they couldn't manage it. There was only one thing left to do: run for it!

Which is how the driver, who had been woken by the voices and clatter in the lay-by, got the shock of his life. Still a bit sleepy, when he climbed down from the cab in his dirty vest, he discovered that the manure hose had fallen onto the ground and was squirting profusely. A bit further away, he saw two running figures and he chased after them, but slipped and fell. Before he could get back on his feet again, he heard a car start and saw two headlights. The next moment, a large vehicle with a trailer swept past, accelerated and disappeared into the night. Somewhat confounded, he just stared after it before shaking his head and going back to the tanker. He had heard the joke about Norwegians who robbed dustbin lorries, but this was a step worse. Stealing liquid manure! He turned off the tap and shook his head. Then he wiped himself down and climbed back into the cab.

When he woke up a few hours later, he was confused. Because during the night he thought he had seen two old ladies running away. Two very old women who stole liquid manure? No, he must have drunk far too much vodka as usual.

When Christina and Anna-Greta drove into the yard at about two o'clock in the morning, they were dirty and very tired. Christina parked the minibus, and as quietly as they could they carried away the siphon pump and the containers.

'You know what, Anna-Greta?' said Christina. 'It was lucky for us that we discovered it wasn't milk.'

'On the other hand, there are so many sorts of ice cream nowadays. With that liquid manure I could certainly have managed to produce something tasty,' Anna-Greta neighed, with a thunderous laugh so loud that Christina had to put her hand over her mouth. But then she also realized that her friend had taken it all in good spirit. And they had indeed done their very, very best – despite not being successful.

21

The next morning, Christina and Anna-Greta slept a long time. Martha looked disapprovingly at the closed bedroom doors and shook her head. They got up later and later in the morning and often ate breakfast on their own. And when Martha came into their rooms and tried to say something, they didn't seem to listen. It was as if they had their own secrets and didn't care about what the rest of the gang were busy doing. Not even Rake knew anything.

Oh well, the main thing was that everybody was happy and was doing well, Martha thought. Nevertheless, deep inside, she felt dissatisfied; in fact, she felt almost like an outsider, and that made her worried. Increasingly, she had to cajole and persuade Christina and Anna-Greta to get her decisions approved. What if Brains and Rake also started to behave in the same manner? Then it would be a problem. She must try to be more sensitive and listen to what the others felt, otherwise it could all end up as a total fiasco.

She put the coffee on, and set out coffee cups and a bowl filled with wafer biscuits. Outside the kitchen window, the sun was shining and she would rather be sitting on the swing seat with an exciting book. But she couldn't do that; there were far too many things that needed organizing.

'Why do we always have wafers with our coffee? I think it would be much tastier with crispy oat biscuits,' Anna-Greta pointed out, when finally everyone was gathered in the kitchen.

'Or if we could at least have some shortbread fingers,' Christina added.

'Yes, yes, of course,' Martha mumbled, her thoughts elsewhere. 'I thought that we should perhaps have a little meeting,' she said, trying to soften that cocky 'organizer' voice of hers.

'Are we going to have another meeting? Kiss my arse!' said Rake, waving his arms.

But Brains understood, and together they lifted a table and chairs out into the garden, placing them beside the sofa swing next to the greenhouse. But nobody else did anything, and it wasn't until she had shown them the cinnamon buns she had baked earlier that morning and put out the bottle of elder-flower juice that the whole gang gathered together.

'We must get more people to move here,' said Martha, pouring the juice. She called her drink elderflower champagne because she added a bit of yeast, just like she had seen on TV. But Christina put her glass down immediately, burped and called the drink balloon juice. Martha raised her eyebrows, but didn't say anything. She just quietly went to fetch a new glass and a carafe with vegetable juice.

'But if people move here, they must have somewhere to live,' said Christina.

'Lots of summer houses are not being used at all after the owner has died, with people disputing the will and arguments within the family . . .' Rake reflected. Being the oldest member of the gang, he sometimes thought about life after death. 'Perhaps something could be done with those houses?'

'You're right, when I was out driving around the area with Brains, we counted twenty-two empty houses,' said Martha, and she fished out a notebook, pens and a heap of postcards and stamps from her large shoulder bag.

'And what are we going to do with these?' Rake wondered, looking at the postcards. They depicted beautiful traditional farmhouses, painted yellow and red with white trimmings, forests, meadows and sunsets.

'We succeeded in getting the names of the house owners. Why not send them a nice picture postcard and suggest that they sell their houses?'

'Oh really? But nobody wants to buy a house this far out in the countryside,' Christina objected.

'But we can buy them,' said Martha. 'If we arrange accommodation for the parents who move here with their children, then Irma at the school can start to take in new pupils this autumn. We've got money in our Robbery Fund, remember.'

'From bank robbers to property owners,' Rake sighed.

'If we're going to save the school, then the families must have somewhere to live, mustn't they? In the long term, we can sell the houses to the municipality or to somebody else who is interested. With more people in the district, the houses will be worth more, and then we'll get our money back and make a decent profit too,' Martha went on.

Anna-Greta looked at her friend in surprise. It was amazing

what a lot of things she was getting involved in nowadays. She was even thinking of their finances.

'Yes, not a bad idea at all to save the district and do some good business at the same time.'

'But the people who move here must have jobs, of course,' Rake pointed out.

'We can use some of the money from the Robbery Fund to support new small businesses,' Martha reflected. 'It isn't really our responsibility, but we can give them a bit of a helping hand when they start up. Besides, we can fork out some money straight away.'

Brains thought about his future pupils. What if they could develop some exciting new products and he could persuade them to start a company?

'Great. We can think up something to write on the picture postcards, then,' Christina said, eager to end the meeting as quickly as possible. She stretched across to reach one of the pens. 'Why not something like this: "Dear house owner, we have fallen in love with your house and would like to buy it. We can pay the top market valuation and can do so straight away. Our offer is valid until the end of the month."?'

'Yes, that sort of thing,' they all mumbled, thinking it sounded good. And then the gang set to work and wrote friendly postcards to the twenty-two house owners. When the cards had been written and Martha had collected them all together, Christina said that she and Anna-Greta would go and post them in a postbox.

Martha thanked them, but then started wondering. Christina and Anna-Greta seemed to be using every possible excuse to vanish off together for a while. Were they hiding something?

No, she dismissed the absurd idea, and started looking through the cards. She picked one up with Rake's almost illegible handwriting.

Dear house owner,

I have passed by your house many a time and to my sorrow seen that it is uninhabited. Such a nice house is worth a better fate, and ought to have an owner who can take loving care of it. I think I am just such a person and would like to buy the house,

Best wishes, Bertil Löv
P.S. You can call me Rake

Martha giggled. 'Rake, that should do nicely, but perhaps you shouldn't use your real name.'

Rake turned bright red and hummed and hawed a long while because he hadn't thought of that and they didn't have any more postcards. But Christina put her arm round him and said that it didn't matter at all, and that what he had written was perfect.

The gang of pensioners looked through the postcards, then discussed when the school was to start and the question of boarding pupils some more. Finally, Anna-Greta rounded off by standing up and singing Cornelius Vreeswijk's song about children in a summer camp. The rest of the gang joined in. The song put them all in a really good mood, and when they reached the end, Christina shoved all the postcards into her bag.

'Right then, now we'll go and post them,' she said, and nodded to Anna-Greta, after which the two of them left the others and went off in the minibus. When they had driven a short way, Christina couldn't restrain herself.

'Uff, Martha has become such a model citizen. Law-abiding, boring and absolutely perfect – buy houses and have boarders. Damn it, she didn't mention bank robberies a single time today. If we're going to have any fun these days, we'll have to arrange it ourselves.'

'Yes, but don't forget that she has said we are going to organize several fun events.'

'Events and entertainment? What's so exciting about that? I want some action!'

Christina drove at a fast pace and didn't slow down until they were approaching the lay-by. She had seen a postbox there the night before, so they could drop the postcards in it and at the same time check that they hadn't left any tracks behind.

When they got there, Christina noticed that there was still a stench of manure in the area. It had evidently taken the driver a while to stop the flow, and even though there had been some rain during the night, it hadn't helped. Unknown to Christina and Anna-Greta, the sleepy driver hadn't been able to fully grasp the fact that somebody had tried to syphon off the liquid manure. Having a fear of being robbed, he had been advised by his therapist to start transporting manure and rubbish instead of other goods. And then this had happened . . .

Carrying the postcards, the two women carefully rounded

the polluted area on their way to the postbox, and once there they dropped the whole bundle in.

'Now we've done our good deed for the day to help the municipality,' said Christina in a satisfied tone, and then they went back to the minibus. But just as they were about to drive off, they caught sight of a car trailing a horsebox. The woman in the car drove slowly and parked quite close to them. She turned off the engine, opened the side window and called out:

'Is there a restaurant or a café somewhere nearby where you can park a car and trailer?'

'Yes, sure, in Hemmavid. At the Danish Pastry café they have hot sandwiches and the best croissants in the world,' Anna-Greta informed her.

'Sounds perfect,' the woman answered, getting out of her car to check the horsebox. She opened the door and peeped in. 'You have to check on your horse so you know everything is OK.'

'Yes, indeed, I just adore horses,' Anna-Greta exclaimed. 'Can I have a look?'

The woman looked at the elderly lady with the friendly eyes and nodded.

'He's so handsome, you can imagine how proud I am of him.'

Anna-Greta looked inside the horsebox and noticed that the horse was a black, long-legged, very stylish stallion.

'What's he called?' she asked.

'Hurricane; he's a thoroughbred racing horse, a real winner, I can tell you!' The woman went up to the horse, stroked his neck a few times and remained standing there. 'Sometimes

I've wished that I'd started a different sport so I wouldn't have to deal with these difficult horse transports. On the other hand, I love horses.'

'I understand that; I have ridden a lot too,' said Anna-Greta.

'The Danish Pastry in Hemmavid, you said? Is it easy to park there?'

'Certainly, you just have to drive straight ahead for three kilometres, and then turn off to the right when you see the sign for Hemmavid. Then you'll notice the smell of something freshly baked,' said Anna-Greta.

The woman raised her hand to say goodbye, got back into her car and drove off. Anna-Greta watched until the car and horsebox vanished from view.

'What a horse! He must be worth several million!'

Christina didn't answer, but returned to their minibus. She didn't open her mouth until they reached the main road.

'You know what! Some racehorses are worth up to fifty million. What if we could kidnap one, and demand a huge ransom?'

'You must be joking. We are going to leave our criminal life behind. Martha has said that we must lie low.'

'Yes, I know, but on a scale from one to ten, how much fun is that?'

Anna-Greta thought about it. She had found it horribly boring, having to take things easy for such a long time, and it wasn't until they had set up the police traffic checkpoint that she had felt that delightful joie de vivre again. She delayed answering, took a very large number of deep breaths, then finally had her say. 'It's a dirty trick to commit crimes, and if you are going to steal, then the profit must go to charitable causes. Otherwise, you most certainly shouldn't do it,' she said firmly.

'Right, but listen to this,' said Christina, putting on a philosophic face. 'If a bank robber steals a few hundred thousand he ends up in prison.'

'Yes indeed, but without cash there would be no bank robbers. Nowadays they are unemployed.'

'But if a bank helps its clients to dodge tax, then it is suddenly OK, even though they have stolen billions of tax money. Talk about crimes!'

'I know that, of course. And then they launder the money for their clients and get paid for it.' Anna-Greta sighed because she thought that the banks had had higher moral standards when she worked in one. 'But what has that got to do with us?'

'Well, then we can steal a horse with a good conscience.'

'You know what, Christina. If Brains and Rake could hear you now, they would talk of "feminine logic".'

'Yes, but –' Christina hummed a little over her dubious reasoning, but then started up again. 'It's a lesser crime at any rate, don't you think? And if we steal a valuable gee-gee worth, say, thirty million or so, then we can demand a hefty ransom.'

'Several million.' Anna-Greta smiled and perked up a bit. 'Besides, we can ride on our booty too. You can't do that with cyber-money.'

At which point they both broke out in jolly laughter – because now they realized that they would soon have even more secrets to share with each other. Martha could be as law-abiding as she wanted, but for them: Adventure was the word!

22

It was one of those lovely late-summer days when the air was crisp and clear and the leaves on the trees had got their first splashes of autumn amidst all the greenery. The morning was cold with dew on the north-facing slopes, and the sun slowly started to bring warmth. Head teacher Irma Höglund looked out across the schoolyard. Autumn term, school start and new pupils . . . just as long as it didn't all go wrong at assembly . . .

Wearing her prettiest dress in shades of blue and grey, she walked quickly through the school building to ensure that everything was under control. Her blond hair was combed in a smart page style and she had put make-up on. While she hurried down the corridor, she rehearsed her welcome speech, well aware of how important it was that she sounded nice and welcoming. She looked about her. Everything was spick and span, and the teachers were waiting inside. In the school lab, the chemistry teacher was prepared; as were the woodwork and handicraft teacher in the workshop; and in the hall, the music teacher played Mozart on the grand piano.

She opened the door and went out. In the schoolyard there were balloons in bright colours, and in a sheltered spot protected from the wind, she had laid out coffee and cakes as well as that elderflower juice which Martha had told her about. She thought again with gratitude of that elderly lady who had come like a whirlwind and filled both her and the school with new energy.

Shortly after Martha's visit at the beginning of the summer holidays, they had met again and divided the tasks between them. While Irma talked to the school board about pupils with special needs, discussed with psychologists and applied for funding for extra teaching resources, Martha and her friends had arranged places to live for the pupils and their parents. The school was now getting fourteen new pupils, and some of them had their family or one parent with them, while five teenagers would be boarding in the former old people's home that was now under the supervision of a sixty-two-year-old lady called Victoria, who would be the housemother there.

When Irma had wondered how on earth Martha had dared to buy houses in a sparsely populated area like Hemmavid, she had looked pleased with herself.

'We purchased those houses so that they wouldn't start decaying, and now they will come into use. Once the district is back on its feet, we'll sell them to Hemmavid, or to the families that have moved in. It's as simple as that.'

'I trust you haven't robbed a bank to finance all of this,' Irma had joked, and to her surprise she'd seen how Martha had blushed before she composed herself and laughed at the idea.

A car drove into the car park and Irma looked at the school clock. The assembly would begin in half an hour. The car stopped and one of her favourite pupils, Jonas Bratt, a short, red-haired, somewhat overweight boy from year eight and his parents got out. He was an incredible nerd and nature lover. There wasn't a plant he didn't know the name of, or an animal he didn't know about. But his dad was strict and he was sometimes beaten. When that happened, he didn't say anything, but Irma understood nevertheless, and tried to look after the boy as well as she could.

Yes, she knew most of the pupils and their parents, but from now on she would face new challenges. What would it be like teaching children and teenagers who were specially gifted? It would be fun and exciting, of course, but the new school year would also mean a lot more work. Thankfully, the gang of pensioners, who had recently arrived in the village, had promised to help. Brains would teach technology, and his good friend, Rake, who had been at sea and was good at gardening, would also contribute his knowledge. This was going to work out OK.

More and more cars drove into the car park, and half an hour later a hoard of expectant youngsters filled the school-yard. Martha helped to serve coffee and cakes, and the pupils who knew each other from before, greeted and hugged one another. The newcomers looked a bit lost, but, when Martha saw this, she went up to them, offered them some juice and chatted for a while. Irma felt the support. Martha and her friends had evidently meant it when they had said they would help her.

When they had all had time to greet each other and chat a bit, the pupils were shown into the hall. Just when Irma opened the door and was about to enter, she heard an unusual noise. It sounded as if it came from the forest not far from the schoolyard. She came to a halt and wanted to find out what it was, but as the pupils had already started to pour into the hall, she had no choice but to hurry after them. When all the pupils had sat down in their places, she went up onto the stage.

'How nice to see you here. You are very welcome!'

Then she said a few words about the school, and what was awaiting them in the coming autumn term. Together, they walked around the school premises and got to know the teachers. When Irma saw the pupils' enthusiasm and heard their happy laughter, she felt a warmth build up inside her. She was needed, the school was needed, and, whatever happened, they must fight hard to keep it.

When everybody had greeted the teachers and looked around, the day ended with Irma giving every pupil a balloon which they released to float up into the blue August sky – an old tradition. Everybody released their balloon, except a group of new troublesome pupils who inhaled the helium gas from their balloons, sang the national anthem with a Donald Duck voice, and then sat on the balloons so that they burst. Finally, the welcome ceremony was concluded with the music teacher playing Evert Taube's 'Änglamark', which sounded really lovely, except for the high-range notes where one of the pupils had taped the keys together.

Afterwards, the pupils and their parents went home, and the first school day was over. Irma waved them goodbye and was just about to leave herself, when she discovered that Martha and the gang of pensioners were still there. She went up to them.

'That was very successful, thanks for your help. This feels good.'

'Yes, I think so too,' said Martha. 'And you know what, when I spoke with some of the parents, it gave me an idea. Next term, we ought to be able to broaden the syllabus even more.'

'In what way?'

'The school could be used in the evenings too. I saw a lot of one-parent families there in the schoolyard: single mums or dads, widows and widowers. They seemed tired and resigned.'

'So what were you thinking?' Irma wondered.

'We could arrange evening courses, obviously. How to make the best of life, your appearance, yes, and how—'

'How to be just as charming as a confidence trickster. Con-man courses?' Irma smiled.

'Yes, that sort of thing.'

Irma didn't have time to reply before she heard that noise again, the sharp cutting sound outside the schoolyard. It sounded as if it came from the forest area where whole classes would often go for walks in the afternoons. She, too, would walk with the children and look at birds and other animals, and teach them about trees, fungi and mosses. The noise sounded like a chainsaw. She felt her tummy tighten and suspected the worst, a feeling that was soon confirmed. The very next moment, there was the loud, screeching sound of heavy crashing. Some idiot was busy cutting down trees in their forest!

Martha and Irma rushed towards the sound, closely followed by the others. When they reached the source of the din, they saw two well-built men wearing helmets with visors and protective clothing standing right next to the old mine shaft from the nineteenth century. The safety railing had been taken away, and the men were busy felling the surrounding trees. Brains glanced at the modern chainsaws and wanted to take a closer look, while Rake scratched his beard and wondered what was happening. Anna-Greta and Christina, who knew that the children often hung around there, looked rather shocked and Irma was in a furious mood.

'This is unbelievable!?' she cried out, covering her face with her hands. Collecting bits of slag, telling them about how mines used to work and looking down into the old mineshaft together with the pupils was often the most appreciated part of the outings, but now the fencing had been torn down and a huge machine was pushing branches and bushes down over the edge of the old shaft. 'What in heaven's name are you doing?'

'We're clearing the area ready for the new council landfill site,' said one of the men, wiping his dirty hand on his face.

'What landfill?'

'Err, we just do what they tell us to do. Skogsås municipality has ordered this; you'll have to ask them.'

'But you can't do this without talking to the neighbours first, that's illegal, you must know that!'

Martha immediately suspected the worst. This could only mean that the municipal council had decided to do something that favoured Skogsås, but was negative for Hemmavid. But establishing a landfill – a rubbish tip – right next to a school, were they out of their minds? While she, Irma and all the others were busy saving the village, somebody in Skogsås was wrecking the place. She must do something immediately. Martha started thinking, and she thought fast. In an authoritative voice she put her hands on her hips and solemnly pronounced:

'You must leave the site immediately. You must have missed the warning signs; I suppose they must have disappeared down into the shaft,' she said, pointing down at the hole. 'Last week one of those fly tippers came with a lorry and the driver dumped barrels of toxic waste into the shaft. He was Polish and hadn't a clue as to what the barrels contained, and just wanted to get rid of them. Then he just scarpered.'

Irma stared at Martha, who was gesticulating with both arms and looked very angry. Brains, Rake and the others took a few steps back and Christina and Anna-Greta winced, horrified. But Martha wasn't done yet.

'When that clown turned up again, we stopped him. We're not going to have any more barrels of toxic waste here, because when they fell down the shaft they broke open and started to leak. So, to be on the safe side, we called in the National Chemicals Agency who immediately closed off the area. Fumes from the barrels can cause lung damage. You'd better pack up and leave immediately.'

The chainsaws were still running, but nobody was using them. The men looked uncertainly at each other.

'You must be careful! That was why we rushed over, we didn't want you to be hurt,' Martha went on. 'But I don't dare stand here any longer. You never know what sort of damage those sorts of toxic fumes can do.'

She went off with Irma and the rest of the gang, and, to be on the safe side, she started coughing and theatrically put her hand over her chest a few times.

'What on earth are you up to?' Rake wondered.

'Toxic waste,' said Martha, but her voice sounded unusually light and happy.

'What toxic waste? What are you talking about?' Irma asked.

'Ah, well, sometimes you have to stretch the truth a little. This was an acute situation. Now we must drive to the nearest scrapyard and get some old metal barrels that we can throw down the shaft. The rustier, the better. That would also explain why the "Toxic" labels have vanished.'

So Martha had been bluffing!? Her friends nodded; now they understood, and Irma started giggling. She went up to her newly found friend and gave her a spontaneous hug. Because now she understood that she had before her a strong and dependable woman who was prepared to struggle hard for what was best for the village.

23

It was raining, so the gang of pensioners stayed indoors and took the opportunity to recover. The tension that had built up before the start of the new school term had been considerable, and now they needed to rest before they planned their next move. They were all unusually lethargic and it wasn't until late afternoon that they set off on their daily walk. In the morning they had even gone on strike when Martha had wanted them to join her for her morning gymnastics, and she had to do the exercises on her own. She had warned them of the consequences if they stopped exercising and just sat at home, but nobody listened. She had now lost her patience.

'You can see for yourselves how lethargic you become if you don't jolly yourselves along with some exercises in the morning,' she said, irritated, when she saw Rake reclining and half-asleep on the sofa and the others wandering around, yawning. 'If you want to skive off from morning gymnastics, you should at least rub yourself down with a towel soaked in cold water.'

'Yes, Martha dear, I *shall* pour a bucket of cold water over myself. Will you be satisfied then?' Brains yawned.

'Should there be ice cubes in it, or not?' Rake added with

a smirk on his face, making the others laugh. Martha smiled too, but remained standing thoughtfully in the middle of the living room. Her friends had become so dreadfully obstinate! Since they had ended up in Hemmavid, the gang had been so much more difficult to deal with. Perhaps she ought to restrain herself a little so that she didn't boss them about too much. But saving the countryside wasn't a children's game; you had to keep in good shape to succeed. Real guerrilla solders trained too.

She wanted to tell them off, indeed to shout at them, but she didn't like people who did that. Lowering her head, she left the room and went up to her bedroom. She pulled a book off the shelf and started to read in an attempt to calm herself. It was called *The Real Happy Pill* and was written by a psychiatrist called Anders Hansen. The subtitle stated: *Power up Your Brain by Moving Your Body* and it was partly about how exercise strengthens a person's brain. So she was right, and she wanted nothing more than that her friends should be in good shape, take care of themselves and be fit and healthy. Yes, so that they could work towards the same goals. But almost every day she felt the irritating opposition that lay in the air. A sudden sorrowfulness overcame her and she put the book down on her knee. She wasn't the sort of person who usually cried, but now she was indeed close to tears. Her friends' disobedience had made her so terribly sad. How would she be able to get them to go along with her again?

She would simply have to do something drastic. With a sigh, she put the book aside, got up and went downstairs. With an artificial smile, she stepped into the living room again. Nobody paid any attention to her.

'Shall we think of something for dinner this evening?' she said, forcing herself to use a friendly voice. The others looked at her in astonishment.

'Are you thinking about cooking? You are not ill, are you?' Rake wondered, having never seen her in front of the stove.

'Everything you need is in the fridge,' said Brains nonchalantly, leaning back.

'Yes, but I think I need a bit of help too,' Martha replied, squirming a little.

Then he came to his senses. 'Yes, of course, let's go into the kitchen and see what we can do,' said Brains, good-naturedly, getting up. He recalled the times when the two of them had planned robberies and worked so well together. What if they could achieve that lovely sense of togetherness beside the stove too?

'Yes, uhm, about dinner . . .' Martha muttered, tired, and she realized that she had painted herself into a corner. Now she couldn't escape. Life was about being able to give and take, so she too must make an effort – and even do some cooking! On more than one occasion, she had succeeded in burning a ready-made pizza – not to mention the pans that had boiled dry or the times she had burnt something on the stove. Sighing, she went into the kitchen together with Brains. But if he assumed that she was thinking of the evening meal, he assumed wrongly. No, she was thinking about how he could help her to produce a cooking app that would provide you with ready-made food out in the countryside.

When Martha and Brains had vanished into the kitchen, Rake turned on the TV and started to watch a submarine film, while Anna-Greta and Christina withdrew to the library.

Christina picked up her favourite book, Ellen Key's *The Abuse of Women's Energy*, and reflected upon how she could organize a mobile library – a book bus – in the district. But she soon came to the conclusion that it was awkward being a guerrilla activist, a villain and a librarian at one and the same time. So, she would quite simply have to delay the book-bus project for a while.

Anna-Greta, for her part, opened her laptop. She had acquired the habit of googling every day to see what people in other parts of the world did to keep their countryside villages alive, before she opened her own anonymous Facebook page. She scrolled around for a while, before suddenly stopping and signalling to Christina to come across.

'Just look at this,' she said, and pointed at the screen. 'This morning I e-mailed two links about boats to Rake. And thirty minutes later I could see adverts for small yachts, sailing dinghies and motorboats on my Facebook page.'

'What about it?' Christina pulled out her nail file and waited for Anna-Greta to continue.

'After that, I did a test, because I wanted to know whether it was a coincidence that those adverts appeared on Facebook, or if something else lay behind it. So I sent him a new e-mail and asked whether we should buy new sails for the sailing dinghies, or perhaps just buy a motorboat instead. He had no idea what I was on about.'

'Of course not; you have always grumbled about being seasick if you get into a boat!'

'Well, anyway, after a while I clicked my way back into Facebook. And, surprise, surprise, my Facebook page was full of adverts for boats.'

'Oops, that's fantastic; God sees you!' Christina let slip. 'Or rather, Google. Weird, don't you think?'

'Indeed! What I do on the computer is thus seen somewhere else and turns into adverts on Instagram and Facebook. George Orwell's 1984 is nothing in comparison.'

'In China they even follow your movements on the streets and can see which products you buy in the shops. The day that technology is used by the wrong people in power, just anything could happen.' Christina wrung her hands so hard that one of her newly varnished loose nails fell off.

'Of course, you can turn your mobile phone off and ignore the Internet, but that isn't feasible when all your bank errands and lots of bureaucratic business must be done over the net,' said Anna-Greta. 'But you know what, we can make use of that to our advantage.'

'What? Should we become spies?'

'No, no, we do this: now I'm going to send an e-mail to Roland to say that I want to start riding again. And that I want to rent a stable stall because I'm going to buy a horse.'

There was a sparkle in Christina's eyes. 'Ah, I'm beginning to get it. Then lots of ads for horses will turn up on your Facebook page, right?'

'Exactly, and then we're going to find a really expensive horse that we can steal and claim a hefty ransom for. So now we'll send e-mails about horses for sale, saddlery, reins and bits and that sort of stuff. We're going to drown in adverts,' Anna-Greta cooed over her own ingenuity.

'And then we'll not only find out what they are worth, but also the addresses. You are a genius, Anna-Greta!' Christina exclaimed. 'So exciting to plan crimes on the Internet!'

Her friend's cheeks had acquired a warmer shade and she looked unusually satisfied with herself. This was actually rather fun, and now she understood that Martha and Brains must have had a whale of a time when they planned their robberies. But stealing horses via cyberspace wasn't so bad, either.

'OK, we'll go for it,' said Anna-Greta and she clicked on *send*. Then, of course, the Internet connection was broken, and Anna-Greta had to go up to the balcony to get a signal so that she could send her e-mail on its way. But an hour later, the coverage was better, and they could work in the library again.

'This is a piece of cake,' Christina joyfully announced when Anna-Greta had clicked her way into social media again, and discovered that her Facebook flow was full of adverts about horses for sale.

'The fact that Facebook have individualized adverts is nothing new. But I doubt whether any oldies before us have used the system to steal racehorses,' said Anna-Greta and she neighed so loudly that Christina had to put her hand over her mouth and say that she wasn't going to take it away until her friend had calmed down.

The two friends spent the rest of the day going through the adverts, noting down the stables with the most valuable horses and listing the stud farms that lay closest to them. Then they printed detailed satellite pictures of the stud farms from Google Maps, and thought about the best way to steal the horse. They were busy doing this and so engrossed in their planning that they didn't hear when Martha entered the room. Her face was red and sweaty, and she had the appearance of having done hard battle with the stove.

'The food's ready. I was beginning to wonder where you were,' she said.

Anna-Greta gave a start. 'Yes, sometimes one loses track of time in front of the computer . . .'

'But you seem to be having a good time. Are you planning something exciting, perhaps?'

Christina and Anna-Greta blushed disquietingly.

'Uhm, we were doing a bit of googling, and then you always get a bit of inspiration,' said Christina, who found it hard to lie, but realized that she must. 'For the time being, we're thinking about things that would attract people to the district.'

'Really, tell me!'

Anna-Greta and Christina looked at each other with embarrassment and struggled for something to say. They must think up an idea, anything at all, just as long as they said something . . . Christina got there first.

'A ghost tour in the old vicarage. That ought to attract people.'

'Great, that's got potential!'

'And we thought that the entrance to one of the old mines could be smartened up and we could make a love tunnel like they have in fairgrounds,' Anna-Greta added, not wanting to seem less committed.

'What a lovely idea.' Martha smiled. 'I'm sure we can make something of that. Could you sketch out a proposal?'

'Yes, perhaps,' Christina mumbled without any great enthusiasm.

'Right then, time for dinner!'

'Coming –' mumbled Anna-Greta with a deep sigh, because she and Christina had intended slipping away to reconnoitre.

On the other side of the valley they had actually found a stud farm with a valuable racehorse owned by the famous magnate and multimillionaire, Martin Borge. He had featured in the newspapers. He had bought several schools, raked in all the school-voucher money for himself and then reduced expenditure by cutting back on teachers, school materials and lesson hours. Then he had sold the whole lot and become fantastically rich. But the schools had been slimmed down to such a degree that they went bankrupt. More than one thousand teachers and ten thousand pupils were affected.

'Good. Then we can steal his horse. That wouldn't harm anybody of limited means,' as Christina had said. Besides, he had also bought cheap forest land and had cleared lots of forest in various places in the district. He deserved to be taught a lesson he wouldn't soon forget. But now, unfortunately, it was time for food – and Martha, who added sugar to the sausage in her very own special recipe which involved hiding the sausage in a thick sauce. Anna-Greta got up with a sigh and accompanied Christina to the kitchen. Her friend turned round.

'Psst. We must be careful,' she whispered. 'We can't forget that we are on the police wanted list.'

'Pah, one robbery more or less won't make any difference. Who on earth would look for us here?'

'What were you saying?' Martha wondered.

'It will be lovely to tuck into your sausage special,' Anna-Greta lied.

The police wanted list . . . Yes, the police had put them on the wanted list throughout the country but had not had any response. The League of Pensioners had disappeared without trace. Freelance journalist Ingmar Sjöberg tipped his chair back and got up. He was beginning to lose patience; he had written that the robbery at the auction house was about to be solved, but then nothing had happened. Nothing whatsoever. And for every day that passed, the harder it would be to track them down, and if nothing was done, then the five oldies would get away with it. He went out onto the balcony for a smoke. It smelt of exhaust fumes, and down below was the noise of traffic. It was already Friday afternoon, and he hadn't achieved very much this week. He picked up a cigarette and lit it. There was so much bloody pressure being the newspaper's star reporter. His bosses were always expecting him to file new scoops. But he hadn't had a scoop for a while, and he found it hard to relax. He inhaled deeply, a bit too deeply, into his lungs, which made him cough. Then he stood for a long time with the cigarette in his hand without being able to come to a decision. The police in Kungsholmen had his flash drive after all, and by now they ought to have found something hot. He ought to remind them again. He determinedly picked up his phone and clicked his way to the direct number to Gert Aronsson. It rang a few times, then he heard the familiar voice.

'Gert Aronsson here.'

'Hello, this is Ingmar Sjöberg. I'm phoning about the flash drive. Have you found out any more about the League of Pensioners? Anything new that I can write about?'

24

Allan Petterson, Skogsås municipality's bigwig, paced back and forth in his mayoral office with his phone in his hand and sounded extremely frustrated.

'Barrels of toxic waste in the mine shaft? Then we can't bloody well use it as a landfill rubbish tip. We could be accused of all sorts of things. Don't you understand? Even if we clean up the site first, leaking barrels can lead to problems in a few years!'

He had felt confident that he had the perfect plan when he asked the forestry workers to clear away the area around the mine shaft so that it could be used for rubbish from Skogsås. Once all the trees were gone and the first lorry loads of rubbish had been emptied there, it would be too late to protest. Damn and blast!

It hadn't occurred to him that the teachers in Hemmavid school had used the place for nature outings, and now some pensioners had been there and stopped the whole thing. His secretary had phoned and said that the forestry workers were very angry. And she had asked him what he was going to do. What would he do? He hadn't the faintest idea. He needed time to think.

'Tell those forestry workers that they will be paid for the job and that we will get back to them later,' he answered, sounding more like a sizzling frying pan than a gentleman. Then he ended the conversation. He didn't want to hear any more because he was hurrying to his next meeting. A mining company wanted to do some prospecting in the district, and if they found lithium and copper, mining activities would provide new jobs. Perfect! Skogsås would expand.

He got up, grabbed his overcoat and hurried out of the room. Then he sat in his red Porsche 911 and drove off.

He accelerated and enjoyed the speed, and all his problems disappeared. The Porsche was his relaxation and made him feel good. He really loved to drive out into the countryside where you could press your foot down and hardly meet another car. A pity that petrol was so expensive; that was really unfair in an area where it was too far to cycle and there were hardly any buses. He turned the car radio on and hummed in time to the music as the trees flashed past.

He drove on a while until he realized that he had forgotten to phone Malin. They hadn't seen each other for a while, and he had promised he would look in at her place on his way home after the meeting. His wife thought he was going to work late. Revived, he pulled out his mobile, and with one hand on the steering wheel and the other holding his iPhone, he pressed the quick dial number. She answered immediately, and he felt his body getting warm.

'Darling, I'm on my way. Shall we –'

He didn't get further than that, having seen a police stop sign held by a uniformed constable stepping out into the road. He braked hard, the tyres screeched and the car skidded to a halt. A police traffic control! Bloody hell! He slammed his hands on the steering wheel and swore out loud, well aware of what the police officer would say. He wound down the side window and the officer leaned forward.

'You were driving rather too fast . . .'

'I have an important meeting!'

'Yes, we all do,' said the well-built police officer with wide shoulders. He had a moustache too, a silly little one.

'I am the mayor of Skogsås, I am out on urgent business.'

'The law is the same for everybody.' Moustache man walked round the car, noted the registration number and wrote out a fine. 'You should be happy we are not clamping the car. Some pensioners did that a few weeks ago when they were playing police traffic checks. The drivers were absolutely livid.'

'Pensioners?'

'Yep, evidently they were making a film.'

Allan Petterson couldn't help but smile. 'The elderly get up to all sorts of things nowadays. I heard about some who stopped the dumping of barrels of toxic waste down a mine shaft the other day,' he said as ingratiatingly as he was capable of, hoping that his small talk would persuade the police officer to tear up the fine. Kurt Löwander's face lit up.

'Did they indeed! How many were they?'

'Four or five, and newcomers in the district from what I've heard. Perhaps it was the same gang?'

'And where are they now?' Löwander had been in a grumpy mood on account of being sent out on traffic control just because his colleague was off sick, but now he perked up. He was reminded about the wanted list and what his boss had said that evening when the gang of pensioners had clamped the lorry wheels and had the fines paid directly to them. His boss had gone on with some fanciful talk about the robberies at the Nationalmuseum and the Grand Hotel, and the jewellery coup at the auction house. The police suspected that it could be the same gang. And there can't be that many gangs of oldies that had moved into the area recently.

'The pensioners? Err, I don't know, but I can find out more,' said Allan Petterson, now in a smooth voice. He had Malin in mind; she would certainly know. Since she and Lilian had opened that café, she had got to know everything about everybody.

'Yes, do that!' said Löwander, and he handed over his business card.

'So perhaps you can overlook the speeding, then?' Allan Petterson pretended to drop a five hundred-kronor banknote on the ground.

'No, certainly not, and you were using your mobile phone too. Nobody is exempt from the law here.'

Kurt Löwander handed over the slip with the fine and then walked away without picking up the banknote. He hadn't gone far before he heard the car accelerate on its way. That very same moment, he realized his mistake. Now the mayor wouldn't tell him anything. And what if those elderly people he talked about really were the League of Pensioners?

25

As yet there had been no snow although it could come any time. There lay a grey mist over the district and it smelt of autumn, forest and moss. Christina looked out across the fields in front of them. When you were in the countryside it was always beautiful, regardless of the weather. It was never like that in cities. She breathed in the cold, fresh air and filled her lungs. Shivered a bit more . . . in a day or two, they would strike. She and Anna-Greta, the fake vets from Veteran Pool Veterinary Services, had increased the length of their daily pole-walk by just over one kilometre. It was a question of getting into good shape.

The two friends always used to feel much livelier after they had been out walking, but recently they had felt rather lethargic, despite the walks. Martha had summoned everyone to one planning meeting after the other, and that had tired them out completely. When you had your own, secret projects, it became very stressful. Besides, Martha was now concentrating on a decidedly complicated plan. A secret venture which would make the people in Stockholm wake up, she had said. Christina pressed down with her poles really hard and shook her head.

'She's dreaming of arranging a power cut, blacking out all

of Stockholm so that the politicians will fathom just where the big cities get their electricity from. Not until then will they understand that they must pay for it, she says.'

'Oh heavens above! Martha's ideas nowadays are so vast in scope. She must be suffering from bank-robbery abstinence!'

'She's welcome to her ideas, but it makes it difficult for others who are preparing their own crimes.'

The two women had put a great deal of effort into acquiring equipment and gathering information about Borge's stable. In Skogsås, they had rented an Ifor Williams horsebox and had even purchased an endoscope, an ultrasound apparatus, special gloves and a number of other items that vets usually have. They would be posing as vets who had come to make a pre-purchase examination of the horses that they intended to get through the guarded gates. Once inside the stables, they would try to kidnap the most valuable stallion without anybody suspecting anything.

They had devoted many an hour to studying everything the experts were expected to do when examining a horse.

'So, we shall examine the horse's back, skeleton, tendons and muscles,' Anna-Greta repeated loudly while she checked what she had learned.

'Yes, exactly, and legs, hooves and teeth,' Christina went on, pressing her walking poles elegantly but firmly into the ground.

'But we mustn't appear to be clumsy. We shall behave professionally; they'll have cameras all over the place, of course. We mustn't forget the horse's joints, flexion tests and that sort of thing.'

'Right, but most important of all – the onion and pepper.'

'Oh yes, our special little kit,' said Anna-Greta.

The two women had also done some secret training with ultrasound and an endoscope in Roland Svensson's stables. They had also given one horse an injection with a sedative – everything to be able to make the right moves with the syringe. But then Roland had started to wonder why the horse, called Drabant, which previously had been so active, had suddenly become so lazy.

'I suppose horses are just like people. Drabant must be getting old,' Christina had said.

'Old? That one is only one year,' Roland had retorted, so, after that, Anna-Greta had suggested that she alone should handle all the horse talk, while Christina was welcome to talk about other things – such as when Roland had asked them if they were going to buy a horse, and she had had to explain that they were busy looking for one.

Christina was impressed by Anna-Greta's calm and her experience with horses, and obviously, without her, the entire project would have been impossible. Her friend had ridden horses up until she was seventy-five years old, after which she had restricted herself to watching show-jumping on TV. Yes, they would take the horse with them.

Christina and Anna-Greta walked a little longer before returning to the house much livelier than when they had left. They ate lunch with the others and in the afternoon sat inside as it had started to snow. The next morning the ground was covered with several centimetres of snow and outside the window you could see beautiful fir trees with their branches weighed down by snow, and white meadows. The two friends looked at each other.

'Oh my God, the horse is going to leave tracks,' said Anna-Greta.

'Then we will have to celebrate Christmas instead,' Christina replied.

'OK, in that case, Father Christmas had better watch out, as here we come!' Anna-Greta said, smiling.

So Christina put candle holders in the windows ready for Advent, and Anna-Greta began to plan a traditional St Lucy Day procession. They drew lots to decide who would be Saint Lucy. Rake, with his chin-strap beard, won, but a lot of persuasion was necessary before he would agree to put a crown of candles on his head. When they had all got dressed up in the white robes and had started to practise singing the Lucy songs, they stumbled across the next problem: they needed an audience, and who should that consist of? In the end, they abandoned the project, and instead went to the school where Irma had organized a Lucy Day procession that was very atmospheric. They were given saffron buns and ginger biscuits, and could listen to the schoolchildren singing with great empathy. The white-dressed angels and the star boys in the procession were rather put off, however, when Anna-Greta suddenly called out 'Louder!', and then Martha had to tactfully put a hand on her shoulder to signal that she ought to remain silent.

Other seasonal celebrations continued with Brains and Rake getting hold of a Christmas tree, and while Rake and Christina decorated it, Anna-Greta played Christmas songs on the gramophone. Martha prepared the food and they all thought it was reassuring that Brains stayed in the kitchen too, keeping an eye on her. Nevertheless, she managed to burn the spare ribs and bump into the soufflé so that it collapsed with a sigh. Shamefaced, she promised to do better for the New Year celebrations. Next, they drove into Skogsås and bought the best champagne they could find and a whole crate of lobsters. But the lobsters were already cooked, and the sauce and the scalloped potato dish had been prepared in the shop. Be that as it may, they ended up with a tasty New Year's dinner. When the holidays came to an end, and they could finally throw out the Christmas tree, Martha sighed with relief. Because now it was high time to plan their next guerrilla project . . .

She went into the living room, sat down in her favourite armchair and picked up her knitting. It was going to be a scarf for Brains. But she didn't knit; instead, she stretched her fingers back and forth in slow, monotonous movements while she thought. The mood in the gang was still not so good, and that worried her. Even though she had made an effort to be calm and sensible for the entire Christmas holiday, she had, nevertheless, radiated impatience.

Brains and Rake had mainly kept to the workshop and Christina and Anna-Greta had walked off to the stables early each morning. Anna-Greta had said that she was thinking of starting riding again and Christina had said that she wanted to learn more about horses. Meanwhile, Martha had sat all on her own. She did, of course, want her friends to enjoy themselves, but it felt almost as if they were deliberately keeping out of her way. Saving the countryside was not something you could do on your own, however; everyone had to do their bit! And that meant they must become a well-functioning team again.

When they had all gathered together in the library after

dinner, Martha made a proposal for the next project. While knitting, and as if the thought had just occurred to her, she said:

'What about a coup against the electricity supply?'

Nobody had the energy to comment. Christina and Anna-Greta didn't seem interested, and Brains and Rake, although not actually protesting, didn't suggest any ideas of their own. They just nodded apathetically, each keeping their eye on the TV, which would soon be showing a football match from some foreign league or other. Why on earth was it such hard work to get them enthusiastic? Martha turned to Anna-Greta and tried to bring her round.

'I've heard that you're going to take up riding again. That's lovely!'

Her friend adjusted her hearing aid, fiddled with it for a moment, but then turned it off.

'Well, I have ridden all my life, and out here in the countryside I must make use of the opportunity. But I do, of course, want to practise properly before I get my own horse.'

'Are you going to buy a horse?' Martha dropped a stitch.

'You bet! I must occupy myself with something now that we aren't robbing banks any longer. And besides, Roland Svensson is super friendly.'

Yes, Anna-Greta had been in the stables quite a number of times recently, and every time she came home, she had told them all how charming Roland was. And Martha had thought the same.

'Lovely to have your riding. Just as long as you have enough energy for our projects too.'

'Look about you. We're all working away, Martha dear,'

Brains broke in. 'The pupils and I, we're really busy. You can't imagine! We've designed some solar panels and worked out a way to make them look like roof tiles. And in addition, we have built a prototype chimney which can absorb the heat from the sun from all points of the compass.'

'Oh my! That's great! Then we can strike and cut off the electricity!' said Martha, pretending to make some cutting movements in the air with a pair of garden shears.

'Why do that?' Rake sounded sceptical.

'The countryside should be paid for the electricity it produces. We must teach the politicians that the *whole* country must flourish.'

'But you're forgetting something; we have democracy here in this country,' Rake protested. 'Not a Martha dictatorship.'

Martha was getting up steam to explain what she had in mind, but Christina and Anna-Greta were already on their way out of the room. Rake and Brains had also got up. Wherever were they off to now? At that juncture she realized that it was going to be a great deal harder being a countryside activist than it was robbing banks. Perhaps she ought to jolly things along with an exciting robbery?

26

They would soon reach the crime scene! They had at last plucked up sufficient courage to dare to strike. Christina and Anna-Greta were on their way to Martin Borge's stables forty kilometres away where the stallion Sharp Eye was for sale for thirty-two million kronor. Christina's hands felt sticky on the steering wheel, and Anna-Greta was unusually silent. They mustn't leave any tyre tracks, but when the snow melted away, the gravel road leading to the stud farm had become full of rain puddles. Christina had tried to avoid the worst of them and had stopped not far from the gate. She glanced nervously at Anna-Greta.

'Now this is for real!'

A man from the stud farm came up to them. He was wearing a black leather jacket on which it said *GUARD* in fluorescent letters.

'And who are you?'

He looked at the minibus which had *VETERAN STABLES* written on the sides, and wrinkled his brow. Christina poked Anna-Greta in the ribs.

'We're here for Sharp Eye. We've been asked to do a pre-purchase examination of him.' Anna-Greta held up her veterinary ID, a document that Christina had created based on models from the Internet.

'Oh right, in that case . . .' said the guard, glancing at his watch. 'He's over there in the stable.'

'Yes, I know,' said Anna-Greta, although she had no idea, but it sounded right. The guard opened the gates and the two ladies drove in with their rented horsebox. They stopped close to the stable, got out and put some documents, the endoscope and ultrasound apparatus on their folding trolley. They looked to all sides. The stable area consisted of a large stable building, a staff residence and, a bit further away, a track where the horses were trained. It was exactly what it had looked like on Google Maps, but walking into it on the ground was something totally different. It was suddenly for real.

They entered the stable building where it felt clean and airy. The central corridor was unusually wide, and there were stalls on either side with the names of the horses on the doors. Each stall had a window, and above was a glass ceiling which could be opened and closed with the help of sensors. The stables were impressively large and Christina immediately felt extremely small. She tried to improve her posture and make herself as tall as possible, as if that would help – but it didn't. She did, however, discover the CCTV cameras in the corner and inside the stalls. She ran her fingers through her hair. It was lucky they had put on plenty of make-up, and were using wigs too. However good those cameras were, not even Martha would recognize them in this guise. When they entered the stables, the guard introduced them to a stable boy in jeans and a checked shirt, and then disappeared. The stable boy was chewing gum and looked at them questioningly.

'Ah, time for an examination?'

'Yes, that's right,' said Anna-Greta and she pointed slightly nonchalantly towards the stall where she knew Sharp Eye would be. 'He's the one we've come to have a closer look at.'

The stable boy went across, untied the horse and led him out.

'The passport, please,' said Anna-Greta as nonchalantly as she could manage – because she knew that the horse passport must be looked at in order to do this properly. When she'd been given it, she asked about the horse's age, pedigree and any injuries.

'Well, that's in the passport,' said the stable boy.

'We are always pedantic about this, and double check,' Anna-Greta said, clearing her throat and making a note.

Then she asked to see how the horse moved – walk, trot, canter and gallop – and they went out together to the yard. Sharp Eye snorted and threw his head wildly, so Christina began to feel worried about how they'd get the horse home. Perhaps it would be best to be on the safe side.

She waited until Anna-Greta and the stable boy turned their backs, then pretended to adjust the ultrasound apparatus. But, instead, she quickly pumped a dose of sedative up the horse's bottom and then hid the syringe in her pocket. Then, as if nothing had happened, she got out the doppler and pressed it against one of the joints. With well-practised movements, she then examined the horse's soft tissue.

'This looks good,' she said after a while, and she pretended to look at the computer screen. Then she took a blood sample and checked it with a dipstick, and mumbled something about the horse not being doped. The stable boy was still chewing the same gum and talking on his phone.

'This looks good too,' Christina muttered, and she made a note.

'Now I think perhaps it's time for the special kit, don't you?' said Anna-Greta, smiling affably and looking about her. The boy was still talking on his phone, perhaps to his girlfriend? Anna-Greta opened her handbag and pulled out some plastic bags containing powder. She handed over the one with onion in it to Christina, while she herself got ready to use the one with pepper in it.

'What's going on over there?' Anna-Greta called out suddenly in a loud voice, pointing in the direction of the exit. The stable boy looked up.

'I'd better go and look,' he mumbled and hurried towards the door. Anna-Greta quickly blew the pepper in front of the horse's muzzle, while Christina pushed some onion powder up his nostrils. Sharp Eye neighed loudly and reared up so that Anna-Greta could barely keep hold of him. Whoops, this was really a great deal more energetic than she had imagined. After she had talked calmly to the horse and had given him something tasty, she regained control of him again.

Then the two women continued to examine the horse's head, nasal discharge (of which there was now rather a lot after the onion), eyes, mouth and teeth, after which they did a laryngeal cough provocation test.

'He's got phlegm in his upper respiratory tract,' Christina announced solemnly and she had barely finished saying so before Sharp Eye started to sneeze. The more pepper Anna-Greta blew in, the more intensive the cough. When the stable boy returned, Anna-Greta looked deeply worried.

'Sharp Eye is not feeling well, he's coughing. This doesn't look good at all. We are sure he has equine influenza.'

The stable boy drew back. 'Oh, Christ no! Not equine flu! That's fucking infectious!'

'Yes, unfortunately, it is a problem.'

'And Dragon Gate and Running Bear are due in soon. They are going to compete this weekend.'

'No problem, we'll solve this,' said Anna-Greta in a loud voice and she nodded to Christina. 'This isn't the first time we've had a situation like this, is it? We remove Sharp Eye from the stables and isolate him in the horsebox. It's as simple as that.'

Before the stable boy had time to react, Anna-Greta resolutely took hold of the horse's head collar and lead rope and led him away from the stables with Christina hurrying behind.

'I must unlock the box first,' she hissed, getting the box door open, and, as soon as Anna-Greta had gone in with the horse, Christina helped to secure the collar rope. When they had done that, Anna-Greta went back to the stables, fetched the endoscope and the bag with the ultrasound apparatus, and checked that they hadn't forgotten anything. It was imperative that they didn't leave any tracks behind them. But at that very moment, just when they ought to be driving off as quickly as possible, she felt it: Oh darn, she had to pee! She looked about her, discovered a toilet, and rushed in.

Perhaps she shouldn't have been surprised, but she was. Even though Martin Borge was a multimillionaire, she had thought that a toilet in a stable would be a simple affair. But no. The room was large, with a washbasin, mirror, shower and colourful porcelain figures on deep glass shelves. Two tall plants stood like thrones and tasteless, kitschy art hung on the walls. Business magnates liked to place their money in works of art and hoped that they would increase in value too. Anna-Greta knew this, but these paintings! It was obvious that Martin Borge didn't have any taste. Amateurish landscapes and cheap reproductions of animals and horses were hung in fancy frames. Anna-Greta stood and stared. The only painting worth looking at portrayed a lady feeding hens. The painting was dirty, the varnish had yellowed and the surface was dark with soot. It didn't have a signature, but it was a nice painting and something that Christina might be inspired by. Anna-Greta pulled out her mobile and took a few pictures before returning to the horsebox.

When she reached it, not only were Christina and the stable boy standing beside the box, but so too was the stable manager. She felt a cold hand squeeze her tummy, because now they were in a pickle. You had to be careful what you said.

'Regrettably, you seem to have a case of equine influenza here. Sharp Eye must be kept in isolation. But at Veteran Pool Veterinary Services we have the necessary facilities to keep horses in isolation. For a small extra fee, we can look after the horse until he is fit again.'

'I've never heard of that service before.' The stable manager looked grim.

'No, it's new, but we are not just any old veterinary service. We've been around a long time and know what it can be like. It's for good reason that we are called Veteran Stables.' Christina smiled as warmly as she could.

Anna-Greta stood in front of the horsebox, put her arms by her sides, and made herself as important and pompous as she could. Her voice sounded resolute and very authoritative.

'I heard that you will be competing at the weekend. It would be unfortunate, indeed, if the infection were to spread to the other stalls, wouldn't it? Then we would, of course, be obliged to report you.'

That same moment, Sharp Eye could be heard coughing and snivelling from inside the horsebox, and it did actually sound as if he was really ill. Christina dug out the report sheets and thumbed her way to a pre-printed form.

'Well, as you realize, this isn't the first time it's happened. We can draw up a contract in which we will have responsibility for the horse until he is healthy. I would estimate that to be the end of next week. It usually takes seven days or so.'

'Err, yes . . .'

'Unless, of course, any complications arise,' Christina added. 'But in that case, we will naturally get in touch. Regardless, we will bring the horse back again and you will avoid all the hassle. I shall send the ultrasound images, and as soon as he is better, we shall do an X-ray and you will get those images too.'

The two elderly ladies smiled in such a friendly and charming manner, that when the tallest of them handed over the pre-printed form with its smart stamps, the stable manager signed it. He then gave them his business card.

'But you must keep a close eye on the horse!'

'No problem. We have cameras in the horsebox, and a guard, alarm and CCTV cameras in the isolation stable. You are most welcome to come and visit us at Veteran Stables. Good luck with the competitions at the weekend.'

The stable boy and the stable manager exchanged quick glances and both of them seemed relieved. Sharp Eye was for sale and wouldn't be competing any more for them. What was most important was that they could sell the stallion for the thirty-two million that they had asked for in the advert. And any prospective buyer could be told that they didn't have time to show them the horse before the following week. Besides, they would want the examination report from Veteran Stables.

On their way out of the yard, they shook hands and Christina promised to contact them when the horse had recovered. They then checked that everything was all right with the horsebox, before getting behind the wheel and driving off. When the gates opened, they waved goodbye, and felt very satisfied with their day.

It was only later, some forty kilometres later, when they drove into Svensson's farmyard, that Anna-Greta gave a screech.

'Oh heavens above! Now I know what we forgot. The bag with the pepper!'

27

'The horse is asleep!' said Christina, looking absolutely terrified. She had opened the door to the horsebox and stared at the animal, which seemed to have been knocked out. The horse's head hung down, he rested on one back leg and his upper lip was floppy. And, what was worse, what a noise! Sharp Eye was snoring – and snoring loudly. Thankfully, he was not coughing so much as the pepper seemed to have stopped working.

'The horse is asleep; I can hear that!'

'But don't just stand there, do something!'

'Do you want me to carry the creature out? I'm not a Pippi Longstocking, you know!'

'I don't understand how this could have happened. We steal a horse worth thirty-two million, and then it falls asleep.' Christina was close to tears.

'You haven't gone and done something behind my back?' Anna-Greta was suddenly suspicious and she looked her friend in the eye.

'Well, nothing more than, well, I was afraid that he would kick out so I gave him a bit of sedative – seven hundred kilos of racing dynamite must be kept calm in some way.'

'Sedative? My God, what sort?'

Christina felt in her pocket and, looking rather ashamed, pulled out the syringe and ampoule.

'Think about it, driving around with a nervous racehorse. If they are worth thirty-two million, then there is plenty of go in them. So, I thought it would be calmer like this.'

'Calm? The horse looks more dead than alive!' Anna-Greta studied the ampoule and shook her head. 'You know what, this is a double dose, the horse could have died. Dear, oh dear, there isn't much we can do now. We must wait until the animal wakes up.'

'Perhaps we can play some rock music? I mean, really loud!'

'And you'll start to rap too, I suppose? No, there is nothing else we can do except drive to the car park and wait until the horse comes to life again. Then we drive to the stable.'

Somewhat dejectedly, they returned to the minibus and drove off to the car park. Everything had gone so well that they had congratulated themselves on having carried out their 'veterinary manoeuvre' whilst they had sung 'Ole faithful', eaten their sandwiches and had a really nice time. After twenty kilometres, feeling happy and jolly, they had stopped by the roadside, changed their clothes and hidden the wigs, becoming their normal selves again. And then they had driven almost right up to Roland's stable where they had intended leading in their newly purchased steed. And they would have done just that, if he hadn't been totally zonked out . . . What a cock-up, when otherwise they had, on the whole, thought of everything. Yes, they had even arranged a pedigree, and had with them a breeding report, with DNA type and genetic panel test. As so often happens in life, things did not work out as planned. There was truth in the old saying: a little stone in the way overturns a great wain (or, in this case, a little syringe knocks out a great horse). Now the animal was far too groggy for two elderly ladies to handle.

While they waited for the horse to sober up, Anna-Greta took the opportunity to show Christina the photos she had taken inside the toilet.

'If the toilet looks like this, then one can hardly imagine what the rest of the rooms in the farmhouse look like,' she said. 'Fancy furnishings, but just look at the rubbish art.'

'My goodness me! You tire of that sort of painting after five minutes, but what's this?'

Anna-Greta leaned forward. 'Yes, the landscape looks French, and I know you like that. Thought it might give you a bit of inspiration.'

'That was nice of you, but we'll look at it later. Now we must rest a while.'

'To be in good shape when we look after the horse.'

Christina stretched to reach a blanket which was large enough to cover them both, and then she leaned against Anna-Greta's shoulder to snooze. Soon they were both asleep.

They got a few hours' sleep in the car park before being suddenly woken by noise from inside the horsebox. The sun had risen, and it was early morning. Sharp Eye was tramping and snorting, and when they peeped in, he was is some strange way lively and dozy at the same time. Slightly frightened, they drove off to Roland Svensson's. Tired and looking rather pallid, they soon arrived and apologized for being late. Or, as they put it, 'they had run into a few problems en route'.

Roland shrugged his shoulders, spat out his snus, adjusted

his braces and helped them lead the horse out. He looked thoughtfully at the animal.

'Wow, that's quite a stylish horse you've got. Black, lively eyes and magnificent, I must say. But he seems strangely groggy.'

'Perhaps he didn't sleep so well last night?' Christina tried, but Anna-Greta immediately poked her in the ribs, terrified that she was going to make a fool of herself.

'Oh, I see, that's a shame. So, what's he called?'

Whoops – they must, of course, give the horse a name. Christina looked at the lethargic animal and tried to think up something.

'Slow Motion,' she burbled on.

'Slow Motion – yes, spot on! And which stables does he come from?' Roland wondered.

Anna-Greta jumped in. 'Asch, we bought Slow Motion from a private seller in Skåne. They have so many horses there, you can't imagine.'

'Ah, I know, then I understand. Golly, you've had to drive a long way.'

Christina and Anna-Greta looked at each other and gave a sigh of relief. It was difficult to lie and almost even harder not to say too much. But they seemed to have navigated those treacherous waters successfully.

They gave the horse some hay and water, and made sure it was comfortable in the stall. Then they left the stallion Sharp Eye – code name Slow Motion – in farmer Svensson's care and promised to return the next day.

On their way home they tried to rehearse what they would say to Martha, and decided that the white lie about Skåne

174

wasn't so bad. But there remained many a thing to do. They must disinfect the horsebox and clean the car. And then they had to work out the best way to get hold of the ransom money and later hand the precious horse back.

'And, of course, you must ride him, even though he's a racehorse,' said Christina with a nervous giggle. 'Otherwise, it's going to look suspicious.'

'A racehorse? Yes, yes of course,' Anna-Greta mumbled. 'That's no problem. But, Christina, was it such a good idea to call him Slow Motion? Couldn't you have found something a bit better? A racehorse which answers to the name Slow Motion . . .!'

'That's just the point. Nobody is going to suspect that he's a racehorse. Perfect camouflage,' Christina attempted.

'Well, so it shall be, then,' mumbled Anna-Greta.

Exhausted after all the tension and a night's bad sleep, they returned home to rest. On their way up the stairs, they met a perky Martha.

'Good morning! Good morning to you! Perfect timing! I understand that you've been in the stables with your new horse, and perhaps are a bit tired. But that makes now an ideal time for us to do our morning gymnastics, doesn't it?'

Christina and Anna-Greta looked helplessly at each other and realized that they were too tired to protest.

28

Sometime later, when they had all done their gymnastics, showered and had had a glass of delightful fruit juice in Rake's greenhouse, Brains suggested that they should discuss what they wanted it to be like in Hemmavid from now on.

'Stealing and bank robberies are brief, quick projects that we are used to, but all this about saving the countryside takes longer and demands more patience. Do we have that?'

'It will be difficult, but it is feasible,' Martha answered, brazen but in a voice that didn't sound entirely convincing. Perhaps it was the uncertainty, because they had all done their morning gym exercises as usual, but they had only dutifully waved their arms; they hadn't done any weightlifting and had skipped the exercises for their tummy muscles. And Christina and Anna-Greta had been entirely in a world of their own. When they had stretched out on the yoga mats to relax for a few minutes, they had fallen asleep! What was going on? Why were they all so lethargic? Martha took a big gulp of juice.

'As you know, there is a great deal we ought to do for the district.'

'Yes, we know, Martha; that's what you usually say,' said

Rake, and the others nodded in agreement. 'But come off it, not even the country's politicians can manage it!'

Martha restrained herself. She suddenly felt as if she was standing in front of a school class with a lot of boisterous layabouts who ignored the teacher. She tried again.

'That's exactly why. The politicians have failed, so we must do battle.'

'Yes, yes indeed; we have understood that that's what you think,' Brains mumbled.

'But we can make a difference, haven't you noticed? Thanks to our police traffic checkpoint, the long-haul lorries avoid driving past here, and we still have Roland Svensson's farm shop.'

Nobody said a word.

'And besides, we got two extra teachers for the school, teachers with special competence. Irma is absolutely delighted,' Martha went on.

'And if we rob a bank or two in the region, perhaps the police will call in some extra resources too. That would mean some new jobs,' Rake teased her.

Martha gave him an irritated glance, but tried to sound calm.

'I am sorry, my dear, but the police are after us. For the time being there won't be any bank robberies.'

'No, one should most definitely not rob banks,' Christina pointed out and lowered her eyes, while Anna-Greta's cheeks had acquired a distinctly red tinge and she looked away.

'If we arrange ghost walks in the old vicarage, we must have guides. Perhaps that would mean new jobs,' Brains reflected out loud when he saw how Martha was beginning to lose her cool.

'And the tunnels of love attraction needs guides too, so I suggest that we employ some handsome young men,' Anna-Greta said with a giggle.

'No, blondes,' Rake broke in.

Martha felt herself becoming increasingly impatient. Nobody seemed to be taking the situation seriously.

'We can start up the events here in Hemmavid straight away. That would perhaps be a nice task for you, Christina?' Martha almost appealed.

Christina, who had been secretly looking at racehorses on her mobile, now looked about her in embarrassment. What had Martha just said?

'Err, yes, of course,' she mumbled.

'Thank you! And then there is the question of the tunnels of love. What a lovely idea you had, Anna-Greta. Couldn't you draw up a plan for how we can arrange it? I mean, should we have romantic lighting in the tunnels, music and that sort of thing?'

'And why not some double beds,' Rake butted in.

'That's enough!' Martha exclaimed.

'Romantic lighting and quiet music, I've nothing against that. I'd be happy to plan some hot meetings in the tunnels,' Anna-Greta said.

'Excellent, let's do that. Then we just have our guerrilla campaign left.' Martha took out some marker pens in various colours, and a flip chart that Irma had given her. While the gang murmured, she hung up a map which showed the district's switchgear and power cables.

'As soon as we have sufficient solar panels and our own back-up, we can knock out selected parts of the national grid.'

They gave each other looks of astonishment. So Martha had actually been serious about sabotaging the power supply? They had thought – hoped, at any rate – that she was just toying with the idea. Now, evidently, she wanted to put it into action. Anna-Greta was the first to react.

'That's clever. It would be good for business. Then we can earn pots of money with our solar panels.'

'But a power cut. Couldn't we think of something more peaceful?' Brains asked.

Martha nonchalantly waved her hand over the flip chart.

'The electricity companies don't pay tax to the countryside municipalities and nor do we get any of the profit from the forest and mining activities. In Norway, on the other hand, thirty per cent goes back to the countryside where the wealth was generated. That makes for a living countryside. That's why we must wake up those in power.'

They fell completely silent, because nobody had thought of this.

'Besides,' Martha continued, 'people living in the Norwegian countryside pay less tax. So they can keep their schools and health clinics and don't need to close down maternity units like we in Sweden did in Sollefteå, for example.'

Martha noticed that the others were listening.

'And the Norwegians also write off student loans for those who move out to the countryside, and they support new companies. They have lower payroll taxes for employers the further away from Oslo they settle.' Martha put her hands together like a church vicar – and dropped her pen on the floor. Rake bent down and picked it up.

'Must the Norwegians have to be best at this too? Isn't it

enough with the oil and all their medals for winter sports? Oh my God, I'm fed up with it!' he muttered.

'But you see, the Norwegians are smart. They give everybody a chance, regardless of where they live. We don't do that here in Sweden.'

Brains squirmed a little.

'But Martha, dear, do we really have to get all political? I think we should limit ourselves to theft and bank robberies.'

'But a gang of elderly pensioners are not the first people the police would look for after some sabotage.'

'Sabotage?'

Martha could hear how they all gasped for breath.

'Yes, what I had in mind was a little guerrilla activity in two stages. First, we write to the politicians in Stockholm and ask them to revise their countryside policy. If they don't do that, we cut off their electricity and threaten not to turn it back on again until they have promised to change it.' Martha now had her hands by her sides and looked very determined.

'But that just isn't realistic. That's blackmail!' Brains gasped.

'And illegal,' Rake added.

'Pah, we'll just give them a little scare.'

'Easy as pie. Shall we black out the whole country or just half of it?' Rake answered, in a voice dripping with sarcasm.

'Hopefully, we won't need to go that far. But lads, you could work out a good way to switch off the electricity if necessary. I'm sure you'll think of something clever and preferably do it legally, if possible.'

'Jesus above!' Brains moaned.

Martha got up and went into the kitchen. She fetched coffee cups, a can of newly brewed coffee, some cloudberry liqueur and some cardamom-flavoured pastries that Christina had baked that same morning. When she came back, they all stopped talking.

'Let's have a little coffee break before we think about this any more,' she said in a mild voice so as not to seem bossy. 'And if you have any good ideas, that's fine by me. It's always best if you do things together.' She sat down on the sofa, picked up her knitting and pretended to be a lot calmer than she felt.

Rake didn't stop fiddling with his scarf, Christina looked stressed and Brains was silent. Anna-Greta hummed a tune from a popular Swedish dance band, and Brains opened his mouth to say something but changed his mind and looked out of the window instead. No response whatsoever. In the end, Martha couldn't restrain herself any longer:

'Now listen to me, if you don't want to volunteer, then I must accept that, but then I'll ask others in the village. Because now this is serious. We don't have much time left; soon half of Sweden will have been closed down!'

With that, she had said her piece and she left the room. Now it was sink or swim.

29

After the meeting, Brains and Rake walked across to Brains's workshop. They entered through the squeaking door, happy to at last have a moment for themselves so that they could talk man-to-man. In the big workshop with its carpenters' benches, lathes, power jigsaws and several work tables, it smelt of metal and sawdust and was rather messy. Brains went up to his secret fridge – behind a bench grinder and an old welder's helmet – and took out two strong beers. He gave one to Rake and then sat down on the bench next to the lathe.

'I don't like this at all, you know. Just because we are men who know about electricity and mechanics, we don't have to become terrorists who sabotage the electricity grid. That isn't a small thing to ask – and besides, it's bloody dangerous. Can't you talk to Martha?' Rake looked appealingly at Brains.

'Talk to her? No way; once she's decided something, that's it.'

'The fact is that women folk are far too emotional.'

'Indeed, but I can understand her. The politicians forget about the countryside.' Brains got up and looked around the workshop. 'But whatever rebel attack we're going to carry out, we must clean up here a bit, otherwise we can't work.'

Rake nodded, and they set to work. While the men cleared

bits and pieces off the carpenter's bench, sorted the nails and screws and hung up the tools in their correct places, they discussed various ideas. They cleaned the lathe and blaster and oiled the circular saw before finishing off by sweeping the floor. Only then did they allow themselves to take a break. Brains fetched a packet of crisps and took two more beers out of the fridge. He gave one to his mate.

'So, we've got to cause a power cut,' said Rake and he took a deep swig of his beer.

'Yes, that's right. We could let a robot lawnmower roll into the transformer station outside Skogsås,' Brains reflected. 'But what would the politicians care about a little power cut? If we're going to do something, it must knock out the entire national grid to have any effect.'

'Can't we think up something else?' Rake finished his Carlsberg and looked unhappy. 'If we cut off the power supply, people will notice it straight away and we'll be caught.'

'You're right, it would only lead to lots of problems.'

'Of course, it is noble of Martha to try to save the countryside, but I've made up my mind. I'm going to refuse.'

'What, are you going to oppose Martha?' Brains gasped.

'I'm not going to sabotage anything; it isn't my style.' Rake sounded resolute.

'But we must stick together.'

'No, Brains, I'm not going to risk having a high-voltage cable falling onto my head. If she wants to sabotage the electricity, she'll have to do it herself. I've got a better idea. We fool her.'

'Fool Martha? Are you completely out of your mind? There isn't a cat in hell's chance of that!'

183

'Pah, this is what we'll do. We won't oppose her but simply say, yeah sure, Martha, we are working on it and then *we don't do shit*! So, we keep putting things off, just like a real politician, and, in the end, nothing will come of it.'

'Rake, you're a genius, that's marvellous!'

And with that, the two men felt relieved and in very good spirits. A weight had been lifted off their shoulders and, for the first time in ages, they felt like young, free men. Martha could babble on all she wanted, but there was no way they were going to obey her.

Chief Inspector Kurt Löwander turned off his mobile and shook his head. He wanted to get in touch with that former police inspector, Ernst Blomberg, whom the boss had talked about. But he couldn't get hold of him. Blomberg had closed down his detective agency and had gone abroad. It had all happened in a great rush, and the person who had taken over his old premises didn't have his latest contact details. He referred Löwander to Kungsholmen police station where Blomberg had worked before he retired.

'They think he has gone off to Russia to do business,' the man on the other end of the phone said, before excusing himself and ending the conversation.

Löwander swore at his own tardiness. Why hadn't he thought of contacting Blomberg earlier? The boss had talked about him. Said that he had become a private detective after retiring, and that he had suspected some oldies of theft and bank robberies, crimes that still hadn't been solved. And now he had disappeared. Perhaps his former colleagues at Kungsholmen might know more? It was at least worth following up.

Löwander got out a pen and a sheet of paper and dialled the direct number of the head of the police department at Kungsholmen, a certain Gert Aronsson. This was more productive, and Löwander found out that Blomberg's office premises had been taken over by a journalist who had handed in a flash drive that had been left behind. Löwander had to ask one more time; this sounded really fantastic. What if he could find something there? After talking a while, he and Aronsson came to an agreement that Löwander would be given access to the information, and, if it should prove useful, he would contact Kungsholmen again. If he came across any new, exciting details, the journalist would have first dibs on the news. The journalist had phoned and nagged them about it recently, and he wanted all the information on the flash drive right away. But that wasn't going to happen. With his slippery voice, Aronsson asked Löwander to keep an eye open and report back if he discovered anything suspicious.

'Sweden is large and we can't be everywhere, can we? But the jewellery robbery at the auction house was carried out by a gang of oldies. It could be the League of Pensioners, so report back if you see anything.'

'Yes, of course,' said Löwander, solemnly promising to get in touch. But, for the time being, he was going to keep all the information to himself. Otherwise, the Stockholmers would take over the investigation. No, first and foremost he would check the information on the flash drive in peace and quiet, and then he would decide how to proceed. Regardless, it would be exciting. He needed something stimulating to happen, his police work had become increasingly bureaucratic. If that gang of pensioners were shady types, then he was going to nick

30

Christina sat in her armchair in the living room with a shawl over her shoulders and a book in her lap. She tried to read, but couldn't concentrate. *Unsuccessful Crimes* was perhaps not the best choice just after you had committed a theft yourself . . . and suddenly realized that you hadn't thought through the crime properly. Because soon Sharp Eye would be missed, and before that happened, they needed to work out how to arrange the ransom payment and how they were going to hand back the horse without becoming suspects. Christina fingered the book in front of her and unconsciously ran her index finger over the title *Unsuccessful Crimes* several times.

'Anna-Greta, you know what? When we've got the ransom money and handed back the horse, we must buy a stylish black stallion to put in Roland's stable instead of Sharp Eye. Otherwise he's going to wonder.'

'True. But first we must compose the letter demanding a ransom for the horse.'

'Why not write: "Give us ten million straight away, otherwise we shall not feed the horse with oats, but with cabbage soup, which will make him gassy",' said Anna-Greta and she neighed in delight over her own joke.

'Or we could write that if we don't get our ten million by Sunday at the latest, then we'll swap the horse for a donkey.'

'No, but seriously. We must think how a real thief would go about it,' Anna-Greta replied.

'He would have sold the horse to foreign buyers, taken the money and done a runner.'

'Exactly, so that's what we shall threaten to do.'

Christina and Anna-Greta sat in front of the computer and tried out different wordings.

Dear Martin Borge,

As you will have noticed, your valuable racehorse has disappeared. If you pay a ransom fee of 10 million kronor to us before 10 p.m. on Sunday evening, then we promise to give the horse back.

'Nice and short, and then we give them the account number that the long-haul lorry drivers swished the fine money to,' Christina said.

'Good idea, and I'll see that it goes via the Dark Web before we transfer the money to our Robbery Fund.'

Anna-Greta and Christina did a thumbs-up and then ended the letter by adding their secret pay-as-you-go mobile phone number which couldn't be traced. Finally, they signed the letter with 'The best for Sharp Eye', and a P.S. in capital letters: DON'T CONTACT THE POLICE. IF YOU DO, YOU WILL NEVER SEE YOUR HORSE AGAIN.

At 11.30 p.m. that same evening Anna-Greta and Christina's mobiles vibrated, and they crept down the stairs as quietly as possible. Without anyone seeing them, they sat in the minibus and drove out onto the big road. Innumerable kilometres later they had posted the letter in Norway (to fool the police), returned to Hemmavid and crept back into their rooms again. The tension had been so intense that they fell asleep straight away, and the next day they woke up embarrassingly late. Neither of them felt like getting up; they stayed between the sheets a very long time. Not until they had got dressed and eaten their breakfast did they have the energy to talk. Christina tapped Anna-Greta lightly on the shoulder.

'Pssst,' she said. 'We have been blessed with a horse. We had better go and look after him!'

When they reached the stables, they met an angry Roland, his hair all dishevelled.

'What the hell have you dragged in here? Slow Motion – what a name! That's quite a joke. The animal has been banging around in his stall all night long, and nobody has been able to sleep.'

'Sorry about that, perhaps he's restless after the journey,' Christina apologized.

'Well, then, it would be best if you took him on a long ride so that he settles down.'

Anna-Greta heard the racket from inside the stall and it made her worried.

'Yes, of course,' she mumbled, but without conviction, because inside the stall it sounded like a gang of workmen trying to demolish the walls. Anna-Greta and Christina turned pale, but nevertheless tried to approach the stall as nonchalantly as they could. They resolutely opened the door, but stopped in their tracks. Sharp Eye was shiny with sweat; he neighed loudly and had a wild look in his eyes.

'Good heavens,' Christina mumbled. 'Do you dare ride him?'

'Sit astride seven hundred kilos of dynamite? Err, I don't intend risking my life unnecessarily,' Anna-Greta whispered and avoided Christina's gaze. Even though she had sat up on racehorses before, this was something completely different. A gentle old racehorse, she could manage that, but not this one!

Before she had had time to think what to do, she caught sight of Martha who was rapidly approaching them. She seemed strangely focussed, and the friends immediately suspected the worst.

'What a fancy horse. Would be fun to ride him,' said Martha, nodding towards Sharp Eye.

'Yes, yes, indeed,' Anna-Greta stuttered in reply, wishing she could disappear in a hole in the ground.

'The fact that this stallion is called Slow Motion must be a joke. Have you checked the chip?'

'The chip?' Christina gasped.

'Yes; it would be a great shame if he is a horse that has not been broken in properly and was imported to Sweden and sold cheaply in the south,' Martha went on. 'Might even be an illegal animal.'

Anna-Greta turned paler. The International Federation for Equestrian Sports demanded that all horses that competed in international competitions must have a chip – because they had to be able to check that the horse really was what the owner claimed. But how on earth could Martha know this? And Anna-Greta turned even paler when she realized that Sharp Eye still had his chip. If the owner became suspicious and came here and checked the chip code, well, then they would be caught! Anna-Greta and Christina exchanged worried looks.

'Ride him? I'm afraid I've got a bit of a backache today; I thought I'd wait until tomorrow or the day after,' Anna-Greta stuttered. 'Yes – before I go for a lovely ride.'

'Careful with your back, my dear, it is probably best that you wait,' Christina agreed in support of her partner in crime.

'Well now, lucky for me, then,' Martha exclaimed. 'If you can't go out riding, perhaps you can help at the school? Irma wants to discuss some new projects. She seems interested in that charm course for singles that we talked about.'

'Charm course?' Anna-Greta gasped, grabbing hold of the door frame, swaying a little and feeling as if she was about to faint. She just couldn't deal with any more at the moment; she was so tired she could hardly stay on her feet. And Christina could see that.

'Pah, don't worry about tomorrow – the day after that, it will be over,' she tried to console Anna-Greta, and she put her arm around her friend.

The door was heard to open, and a familiar figure came into the café. His dark hair, his charming smile and that erect, self-confident posture was unmistakeable. And he was so elegant in his grey overcoat with the matching grey-blue scarf. Allan Petterson! Malin blushed and quickly looked about her.

'But, Allan, what are you doing here?' she stuttered when he stepped up to the glass counter to order.

'A cup of coffee and a hot cheese sandwich, please!' He winked at her.

191

Malin looked around. Thankfully, there were only two guests inside the café and they weren't locals. Lilian had gone off to the school and would be away for an hour or so. They must be careful. Although, if Allan had come here, it must be something important. What if he had come to an agreement with his wife? She made the coffee, warmed the biggest and finest cheese sandwich she had, and put it all on a tray. When he paid, she gave him a questioning look.

'Is it something special?'

'Yes. Have you got a few moments?'

They sat down and she enjoyed being close to him. Would he raise the question of moving to Skogsås again? But she had already said that she didn't want to leave her sister in the lurch. They had run the village shop together, and now they ran the café together. No, she couldn't move to Skogsås, however much he wanted her to.

'How are you?' She felt his hand under the table and nodded. Would his wife be going away so that they could meet in his house? Or what? He caressed her gently and leaned forward.

'Well, I was wondering if you could help me with something . . . it's about a gang of pensioners. Do they come to the café?'

'There are a lot of people here who are a bit older. We have some newcomers, of course, who sometimes visit the café. The ladies like our croissants and love the hot cheese sandwiches. The men usually hang around the pinball machine. But, well, I don't know . . .'

'The ones who have recently moved here, can you tell me any more about them?'

'Well, there are two elderly men and three women. One is tall and thin as a drainpipe, and another one is always very

192

elegant. They are not always together, but I think they know each other from before.'

'How old are they?'

'Hmm, about seventy-five, or eightyish, I should think.'

'Do you know where they live?'

'It is rumoured that they have moved into the old bank. I think it's them.'

Petterson felt how it all fitted. They could be the five elderly pensioners who had stopped the rubbish tip in the old mine shaft and who the traffic police officer had talked about. When he had phoned him later to discuss the fine, Löwander had again asked whether he knew anything about the oldies. And he had sounded extremely keen to know more. Admittedly, Petterson had been fined despite his 'small talk', but a fine could perhaps be made to disappear. I scratch your back, you scratch mine. Allan Petterson felt in his pockets. He hadn't emptied them, perfect; the business card was still there. If he tipped the police off now, it might serve him well in the future. Quickly he picked up his mobile and punched in the number.

'Allan Petterson here, well, it's about some pensioners,' he started off. 'I thought you might be interested . . .'

31

A whole week had passed but no horse owner had been in touch and Christina and Anna-Greta were becoming increasingly nervous. The silence was the worst. What did you do when you were expecting a ransom sum and the victim didn't get in touch? Besides, Roland Svensson had said that Slow Motion was such a problem that Anna-Greta must immediately look for a new place to stable him.

Christina and Anna-Greta felt under pressure. They couldn't send a bloody horse head, like they did in *The Godfather*; what should they do instead? And also, the two fake veterinarians from Veteran Stables had promised to take the horse back after one week – and that week had already passed. So, when Martin Borge's stableman had phoned, they hadn't answered. The two vets at Veteran Stables had simply ceased to exist – even though the horse was still there.

Christina and Anna-Greta suffered and found it very hard to concentrate. They walked across to the stable, mucked out the stall and made sure that Sharp Eye had hay and feed, but just being there made them nervous, so they went home, read books and played games on their mobile phones. But this didn't help, and Anna-Greta clicked randomly among her apps, e-mail and photos. Late one afternoon when she was lazily looking at her phone, she happened to click on the photos of the painting in Borge's stable toilet. She stopped there.

'Christina, do you know what? This painting is really very good. Perhaps you should paint a copy?' she said, showing her friend the photos on her phone. 'It would fit in nicely above the *David and Venus*.'

'Why not? Can you send me the pictures?'

'OK, I'll send them to you.'

Anna-Greta went up to the balcony, got a good signal and sent them off, while Christina went to fetch her laptop. Then they both sat down in the living room.

'The painting is dark and dirty, but if it was cleaned, perhaps it would be a true work of art,' Anna-Greta said, pointing at her computer screen. 'But we can't exactly go there with a scrubbing brush, can we?'

'I wonder who has actually painted it. I can't see a signature.' She zoomed in on the corner, but couldn't see anything. 'It could be hidden under all the dirt, of course. Let me work on the image in Photoshop. That can do wonders.'

Anna-Greta examined Martin Borge's painting in silence. Then she called out.

'Christina, this painting is good. What if it's worth lots of money?'

Chief Inspector Kurt Löwander turned off towards Hemmavid and drove slowly down the main street. The little village was in darkness and only a few of the street lamps were working. The houses lining the road had no lights on, and the café was closed. He looked carefully on all sides. Löwander had received a tip-off about five pensioners who had recently moved into the area and were said to be living here; five active oldies who could be the same gang that had set up that traffic checkpoint. Now, the mayor, Allan Petterson, had told him that they had visited Lilian's and Malin's café, and that they lived in a building on the road through the village. It had once been the village bank, but now the newcomers had bought the building. He drove closer, slowed down and pulled into the side of the road. There were some lights on in the old timber building.

This was the place. Worth staking out for a few hours, Löwander thought. He turned off the engine and pulled out his binoculars. The current attitude in Stockholm was that they didn't give a damn about thefts. Nowadays it was only terrorists and crimes of violence that were given priority. But he was going to show them; he would gather evidence and nail the thieves himself, and then the snooty Stockholm police could come and fetch them. Villains should be behind bars; it was as simple as that. He focussed his binoculars on the windows.

The oldies inside were clearly visible – indeed, so clearly that he could see what they were wearing. A flowery dress, an old 1950s jacket . . . he could keep a good watch on them from here. Löwander felt a shiver of excitement and his mood improved. Here he could find the proof he needed, and he reached out to pick up his camera from the passenger seat. With a really good telephoto lens he could even get their faces. He picked up the camera and pointed it towards the windows.

But then, at that very moment, the Venetian blinds were closed. In all the windows. And the lights were turned off. Bloody, bloody hell!

32

A lot of hammering could be heard from the workshop, and the jigsaw made a hell of a racket too. Brains went around among the pupils and handed out protective acoustic earmuffs, but the pupils hardly took the time to put them on properly before again bending over their workpieces. He looked out across the workshop and couldn't help smiling. A gang of teenagers worked at every table and there were heaps of planks and various metal parts on the floor. It wasn't obligatory to take part in Brains's experimental workshop, but now almost all the pupils came there after the school day.

He usually had two hours of teaching and practical work, including a little break with the pupils when they discussed various ideas. Never before had he felt himself to be so needed, and he praised Martha for having encouraged him. She had insisted that both Brains and Rake should get lots of money for their activities.

'We'll dip into our Robbery Fund since this can contribute to creating jobs in the countryside,' she had said.

The Robbery Fund was admittedly the League of Pensioners' holy Robin Hood money which was for culture, health and care, and for people who couldn't make ends meet. But, as Martha said, you also had to invest in the future.

Thanks to that money, Brains had been able to employ craftsmen to convert the old stable row, so now the pupils had their own work benches and tools. There was a flood of creativity. He so enjoyed being with the teenagers that he found himself wondering if he too had ADHD, or whatever it was called. But what did it matter? It was just a combination of capital letters, he thought. What was most important was that you had a good life and didn't make problems for other people. These teenagers were admittedly a bit difficult to handle now and then, but they had so many delightful ideas.

Brains purchased equipment, material and the tools necessary, and was pleased to see how thrilled the teenagers became. It was a bit like reliving his own youth in Sundbyberg, outside Stockholm, when he had experimented in his father's workshop. But now he didn't need to be on his own; instead, they were a gang who created things together. He was just going to fetch the bag of sweets he had hidden away and the fizzy drinks for their break, when he caught sight of Martha.

'I was curious to see how you're getting on,' she said and came up to him.

'Yes, as you can see, this is a hive of activity!'

He took Martha under her arm and guided her to one of the carpenter's benches where a youth was busy working with solar panels. Next to the bench, which was covered with battery cables and junction boxes, stood a utility moped – one of those with a platform at the front. At first, Martha hadn't a clue as to what it was doing there inside the workshop, but when she got closer, she understood. The platform was covered with solar panels.

'Wow, that's a fancy moped,' said Martha, nodding towards the vehicle. The boy called Kalle was about fifteen years old. He had a thick head of blond hair, red cheeks and an intelligent gaze.

'That's handy when there's a power cut,' he said, patting the moped. 'I've got the batteries here under the solar panels. If there's a power cut somewhere, I can drive there and they can connect to my batteries.'

'Gosh, that's clever! Your idea ought to be developed. Why not put solar panels on car roofs?'

Kalle looked at Martha with new respect. The old lady seemed to grasp what he was doing.

'Yeah, that ought to work,' he said and nodded.

Martha smiled and would have liked to have run her fingers through his unruly hair. The boy reminded her of the son she had lost when he was only five years old. He had drowned and that was a sorrow that she always carried with her. Kalle reminded her of him. He was shy, almost a bit moody, but his eyes were full of vitality. Brains had told her how he was always in the workshop; he was usually the first to arrive and the last to leave. His mother was dead, and when his father became unemployed, they had moved to his grand-parents' farm outside Skogsås. There, his father had opened a garage for car repairs next to a scrap-metal yard, and ever since his early teenage years, Kalle had spent lots of his time looking for different metals, cables and various bits and pieces which he had played or experimented with. And his father had taught him to work with carpentry tools and lathes. No wonder he had become so clever. He fingered one of the solar panels.

'They can lay out rolls of grass turf,' he reflected. 'What if you could have a sort of solar panel roll that you could lay out and connect up when needed?'

'Excellent! You must work on that idea!' Martha said.

He brightened, and she felt like giving him a hug. A big hug. Like she once used to hug her son . . .

'Martha, come and look at this,' Brains called out, and he dragged her over to another bench. Amanda was standing there, a seventeen-year-old girl with brown hair. She had beautiful dark eyes, and her hair in two long braids. She was busy working on something that looked like an ordinary kitchen cutting board.

'What have you got there?' Martha wondered.

'This is a cutting board with a built-in scales, so that you can weigh what you cut up directly.'

'That's ingenious. Could you make one for me, and I will buy it!' said Martha, thinking that it would be useful in the kitchen.

At the far end of the workshop, two benches had been pushed together into one big workbench. Two boys and a girl were busy there working on something. Martha could see a weird contraption which looked like a large, flat jellyfish. She gave Brains a questioning look.

'That's a drone. Sixten, Lasse and Sophie have been working on that for a long time.'

'Yeah, we're thinking of opening a drone bureau,' said Sixten, who was called Sixten Crewcut because he had his hair cut very short and just had a little lock of hair on his forehead.

He was the oldest of them. 'We thought we could offer a local transport service for post, medicines and that sort of thing.'

'A drone service where we can handle larger packages too,' Sophie added, with a look of satisfaction. She had dyed her hair purple and had a ring in her nose.

Martha glanced at Brains, and saw how proud he was. The workshop and the teenagers who liked being there, this was his doing. At that moment she was filled with warmth, and she understood why she had got engaged to him. Brains was a man who did something for others, and now he had taken these pupils under his wing and had got them to flourish and develop. He had talked about concentrating on the young people to save the countryside. Taking what is best, and what is traditional in a district – but also creating something new together with a younger generation. She looked at him and squeezed his hand, followed by an extra little caress on the inside.

When he felt it, he immediately looked very happy; he felt warm, and as if he had been given super powers.

33

You couldn't see who had painted that picture. Christina had worked with Anna-Greta's photos in Photoshop, but had not succeeded in making a signature visible. She gave up and instead decided to copy it. Because she liked the painting so much and it would soon be Rake's birthday. It would make a fine present.

She started the next day and stretched a canvas on the easel before her. Then she cheated a little and projected, with the computer's help, the motif onto the canvas. She didn't usually do that, but this was going to save time. Because, just now, there was so much else she had to think about. And Rake's birthday couldn't wait. The motif with the woman feeding hens on a farm somewhere in France inspired her, and Rake would certainly like it. Most of the time she used watercolours, but she was good with oil paint too and could even mix her own oil paint in various shades. If she managed to make a decent copy, it would look really nice above the *David and Venus* sculpture – unless, of course, Rake wanted it in his bedroom. Martin Borge didn't have a clue. How on earth could you restrain yourself from having such a beautiful painting cleaned, and, even worse, hanging it up in the loo?

While she painted, she listened to records of Edith Piaf and Jacques Brel, and ate a French croissant. She painted intensively all day long, and, dressed in her smock which was stained with paint and with brushstrokes on her nose, she showed Brains a photo of the picture frame and asked him to make a similar one in secret.

The following day, he came in with the frame he had just made, and helped her to frame the oil painting. She gave a laugh, because now it looked just like the painting on Anna-Greta's photo. Just as they were finishing, steps were heard in the doorway and Martha came into the room. Christina stroked the frame with her hands.

'What do you think? A nice birthday present for Rake, isn't it?'

'Absolutely; it looks like a French nineteenth-century painting. He likes the sort of paintings where you can see what they represent.'

'Anna-Greta was going to give him a crate of jazz records, and Brains, for his part, had bought a humidifier for the greenhouse. Have you got something nice for him?'

Martha blushed. She had been so preoccupied with her own projects that she had completely forgotten that it would be his birthday – and hadn't thought of anything.

'Err, why not a model boat or perhaps something for his greenhouse?' she mumbled.

'Yes, I'm sure they'd be nice presents, but you know what he would like most of all?'

Martha shook her head.

'Peace and quiet. He is very disturbed by the way you are always having meetings and starting new projects. You must remember that he is over eighty, and that is quite old for a man who pretends to be sixty-five.'

Martha had to admit it to herself. Yes, she certainly did want to activate her friends all the time, but the countryside in Sweden – and in many other countries for that matter – was really under threat. You had to react!

'All right, then, no meetings on his birthday, but instead good food, flowers, champagne and a peaceful, silent present. Perhaps that would be in order?' Martha summarized.

'Sounds fine. Then he'd be happy, and understand that you have really made an effort for his sake.'

Martha went out into the kitchen, fetched a cup of coffee and thought about it. But just being silent and not doing anything wasn't a nice birthday present, not at all. It sounded terribly boring! Couldn't she give him a quiet and peaceful present in some other way?

She looked out of the window. The sun was about to set and it glowed like a red ball of fire over the landscape. She washed up the coffee cup and watched as the sun sunk lower and lower down towards the horizon. Silent and beautiful. Something like that; what if he could be given something as peaceful as that as a present?

The fillet steak with tomato and cheese, green salad and scalloped potatoes were ready, the cake baked, and the champagne and glasses waiting. In addition, Martha and Christina had made a prawn-salad mix which they had put on home-baked dark bread. It was all laid out on the dining table and Rake's presents lay on the shelf under the *David and Venus* sculpture. Martha had her present ready too. It was that beautiful sunset that had inspired her.

'Lovely, now we're ready. I'll just prepare the little surprise I have in mind for him,' said Martha, and she went out to the porch.

'Tell us, what is it?' Christina asked her.

'No, it's a secret. I'll soon be back and then you'll understand.' She put her coat on, stepped into her boots, put on her rucksack, then went out – quite looking forward to the reaction of Rake and the others.

While she walked quickly along the forest path, she reminded herself of everything she had learned about Thai lanterns, that special sort of paper lantern that many Swedes now used on New Year's Eve instead of fireworks. No explosions and screeching sounds here, certainly not, but instead it would be silent and peaceful! And dignified! She patted her rucksack. She had everything she needed in it!

In the forest behind Roland Svensson's farm lay the little forest glade she had chosen for this. It was just right! Martha headed for it, stopped, looked about her and took a deep breath. There was nobody around, nobody who could disturb things. But the wind? She looked up in the trees. The wind was blowing towards the farm so Rake ought to be able to see the lanterns when they floated past above their house. It would be lovely! She took her rucksack off, carefully extracting the first delicate Thai lantern of flameproof paper. All she needed to do now was to light the paraffin in the holder underneath, and then release the lantern. To be on the safe side, she checked the instructions a final time:

1. *Take the lantern out of the package.* (Yes, she had done that.)

2. *Carefully unfold the lantern to full size and turn it upside down.* (Exactly, she was just about to do that.)

3. *Light a corner of the fuel pouch and make sure it catches fire properly.* (Yes, right, she would light the corner of that bit of paraffin; that would work best.)

4. *Turn the lantern the right way up, so that it can fill with hot air, but don't let the flames ignite the paper in the lantern.* (No, indeed not, that would spoil it all!)

5. *Release the lantern when you feel that it has sufficient power to rise and float away. Enjoy it! And why not buy some more and become so proficient that you can teach your friends!* (That would have to be something for later.)

Martha took the box of matches and lit the fuel pouch soaked in paraffin, then held the lantern frame over the flame until she felt that the lantern wanted to lift off. Lanterns like this have existed for more than a thousand years; they flew well, and radiated peace. Rake would be satisfied!

There you go! Now the wind had got the right direction and strength. She felt how the lantern wanted to rise, she took aim for the house and let go. The Thai lantern rose up into the air in a slow and dignified manner, and she followed it with her eye while it gently blew in the direction of the house. The beautiful lantern was, in Thai tradition, a declaration of love for your darling. And of course things sparked and glowed when you were in love, but now this would cause Rake to spark, because it was his birthday! She smiled to herself and joyfully anticipated his reaction. Rake would understand that even though they quibbled sometimes, she was very fond of him. So fond, indeed, that she had made this effort to give him a beautiful and peaceful surprise. A sort of meditation of celebration. But then, at that very moment, there was a strong gust of wind. The lantern swayed, changed direction, and floated off eastwards past the power line and high above the forest.

Oh well, thank God she had another lantern. She quickly pulled out lantern number two, unfolded it and lit the paraffin-drenched block. And this time the Thai love lantern floated straight towards the house without being blown off course. Pleased with herself, she followed its progress until suddenly yet another gust of wind blew. The lantern changed direction and glided away in the dark towards Roland Svensson's stables and privy. She just had time to hope that nobody was going to be scared, before the lantern disappeared. She continued to stare after it as if she could make it come back with her strong will, but no. Both lanterns had sailed away out of her control and so she gathered her things together. After this unexpected turn, how was she going to celebrate her friend now? Disappointed in herself, she walked back to the house, and had almost reached the yard when she heard a crackling noise and saw sparks over by the power line. The next moment, everything turned black. And the whole district lay in darkness.

34

Oh goodness gracious, that was quite a bang; what if it had caused a power cut everywhere! That hadn't been the intention, Martha reflected. She'd just wanted to celebrate Rake's birthday!

As soon as she got inside the door, she hurried up to her bedroom, took off her jeans and pullover, and put on a dress instead. She would at least look nice for his birthday dinner! But this was just typical. When her friends had asked her to celebrate Rake with dignity, she had succeeded in closing down the whole district! It was still dark, and she couldn't find the matches. She ought, at least, to put on some make-up. Then she heard a familiar engine sound and the light flickered on. Lovely! Brains, of course, had started the generator. Quickly she put on her lipstick and some mascara on her eyelashes, then, without letting on where she had been, or what she had done, she went down to the others, cleared her throat in a suitably nonchalant manner and exclaimed:

'God, what a nuisance! There are so many power cuts out here in the countryside.'

She pretended to take it in her stride and looked out of the window. It was still pitch-black out there.

'Lucky that we have our generator. It was running out of petrol, but I've just been out and filled it up.' Brains smiled at her. Now they had lighting again. On the other side of the road, some candles flickered in the windows.

'What about Kalle's utility moped? Perhaps he could help somebody?' Martha suggested.

'Pah, the power will soon be back again,' Anna-Greta said.

'It isn't sabotage, is it?' Christina sounded worried.

'No, my dear, why should it be?' said Martha suspiciously quickly while her brain was working at full speed. What if the first lantern had bumped into one of the power lines in the grid? A Thai lantern could burn for fifteen to twenty minutes and fly a long way in that time, so it wasn't impossible.

'Perhaps we should listen to the local radio station and find out what's happened,' Anna-Greta proposed.

'Yes, lucky we have a battery-driven radio,' said Christina.

Martha turned on the radio with a sinking feeling in her tummy area.

At around seven this evening, there was a power cut in Skogsås and the surrounding district. Approximately two thousand households are affected. It is not yet clear what has caused the power cut. Technicians from Fortum are working flat out, but can't yet say when power will be restored . . .

Martha avoided looking the others in the eye and hummed slightly nervously, while Christina went to the kitchen to get some tealights. Rake stood by the window and looked out. It was still dark.

'Trains won't run, traffic lights won't work, everything will thaw in freezers, and you can't use your bank card,' he muttered. 'But, worst of all, what about my plants? I try to maintain an even temperature in the greenhouse!'

'And you can't go shopping or fill your car with petrol,' Rake added.

'Not to mention the Internet . . .' Anna-Greta pointed out.

'But this is what it is like in the countryside sometimes. The electricity grid breaks down and the politicians don't care,' said Martha, still without daring to look the others in the eye. 'Do you remember that big black-out in the 1980s? Something happened in a transformer station and it became dark in almost the whole of Sweden. There was a hell of a fuss about that, but when it happens in the countryside, well, then people just shrug their shoulders . . .'

The extent of a power cut in a blacked-out community gradually sank in and they sat there in silence for a long time, until Anna-Greta straightened her back and said in a voice that breathed opposition:

'Martha, you talked about how we ought to sabotage the grid; do you still stand by that?'

Martha wrung her hands, blushed more than she had done all her life and hummed and hawed a long while before she could get her voice back.

'Well, if you are going to do something like that, it must be part of a brief and limited sabotage for a particular purpose and not harm anybody,' she said. 'But now I think we should sing for Rake, it's his birthday after all!'

She lifted her champagne glass and started to sing 'Happy birthday to you' with the others, after which they all toasted and cheered. They sat down at the dining table, but the food had now become cold. They ignored this and started eating anyway, but after a few mouthfuls Martha put down her knife and fork and said:

'I wonder how Roland and the horses in the stables will manage, but I suppose he has a generator.'

Anna-Greta suddenly woke up. The horse! Oh my God, the stall where Slow Motion was kept had an electronic lock. Their kidnapped racehorse could walk out any time at all . . . Anna-Greta poked Christina in the ribs and said in a low voice:

'We must go and check up on Sharp Eye!'

Christina looked aghast because she too immediately realized what could happen. Roland Svensson had been so proud of his new, expensive electronic locks and had boasted that they were so good that he didn't need anything else. He did, of course, have a battery back-up, but had he got round to installing it? Christina got the shivers. What if Sharp Eye had gone, and their thirty-two million kronor had run out through the stable door . . .

211

35

'Oh God, the horse!' Christina shouted out and jumped up at almost the same time as Anna-Greta. Without explanation, they rushed out into the hall, hurriedly pulled on their outer clothes, took head torches with them and rushed off to the stables. Martha watched them in surprise. She just couldn't understand her friends' relationship with that horse. On the one hand, they had bought it because Anna-Greta wanted to start riding again, but on the other, she hadn't yet mounted it. She'd blamed her back-ache. And there was something weird about the stallion. It was as if it had been spiked with ginger, a bit like the horse dealers in bygone days had done when they wanted to liven up their horses before selling them. Slow Motion had been such a bother in the stables that Roland was near the end of his tether.

'Slow Motion,' he had scoffed, 'that name is about as accurate as calling a Formula One car a tractor!'

The horse had probably become even more nervous now that the power had gone. Martha got up. Christina and Anna-Greta might need some help. She had better go and see if she could give them some assistance! Martha hurried after them and reached the stables just as Christina and Anna-Greta were coming out of the main door. There was very little light and it was hard to see, but Martha recognized their voices. Christina was crying and Anna-Greta was in a dreadful state. They were so upset that neither of them noticed her.

'What chaos! Several horses have run off,' Anna-Greta moaned.

'Which way do you think they will have gone?'

'Horses tend to return to the farm they come from. Holy shit! In that case we've lost a fortune!'

Martha remained standing where she was without making her presence known. What were they talking about? She crept up closer to hear more. Their head torches swept around as if they thought they would find the horse somewhere nearby.

'Roland should have an emergency generator; why hasn't he started it? And where are the stable boys?' Anna-Greta sounded really angry.

'It's all Roland's fault, he ought at least to have kept the padlocks. His own animals will probably stay close to the farm, but Sharp Eye!' Christina's voice quivered.

'Slow Motion . . .' Anna-Greta corrected her.

But Martha had already heard the name. Sharp Eye – where had she heard the name before? Wasn't it the name of one of the racehorses they had on the stud farm the other side of the valley? She became suspicious and followed her friends at a distance.

'I thought we could support the district our own way,' she heard Christina say. She was in tears. 'But what will we do now?'

Agitated voices could be heard outside the stables and Christina became quiet. It sounded like Roland and the stable boy. The voices came closer. Martha withdrew further into the darkness, and Christina and Anna-Greta turned off their head torches. When the men had gone past, they left the stables, as did Martha, who quickly slipped away. She didn't get far before she heard a humming sound and the lights came back on. Roland had generators of course. But what on earth were Christina and Anna-Greta up to? Had her friends laid their hands on a valuable racehorse which had now run off? It seemed so. Martha couldn't help but smile. They had become so cunning, her friends. What a contrast to what they had been like when they had lived at the Diamond Company old folk's home. And they had done this all by themselves too! She almost felt proud of them. On the other hand, everybody in the League of Pensioners must stick together. She decided to confront them.

When Christina and Anna-Greta came in through the door a bit later, they saw to their surprise that Martha had laid the kitchen table with home-made scones, tea and a bottle of cloudberry liqueur. There was a lighted candle on the table too, and Martha gave them a friendly smile.

'Welcome!' she greeted them. 'The others went into the living room, but we three can have a nice little chat here, can't we?'

'That's kind of you, but we're just on our way to the minibus. Our horse has run away, so we thought we'd go out and search for him straight away,' Christina said, thinking to excuse them both.

'So, you're going to look for Sharp Eye, right?'

Martha had slipped in the real name of the horse, and when Christina spontaneously answered:

'Yes, he's run away –' No more words were necessary. It wasn't Slow Motion but a valuable racehorse that had been boarded in Roland Svensson's stables. Martha leaned forward.

'OK, your millions have galloped out of the stables and now you're in a pickle. And you have no idea what to do about it. That's the situation, isn't it?'

'I don't understand what you're talking about,' Christina ventured.

'What do you mean?' Anna-Greta protested.

Martha ignored their objections. 'You want to get the horse back, of course, and I've got an idea for you. We can work together. The members of the League of Pensioners should support each other, don't you think?'

'Hmm, we always work together,' Christina mumbled, embarrassed. 'But our thirty-two million has gone up in thin air . . .'

'If Sharp Eye is worth thirty-two million, then I suspect you could get a ransom sum of ten million for him,' Martha carried on. 'That would be ten million for the Robbery Fund. In which case, we have no time to lose. I suggest that we leave immediately. It's delightful that you took the initiative for a little theft. That warms my heart. I was just thinking that we ought to strike again, and now I've discovered that you already have done! Respect!' Martha raised her glass of cloudberry liqueur.

Christina and Anna-Greta exchanged confused glances.

'Well, we demanded ten million, but so far we haven't received anything. And now the horse is missing,' said Anna-Greta, who realized that Martha had seen through them. And not only that, she wasn't angry but wanted to help them. In the stressful situation they now found themselves, it was actually lovely and liberating.

'Everything goes so much better if you help each other. But we must hurry. Sharp Eye is not exactly a slow creature. We must get hold of him before he gets too far away!' said Martha.

'But Rake's birthday . . .'

'Oh, when we get back, we'll have another birthday party for him!'

Christina and Anna-Greta hurried off to fetch some warm clothes, a box of protein bars, something to drink, some rope, string and gaffer tape. They quickly put it all into a shopping trolley and hurried down the stairs. Then Christina looked into the living room, told the surprised men that she was sorry that they must leave immediately, but she would explain it all later. Pressed for time, she encouraged Rake and Brains to celebrate the birthday by themselves until they came back. And before the two men had properly understood what was happening, the ladies were on their way out of the house. Christina and Anna-Greta drove to the stables and hitched the horsebox onto the minibus, while Martha crept into the stable corridor. There she looked for Sequin, a stylish young mare she knew from before.

Thank God Roland and the stable boy had gone off, so that she could lead her out into the yard. Sequin seemed to trust Martha and didn't protest at all, and that suited Martha perfectly since the mare was needed just now. Martha knew enough about horses to know when a mare is on heat. And a few days earlier she had seen that Sequin showed all the signs.

216

As soon as they managed to get Sequin into the horsebox, they drove off to look for Sharp Eye. While Martha drove, Christina and Anna-Greta told her about the theft but emphasized that their little attempt to get a ransom had been for the sake of the village. Ten million was just as much as a complicated bank robbery, and they thought they had been smart when they had stolen the horse. The problem was only that the owner refused to pay. Martha praised them for their inventiveness and mumbled something about how tricky it was to be a villain, but that now what was necessary was *taking action*.

When they drove off into the night, the power still hadn't been restored, and the only difference was that, thankfully, it had started to become light. With a bit of luck, they would surely catch sight of Sharp Eye. While they sat in the minibus, Martha thought that she ought to confess to having messed things up with the Thai lanterns, and she was just about to tell all, when Anna-Greta turned the car radio on to listen to the local news: *Fortum have localized the damage which blacked out two thousand households in the Skogsås district. At first, the company had no idea what had caused the power cut, but they have now succeeded in identifying the fault . . .* At this point, Martha started to have difficulty breathing and she quickly wound down the side window to get some air. *According to Fortum, the power cut has a natural explanation. A beaver had felled a tree which landed on a cable, which, in turn, took with it other cables that were connected to a transformer in the area. That was why the power cut was so extensive. But now the technicians on the spot estimate that power will be restored by lunchtime . . .*

'Oh, fantastic! It wasn't me!' Martha exclaimed, and then couldn't refrain from laughing.

'What on earth are you laughing at?' Anna-Greta wondered.

'Pah, Christina said that Rake thought I ought to calm down a bit. So, I thought I would celebrate his birthday with Thai lanterns instead of fireworks. But the lanterns blew away and when there was a power cut, I thought that they had got caught on a power cable or in a transformer station. But it wasn't me, it was a beaver!'

'So you thought . . .' Christina was all eyes.

'Indeed, I did, but I am completely innocent, so now we shall party!'

'That's worth a toast, certainly. Do you remember in our youth when we were up late partying?'

'In the days when we were chasing men?' Martha asked.

'Yes, but now we are chasing a horse!' Christina started to giggle.

'With our minibus specially adapted for oldies. Times change,' Anna-Greta interposed.

'Well, at our age you have to adapt,' said Martha.

Martha and her friends kept to the gravel roads in the forest to see if they could catch sight of Sharp Eye there. After two hours of this, without any success, they decided to sleep in the minibus and continue to search the next day.

'What if we could find the horse and get our ransom money of some millions? I would call that a good night's income for three ancient ladies,' said Anna-Greta producing one of her customary horse neighs – and then the others smiled, even though they were so tired.

After looking around for a while they parked at the side of

the road, to bed down as best they could. But then Anna-Greta remembered the horse and went out to the horsebox. When she reached the back door, she opened the upper hatch so that Sharp Eye would pick up Sequin's scent. That ought to attract Sharp Eye as quick as a flash. Martha, for her part, thought about the menfolk back at home. She phoned Brains so that they wouldn't be worried.

'We're fine. We haven't found the horse yet, but soon will. Don't worry. Sleep well!'

Then the three ladies folded back the seat, pulled a warm blanket over themselves and were ready for sleep. Round about them, they could hear the sounds of the forest; out here there was none of the noise of a town. That's what is so wonderful with the countryside, Martha thought; it is so silent here. Really silent. And within a few minutes, she had fallen asleep.

Rake and Brains woke up in a house that was empty and abandoned. Confused, they brewed some coffee and buttered a few slices of bread.

'They've gone off! What the hell should we do? What if they get lost in the forest? We ought to have been there for them,' said Brains, who was really rather worried.

'Yes but, they simply went off, so they only have themselves to blame,' Rake said, still indignant over having been abandoned in the middle of his birthday party.

'But, mate, it was about millions, Martha said. You mustn't be angry until we've heard their explanation.'

'They can't explain this away! You only have a birthday once a year. I'm going out to the greenhouse.'

'You do your planting, and I'll hold the fort here in the

kitchen. Martha and the others would never have gone off like that unless they had to. In the meantime, let's enjoy being alone at home.'

'What's to enjoy?'

'No ladies to boss us around, of course!'

Martha phoned home the next day and noticed that Brains now spoke in a more loving tone of voice. Perhaps it wasn't such a bad thing for the menfolk to miss them a bit . . . and she couldn't say what time they would be home again.

'Perhaps Sharp Eye has already been caught,' Christina sighed late in the afternoon when they still hadn't seen the slightest trace of the horse. After driving around for three hours on forest roads, they had stopped for a rest, made some coffee and each eaten a protein bar. 'Shall we give up?'

'No way. You have to be prepared to make a bit of an effort to get hold of ten million,' Anna-Greta protested.

That very moment, before they had started on their snack, they heard a familiar neigh. Sharp Eye was standing just a few trees away.

Anna-Greta nipped out and had something tasty to tempt him but there was no need for that, because Sharp Eye was already intent on reaching the young mare in the horsebox. As quick as a flash, Anna-Greta opened the horsebox while Martha hooked a long, wine-red rope onto the halter. At the last moment they managed to get Sequin out into the glade before Sharp Eye started his raging attentions.

'Now we've got him,' Anna-Greta exclaimed, but an almost 700 kilo racehorse couldn't be handled any old way, and the gang of pensioners had to hurriedly save themselves as best they could. It thus took quite a while before Anna-Greta managed to fasten the rope in Sharp Eye's halter, and it wasn't until Christina surprised him with a jab of sedative that they jointly succeeded in coaxing him into the horsebox. A somewhat dazed Sequin now stood close by, next to a fir tree, and with the help of a fistful of tasty horse goodies and lots of patting and stroking, Anna-Greta could finally mount her.

Then Martha drove slowly in the direction of Martin Borge's stud farm, while Anna-Greta rode on the mare behind the minibus. When they were close to the stud farm, they stopped and took Sharp Eye out of the horsebox.

'Can you manage him?' Christina asked anxiously when Martha took hold of the halter to lead him into the yard.

'Your dose of sedative still has effect,' said Martha and she gave him a handful of horse goodies. 'This is going to go well.'

And while Martha walked up to the stud farm, Anna-Greta rode to the minibus where she and Christina put Sequin into the horsebox.

It was still light and the two of them sat on the front seat with a pack of cards. They thought that a round of canasta would be nice while they waited, but in the state in which they found themselves, they couldn't even manage to play snap. They put the cards aside and stared up at the stud farm. How on earth would Martha manage this?

36

Oh my goodness, this was harder than she had expected. Martha was suddenly gripped by a great uncertainty. She didn't know which was the most difficult, to hold the horse or to confront the lord of the manor. Even though she had grown up on a farm and knew a thing or two about horses, she was decidedly nervous when she led Sharp Eye on to Martin Borge's property. She cautiously approached the fence, and when she reached the gate, Sharp Eye became nervous. The stallion neighed and was almost impossible to hold, and it wasn't long before a guard was seen inside the gates.

'I found this horse in the forest and it wanted to go this way,' said Martha with a friendly smile.

'Sharp Eye!'

'Oh really? The famous racehorse? Well, having grown up with horses, I immediately saw that this was a valuable specimen,' Martha began, leaning her head to one side and trying to look knowledgeable and special. 'Yes, so I fed him and tried to find out where he came from. I made a few phone calls and found out that here at the stud farm there was a horse missing. So I made my way here to ensure that he passed into the right hands.'

'Fantastic!' the guard exclaimed. He pulled out his mobile phone and rang Borge and the stable manager. While they waited, he told Martha of how the horse had been stolen and that they had all been very worried. The villains had even demanded a ransom sum, he let on. Martha listened and gave a friendly nod as if this was the first time she had heard about it. The two stood talking a good while until they heard some voices. Martha turned round and caught sight of the stable manager and a short, fat man who said he was the owner of the estate, Martin Borge. He almost ran up to the horse.

'Sharp Eye! Wow, fantastic, to think that you're back!'

'Yes, I found him,' Martha commented, but the man didn't seem to hear her. He looked almost moved and patted the horse time and time again on its neck. He didn't care about Martha, didn't care about the stable manager – or the guard, for that matter. He was completely engrossed in his own bubbling joy. Martha went forward and introduced herself as Inga Svensson and said in a loud voice:

'Sharp Eye is a fantastic racehorse. You don't leave a fine horse like this to fend for himself, I thought, so I realized that something must have happened.' She paused for a moment while she examined every change in his countenance. But the multimillionaire didn't say anything; he just started to walk round the horse to see if there were any injuries. There weren't.

'Not a scratch. I don't understand where the horse has been,' he said.

'With knowledgeable horse thieves, of course. Otherwise, they wouldn't have demanded a ransom.'

The estate owner looked angrily at the guard. This was

223

evidently information that the guard should have kept to himself. Martha saw the opening.

'I heard that they demanded ten million, so perhaps you could consider a hefty finder's reward for me? That wouldn't be more than fair, don't you think?'

Martha tried to look as innocent as possible, and gave him the fairest smile she could manage. Borge muttered something, ordered the stable manager to lead the horse into the stables, and then turned back towards Martha.

'So you want a reward, you say?'

'I'm not insisting, naturally, not at all – but my house in the south must be renovated and pensions nowadays are so low. So, you understand . . .'

The man felt in his pocket for his wallet, dipped into the wad of banknotes it contained, and handed two five hundred-kronor notes to Martha.

'Well, thank you very much for your help, then.'

Martha gasped. The bastard was a billionaire! But Martha wasn't going to give up. She dug out a piece of paper from her handbag and jotted down the secret pay-as-you-go telephone number on it.

'I am sure you will have second thoughts when you've had time to reflect upon this. You have just got back a horse worth more than thirty million, isn't that right? A hefty reward would help an unfortunate poor pensioner – and it is so very simple to transfer money nowadays with Swish via the phone. I look forward to hearing from you!' Martha raised her hand in farewell and went on her way.

*

'How did it go?' Christina asked when Martha was back with her friends.

'A stingy type, he is that!' she said, almost in tears, when she got into the minibus. 'He's rolling in money but he only offered a thousand kronor! Now he only has himself to blame.'

'What do you mean?' Christina asked.

'He will find out. I have a plan B, but first we must take Sequin back.'

They led Sequin out of the horsebox, and while Martha and Christina drove homewards, Anna-Greta rode Sequin back to Roland Svensson's land and let her go there. Martha and Christina picked up their friend and forewarned Brains and Rake as to their imminent arrival.

'It will be lovely to have a shower and change clothes,' said Christina.

'And catch up on sleep in a proper bed,' Anna-Greta said.

When they drove into the yard, Rake and Brains were standing in the porch looking very resolute.

'You're crazy, just going off like that!' said Rake, but he helped Christina off with her overcoat. There was more worry than anger in his voice. 'Anything at all could have happened!'

'Yes, where have you been? We were so worried,' Brains complained, even though Martha had actually gone to the trouble of phoning him several times. She was just about to protest, when she noticed that Rake was wearing his barbecue apron. She looked at the men with amusement and gave them a big hug.

'Sorry that we disappeared just like that, but it was the

power cut. It was a matter of ten million! But now we shall celebrate your birthday, Rake, and do so really properly.'

'Yes, we have decided that we shall celebrate for two days instead of one, since we went off in such a hurry,' Christina added. And they all hugged one another for a long while, until Rake managed to get his act together.

'Well, yes, we've already got grub for today. So sit yourselves down before the food goes cold. Take your seats, my friends!' he urged and preceded them into the kitchen.

There was a smell of grilled meat and on the table stood a bottle of wine next to a large platter filled with thin slices of beef, fried onion, gravy and mashed potato. And in a bowl beside them, there was also a Greek salad for Christina. The gents had made them a delicious dinner, and that made Martha realize just how much they had been missed.

They sat down and when Christina and Anna-Greta told them about Sharp Eye and the hunt for the ten million kronor ransom, all the tension dissolved and the men got answers to the many questions they had waited to ask. It was a cosy dinner with lots of chat and many stories, and when Rake burped, nobody said anything, they were all just so incredibly happy to be back together again.

After the meal, Martha started to brew the coffee, and while the gang waited for it to be ready, Rake pulled out a newspaper cutting. He placed it on the table and put on his reading spectacles.

'You know what, Martha,' he began, 'I saw this letter to the editor the other day, and both Brains and I have read it. Bank robberies seem rather pathetic in comparison.'

'Now I'm getting curious,' said Martha. 'Read it out loud so we can all hear.'

Rake looked at Brains, who nodded, and then began to read in a loud and dramatic voice: '"*I live in Sweden's richest municipality, Ragunda –*"'

'Yes, right, that's quite a long way from here – but read on. It's a sparsely populated area just like here,' Anna-Greta interposed.

'Yes, well, this is what she has written, this pensioner,' Rake went on, and he cleared his throat a few times:

'"*They damned up the waterfalls in Indalsälven river, nine hydro-electric plants which give billions to the state, while property taxes give a few hundred million more. We also have hundreds of wind turbines which deliver electricity down to the south, but the profits don't end up here, instead they go to Germany or some other place. The same applies to the forest. Most of the forest is owned by Sveaskog, SCA and the Swedish Church, but we don't see any of the income here. The state has closed down the social security office, the employment exchange, the MOT testing centre and the dispensing chemists. The door to the police station is locked, and they have gone home. There are, admittedly, two railway stations, but no trains stop at them, so we must make a round trip by car of a hundred and eighty kilometres, if we want to get on the train.*

'"*We have horribly bad roads, and we never see a snowplough. Mobile phones don't work and the local bank branch has closed down. I must make a round trip of two hundred kilometres by car to visit the bank. And I need hardly mention that the health clinic has closed. Petrol has gone up in price, but my car, which takes me to my job, uses just as much fuel as before.*

227

'"I want to live in the countryside, but what should I do to be able to stay and live here?"'

And it was signed:

'"A pensioner in the countryside who can only just scrape a living together."'

Rake pointed at the letter and looked at Martha.

'It isn't only us here in Hemmavid who have it like this, but also people in other districts in Sweden. And abroad, too, for that matter. You were right all the time, Martha, and I'm sorry if I've been so slow to fathom it.'

'And I don't think I've really understood how serious the situation is,' Brains interposed. 'But now Rake and I have talked it through and you can rely on us. We stand behind you.'

'And we do too,' Christina and Anna-Greta agreed, and that was just too much for Martha. She had struggled hard to get them all to go along with her, and now that she had finally succeeded, she was close to tears. She had always tried to hide her feelings, but deep inside she had been very sad when she hadn't got the gang on her side. Previously they had always striven for the same goal and had stuck together against the world outside; without her friends she had felt so lonely. Martha cried and sniffled, and when Brains, Rake, Christina and Anna-Greta put their arms around her and tried to console her, she sniffled even more and couldn't say a word. She sobbed like a little kid, and was ashamed of not being able to control herself. But the others just smiled and let her cry away. Then Christina said:

'You know what, we must celebrate this. Liqueur or champagne?'

'Liqueur *and* champagne!' they all shouted. And they had both. They each took a glass of champagne as well as a wee glass of Irma's blackthorn liqueur to go with the coffee. And soon the after-effects were evident. One after the other, the ladies crept off upstairs to have an after-dinner nap, and Martha, who had intended doing lots of useful things, had no energy for anything. She stumbled into the shower, and barely had time to get back into her bedroom again before falling asleep with a contented smile on her lips.

37

The following morning, when Martha woke and went down to the others, she was still in a radiant mood, happy that she and her friends had found each other again. But she had only just entered the kitchen when she met with an angry Rake.

'The police were just here and were looking for you.'

'The police!' Martha sucked in some air and found it hard to breathe.

'Yes, it was a man with a little moustache who asked if you were here. Lewander? Löwander? Or whatever he was called. I thought I recognized him from the police traffic-control thing. But he wasn't in uniform.'

'Mysterious!' A thousand ideas rushed through Martha's head. Had the police managed to trace the payments of the fines that Christina had demanded from the worst of the traffic violators? But that ought not to be possible with Swish . . . hmm, while they had been searching for Sharp Eye, the three friends had had time to talk about so much. Christina had described how she had been carried away by the excitement of the moment, and asked the drivers to Swish the fines – via their secret telephone number – to their Robbery Fund. And this was something they wanted to do again.

Because, as she said, once you had committed a criminal act, then it was easy to do so again, and keep on doing so. But if that cyber money was untraceable, why had the policeman turned up? Had someone secretly tipped him off? Or had the police stations across the country received an updated wanted list? There couldn't be that many elderly gangs running around in the kingdom of Sweden of course, and it was bad enough that one of those constables had caught sight of them. Martha breathed heavily. Perhaps they shouldn't have carried out that traffic check, because on that occasion all five of them had been there – five oldies. Just like with the League of Pensioners . . .

'Well now, Martha. Now everything depends on you!' said Rake, clumsily putting his arm around her shoulders.

'And, Martha dear, are you going to be nice and friendly towards the police?' Brains appealed. 'You mustn't make him angry, because then he might get us put behind bars straight away.'

Martha tried to refrain from showing her worry, despite feeling decidedly uncomfortable about it. Shaky, she tried to inflate herself and nonchalantly shrugged her shoulders.

'Pah, I shall talk him down!'

'I don't doubt that,' said Rake, and immediately looked relieved. And then the others smiled and relaxed too.

Martha pondered a long while as to what she should do, but finally decided that prevention was better than a cure. If she went to the police station herself, it would make her seem less guilty than if she waited for the constable to return. So she asked Christina to style her in typical old-lady clothes, wave her hair and find some sensible walking shoes, so that

231

she would end up looking the equivalent of an even older model of herself. Christina was really inspired.

'Right you are, Martha, I shall transform you!'

Christina arranged Martha's hair in an old-lady coiffure, and then started on her make-up. She sung quietly to herself while looking for powder, eyeliner and lipstick until she happened to catch sight of herself in the mirror. Then she stopped abruptly. Christina knew that she was exceptionally vain, but, nevertheless . . . her hair had become so dry!

'It really is bloody irritating. When you grow old, you lose your hair and get sagging breasts,' she sighed.

'Yes, but think about it; it's much better to lose your hair than your breasts. You must see the positive side, my dear,' Martha said.

And Christina couldn't help but smile. It reminded her of another of Martha's sayings: Nobody reflects upon the fact that a nose only grows to a limited length. But you ought to be grateful, because otherwise you could have ended up looking like an anteater!

'Now then, which clothes shall we choose?' she wondered. Together, they examined the wardrobe with the fancy-dress clothes before settling on a magnificent flowery dress in pale blue with a round neck, long sleeves and pockets. To go with it, Martha found some suitable footwear with a wide heel and plenty of room for your toes. With a sigh, she realized that she, as usual, would have to leave her belt bag at home, and she kitted herself out with a vintage handbag, black with flowers on it. Now Martha thought that she looked very innocent and, to further reinforce her guileless image, she took the bus to Skogsås. Because harmless old women didn't have their own car, they waited faithfully for the bus, Martha thought.

When she had walked from the bus stop to the police station, she remained standing outside for a long time with her mouth full of Jungle Roar pastilles, before she dared to enter. She took a few deep breaths. What if the police had actually found the League of Pensioners and wanted to put them in prison? No, it was better to nip this in the bud. With firm steps she walked up to the front door and rang the bell. The door opened and a female receptionist greeted her.

'Good afternoon, my name is – I mean, I would like to talk with a Lewander,' said Martha.

'Löwander?'

'Yes, perhaps that was his name. He was looking for me the other day, and since I had an errand in Skogsås anyway . . .'

The receptionist phoned up to the chief inspector and Martha heard them talking for a moment. Then Kurt Löwander made his appearance in police uniform and shiny shoes. Martha gave a hearty smile but quickly lowered her gaze. What a ridiculous moustache he had; yes, he looked a sight! Who did he think he was, a new Errol Flynn?

'I heard that you were looking for me,' she began.

'Yes, I was given your name at the school. There are some things that are unclear that I would like to talk to you about,' he said, and showed her into his room.

Martha fidgeted with her handbag. This didn't sound good. Irma had given him her real name, so he had been able to track her down. But she had told her in confidence! Irritated and disappointed at the same time, Martha delved into her handbag for more Jungle Roar sweets. This might be trickier than she had anticipated. She held up her packet of sweets.

'Constable, perhaps you would like something to suck on?'

Kurt Löwander shook his head, cleared his throat and put his hands together in front of him on the desk. Then he changed his mind and stretched out his hand, upon which Martha filled his palm with her favourite goodies.

'These are yummy; something sweet keeps one in the best of moods,' said Martha, with forced jolliness. Löwander nodded, put a few sweets into his mouth, and looked her in the eye.

'I've been thinking about that police traffic check a while ago when we last had contact with each other.'

'Ah yes, I remember that. You were so nice and polite!'

'So it was you and your friends who carried that out, is that correct?'

'No, no, not at all. I had booked some actors from Poland. Yes, I'm sorry, I know that you shouldn't fetch cheap foreign labour from abroad, but cultural activities – as you will know – never get any funding, so I solved it in my own way.'

'Actors from Poland?'

'Yes, though really they were extras. They don't actually say very much in the film, they had walk-on parts; they only needed to do what I told them to. No Marlon Brando and Elizabeth Taylor there, no indeed.' Martha laughed as naturally as she could.

Löwander wrinkled his brow and popped a few more Jungle Roars into his mouth. Actors – or extras – that was not a scenario he had thought about. Rather, he had assumed that it was a gang of pensioners who had known each other for a long time, just like the League of Pensioners. Martha saw his hesitation, sat up straight, and gave him a stern look.

'You disappoint me. When you came looking for me, I thought that perhaps you wanted to act in our next film, the one with Vikings, you know. You radiate such delightful manliness and I can see that you obviously go to a gym several times a week.'

'Errr, yes, that's correct, yes . . .'

'Muscles and moustache – not bad at all. Constable, you would be a fantastic Viking chieftain. But then, of course, you would have to grow a beard too, to look really warrior-like. My God, you would look so stylish! And you can borrow a sword and shield, if you want.'

Löwander lost his thread and fumbled with some sheets of paper on the desk before composing himself again.

'We have heard that you levied fines on those long-haul lorry drivers. That is illegal, as you might understand.'

'We haven't collected any fines; are you out of your mind?'

'Some drivers phoned us and complained.'

'Pah, do you really believe those villains? They are a bunch of liars, the lot of them. Do you know why they've complained? Well, it's because we attached a GPS transmitter to the vehicles we waved in. We wanted to see exactly how many hours they had driven, and to check whether they have worked illegal driving shifts in Sweden. And the drivers don't like that.'

'You did what?'

'The drivers are only allowed to spend three days here in Sweden, as you know, but a lot of them ignore the regulations and take jobs from Swedish carriers. But our data exposes them. One or two of them must have found the GPS and phoned the police to discredit us. To make you think that we can't be relied on. But those mafia drivers are really shady types, believe me. You ought to set up more traffic checks and lock them up!' Martha snorted and slapped her handbag down on the desk (it was, at least, good for that).

Kurt Löwander was confounded by the elderly lady who had come in so meek and mild, but who had got up steam and now had become really angry.

'But why did you attach a GPS?'

'For the film, of course. It has to look realistic, otherwise you can't win a Golden Palm award at Cannes. You see, chief inspector, even though it is a pensioners' film, we nevertheless want it all to be credible and realistic. We do have our pride, you know!'

Chief Inspector Löwander continued to question Martha a little longer, but made no progress. He who had dreamed of having found a member of the League of Pensioners seemed to have got hold of the wrong old lady. What sort of false tip-off had the town mayor given him? This old lady even promised to give them more information about how the various long-haul lorries had been driven and offered to help them as best she could. The chief inspector only had to tell them, if the police needed a helping hand. And however much he asked, cajoled and persisted, he didn't manage to get any further information about the notorious League of Pensioners. Instead, he took a gamble.

'Do you know about the theft of diamonds at the Stockholm auction house?' he ventured. If she had been involved, then she might give herself away. You never knew.

'Stockholm? You mean that big theft that has been in the newspapers? Were you involved?'

'No, not me, no; I just wondered . . .'

'Oh, you know what? They ought to make a film about that too. Would you like to be in that, then?'

Löwander looked helplessly at the scatter-brained old lady. He wasn't getting anywhere. He had nothing on her, nothing whatsoever, and she was driving him mad. Unfortunately, he must let her go. She didn't even have a belt bag, a detail that had been talked about at the station. And now he had had more than enough for the day. He had a headache and was beginning to get a bit of a tummy ache from all the Jungle Roar sweets. Mumbling, he got up, thanked her for coming in, and accompanied her to the entrance hall.

'I promise to get in touch if we make another film,' she chirped on her way out, and curtsied politely when she said goodbye. He swallowed a sigh and held up his hand in farewell. Then he returned to his room, picked up his washbag and went into the toilet. Wielding a toothpick as well as a toothbrush, he tried to prise out all the Jungle Roar pastilles that had got stuck between his teeth. Then his mobile rang. It was Bettan; she would be wanting to know what time he would be coming home, and if he could do some shopping on his way. Löwander resisted the impulse to click off the call. She spent all day at home, couldn't she do the shopping? He breathed deeply a few times, then answered as calmly as he could:

'Hello, darling, I haven't time to talk at the moment. We've so much on at the station. But I'll come home as soon as I can, I promise . . .'

*

'How did it go?' they all chorused when Martha arrived home four hours later – it took a long time because she had to wait for the next bus. They sat in the living room and drank tea, watching the end of *Ocean's Eleven* with Brad Pitt and Julia Roberts. When Martha entered the room, they pointed at the TV, watched the final scene and then turned it off.

'Good film, but our own robbery of the casino in Las Vegas was even smarter,' Brains said. 'What did the police say?'

'Well, I think I talked him down.' Martha looked pleased with herself.

'That wouldn't surprise me,' Rake said and he smiled.

'But from now on, we must teach you a few words of Polish. I said that you were actors from Poland. Anything so that the police wouldn't connect me with you – that is, the criminal League of Pensioners who did a runner from their retirement home and who have committed so many crimes, you know . . .'

'Well, well, nice one!' said Brains, and Rake too seemed relieved. 'Good work, Martha.'

'And you know what? When I was at the police station, I had an idea.'

'And what might that be?' Brains wondered, sounding suddenly rather worried, afraid that she might be cooking up something trying.

'We'll travel to Stockholm and demonstrate on behalf of the countryside. We shall try to get as many people as possible from here to go along with us, and then we'll do the same as the farmers in France when they protest against the politicians.'

'Tip a load of tomatoes outside parliament, you mean?' Anna-Greta wondered.

'Yes, that sort of thing.'

'But don't you think the Stockholm police will recognize us?' said Christina in an anxious voice.

'Pah, we've got our wigs and fancy-dress clothes. No policeman would think that we are bold enough to show ourselves in Stockholm. Villains don't usually return to the scene of the crime, you know.'

'Exactly, and there are good reasons for that,' said Rake.

38

The days grew longer and it was getting slowly warmer. Soon the trees would come into bud, and before them lay a season of light expectation. Indeed, this time of the year Martha always felt especially optimistic, but now she was worried. It was a big project that she had started up, perhaps far too big. She looked up at the red-painted house where Roland lived. He must support them; it wouldn't work without him and the cooperation of the others in the village and surrounding district. She walked up to the front steps and knocked on the door, her jaw firmly set. She had to deal with two complicated things that she must talk to him about. She would serve him a big lie, while, at the same time, asking for his help. Two things not always so easy to combine.

'Ah, it's you,' said Roland with a happy smile when he saw it was Martha. 'I was just on my way to the cowshed.'

'Righto, let's go together,' Martha said, and she waited while he pulled on his overalls, got his boots on, slipped his gloves into his back pocket and put his cap on.

'I'm sorry about what happened with Slow Motion,' he started up when they reached the stable yard. 'I hope there won't be any damages to pay. I'm thinking about the locks on that unfortunate night. It was all my fault.'

'No, no, it sorted itself out! We found him. But there was something weird about that horse. I do actually believe he must have been smuggled to Sweden, because his horse passport was a forgery. As luck would have it, we managed to catch him and transport him back down to Skåne.'

'Oh my word, to Skåne . . .'

'Yes, we wanted to get to the bottom of it all, and seek out the former owner. He was surprised to see us and denied that the papers were fake. But then we threatened to report him to the police if he didn't let us return the horse and get our money back. In the end, we managed that.'

'That you dared –'

'It has to be fair and proper. And I don't suppose he wanted the police – not to mention two angry old ladies – after him.'

'Yes, it is evidently a good idea to keep on good terms with you,' Roland laughed, and Martha found herself yet again feeling sympathy for him. He was so easy-going and positive, and looking at him there in the farmyard in his overalls and his dark, curly hair, she was reminded of the former prime minister, Thorbjörn Fälldin, who was a farmer too. Back in those days, a lot of people felt safe with him even though they didn't know him personally. Roland Svensson wasn't a politician, but a down-to-earth person who made people feel comfortable. Just the fact that he had agreed to arrange that crazy cow bingo! Perhaps she could cooperate with him again? Because now she needed tractors and hay carts for the plan in Stockholm.

'I think we ought to do something for the countryside,' she

began. 'Why not travel to Stockholm and demonstrate? There would need to be a lot of us in the procession. Can you help to get local people to become involved?'

They went into the cowshed and Roland fetched a neat little milking machine which he wheeled up to one of the cows. Martha recognized Maj-Ros, the cow which had been involved in so much unsuitable behaviour during the cow bingo. Martha was reminded of the power cut. It was lucky that the local farmers were accustomed to power cuts and had their own generators. They had padlocks and battery back-ups in their stables – though, on that particular evening, the generator at Roland's farm hadn't worked properly. But a power cut in the Stockholm area would be a lot harder to deal with. There, many people lacked generators, stoves and fire-places, and even tealights.

'What sort of demonstration were you thinking of?' Roland wondered, while he attached the milking machine.

'We ought to do something special, something flamboyant. Our Swedish demonstrations are always so tame and cosy.'

'Liven things up a bit, you mean?'

'Yes, exactly. Why not do something like they do in France? Become more revolutionary, tip rotten tomatoes, manure, do something so that people notice us.'

Roland Svensson turned the milking machine on, and stood silently beside Maj-Ros for a few moments.

'Pensioners who throw manure about, that would be a sight . . .'

'We could, of course, use rotten apples too. Regardless, we need a few tractors with wagons which we can fill with our "demonstration material".'

Roland Svensson gave her an amused look.

'All right, hay wagons and tractors, I ought to be able to arrange that.'

'Meanwhile, the rest of us can paint signs, think up slogans and plan the journey to Stockholm. Then we'll fill the wagons with whatever we are going to dump on the front steps of the Riksdag building.'

'And why not take along some animals? A few cows and sheep outside the Riksdag ought to give people something to think about.'

'Excellent, and why not hens and cocks too?' Martha added with a smile. 'What a good idea!'

Now Roland took a step forward and gave her a big hug.

'I'm so pleased that you and your friends are doing so much to help the district. There should be more like you!'

Martha was so flabbergasted that she was speechless. She had feared that he would think she was a nutcase, but instead he wanted to help her. She felt warm all over, and noticed that she was blushing.

On her way home, Martha felt guilty about Brains. It used to be the two of them who planned the bank robberies together, but for this project she was simply forced to involve the nice farmer next door. The League of Pensioners didn't have any animals, nor did they have tractors or farm wagons.

When she got home, her friends were sitting out in the garden with pen and paper at the ready. It looked as if they were drawing up plans, and that was very cheering to see. They wanted to be involved in the planning – wonderful! Exhilarated, she went into the kitchen, brewed some coffee, got out the wafer biscuits and oat cakes and a large carafe with elderflower juice. Then she put everything on the newly purchased dining trolley and wheeled it out into the garden. Rake saw her coming and poked Brains with his elbow.

'Ahah, I bet she's got something new in the offing.'

Martha served the coffee and gave them refills, and they enjoyed that for a while until Martha put her cup down, dried her mouth with her serviette and cleared her throat.

'Roland is ready to help us with that demonstration outside the Riksdag building in Stockholm.'

'So you were serious, then. Well, Stockholmers had better take cover, here we come!' Rake exclaimed spontaneously. 'The yellow vests – or whatever we'll call ourselves.'

'Hmm, I think we should concentrate on placards. What about wording like: *"The entire country shall live"* and *"Sweden will grind to a halt without farmers"*?' Martha suggested.

'Or what about this: *"The entire country shall live, but Sweden will grind to a halt with politicians"*?' Rake seemed pleased with his own inventiveness.

'No, we mustn't be nasty. We shall be international. Think about the French Revolution. They know how to demonstrate in France.'

'So what do you have in mind – the guillotine and bayonets?'

'Rake, stop teasing, this is serious now,' Christina broke in.

'Why not hooting tractors, and a mountain of manure and tomatoes on the Riksdag steps?' Brains suggested.

'But will we only throw tomatoes, or rotten apples and potatoes too?' Anna-Greta wondered, wanting to know exactly what they were going to do.

'It's better to use potatoes to make into vodka!' Rake protested.

'But manure is good. Angry farmers in France usually throw shit when they have a grievance with the politicians.'

'Hang on a moment, we need the cowpats for cow bingo,' said Anna-Greta and she laughed at her own joke.

'But talking seriously. The entire demonstration is about showing the politicians that they must save the countryside,' said Martha.

'I know!' Anna-Greta exclaimed. 'Instead of manure, we'll fill the farm wagons with thistles and stinging nettles that we'll tip into the square outside the Riksdag.'

'No, goodness me, no! Nettles are packed with vitamin C, iron, potassium and calcium. They are really good for you, and you can make a yummy nettle soup and a lovely salad from them too. No, we mustn't waste nettles,' Christina said.

'Thistles, then?' Martha suggested as a compromise.

'Thistles? Stop there and justify it! You can't imagine just how beneficial they are for butterflies and bees,' Christina continued.

'Humph, now we'll vote on it,' Martha said, having tired of the discussion.

Finally, with a majority of four to one, they agreed that thistles and nettles could be a novel and refreshing element in the demonstration and might, in fact, even be something that the press could pick up on. Then Martha told them about the animals that Roland would take to Stockholm.

'But releasing animals on the asphalt won't make it feel like the countryside,' Rake objected. 'We must create a bit of the countryside outside the Riksdag too. You know, animals, greenery and bushes, that sort of thing. Otherwise, people won't fathom it. There is some nice turf we can use.'

'What an excellent idea!' the others agreed.

'I propose that we buy two pallets of lawn turf, about seventy square metres each, and that we unroll them outside the Riksdag building,' Rake went on. 'Then we can take along a few plants and some bushes too – I've got some in the greenhouse. And when we are ready, along comes Roland with the animals. That would work well, don't you think?'

'Rake, that's not a bad idea! Let's do it!' exclaimed Martha, and she went to fetch another dish of wafer biscuits and a bottle of elderflower champagne. They toasted the idea and wished each other luck for the demonstration of the century in the capital. As a final note, Anna-Greta started to sing a revolutionary song about clenched fists, but stopped as abruptly as she had begun when she realized that she had made a mistake. What she had sung wasn't a revolutionary song at all, it was the Christmas song of the Swedish temperance movement.

The following day, the League of Pensioners invited Roland around for coffee, and they agreed that he would organize the animals and transport, while they would try to get people to join them, write press releases and invitations, make placards and think up slogans. Rake and Christina promised to arrange the logistics of the lawn rolls and the bushes. They would need time to organize it all, but in four weeks from now, they – and as many as possible from Hemmavid and the surrounding district – would travel to Stockholm and demonstrate. In a completely new way.

39

At last they were on their way! Martha looked in the rear-view mirror and saw a long row of tractors and farm wagons behind them, while the busses that Brains and Rake had arranged could be seen at the very back. Roland's two cattle trucks drove slowly and couldn't be seen, which was fine. Then they would have time to unroll the turf unhurriedly before the animals arrived. She smiled to herself. Now the people in the nation's capital would have the experience of their lives!

The gang of pensioners hadn't put on yellow or purple vests, caps or other symbols; they had stuck to ordinary clothes, since this was a demonstration that affected everybody. They did, admittedly, have their usual disguises, but they were ordinary clothes for old men and old women. And they were good at acting as such. Martha adjusted the rear-view mirror and glanced at her friends in the back seat.

'How are you doing, girls?'

'Fully charged, and more besides!' Anna-Greta answered, with Christina showing a thumbs-up at the same time.

Martha saw that they were raring to go, and she herself was also in an excellent mood. She could feel that lovely shiver in her body just like when she had robbed banks – a feeling she had missed. It was just a pity that demonstrations cost money, rather than providing revenue. In the long term, this ought to provide income for the district, albeit in a calmer and more bureaucratic way.

It had taken time to coordinate the demonstrators, and it had not all been clear running. The idea of applying French demonstration habits on the people in Hemmavid was not something that the villagers accepted just like that. But, after an open meeting at the Danish Pastry café, where Roland had talked and supported the plan, they had managed to get a majority of the villagers to join them. The idea of tipping thistles outside the Riksdag building met with firm opposition, and it wasn't until Martha pointed out that it was better than wasting good apples and tomatoes that it was approved.

It was not yet six in the morning, and Christina and Anna-Greta were squashed in the minibus together with various placards and banners proclaiming SAVE THE COUNTRYSIDE and SWEDEN CAN'T SURVIVE WITHOUT FARMERS. Slowly, they approached Stockholm where the procession of vehicles met with some unexpected problems. To start with, they got lost among all the roadworks and drove too far, so that they became caught up in the new Slussen junction, and then it took some time before they could find suitable roads into Mynttorget. But, finally, they reached their destination and Martha parked, while the busses with all the demonstrators parked outside the royal palace, and the tractors and cattle trucks drove on to Riddarholmen.

Even though it was still early in the morning, tourists and other people out walking early could be seen outside the Riksdag building. They strolled slowly across the bridges, enjoyed the views and stopped now and then to take pictures. A bit further away, beside the Strömmen canal, you could see fishermen in their boats, and there were some early-risers paddling their canoes towards the town hall. It was sunny and very peaceful. After a while, the demonstrators arrived and with a combined effort, the 140 square metres of turf were unrolled outside the Riksdag steps, enclosing the area. Meanwhile, the League of Pensioners unpacked placards and banners.

'It's going to go off soon!' said Martha, who was keeping a watch out for guards, police or somebody from the security services. But, so far, everything was quiet.

'"Go off"? Perhaps more than that,' Christina muttered.

When the lawn was rolled out, Martha texted Roland, who was on Riddarholmen, and gave him the start signal for the animals. He opened the doors to the cattle trucks, and soon you could hear noisy mooing when a herd of cows waddled along Myntgatan in the direction of Mynttorget square – followed by various bleating sounds from a flock of sheep. Roland and his assistants managed skilfully to manoeuvre the larger animals towards the steps, while the cocks and hens, amidst loud cackling, were let out of their cages next to them.

'We've got the countryside here!' said Roland, pleased with himself, and he gave Martha a victory sign which she happily replied to with her long finger and index finger raised in a V. She still hadn't spotted anyone from the security services.

When the first politicians turned up, about half an hour later, they couldn't believe their eyes. They were in the very centre of the Swedish capital city, but had in some mysterious way been transported out to the countryside. There were cows and sheep grazing on the grass in front of the Riksdag building. Various loud moos and bleats could be heard between the buildings. A cock had got loose and was chasing a cackling hen, while a nosy sheep was trying to nibble a passing Green Party member. Not far away stood a horde of demonstrators who were handing out flyers, while others were chanting slogans and holding up placards. The largest ones proclaimed: *NO FARMERS; NO FOOD, FOOD DOESN'T GROW BY ITSELF* and *DON'T SHUT DOWN HALF OF SWEDEN!*

Members of parliament tried to hurry up the steps into the Riksdag building, but were immediately stopped by some sheep which butted them at waist height. The sheep were followed by three old ladies, and the tallest of them shouted out: 'Think about the climate. Save the countryside! All of Sweden shall live!'

The members of parliament rushed on, but that was not a good idea, because that made Martha angry. Really angry.

'You bureaucrats sitting behind your desks must think that all milk comes with the stork, and that cows give birth to fish fingers. No, indeed, now you'll see for yourself!' she hissed, and raised a clenched fist. Then she pulled out her mobile and sent a text, this time to Brains: *Action!*

Soon the rural engine sound of two impressive Massey Fergusons approached the Riksdag and drove right up to the site of the demonstration. The huge tractors led the way to Mynttorget where a group of well-built farmers from Hemmavid unloaded the wagons. They tipped the whole load of weeds and thistles into the square, and the cows and sheep immediately helped themselves to the huge mountain of greens. Anna-Greta started the chants again, and this time she wanted it to be louder, so she borrowed Roland's megaphone: *'Better to have cows in the countryside, than to be milked by the Riksdag!'* she shouted into the funnel, and they all looked at each other in surprise because that was not what they had practised; it was something she had been inspired to shout in the heat of the moment. But the rest of the choir quickly started up: 'Without cows, Sweden will grind to a halt! And don't shut down half of Sweden!'

Now the demonstrators had really got up steam, and were shouting so loudly that they didn't hear how the wind was blowing up, or notice how one of the sheep had managed to open the clasp that kept the provisional fencing in place. Before anybody had time to react, the wind caught up the heap of weeds and blew it across towards the water, followed by some bleating sheep who wanted more greens to munch on. And while the animals went off towards the bridge, the heap of thistles spread across Mynttorget and in the direction of the Strömmen canal. The abundant installation of greenery – which would have been a worthy feature in any art museum – fell into the water and floated away majestically on the surface before it seemed to give up, collapse, then slowly sink to the bottom.

Martha put her hands over her face and moaned: 'But there aren't any members of parliament down there!'

Fisherman John-Olle, who caught bream and pike from his flat-bottomed green boat in the Strömmen waters, had drunk a few strong beers and had been singing to himself. He was a weather-beaten figure in a worn-out leather jacket, and now and then he dipped his large scoop net into the water.

251

Now he was hoping for a big catch, and he waved happily to the people watching from the quay. Resolutely he lifted up the net to pick out the fish, but just as quickly dropped it back into the water. Stinging nettles and thistles! What the hell?! No, it was time to go home and sleep off his hangover.

Meanwhile, Roland was trying to get the animals under control. Even though the gate was open, some of the cows stayed inside the area and grazed peacefully, while others happily trotted towards the royal palace. The sheep that had got out in Mynttorget looked around, curious about their new surroundings, and when some members of parliament hurried up the steps, the ewes followed on their heels. One of the stressed members forgot to close the door behind him, and that was all that was needed for the sheep to get in. Since there was a bowl of fruit on the reception desk, what followed was not surprising. Soon the receptionist was surrounded by a flock of bleating sheep who were guzzling the fruit, and only at the last minute did she manage to run up and close the door to the debating chamber. Otherwise, it would have been the first time in the history of the Riksdag that *real* sheep had sat there.

The procession of demonstrators, with more than one hundred farmers, business people and workers from the district around Hemmavid, saw what had happened and tried to get things back into order, while some men from the security services looked at a loss. Roland apologized for the chaos and asked for their help, and together they soon caught the animals. Then the next problem arose. On Mynttorget, hordes of youngsters appeared, taking part in a strike.

SCHOOL STRIKE FOR THE CLIMATE, it said on several placards, and in just a few moments this demonstration had
attracted so many people that there was no longer any room
for Martha and her friends. They all thought that they had
demonstrated sufficiently, and Roland and his men hurriedly
shepherded the animals back to the cattle trucks for their
return journey to Hemmavid.

'Moving out to the countryside, preserving the forests and
supporting small farms helps the climate!' said Roland. 'That's
why it's so important to be able to continue to live and support
ourselves there.'

Then Anna-Greta again took the megaphone, shouting her
practised slogans right into the funnel:

'*The entire countryside must live! Otherwise, what is going to
happen?*'

'We won't get any food!' the choir answered.

'*Support all small farms! Otherwise, what is going to happen?*'

'We won't get any beer!' Rake shouted out.

Then they were lost for words, including Anna-Greta, who
was so astonished that she forgot the next slogan.

'Now that we've done our bit for the countryside this time
round, it's time to travel home,' Martha noted.

'You can go, but Brains and I are staying in Stockholm,'
Rake said suddenly and most resolutely, winking to his mate.

'What on earth . . .?'

'You've said that it isn't a good idea for the five of us to be
seen together. So Brains and I are going to do a round of the
pubs this evening. We'll follow you tomorrow.'

Martha looked down at the ground to hide her disappoint-
ment. The menfolk evidently still wanted to do their own

thing, even though she had finally got them involved in the struggle for the countryside. Oh well, if they wanted to be on their own and enjoy themselves the way menfolk usually did, that was up to them. Although she had expected them to follow them straight away, she very much wanted them to feel good, so she collected herself and said as cockily as she could:

'Of course, if that's what you want. Have a nice time, see you tomorrow!'

And that's what they did. The gang from Hemmavid withdrew to their buses, and Martha and her friends returned to their minibus with its false registration plates.

'Say what you want about today, but we have learned quite a lot,' said Martha when they drove up the E18 motorway northwards, tired after the great tension.

'You can say that again!' said Anna-Greta. 'And, hopefully, the politicians fathomed something too.'

'But have you thought it through? Demonstrations are not going to be enough. We ought to do more,' said Martha. 'So far, we have worked with the school, tried to create new jobs, and we have staged various events. But in the final analysis, it's all about politics. What have the powers that be done for the countryside?'

'Not very much, if you ask me,' said Christina.

'Exactly; nothing very much has happened. So, what we need to do – err, hang on to your seats! The politicians . . . Guess what, I've thought up something drastic. What about a kidnapping?'

'But Martha!' said her friends, gasping audibly.

'Pah, I was just joking,' Martha laughed and accelerated

past an old Volkswagen that was belching out fumes in front of them. But in the back seat, Christina and Anna-Greta immediately felt uneasy. Because they knew that Martha never said anything unless she meant it . . .

40

Brains and Rake weren't thinking of either the countryside or the climate. Instead, they spent the entire afternoon wandering around in Stockholm, looking at the crowds and especially the pretty women. Then, of course, they made a visit to Clas Ohlson and checked out their stock of new gadgets before they strolled out onto the street again and had a few beers at a restaurant where they could sit outside.

'This is how we should always have it.' Rake beamed, knocking his big tankard against Brains's so that it splashed a little. The two friends sat in Kungsträdgården, each with a Carlsberg, and waited for the Operakällaren restaurant to open. They planned to have something tasty to eat while looking across to the palace and the Riksdag building – feeling in an especially celebratory mood after the demonstrations earlier in the day. They had time for two strong beers before the restaurant opened.

Moments later, they were brusquely stopped at the entrance by a tattooed doorman who claimed that it was fully booked.

'What the hell!' exclaimed Rake when he looked in at the almost empty dining room.

Brains put a fist on his shoulder and mumbled something about them perhaps not wanting any pensioners there.

Regardless of how much Brains protested, Rake didn't budge an inch, and since Brains didn't want to be left by himself, he eventually gave in. The idea of going to the Grand Hotel, where he and his friends had once stayed at the time of the art theft at the Nationalmuseum, made him nervous. Because on that occasion they had also plundered the hotel's guest safes and had run amok in the Princess Lilian suite. They were, of course, in disguise now, but sometimes people could recognize you from your posture or the way you walked. To be on the safe side, he decided to pretend to be lame.

The two men walked to the hotel and ascended the front steps as nonchalantly as they could, and Brains limped very credibly into the Cadier bar. Expectantly, they settled down on the high, green leather chairs by the bar and ordered a beer for each of them. People were standing, holding their drinks, engrossed in lively conversation, and all the tables were occupied.

'There you are, quite a party here!' exclaimed Rake, and not many minutes passed before he started chatting to the first pretty lady by the bar. He smiled, and flattered, and told her of many storms in the Atlantic, but she was unusually hard to flirt with this evening. Rake, who was accustomed to women falling for his charms, didn't give up, but boldly continued to try to charm one woman after the other. He was, of course, fond of Christina, and he knew that he would never be able to find a woman as wonderful as her, but it was so exciting with all these beautiful apparitions on every side. He was so keen that he ended up winding his scarf so many times round his neck that it was beginning to leave a mark. Tirelessly, and with a smile on his face, he went back and forth along the bar with a beer in his hand, while starting conversations, giving compliments and feeling himself to be in superb form. Unfortunately, the members of the fairer sex seemed to be extremely busy with one thing or another, or they were just about to leave. And he had also forgotten all those hidden cameras that were everywhere, those which showed what you looked like and how you moved. When Rake drank beer and admired the ladies, he didn't think about such things.

'Oh well, let's move on and kip down for the night, and then we can go home tomorrow morning,' Rake yawned an hour later with a wrinkled scarf and his shirt partly unbuttoned. Brains nodded, relieved that they would finally be able to go to bed, and got down from his bar stool. Rake needed a helping hand, so Brains put his mate's arm over his shoulder and paraded out with him, without limping. His steps were firm and he took Rake out into the street where he stopped a taxi. But, before he had opened his mouth to say where they were going, Rake ordered the taxi driver to take them to the casino on Kungsgatan. Now they would get the roulette wheel spinning, that was for sure!

Once inside, they each got a beer and Rake then gambled away all the money he had with him. If it hadn't been for Brains, who slipped him a few five hundred-kronor notes, he would have made a loss that evening. Thanks to the extra money, he was able to win back all that he had lost, and as the night wore on, he ended up with about what he had started with. Brains managed to stop him and together they returned to Stureplan, where they checked in at the Kung Carl Hotel. Contented and happy with their experiences, they went to bed and slept until late the following morning.

They had had a very good time, but had not gone too far,

and now it would be nice to see their own ladies again. Rake was already longing to get back to his Christina, and Brains was looking forward to seeing Martha again.

As soon as they had finished breakfast, they visited the big NK department store round the corner, and bought presents for their women before catching the bus home.

While the menfolk had been amusing themselves in Stockholm, Martha, Christina and Anna-Greta had driven back to Hemmavid, where they gave a crate of beer to Roland to thank him for his help.

'Now we have started a protest movement!' said Martha, contented. 'From now on, people in the countryside are not going to put up with the politicians' prattle any longer.'

'No, I don't think they will either. The demonstration could be heard all over Mynttorget,' Roland said, smiling. 'But my favourite was the thistles, a real installation of greens. Have you ever thought of studying at the art college, Martha?'

She started to giggle. 'You know, your cows and sheep were quite a success too!'

'The reporter who was going to write a piece about the climate strike took some pictures of our demonstration as well,' said Anna-Greta. 'The placards and banners were very visible on TV, so there will probably be more of us demonstrating next time.'

They chatted away a little longer and then said goodbye to Roland. Martha gave him a warm smile, and they remained standing facing each other for just a second too long.

'Keep at it, Martha, we need people like you,' he said, and gave her a hug. 'To think what you've started up!'

He always makes me feel good, she thought for the umpteenth time, while they walked home. She was, of course, fond of Brains, even though his saggy 1950s trousers, old nylon shirt and shabby slippers would drive any woman to tears. But he was a fantastic person, there was nobody like him, and she loved him. However, she did miss their cosy moments when it was just the two of them, because nowadays they didn't seem to do much together any more. Apart from the demonstration in Stockholm, Brains was mainly with Rake and the teenagers, and he spent all his time in the workshop. He often sauntered into the bedroom late in the evening.

'Well, goodnight then,' he would say after pulling on his pyjamas (which had become all shiny over time), and giving her a peck on the cheek. Then he lay down, pulled the covers up to his chin and, shortly afterwards, snored as if he had a whole set of drums in his stomach. Martha sighed. Couldn't he be a bit more charming? Couldn't he at least try to look a little more like James Bond? Although, of course, she had to admit that she wasn't exactly a Miss Universe . . .

Martha and her friends were extremely tired, and after their long day in the capital, all three of them went to bed early. They slept undisturbed until late in the morning the following day.

Martha was the first to wake and she and Christina went down to the kitchen to prepare breakfast. They laid the table with a butter dish, cheese, ham and marmalade; they put some slices of salmon on a pretty ceramic plate, and added a green salad and a bread basket full of toast. Then they heard footsteps from the stairs, and Anna-Greta appeared in the doorway.

'Oh, yummy. Have you got toast with honey and marmalade too?'

'Yes, for sure, just tuck in.' Martha smiled and held out the bread basket. Anna-Greta sat down at the table.

'What do you think about yesterday?' she asked, spreading a lot of butter and honey on the bread.

'I looked on my iPad: apart from that little item on TV, there was a three-column article in *Expressen*,' Christina said.

'That's not bad at all, and there's something about the demonstration on social media too! Several of the people who were in Mynttorget have uploaded photos,' Anna-Greta added, as she hadn't been able to resist looking at her tablet either.

'I hope it's good stuff; nothing embarrassing, is there?'

'Uhm, you can see for yourself.' Anna-Greta held up her tablet and showed a picture of Martha when she leaned over the railings with her hands stretched out. 'You look as if you love thistles and want to take the entire green installation home with you. Or were you trying to catch a bloke?' Anna-Greta neighed in delight and Martha blushed as though she had been caught in the act.

'Anyhow, thank God there are no photos of the five of us together. That's good,' said Christina, who couldn't stop thinking about how they were still on the wanted list.

'We will have to work like this in groups, to be on the safe side. Thankfully, it isn't so easy to identify old ladies. The police probably think they all look the same.'

'Like old ladies, yes, but you don't have to look like that,' said Christina with an unusually authoritative voice, adjusting her hair and pulling out her lipstick. 'You can make yourself look better!'

'Yes, yes, I suppose so,' said Anna-Greta, and quickly she ran her fingers through her hair. 'But we have more important things to think about. We need money and we still haven't received our reward for Sharp Eye yet. We must do something about that . . .'

Late in the afternoon, Brains and Rake returned and apologized for having been away so long.

'Goodness gracious, what on earth have you been doing?' said Martha when the two comrades came in through the door with a bit of a hangover and very ruffled hair. Rake had lost his old scarf. Brains's shirt was covered with beer stains and both of them were wearing trousers full of creases. Rake had also bumped into a newly painted door so he had some blue paint on his bottom.

'We had a lovely day in the big city, I can tell you that,' he said, handing over a bottle of perfume and a bunch of roses to his beloved Christina.

'It was great to hang out there a while,' Brains added, and he handed over a pair of sensible walking shoes to Martha.

Martha looked at the two gentlemen and their gifts, and couldn't help but smile.

'Thank you,' she said. 'Lovely that you could amuse yourselves; now make sure you get some rest. Then you can have a shower and throw your old clothes into the washing machine before we get together for another meeting. There's a lot on the programme.'

'Not today, surely?' Rake sounded worried.

'No, recover first, but then we'll have to discuss what we are going to do next. And we need you for that.'

The point about recovering first was something the men considered a pleasant admonition because they were indeed very tired. Gratefully they went upstairs to rest, and soon noisy snores could be heard from their rooms. Martha tiptoed up and carefully closed the bedroom doors. Then she came down the creaking wooden stairs and into the kitchen, where she poured out two glasses of elderflower champagne and one glass of vegetable juice and took them into the living room. She put the glasses on the coffee table and called to Christina and Anna-Greta, after which she fetched her knitting with the half-finished pullover for Brains. While she waited, she looked at the *David and Venus* sculpture on the top shelf and smiled to herself: an interesting plaster sculpture; nobody could guess what it contained. It was just a pity that they couldn't try to sell the earrings yet. Because they were in great need of money . . .

'What did we gain from the demonstration in Stockholm, do you think?' she asked them a little while later once the others had got comfortable.

'The grass and the animals were a real hit,' said Anna-Greta, contented.

'Nobody would have missed the fact that we were demonstrating for a living countryside. But we need to see results too,' Christina said.

'So we must continue the struggle. And for that we need cash. I can't see any other way just now than that we must get Borge to pay us a reward,' said Martha.

'Hmm, that sounds risky!'

'If only we could find a signature on that painting,' Anna-Greta sighed. 'I've got a feeling that it's painted by a real artist.

264

What if it's worth a lot of money? Then we could steal it and sell it.'

'Well, a little robbery might improve my blood pressure.' Martha turned her knitting over and looked at the half-finished pullover for Brains. She had chosen a complicated pattern and it seemed to be taking ages to finish. Next time, she would probably opt for a single colour, or a pair of mittens.

'I've looked and looked for a signature, but I couldn't find one. Perhaps if I use a higher contrast in a really advanced image-processing program,' Christina pondered. Martha cleared the glasses away.

'Try again. Why don't you fetch your laptop?'

Christina nodded, and returned a few moments later carrying her computer. She had several image-processing programs but hadn't been interested enough to test them all. She click-started the computer, and Martha and Anna-Greta watched as she tried different colours and contrasts.

'I can't find anything now either,' she stated a short while later.

'But not all artists sign their work at the bottom of the painting – or in the right-hand corner,' said Anna-Greta. 'Try in the left-hand corner or somewhere else. It's a nice painting, and even if it wasn't painted by a French Impressionist, it's very classy.'

'What if it was painted by one of those Nordic artists who travelled to Paris at the end of the nineteenth century?' Christina asked. 'Carl Larsson had an oil painting in the Paris Salon in 1883; I know that.'

'Well, then, don't give up!' Martha put her knitting aside and stared at the computer screen. 'If it's a genuine painting, it could be worth a pile of money.'

Christina increased the contrast and they all felt the excitement in the air.

'It looks to me like there are a few lines in the left-hand corner,' Christian mumbled. 'That could be a letter or the beginning of a signature. But I can't get any closer than that.'

'So what do you say, girls? Has the time come for a little theft again?' Anna-Greta laughed a little nervously.

'Do you mean that we should steal something when we don't even know if it's worth stealing?' Martha summarized.

'Yes, why not? It makes it all the more exciting and what have we got to lose?'

41

When Brains and Rake had slept off their Stockholm adventure, they thought that everything would return to normal. Brains was looking forward to meeting his pupils again, and had prepared a lesson about how to use a lathe, and Rake, for his part, was going to experiment with new herbs in the greenhouse. But when they came down into the kitchen, the womenfolk were already sitting there and they looked worryingly energetic.

'We must plan a little robbery,' they said in unison when the gentlemen had drunk their first cup of coffee and each had been served a newly baked cinnamon bun.

'A painting. It might fetch millions,' Martha went on, and then Christina and Anna-Greta described their thoughts about the painting.

'You don't need to take part if you don't want to, of course,' Martha concluded. 'But we'd be grateful for help with the planning.'

'Planning?' Rake took a large bite of his bun and then put it down on the plate again. 'As I understand it, most of the work has already been done.'

The others looked at him, not understanding. He stretched his hand towards Christina.

'The painting that I got as a birthday present, my dear. You said you had copied a fine painting at Martin Borge's. All we need to do is to dirty your painting a bit, then we swap them.'

There was silence for a moment and then they all cheered. Christina had unknowingly – or was it subconsciously – already prepared the robbery. If you simply dirtied the painting with a bit of soot and imitated the yellowed, dark varnish, you would be able to use it. And then there was the frame, of course. That must be patinated a bit. So, while Martha did the washing up, the others hurried off to the workshop.

With steel wool and very fine sandpaper, Rake helped Christina to 'age' the canvas on the back, while she herself worked with a darker varnish and some ashes from the fire-place. Soon Christina's painting looked really antique, and it was so well done that Brains stood in front of the painting and hummed.

'You know what, in this case the aging didn't sneak up on you as a surprise. It happened in a flash!'

But the members of the League of Pensioners weren't ready yet. The painting had to be transported, and how do you sneak a painting into somebody's home without being seen? And then carry out another one, so that nobody notices anything?

'So we have to go into the loo with Christina's painting, and swap it with Borge's,' said Anna-Greta. 'Rake, you are clever at sewing sails. What about sewing some hooks on the inside of an overcoat?'

'No problem, but the painting will be visible nevertheless.'

'Not if we use two overcoats. I have several old ones that

268

we can use,' Brains added, understanding what Anna-G
was thinking.

'That's a good idea; I think we can manage this,' sa
Christina.

The friends then devoted most of the day to preparing the
coup. Brains patinated the picture frame, and when he had
finished, he framed Christina's picture again. By then, the
others had already chosen two overcoats and Rake had sewn
hooks inside the old beige coat that Martha would wear inside
the other. Finally, Brains carefully hung up the painting on
the hooks, after which Martha put the coat on. And an outer
coat on top of that.

'Usch, it rubs against me and it is going to be hot – but
I will do anything for art,' she said and made a victory
gesture.

The next day passed unusually slowly, and Martha dropped a
lot of stitches when she tried to follow the pattern for her
knitting. But then it eventually got dark and the time had
come to set off. Rake and Brains had discussed whether they
should go along or not, and decided that it would look more
innocent if the stud farm got a visit from three elderly ladies
than two men. So they stood on the front steps and waved
when the minibus drove off.

Martha and the other two had barely vanished from sight
when there was some heavy knocking on the front door. Rake
and Brains looked at each other and hesitated. It couldn't be
the police, could it? But then they heard Irma's voice. She
stood in the porch and told them about a water leak in the

269

school. She wondered whether Brains and one of his pupils could perhaps help.

Brains and Rake put on boots and raincoats and followed Irma. On their way to the school, they knocked on the door where Kalle with the utility moped and his mate of the same age, Sixten, lived. They were two of Brains's pupils who had shown themselves to be especially inventive. Or, as Brains panted as they approached the house, 'They are smart lads, those two, I'm sure they can help us!'

Kalle pulled on a jacket and boots and was ready straight away, while Sixten was slower and must first close down his computer. He had been busy working out how to construct a powerful, robust drone which could carry larger deliveries. He put on his cardigan, waterproof over-trousers and boots, and joined the others.

When they reached the school, Irma took them round the building to look for the leak, which wasn't so simple, as there were many rooms and the water pipes were hidden behind panelling and junk. They found the leak in the chemistry lab; it was a bolt in the joint between two water pipes that had ruptured and water was spraying out. Water was trickling along the wall and floor and down into the cellar.

'Best to seal that straight away. Can you manage it, Kalle?' Brains asked, thinking that this would be a good task for him.

He wiped his blond locks from his forehead, examined the rusty bolts and nodded.

'If you turn off the water, I'll seal this,' he said. 'Really, both the pipes and the joint need replacing, but I can do a temporary repair.'

270

'Do you need hemp and sealant?' Brains asked.

'Nope, it'll work with a new bolt, nuts and a repair clamp. Then a plumber can fix this in the morning.'

Brains had thought that Kalle, who had moved to Hemmavid with his father during the autumn, had a nerdish interest in electricity and solar cells. But no, he could do so much more than that.

'OK, if you do that, then the rest of us can check the cellar.'

They went down the steps and when they reached the cellar door, they saw that water was trickling under the door. Rake pushed it open and Irma gasped. The water was ankle-deep in there.

'Oh heavens above! We can't deal with this!'

'Oh yes we can, I've got a water pump. Let me solve this,' said Rake, ready to serve; he mentioned something about ships that started leaking and hurried home. Under one of the work benches in the greenhouse he took out his water pump, got it onto a trolley and dragged it off to the school.

He whistled to himself, feeling needed and clever at the same time. He was happy to be able to fix things that Martha could never manage. That felt in some way especially delightful.

When he got back to the school, the others were busy emptying the water with buckets, and Sofia – the girl who worked with Sixten in the drone group – had cleaned the drain so that the water level was starting to sink. But a water pump was necessary, and when he had got that working, he quickly pumped out the rest of the water.

'That's great; all we need now are hot-air fans to dry this out,' Irma said.

They opened the cellar windows. Brains took two big

construction fans from his workshop and when they started up, everybody went upstairs to the common room.

'To think how well it can go when everybody helps,' Irma said. 'Thanks to your workshop, Brains, the pupils have acquired a lovely self-confidence. It feels as if we can deal with anything.'

And when she fetched some lingonberry juice and a bowl of fruit for everybody, she was filled with a sort of joy deep in her heart. It felt as if the school, with its old and new pupils, would never be shut down. The villagers' joint strength was too much.

When Brains and Rake got home again, they each got out a beer and felt very satisfied with themselves. The girls might well be out trying to steal the painting to bring in money to the village kitty, but they themselves had made a hefty contribution to Hemmavid and the school in their own way. And it was lucky that they had been so busy, because deep inside they were both very worried about their friends. Martin Borge had a reputation for being a tough guy. And if Martha and the other two messed things up, he could really make life difficult for them!

42

In the minibus all was quiet for a long time, but when the gang got closer to Martin Borge's stud farm, Martha suddenly began to feel uneasy. She thought about Christina, who had worked so hard on Rake's painting.

'I hope you're not sorry that we've dirtied your painting, my dear? I thought that when this is over, we can buy you some new paints and canvases.'

'No, I'm not sorry. That painting was fake anyway. And now at last we have the chance to recoup some money from the horse theft!'

Martha and Anna-Greta exchanged glances. Christina was so easy to deal with nowadays; she had really toughened up. But they themselves were nervous, and when they stopped some distance from the gate to the stud farm, they all felt a bit wobbly on their legs.

'You'll pull this off, Martha, you always do,' said Anna-Greta in an attempt to encourage her.

'And good luck, my dear. We're behind you. You're going to do a great job!' Christina agreed, and she pressed her thumb against Martha's.

'Thanks!' Martha mumbled in what was, for her, an

unusually weak voice. She carefully eased herself out of the minibus. The painting felt heavy as it rubbed against her back, and she wondered how long she would be able to carry it. She looked about her. It was almost black outside and it felt a bit spooky. The stud farm was in darkness, but one or two windows were lit up. She smiled bravely at her friends and gave them a victory sign. Then she adjusted her overcoats, went up to the gate, and rang the bell.

'I'm looking for Martin Borge.'

The guard leaned forward and asked the obvious: 'And who shall I say is asking for him?'

'Just say that I'm an old admirer who would like to meet him.'

'Anything else?'

'Tell him that I am the sweetheart of his youth. He will know who I am.'

The guard phoned through to the house, and Martha heard somebody answer. She couldn't really follow the conversation, but it ended in a decision. Martin Borge was on his way.

Martha stood inside the gate and talked with the guard while she waited. When the estate owner became visible on the gravel path, she stepped forward.

'Ah, there you are, how lovely!'

Borge slowed down and came to a halt when he saw who it was.

'Yes, it's me again, the woman who found Sharp Eye. I thought that perhaps you had changed your mind about the reward. It might be that you're not so clever at using Swish to send the money, so I thought I would come personally instead.'

Martin Borge groaned, disappointed not to be meeting the woman from his past.

'But I gave you two five hundred-kronor notes.'

'Can't you remember that I wasn't satisfied with that? I thought that you might be able to pay a poor old woman a bit more. After all, the horse is worth thirty-two million kronor, and without me you wouldn't have got it back.'

'Sorry, I'm not made of money.'

'My husband is dead and I have worked as a nursing assistant. I can't live on my pension.'

'All right, then.' Martin Borge took out another five hundred-kronor note.

'Thank you so dreadfully much,' said Martha, and she curtsied. 'But don't forget my account number if you should change your mind and want to contribute more.'

Billionaire Martin Borge took a few steps forward, to show Martha that it was time to leave now.

'Excuse me, but I am a long way from home. Could I use the toilet?' Martha said in an appealing voice, pressing her legs together in a classic I-must-go-to-the-loo gesture.

Borge gave her an irritated look. 'If you really have to, then! Show her the way.' Borge nodded to his stable manager. 'Thank you very much for coming with the horse, as I said, but now I think we have concluded our business!'

'No, not yet,' said Martha, but so quietly that he didn't hear her.

Once inside the toilet she saw to her relief that she had ended up in the right place among fancy mirrors and tasteless art. She looked all around her in the room, but stopped abruptly. Where was the oil painting hanging? It wasn't there!

Had that stingy Borge suddenly realized that he had a rarity and put it aside? She looked again. No, it wasn't there. That very same moment, someone knocked on the door.

'Are you finished?' Martha recognized the stable manager's voice. They evidently wanted to be rid of her as quickly as possible.

'Just a moment,' she called out through the door, then she flushed the toilet and went up to the washbasin where she turned on the cold-water tap. Irritated, she glanced at herself in the mirror, and swore like a trooper. They had wasted their time and thought they were on to a good thing, but now the painting wasn't even there. She adjusted her hair and was just about to leave when she saw something in the mirror. In a corner furthest away, there were two paintings leaning against the wall. She let the tap run, and hurried across. The first painting depicted a hunting dog and a huntsman, but the one behind it was the French painting. She checked there were no cameras by the ceiling, couldn't see any, and took a little cotton bud and the container with linseed soap out of her pocket. She carefully rubbed the bud in the corner closest to her and noticed that it became dirty. Dirt and old darkened varnish . . . It was either a contemporary copy or perhaps the painting was genuine! Quickly she took off her overcoats, loosened Christina's painting from the hooks and put it down on the floor. Then, with a well-rehearsed movement of her hand, she hung Martin Borge's painting inside the coat. She then put both coats back on, and put Christina's painting in the corner behind the other picture. Out of breath, she straightened her back, put the linseed soap container into her pocket, turned off the tap and let the water out of the washbasin.

'Thank you so very much, so kind of you,' she said when she came out. 'Be glad that you are young. We elderly have to pee far too often.'

Then she said goodbye, left the stable manager and the stud farm and walked out to the road where Christina and Anna-Greta were waiting.

'Now,' she panted, 'now let's get out of here!'

When they got home, the men were waiting for them in the living room where the *David and Venus* sculpture was uncommonly conspicuous on top of the shelf. While they had been away, the two men had not only dealt with the water leak, but Brains had also installed yet another spotlight above the plaster sculpture. He had also lowered the shelf so that there would be room for Borge's painting above it. Martha noticed this, and gave him a quick hug.

'We did it!' she said, 'but, gosh, I was so nervous!'

Brains was about to say something but was interrupted by Anna-Greta's lively shout.

'Now you'll see something, lads,' she called out when she stormed into the room with the painting under her arm. 'Here you can see art of the highest class.'

She held up the painting so that the old men could see it, and while Christina fetched linseed soap, Brains and Rake checked the frame and the back of the painting. Christina returned with some sheets of newspaper that she spread out on the table together with brushes, cotton buds and wads of cotton wool. Carefully she started to clean the canvas in the upper right-hand corner. Everyone was silent while she slowly tested what would work. The cotton wool turned dark from

277

the dirt. Then she tested the lower right-hand corner, but couldn't find any signature. Then there was the left-hand corner. The friends exchanged expectant glances. This was the crucial moment. Christina leaned forward and used a bit of cotton on the left-hand corner. Her breathing speeded up, and the gang all leaned so close that the whole table almost tipped over. Slowly, ever so slowly and carefully, yes, but there was a C, followed by an A, an R and an L. Christina finally managed to make the entire signature visible.

'Oh my goodness!' she exclaimed. 'It's a Carl Larsson!'

'There are only a few works by him in oils, and just recently one of them was sold for almost eight million,' said Anna-Greta, who spent a lot of time doing research. 'And I hope you won't be offended, Christina dear, but we can safely say that your copy isn't worth quite so much.' And then she laughed as only she could, and ended her announcement by calling out for champagne.

Rake hurried into the kitchen, opened a bottle of genuine, sparkling champagne and filled five tall glasses, which he then carried out on a tray.

'Cheers, everyone,' said Martha. 'It is strange indeed, but this theft feels especially successful, since we have tricked a stingy devil. If only he had been a bit more generous, this would never have happened.'

'Good for us that he wasn't. Because this must be the perfect crime! He isn't even going to realize anything's been stolen, so we can never be accused of theft. And at the same time, his painting is going to contribute some extra millions to the countryside. Could it be better?' Brains wondered.

'Oh yes it can, because now we are going to sing "The

Champagne Gallop". Like after every successful coup!' said Martha.

So they sang and toasted, and when Rake and Brains told them about the water leak that Kalle had repaired, there were a few more toasts. Then they all went to bed. But, just as Martha was on her way up the stairs to her bedroom, she saw something flash outside, like a reflection from a mirror, or possibly a pair of binoculars. It came from a car parked some way away. Weird! She closed the blinds to be on the safe side. And thought about whether or not she had seen that car before.

43

The sun warmed things up and it felt nice to be outside. Light, high clouds, no rain and summer approaching. Rake had made the yard really nice and now they only had to get the borders and gravel paths into shape. The entire gang were out in the garden helping. While they tidied the area and raked lawns and paths, they talked about the future.

'We can't be carrying out thefts all the time; above all, not now when we have to wait before we can sell the booty!' said Martha as she straightened her back. It felt like she was getting a blister on her hand from the rake handle. Why did you have to rake gravel paths? She didn't like gravel paths that always had to be kept raked so that they looked nice and tidy.

'It's boring, having to keep our heads down,' said Christina. 'It is much more fun committing crimes, because then we can do something for others. It feels lovely to give away robbery money!'

'But crime isn't enough, and now we need lots of dough,' said Brains, moving the wheelbarrow. 'How else are we going to be able to develop Hemmavid?'

'If we can attract tourists and investors to the district, that will bring in cash.' Martha looked out across the yard where they had managed to clear away the worst of the weeds. The borders around the main building would need weeding too, but then it would be ready. It was so delightful when the light and the sun returned. But all this gardening work . . . it demanded so much time just when they needed to plan new projects! Martha had promised herself that she would do her bit for the others, not just decide everything herself and boss them around. She would have to accept the situation. And, so far, they had actually achieved a great deal. Nowadays, the long-haul lorry drivers avoided the roads around Hemmavid, and several families had moved into the village and put their children into the school. They were making progress, but it wasn't enough.

'I vote for us to have some magnificent events again. Not cow bingo, but it would be great if we could do something original that doesn't happen anywhere else but in Hemmavid!' said Anna-Greta.

'Yes, I think so too,' said Rake, and the others nodded in agreement.

'Excellent; you plan around that, and I'll go and do some shopping in the meantime,' said Martha, before taking off her garden gloves and going into the house. Carefully she washed her hands, combed her hair and put on her pale blue cardigan, a colour that she knew suited her. Then she went off to the farm shop.

Roland was busy with a customer, so she had time to pick up several items while she waited. From having a little shop with his own produce, he had now extended the premises into adjoining rooms and sold other items too. He had a lot more on the shelves and in the freezer now. He got beef, pork, lamb and even chicken from a local farm abattoir. And, of course, he still had his fresh milk, cheese and local eggs. His sister had made elderflower juice which she had bottled, and he sold plenty of that, and yeast too. For the summer season he was also thinking of selling apple cider. When Martha saw that he was on his own again, she went up to the counter.

'As you see, my basket is full. Things are going well for your shop now, aren't they?'

'They're getting better and better. The newcomers in the village mean a lot. The Sandberg family fish for us, and they also make wonderful cheese from goat's milk. The Hedins have built a hen shed and we get fresh eggs from them. And now a family with two children in the school have opened a bakery. So I sell their bread here too.'

'It sounds lovely. I hate fish and chicken which has been transported across half the world before getting here.'

'It's meant more work for me, of course, but my wife helps and now my son and his family have started to give us a hand too, so I get help on the farm.'

'It's going in the right direction!' said Martha, putting her shopping on the counter. She looked at him while he rang up her items on the cash register. Roland Svensson was a really special person, and without him they wouldn't have managed either the cow bingo or the demonstration in Stockholm. A man who solved problems, who was always good-natured and happy. She felt almost guilty as she dallied at the counter. Because now she was going to persuade him to be in on the next project.

'Yes, things are certainly going better for the district now, and that's great, but it isn't enough,' she began. 'I was wondering if we could arrange some exciting events for the summer, things that would attract a large public.'

'You mean dance-band music, flea markets and that sort of thing?'

'Yepp, but preferably something extra special, which puts the village on the map, which only happens here and which the newspapers will write about. Can you think of something? I'll talk to Irma, too, and then we'll see what comes of it.' She paid, put her shopping into her bag and went towards the exit.

'I can see what you're after. It has to be something really special,' he said, and he gave her a wink. And then she felt that warmth and mutual understanding that you have with only a very few people in your life.

After visiting Roland, Martha went to the school, and – as usual – Irma came on board. She offered to help with staff and logistics, and she would also try to get money from the council. They each took a cup of coffee in the head teacher's office, and chatted until Irma had to go off to her next lesson. When Martha left, she was very satisfied. The two probably most important people in the village were receptive to the idea. Now it was a question of thinking up something good that would attract the public – but which would not attract the interest of the police.

Freelance journalist Ingmar Sjöberg glanced around the newspaper's editorial office. It was hot and most people were in T-shirts or had taken off their jackets, and those who were rushing between the news desk and the editing side, smelt of sweat. He often worked from home, but sometimes he had to visit the newspaper offices for various meetings, something that he would have liked to avoid. He got up, took his mobile with him and went into the silent room. He carefully adjusted the chair, took out a pen and keyed in the number to the police. This time, he wasn't going to back down. Those idiots at the Kungsholmen police station must now at last give him something to write about. He couldn't wait any longer. He impatiently held the phone close to his ear while he listened to the ringing tone. After three rings, he recognized Aronsson's slurry voice.

'Gert Aronsson.'

Ingmar Sjöberg began with a few polite phrases, but then got straight to the point. 'How are you getting on with the jewellery theft at the auction house?'

Aronsson cleared his voice at the other end of the call. 'We've found lots of interesting things on Blomberg's flash drive. Links to banks and shady deals in Russia. We're working on it at the moment.'

'But the League of Pensioners – you said it was only a matter of time before you could get them behind bars . . .'

'Yes, but we are short of staff. We're dealing with the Russian stuff first. That's really hot. We are counting on the oldies making a mistake soon, and then we'll nick them.'

Ingmar Sjöberg was about to put his feet up onto the desk, but he resisted the impulse. 'But you promised me a scoop.'

'You'll get it, you'll get it! Don't be so impatient, young man. But at the moment we are tracking Blomberg because he will certainly know more about the accounts in the Russian banks – and all the rest of the stuff on the flash drive, for that matter. But, unfortunately, he's hidden himself away somewhere. A cousin thinks he's gone to Belarus. And who the hell can track him there? It's very frustrating, but we're chasing him, I promise . . .'

'But what about the League of Pensioners?'

'We haven't forgotten about them, don't think that. We've got surveillance at all the auction houses, in Sweden and abroad. Sooner or later, they will try to sell the stolen property and then we'll get them. And we have circulated their details to all the local police stations. If we hear anything from them, well . . .'

Ingmar Sjöberg angrily kicked the waste-paper basket under the desk. He felt he had been tricked. He had given them Blomberg's flash drive full to the brim with information, but so far, the police hadn't given him material for a single article. Not one! He ought, in some way, to get things moving. He wasn't bloody well going to give up!

Martha and Brains had prepared lunch together and used almost everything that Martha had bought at Roland's farm shop. They had made steak tartare with tomatoes baked in the oven and fresh vegetables. It had been really tasty! No processed ingredients, or that sort of fish that had been filleted in China and then transported to Sweden. Now, after a very satisfying meal, they were sitting in Rake's greenhouse with a cup of coffee, a plate of wafer biscuits and a bottle of cloudberry liqueur. Martha inhaled the sweet aroma of flowers and herbs.

It had been a mild winter, and Rake's plants were doing well. He hadn't had much heating turned on, so now crocuses, winter aconites and narcissi were flowering, as were the red and white barrenwort plants. It was so beautiful and smelt lovely! In the Diamond House retirement home, he had had several pots with flowers and herbs on the balcony, and they had done well too. He had been a seaman, but he had green fingers too!

While they drank their coffee, Martha told them about her meeting with Roland and the idea of organizing something nice in the district. She hadn't forgotten the car she had seen outside the house, but she hadn't seen it again. It was probably just something she had imagined. It was so easy to get all jittery when you were on the wanted list . . . whatever, it shouldn't get in the way of their next project. She drank a gulp of coffee and turned to the others.

'What do you say? Do you have any tips, something that would attract tourists of all ages?'

'Tourist events? I know, beautiful old veteran cars,' said Brains. 'Then you can drive around with the tourists.'

'Sounds nice.' Martha noted it down.

'But I vote for love. That's very popular now. Just think of all the programmes on TV,' said Anna-Greta. 'I remember the Tivoli in Copenhagen with its love tunnels. Why not do something useful with the mine tunnels here, and turn them into love tunnels?'

'We could turn them into a labyrinth so it would take a bit of time for people to get out. Then there would be even more love–' Anna-Greta giggled.

'And why not let in pretty gals in one end of the mine, and bachelor boys in the other. And then we can have a "sleep in" in one of the mine shafts in the middle,' Rake added.

Rake and Brains looked at each other and grinned. Martha gave them a tired glance.

'What about the wife-carrying contest that we talked about earlier?' said Christina.

'And the ghost tours,' Anna-Greta added.

'Wife-carrying and ghost tours sound fine. OK, so who wants to work with what?' Martha asked.

'I can keep watch in the love tunnels,' said Rake.

'And I can arrange ghosts in the ghost house,' said Brains.

'Ghosts, yes; what do you say, ladies? Will you do it?' Rake winked at Brains.

'For heaven's sake, this is serious,' said Martha, and she put her coffee cup down so hard that the spoon on the saucer rattled. 'You can do some planning, and I'll do a few other things in the meantime.' She got up and quickly left the greenhouse.

'Oops, what's got into her?' Brains wondered.

'Of course we'll help her if necessary, but she bloody well proposes new projects all the time. It's utterly exhausting,' Rake sighed.

'We might as well take a break and rest a little, and then we can pick up the thread again tomorrow,' Anna-Greta suggested, and the others thought that was a good idea. Heading back to the house, they put the coffee cups in the dishwasher and then went to their respective rooms.

When Brains was on his way up the stairs, he glanced out of the window and caught sight of Martha. She seemed to be on her way towards the neighbouring farm. He stopped. What on earth was she going to do there?

*

A little while later, Martha knocked on the door of Roland Svensson's farmhouse, and Edit, his wife, who was five years older than he was, opened it. She looked tired.

'Is Roland at home? It will only take a few minutes,' Martha said, apologetically.

'A few minutes? It doesn't usually take –' she broke off mid-sentence the very moment Roland appeared in the doorway. He looked pleased.

'How nice to see you. Would you like some coffee?'

Martha smiled and they went into the kitchen and sat down. It was newly renovated with shiny, plasticky cupboard doors, an aluminium sink unit and large patterned tiles. There was a kitchen island in the middle of the room.

'I wonder if you've thought over that idea of various events? You know, what we talked about,' Martha started.

'Oh yes, I have. Why not turn it into a big event and call it "The Countryside Day". I can set up some market stalls and make a clearing for car parking. We can rent out the market stalls, but the car park ought to be free. On the other hand, we can take a certain per cent of everything that is sold.'

'Wonderful!' Martha felt warmth and happiness deep inside. He made it all sound so simple. You set it up and then it's ready . . .

'OK, we can do it together. If you and Irma work on the logistics, my friends and I will try to create some impressive events.' Martha smiled and suddenly felt elated. 'This could be really great fun!'

'Of course, with you it's always fun!'

They looked at each other and fell silent, as if they had said too much. That very same moment, the door opened and Roland's wife came into the kitchen.

'Yes, I think that's everything. I was just about to leave,' said Martha and she got up. Roland followed her to the hall.

'Right you are, "The Countryside Day", that's what we'll concentrate on.'

On her way home, she thought about Brains and Roland, two men she was terribly fond of. She liked them both, but Brains was her own fiancé, nobody else's. And Roland had his own life. She mustn't forget that.

44

The next day, Martha got Brains and the others to join in the project, and after some discussion they had agreed on a nice programme with Roland and Irma. Now the preparations began. Irma issued a press release and she and Roland talked on the local radio about how important it was to attract tourists to the district. It would provide temporary jobs, but could even lead to future work opportunities. In fact, the two displayed such enthusiasm that soon most people in Hemmavid were involved in one way or another.

Roland Svensson and his friends cleared the area around the common to make room for parking spaces, market stalls and caravans. And Irma, for her part, suggested that her pupils should help to get the Ghost House to work.

She had soon got in craftsmen who renovated the old vicarage so that it would be safe to be there. They removed rotten floor planks and repaired the staircases so you wouldn't fall right through them, after which some pupils took care of the cellar. They cleaned it and in jolly spirits painted the walls black and decorated them with cobwebs. The short, slightly overweight pupil, Jonas Bratt, whom Martha remembered from the first school day, had also arranged a room on his own initiative. He loved crime fiction and thought that they ought to have an especially scary room in the Ghost House. Without telling anyone, he had created a bloody crime scene and filled it with cobwebs, skeletons and murder weapons, which he thought would attract lots of tourists.

Rake, for his part – and here Martha had thought carefully about this before assigning him the task – had been authorized to convert the hundred-year-old mine tunnels and turn them into love tunnels. They lay some distance from the mine shaft where the toxic barrels were meant to be, so it shouldn't present a problem. The energetic mayor, Allan Petterson, had also abandoned the plans for a rubbish tip there and had instead planned a new area north of Skogsås. So he shouldn't be a problem either.

Full of enthusiasm, Martha and her friends set to work.

Brains asked his pupils to help him empty and clean up the tunnels, after which Roland's son, an electrician, set up lighting.

'The mine tunnels should bathe in red and green romantic lighting,' Rake explained, throwing up his hands. 'And then we'll have lovely music coming out of discreet loudspeakers.'

'But if it's going to be romantic, shouldn't it be dark?' Brains wondered, and Rake hesitated.

'Well, I didn't mean cascades of light down in the mine rooms, but enough light so that you don't take the wrong dame,' he pointed out in an attempt to explain.

Anna-Greta saw how enthusiastically he started to decorate the old mine tunnels and was rather miffed, because the love tunnel project had originally been her idea. She didn't give in so easily. Music and an exciting lighting arrangement was, of course, good, but she thought it could be spiced up a little. The thing was, she had found out that you could buy hormones on the Internet that facilitated amorous feelings, and what could be better in a love tunnel? So she googled around for a while and found something called pheromones. They were for cats as well as for men and women.

Without telling anybody, she bought several bottles, and, to be on the safe side, several different types. Most of what she bought was the perfume which was advertised as *This is the perfume that will guarantee you a date – it works 100 per cent*. For a while she was tempted to try it herself, but since she didn't have a bloke for the time being, she didn't bother.

She thought she would wait until the big market day before she went down into the mine tunnels and splashed the aphrodisiac all around – because it would be very irritating if the tunnels became venues for Hemmavid's copulating couples before the big opening day. But she did, however, go across to Roland Svensson and secretly tip him off about how there would certainly be a lively amount of love traffic down there. And she told him that she could recommend a product he could earn money on. Roland took the bite.

The day before the big event, he and Anna-Greta set up discreet perfume holders here and there in the mine tunnels; he had already purchased several automatic dispensers. He filled them with Amor's Drops and another perfume called Horny Little Devil and placed them at the various mine exits. In the farm shop, he also arranged the sale of red roses and bunches of flowers. He was looking forward to the big day with expectation . . .

*

It was raining in Stockholm and inside the Grand Hotel there was a smell of wet textiles. About twenty lunch guests were eating in the dining room or having a beer in the bar, and in the office upstairs the security guard Per Olsson was looking through the last weeks' CCTV recordings. That had been his job for the last few years. Unfortunately he had been sick and was behind on the schedule, but now he would make up for that. He had to check the cameras inside the hotel as well as those out on the street. He yawned. This was the most boring part of his job. All these images of people hanging around in the bar, businessmen talking business with a glass of beer in their hand, or drunken bar guests who knocked back a variety of drinks as long as they had a high alcohol content. Sometimes it was exciting to follow the elderly gentlemen who tried to pick up young dames, of course. Then you could see how some of them patted the girls on their bottoms or touched their breasts and got a mouthful of abuse in return. Some angry gals quite simply poured the beer down the front of the people who were too intimate, while others allowed themselves to be charmed by gentlemen with fat wallets. But after the #MeToo movement, the guys at the bar had become much more careful and the CCTV images were thus more boring.

The security guard quickly scanned through the material. With a bit of luck he might discover a few pickpocket thefts or something suspicious, though apparently the weeks had been quiet. But Friday evenings were often a bit livelier, and he was grateful for that. He was still scrolling when suddenly he noticed a gentleman in his eighties who had a patterned scarf around his neck and was working hard chatting up the dames beside the bar. During the evening he became all the

45

The night before the Big Day, Martha found it hard to sleep. She had qualms about what she had done, and thought about all the people she had got involved. Now it wasn't just her friends in the gang of pensioners that she would have to justify herself to. She had roped in Roland, Irma, the school pupils – indeed the whole village and district.

She made her way slowly down the stairs in her old dressing gown and yawned audibly. The others were asleep or, at any rate, still in bed taking it easy, but that didn't bother her. It was often Martha who prepared breakfast. She thought about what Christina usually excused herself with: *I haven't felt so well today. I was in bed already when I woke up.*

Martha couldn't help but smile at that. Christina was sweet, you couldn't be angry with her. She often slept until late in the morning, and got very little done before lunch, but she was a fine person who always pulled her weight. And her artistic talent was something very special. Without her, the League of Pensioners would never have been as successful as they were now. And anyway, as for having a bit of a lie-in in the morning, it was perfectly OK to indulge yourself on the days you weren't committing a crime.

In a sort of semi-conscious mist, Martha fumbled with the coffee machine to get it going and pottered around in the kitchen, going back and forth between the cupboards and the sink before, finally, she could sip her first cup of coffee and thus think clearly. Then she laid the table for the others, made the porridge and put out bread, ham, marmalade and cheese. When the others appeared a little later, she was already in a good mood.

'Good morning, all! Breakfast is ready. Today we're going to have fun!' she said, and fastened the programme for the day on the fridge door with a magnet. 'I don't think I've forgotten anything. Must go upstairs and get dressed now!'

'Bubbling with energy . . .' Rake muttered.

'But, thankfully, no gymnastics today. Try to be a bit positive, mate!' said Brains.

'Oh, come off it,' Anna-Greta interposed. 'We're going to have lots of fun.'

Unless it ends up a fiasco, Christina thought, but she didn't say so out loud.

A bit later, steps were heard on the stairs and Martha poked her head through the doorway.

'Must just do a final check, so I'll see you on the common in a while,' she said in a buoyant voice and she rushed off in a flowery dress with a matching light-blue cardigan.

'I bet you she was born with ants under her feet,' Rake sighed.

'Oh no, a whole ant hill!' said Brains.

On her way to the common, Martha looked in at Roland Svensson's farm shop. He had stocked up with fruit, cheese, sausages, bread and sandwiches. The freezers were filled with ice cream and the rest of the floor area was covered with crates of beer. He was red in the face and looked really enthusiastic.

'Hi, Martha, lots of people have already come. Wife-carrying and ghost walks – to think that tourists are so keen!'

'In the summer people want experiences.'

Roland stopped, holding a crate of beer.

'And how about you, everything OK?' He gave her a broad smile and put the crate down. Then they briefly looked again at the programme for the day, after which Martha wished him luck and went off to meet up with Irma. As the head teacher, she was used to organizing things, and she had roped in many of her pupils and even a brass band. There, too, most things seemed to be under control. Satisfied that it was all running smoothly, Martha returned to the farm shop to buy something to drink and a snack for later. When she went inside, Roland welcomed her with a smile and handed over a cloth bag.

'I don't suppose you'll have time to think about this. So here is something to keep you going during the day!'

She opened the bag and saw that he had put in some packed sandwiches, fruit and a mild beer.

'Oh, thank you, so kind of you,' she mumbled, happy and confused at the same time. So sweet of him! He looked at her and she remained standing there with the bag in her hand.

'Good luck,' he said. 'Today's party in the village is all thanks to you. You have inspired everybody!'

He took a step forward and she thought that he might be about to hug her, but at that same moment the door jingled and the rest of the gang of pensioners came in.

'Ah, so this is where you are. We just wanted to take a bit of grub with us and something to drink,' said Brains.

'Yes, best to have some provisions with us,' Rake added.

'I've got lots here,' said Martha, and she held up the cloth bag. 'Roland's treat.'

Her friends looked at each other. It was just like Martha had said. The whole village was committed. And to something that they themselves had started.

Martha and the others wished Roland good luck, and then moved on to the village common. Martha hoped it would be full of people, seeing as there were so many summer visitors in the area, and her hopes were fulfilled. When they reached the car park, they saw that it was filling up. A bit further away, people were setting up their wares on the market stalls, and a smell of candied almonds and hot sausages was slowly spreading.

'It won't be long before everything starts up,' said Brains and he put his hand in Martha's.

'Right, and then we'll no longer have any control . . .'

The friends walked around and looked at what people wanted to sell and made notes in their mobiles. Elderflower juice and local honey, but also jewellery, small items in wood and wrought iron. In the car-boot flea market, people were already loading up with vinyl records and old TV games, while others were filling their baskets with vases and ornaments. Gathered closely together in front of a 1950s van was a group of the district's former *raggare*, rockers who loved classic American cars. They were busy rummaging through spare parts and tools, and seemed to be enjoying themselves. Martha felt the expectation all around. To think that there were already so many people there, although the day had hardly begun!

Half an hour later, it was time to formally give the visitors a hearty welcome. In the part of the common that was closest to the entrance, and where the market stalls had been set up, Brains and some of his pupils had constructed a wooden podium. Christina had decorated it with birch twigs, leaves and meadow flowers, and Roland's son had set up a loud-speaker system. Martha climbed up onto the podium and went up to the speaker system. She looked around and did a sound check by tapping the microphone so that everybody gave a start.

'So fantastic to see so many here,' she began, and welcomed them all to the market. Then she told them about all the events, ranging from wife-carrying and ghost trails, to dance-band music and a flea market. There was an expectant murmur from the public, and in high spirits she waved to Christina to come up onto the podium.

'And now we shall hear a bit more about the first event of the day,' she announced, before handing the microphone over to her friend. Christina had make-up on, and wore a tight-fitting red dress with a hat and earrings. She received the microphone with an elegant gesture and turned towards the public.

'At twelve o'clock, dear friends, we shall meet by the obstacle course where we shall see something new and exciting,' she said. 'For the first time ever, we are going to have a national championship contest in Wife-Carrying – or Partner-Carrying, as we have renamed the event for the day. You are all heartily welcome!'

Over on the common, Martha and Christina had marked out an obstacle course with a large sand pit and a deep-water jump. The course was 250 metres and included two steep upward slopes. Martha had, at first, been a bit hesitant about this event since she had heard that the menfolk threw their women over their shoulders like a sack of potatoes – and then ran off with them. And she wasn't sure whether they carried their darlings on their backs any old how, or let them hang upside down with their face banging against the bloke's rear end. And that wasn't any better . . .

'Men have such strange ways of handling women,' she sighed.

'I know better ways,' said Rake.

'But this sport is big in Finland, in Sonkajärvi,' Christina pointed out. 'And the winner gets his woman's weight in beer.'

'Equalitarian or not, we're ready to go,' Anna-Greta exclaimed.

Hemmavid's very own greatest singer, Siva Öst, who had an operatic voice which few could equal, had been chosen to be the master (or rather mistress) of ceremonies for the day. Locally she was known as Siva Diva.

'She has such a high and penetrating voice that it makes people pay attention. And even if the microphone packs up, it will work anyway. Thanks to her, we'll get lots of spectators,' was Christina's opinion, and she had decided that the League of Pensioners should book her for the day.

But when the famous opera diva tested the microphone, and shouted: 'Ready, steady, goooo!', the spectators stumbled backwards in terror, and two wife-carrying blokes dropped their women there on the starting line. Then Christina suggested that Siva Diva should discard the microphone and just talk without it, and after that it worked perfectly. The competition could begin and Siva Diva filled her lungs.

'Ready, steady, goooo!' she shouted out again, but this time without the microphone, and now the twenty competing couples set off along the obstacle course cheered on by the public. A young-looking middle-aged man took the lead with a delicate girl on his back, while the former muscle-builder Herbert, who loved beer, tried to keep up, panting heavily. He had chosen to compete with the heaviest woman he knew, and was looking forward to many crates of beer as his prize. Now he optimistically bumped along with his wifely burden on his back, but it was a burden that seemed to get heavier step by step. After a few metres, she had slipped down towards the curve of his back, and on the first slope she hung down in the vicinity of his knees. She was ticklish too, and she giggled and squirmed so wildly that in the end he was obliged to put her down. The couple were disqualified.

The man who had taken the lead with his woman was Mayor Allan Petterson's son, Alfred, who had a strong competitive instinct and struggled away. So did all the others, but the further they got, the wobblier their progress. The first lap went fairly well and competitors were in a jolly mood, but on the second lap, they started to tire. Things didn't improve when two couples collided in the sand pit and fell down, and one bloke dropped his wife in the water jump – which resulted in a time penalty. And as if that wasn't enough, three blokes got lost in the terrain so that Brains had to run off and look for them. In the end, the mayor's son Alfred won and when he crossed the finishing line with his soaked female load, he clenched his fist in a happy victory gesture.

'Now I want my wife's weight in beer,' he called out in a loud voice, and didn't become quiet until he and his wife were each given a crate of Carlsberg.

'Thank God for the right winner,' said Roland Svensson, content because Alfred's wife only weighed fifty-two kilos and the beer in the crates was beginning to run out.

Then people ate lunch and strolled around the common for a while until Martha asked Siva Diva to announce the next event. This was a visit to the Ghost House. Siva Diva stood next to the microphone stand.

'We are going to have a ghost trail in the old vicarage. It is rumoured that a vicar's wife, who disappeared in the eighteenth century, haunts the place. This will be exciting!' she cried out, and the spectators reeled back yet again.

But they were all very curious. There had never been a ghost house in the district before, so the first ghost trail was soon fully booked. But since the guide they had booked had been taken sick, Siva Diva would now be the guide for the ghost trail too, which she was only too happy to do. She briskly gathered together the participants outside the creaking old timber house and led them, one after the other, into the dark and frightening entrance hall.

'I hope you don't get easily scared,' she joked and then started a trail that nobody had ever experienced before.

She guided the participants around with a dramatic voice, while Beethoven's Fifth and muffled doomsday music could be heard from the loudspeakers. Somewhat jittery, the visitors were herded through the rooms and frightened now and then by ghosts and other horrible apparitions that the school's pupils had positioned here and there, when they least expected them. Unfortunately, nobody had warned Siva Diva about the room that was decked out as a bloody crime scene, so when she entered with her group of twelve people, she screamed so loudly that two of them fainted on the spot. Somewhat shaken, Siva Diva had to sit down, but she happened to do so on a pool of ketchup blood. She then jumped up in panic, tripped over a skeleton and ended up face first in a tangle of cobwebs. Luckily, Brains was in the group and he could calm her down.

Things were a lot jollier in the love tunnels, where, early that morning, Anna-Greta had nipped in and splashed hormones all over the place, and Brains, with Rake's help, had got the technical stuff working. Romantic music poured out of the loudspeakers, and the tunnels were filled with the most wonderful colours. They were all sorts of shades and they became more intense and redder the further along the tunnels you went. Instead of damp and the smell of iron ore, there was a strange cannonade of aromas that made people amazingly happy and exhilarated. Married couples who, earlier in the day, had argued, now acted as if they had just fallen in love, while widows, widowers and other singles were attracted to each other in the most inappropriate manner. Mayor Allan Petterson, who had sought out the love tunnel after the wife-carrying contest and put his arm around Malin, from one moment to the next lost all sense of propriety. First, he offered to buy the café – which he thought they could run together – and then he sort of danced forward. And before he had even left the love tunnels, he had proposed to her four times. When he unwillingly exited from the mine tunnels, tipsy with merriment, he immediately bought double portions of Amor's Drops, an economy pack of Horny Little Devil and an enormous bunch of flowers for his dear mistress. He had only just handed over the flowers, when he heard a very familiar voice behind him: his wife's.

'Darling, so that's where you are. What about it, Allan, shall we go for a tour down in the love tunnels? Wouldn't that be so romantic!'

Allan Petterson pulled himself together as best he could, and said that he had just heard that at the far end of the tunnels the roof had caved in, but that they could go and play darts in one of the market stalls instead.

'No way,' his wife replied. 'Now we're going to have a really cosy time down the mine, aren't we?' Upon which she grabbed his arm and marched off with him, while Malin dejectedly made her way back to the café.

As a finale for this Countryside Day, two of the district's best dance bands had been booked and, at seven in the evening, they started playing. By then, Siva Diva had softened up the public with popular excerpts from *Carmen* and *La Traviata* – without a microphone – so that everyone was in a good mood. But the thought of dancing wasn't as popular with everyone.

Brains complained about a painful foot, with the result that Martha looked for Roland or some other suitable dance partner. But nobody could be seen, and nobody asked her to dance. For the love of God, where was everybody? The dance floor was full of people but she was on her own. She slowly moved closer to the exit and stood there. There had been so much work that she hadn't had time to take part in the events

304

or celebrate, but now, when she had the chance to enjoy a dance, everyone seemed to have disappeared. She sighed, and immediately felt herself abandoned.

A while later, she caught sight of Malin and Lilian, who were wandering around in the festival grounds. They had closed the café and Martha noticed how they were critically examining a camper van where visitors were being served coffee and waffles. Lilian was accompanied by a man, but Malin seemed to be on her own. She was looking around as if she was trying to find somebody, but had not found the person she sought. Martha had seen her talking with the mayor . . . was she looking for him?

Martha, for her part, was waiting for her friends, but when they didn't turn up, she contemplated going home. At that moment, she felt a sweaty hand on her shoulder. A well-built man with shiny cheeks asked her – in his Stockholm dialect – for a dance, and before she had a chance to answer, he had dragged her out onto the dance floor.

'Hello there, you must have been a really pretty lass when you were young!' he said, squeezing her tightly around the waist. Then he twirled her around at a great speed and leaned close so that a smell of sweat and old beer washed over her.

'Jesus, you're not even out of breath. Are you one of those people who eat sensibly, do gymnastics and live soundly?' he asked.

'Yes, I try.'

'Perhaps you do some weightlifting too?'

'Not really.'

'Then you won't have heard of weightless dumbbells?'

Martha shook her head.

'Fantastic, if you want to do some bodybuilding,' he laughed hilariously and, panting heavily, pressed his round belly against Martha's so that she lost her breath. At that moment, thank God, the music came to an end, so she thanked him for the dance and quickly retired before the band started to play the next tune. Then she caught sight of her friends. Rake and Christina were dancing in a tight embrace on the other side of the dance floor, and Anna-Greta had also been asked to dance. A bit further away, Brains was standing talking with some of the teenagers. They all seemed to be fully occupied.

She waited a while, then decided to go home. That very same moment she caught sight of Roland, yes, it was him! She smiled inwardly and was just about to approach him, when he moved onto the dance floor with his wife.

46

The following day, everyone agreed that it had been a very successful event. Roland and Irma were satisfied too. It should, of course, have been Martha who was happy, but she felt low and strangely melancholic. The Countryside Day had been an exceptional effort but now, suddenly, she felt only emptiness. What would she do now? It was not until Malin at the café complained that she hadn't sold more of her buns and croissants, that Martha pulled herself together and became her usual old self again. She had offered Malin and Lilian a market stall where they could sell snacks, but they had declined the offer. They had only themselves to blame, she told Malin.

Time passed and things were more or less calm. In their back garden the borders were in flower. Inside the greenhouse, Rake had planted lots of herbs and Martha couldn't resist tasting them. She tested rosemary and thyme, oregano and lemon balm in lots of ways, and nowadays her dishes were beginning to be rather tasty. But, to be on the safe side, Rake made sure that there were always spices on the table.

During this period, Martha remained surprisingly inactive.

At first, they all thought she was ill, but when she forgot her knitting on the sofa, dropped stitches so that Brains's jumper acquired the weirdest of shapes and even, yawning heavily, happened to pour out the cloudberry liqueur into the washing-up water, they realized that she was simply exhausted. And then, as if in silent agreement, they all rested in the quiet before the storm. Because she would certainly be on the go again soon.

Thanks to the Countryside Day, the petrol station had been temporarily opened, the farm shop had made a profit, and the income from parking, the stalls and other attractions had done a lot to fill the village coffers. Because of this, Roland, Irma and other important figures in the village thought that they should also have a Countryside Day the following year. They would then retain the ghost trails and the love tunnels, but re-think some of the other activities. Some people had questioned the partner-carrying contest. The opinion of the majority of the local men was that if there was to be any point in having the event, then it should be called wife-carrying, and a bloke who had dropped his wife in the water jump demanded that the contest should only be arranged with a rescue team at the ready.

But the people in the district all got to hear that the money from the event had been used for what was best for Hemmavid, and the pensioners noticed this. More of the locals greeted Martha and her friends in a friendly style and obviously recognized them. This was nice, of course – but perhaps it wasn't entirely a good thing. Because now people had started to notice them.

So, for a while, the League of Pensioners decided to lie low and stick to domestic projects at home. Rake and Brains jointly extended the old greenhouse so that it came closer to the main building and provided shelter from the wind, and now you could walk straight into the greenhouse from the veranda. In addition, Rake had hung up a hammock which looked very comfy with its white sail canvas and marine-blue cushions with yacht patterns. The only problem was that nobody dared use it, let alone admit the fact. Because if you were over seventy, then you really shouldn't fall out of hammocks. So, they all praised Rake for his fancy model, but sat down on the sofa swing instead.

A few weeks after the Countryside Day, Christina was sitting in the greenhouse relaxing. The door was open so that it wouldn't get too hot inside, and Rake was busy seeing to his plants. Nowadays he didn't just have cherry tomatoes, cucumbers and chillies; he had also decorated the greenhouse with orchids. But he was humming and hawing so much that Christina suspected something was in the offing. When he was busy pottering in the greenhouse, he was always in a good mood, but now he seemed tense. And she could guess at the reason. Head teacher Irma had asked Rake for help in organizing that charm course.

'What a challenge. I can arrange that as easy as pie!' he had promised and had become so terribly proud that he felt important for several days afterwards. But now it was time to deliver.

'Rake, how are you getting on with that course?' Christina asked.

He gave a start, and then stood still with his little trowel up in the air. 'Ah, yes, it's keeping me busy,' he said.

'Do you want to talk about it?'

Rake fetched his notes and sat down beside Christina. He quickly glanced at what he had written down:

Welcome to a unique course in personal development for Panthers!

Panthers? The elderly were evidently called something like that nowadays. But what if somebody thought it was a nature or animal-care course of some sort? No, he must think up something else. Irma had talked about a course where you could teach single elderly people to become more attractive so that they could break out of their isolation. So it was about people who weren't doing so well, who could be encouraged to do better. But then the participants must learn decent behaviour – or charm.

Charm those around you, and have some fun!

Yes, well, he'd written that, but such a course sounded far too frivolous . . .

Liberate your inner strength! Welcome to a course where we seniors get to know ourselves and our fellow beings.

That sounded better, but what next? He glanced at Christina. He had already had a good look on the Internet and had written down some sentences from those self-help books. But he was definitely going to need her help.

'Christina, listen to this,' he said, looking at his notes and picking out something that sounded fancy:

'*Only with both feet on the ground can we interact with the here and now . . .*'

'Err, yes?'

Uhm, that was the problem. What the hell did it mean? It's obvious you have both feet on the ground, unless you're an astronaut! Even Miss Universe had her feet on the ground . . . This was more difficult than he had expected. But Irma had asked him, she must have seen his social competence and she had faith in him. And that meant he had to show results . . .

Rake tried to jolly himself along. What if he made use of a genuine confidence trickster? Then, wow, the course participants would learn how to charm those around them. Jeepers, that would really get the course moving! But, on the other hand, what would happen afterwards when the participants started to cheat and swindle people for real? What if the most gullible individuals in the district were cheated of money and property . . .

No, when Rake sat there, he realized that it was best to cooperate with Christina. She could give the participants tips on how to smarten up their appearance, while he would teach them social competence, clothes style, etiquette, the art of conversation, finesse and elegance.

'Well, err, Christina –'

She looked up from her glossy ladies' magazine and gave him a warm smile.

'Yes? How are you getting on, my dear?'

'It's difficult to teach charm, but we must get each and every one of them to develop the best they have in them.'

Christina put her magazine aside, and went to fetch her iPad.

'If we're going to talk about charm, we must know what it is,' she said, sitting down next to Rake again. 'Perhaps I should read out loud from Wikipedia.'

Rake nodded, and Christina adjusted her spectacles.

'*Charm is a quality in certain human personalities that includes a "magnetic" quality . . .*' she read.

Rake ran his fingers through his hair and waved his notebook. 'Yes, some have it, others don't . . .'

311

'We can teach people to keep in good physical form, to think about their appearance, to listen and care about others – and not just talk about themselves. Then they will immediately become more attractive,' Christina went on.

'Absolutely. And you should put your arm around the person you like if you want to get an even better response,' Rake added. 'Skin contact is super important.'

'And we must teach folk to dress attractively, wear nice clothes, be well washed and smell nice. And men mustn't splash on too much aftershave of course . . .'

'Smell nice? What about Horny Little Devil?'

'Pah, are you going to go on about that again!' Christina muttered. 'Don't forget that the inner qualities are most important.'

'Inner? Oh yes, sure!' said Rake and he recalled one of the beauties beside the bar in the Grand Hotel. Her magnificent bow would have been able to sink any old Atlantic steamer, but he knew nothing about her inner – then again, he hadn't prodded her by mistake, had he? What if there had been CCTV cameras and he suddenly got one of those #MeToo accusations against him? But no, he had certainly behaved properly – even though he had walked back and forth along the bar. But CCTV cameras, that made him think of . . . Rake froze. Oh my God, what if they had had cameras in the bar . . .

'Write down your suggestions and give them to Irma, and then we'll work together when it's time for the course. If you teach the men, I can take the women, and then we can combine the groups at the end of the week.'

'Yes, right, Christina.'

'Perfect, Rake, I'm so pleased we're on the same wavelength. This is going to go really well.'

And then Rake blushed and felt good again. At least he did so until he found himself thinking once more about the CCTV images.

47

Work was finished for the day and Chief Inspector Kurt Löwander put on his overcoat. He glanced out of the window and thought. Outside, an enormous full moon was rising like a fireball over the treetops, and it was so radiantly magnificent that he had to catch his breath. He would have liked to have gone out onto the balcony to enjoy the beautiful sight, but they were going to have an office party and he had promised to do some shopping for it. Mind you, he could see the moon from the road, of course. Nowadays he missed the countryside, because Bettan had persuaded him to sell their house and move to a luxury two-storey town flat outside Skogsås. It was a new building with a spa, sauna and lots of other modern conveniences. But even though it had a balcony and large windows, he missed the changes of season and having nature on your doorstep.

But now he would have a wild party with the lads, and that suited him well because he was in a good mood. Recently he had not been sent out to carry out traffic checks and he had been able to concentrate on his reconnaissance work. Allan Petterson had also supplied him with information about a gang of pensioners that had recently moved to the district.

Löwander – after struggling with his conscience – had agreed to 'mislay' the speeding ticket, and since then had received many tips from Petterson. Löwander knew that the mayor habitually nipped into the Danish Pastry café and could obtain information from there, so he wouldn't have to go himself. Petterson was a reliable source of information and he had extended Löwander's tentacles. It meant that he could relax more, like now, when he could have a party with the lads at the police station. Bettan would, of course, complain about him coming home late, but she ought to make allowances for this annual get-together, a traditional Swedish crayfish party. The others would buy the vodka, but he had promised to buy the dill and the crayfish. So he had phoned Roland Svensson's farm shop and ordered three dozen Swedish crayfish. And, to go with them, some freshly baked bread, a pie made with Västerbotten cheese, and those delicious local vegetables.

He hurried down the stairs and out to the car park. And, in a happy and exuberant mood, he got into the driver's seat, started the car and drove off towards Hemmavid. On his way, he passed the place where the pensioners had arranged their traffic checkpoint. A film recording and Polish actors, was what she had told him, that scatty old lady. And he had kept his eye out for Poles in the area, but had not come across any. On the other hand, they didn't usually stay very long in Sweden. But Allan Petterson had told him about several oldies who had been to the Danish Pastry café, and who had also run around between the market stalls and various events at the Countryside Day. They had been very involved and they spoke Swedish.

Löwander was all the more convinced: he was on the track

of the League of Pensioners. He should phone Kungsholmen and make sure that he got those CCTV images from Blomberg's flash drive. Perhaps he could enhance the image quality too, and now that he knew which people he was looking for, he ought to be able to find them there. Several oldies had been involved in the theft at the auction house in Stockholm too. It could be the same gang! And perhaps there were also new CCTV recordings that could be of interest? He had better check up on that.

When he entered the farm shop, he breathed in the smell of freshly baked bread and immediately felt hungry. He knew that some shops used the aroma of freshly baked bread to make customers more inclined to buy things, but this was the real thing and the bread had just been delivered from a newly opened local bakery. Besides the crayfish, he bought some dill, the cheese pie and vegetables he'd ordered, and a home-made vanilla and strawberry ice cream that the farm shop had started to sell. He paid with his Visa card, and was just on his way out when he noticed a colourful advert in the form of a watercolour that had been pinned up on the door:

LIBERATE YOUR INNER SOUL!

WELCOME TO A COURSE WHICH
WILL MAKE YOU FEEL GOOD

Löwander stood there and looked at the advert. What on earth was this? When he read further, he saw that it was a course on personal development. You could get to know yourself and liberate your attractive personality. And the course also invited participants to a new sense of community and a new life full of meaningful content. Well, I never, he thought, the school had evidently organized a sort of feel-good course for the locals! If he signed up for such a course, he could get away from home a while. But to *liberate your attractive inner personality*? – damned silly, as if he didn't already know how to do that!

On the other hand, he only had one year left till his retirement, and then he would be lonely. His son had left the nest and he and Bettan didn't have so much in common; it had got even worse since they'd closed down the health clinic and she had become unemployed. It had made her depressed and she hadn't had the energy to look for a new job but had only gone to seed at home and not been able to pull herself together. In the end, they didn't have very much to talk about at the dinner table, and at the same time she had begun to be more jealous. No, he thought to himself, you only have one life and he wanted to make his remaining years as pleasant as possible. If he went to a course like that, perhaps he would meet a woman – one who was a good cook and who liked to watch football. Or with whom he could share a bottle of wine . . . Löwander remained standing in front of the advert. Did he dare? He was a police officer and a lot of people might recognize him – but, of course, he wouldn't be in uniform.

He would tell Bettan that he was out doing surveillance – and that was true in a way – and if anybody confronted him, he could say that it was work. So why not? At a course like that, he would come into contact with local people who, normally, might not be seen out and about very much. They might have valuable information about the newcomers, the

48

It was overcast and the wind blowing across the lake caused the water surface to ripple. It was cool, but not so chilly that you needed an overcoat. That's nice, Martha thought, as she often felt the cold.

She and her friends had gone to the little lake, Låmmen, close to Hemmavid, where there was a boathouse, a bathing jetty and a little sandy beach. By the jetty were eight newly purchased sailing dinghies owned by Hemmavid Sailing School, which was now affiliated to Irma's school. Rake had been inspired by the successes in Brains's workshop and had persuaded Irma to let him teach pupils seamanship. Because, as he said, the sea did you good and if any of the pupils wanted to work at sea, there was plenty he could teach them.

'Just think, before these kids have left school, you are going to turn them into sailors,' said Christina, looking at the moored boats. 'And you, Brains, teach them skills and entrepreneurship. Hemmavid will soon be a model in the countryside and a place that everybody ought to visit.'

'Exactly. Rake's pupils might become seamen, and mine engineers who start their own companies,' said Brains, sounding rather proud. 'Some have already started a business. That's fantastic, isn't it!'

'We ought to take politicians out into the countryside and let them see that it's possible to have innovation here – yes, to tell them about the opportunities,' Anna-Greta reflected out loud, and realized that she herself sounded like a politician.

'But how can we go about that? The people in power are stuck to their Riksdag benches – with superglue,' said Christina.

'Actually, there is one way,' said Martha and she wrung her hands as if she hardly dared say what she had in mind. Rake sat with his legs hanging over the edge of the jetty and glanced worriedly at Brains. Because when Martha wrung her hands like that, and looked as if she wanted to say something, it meant that she was ruminating on a big project. He lightly touched her shoulder.

'Out with it, Martha, what do you want us to do?'

'A kidnapping,' she answered.

'Kidnapping? Oh Jesus! You can't be serious!' exclaimed Anna-Greta. But Brains remained calm and held up a hushing finger.

'Elaborate on that, Martha dear,' he said. 'You propose a kidnapping, but you must explain what you have in mind,' he said and he sounded very understanding and friendly. (He had sneaked a look at Rake's and Christina's notes about a charm course, and it had made a great impression on him.)

'What I mean is that we must get them here, the people in power – the politicians who decide, that is.'

'Now listen, there are three hundred and forty-nine members of parliament in the Riksdag!' Rake sighed.

'That's precisely why we must think up something cunning.'

'But how on earth are we going to get them here? They don't even go as far as the Stockholm outer suburbs, from what I've heard,' said Christina.

'Well, we could say that we are from a huge mining company and have found valuable ore deposits,' Brains suggested. 'We offer to share the profits fifty-fifty, and then they would have to come here and take a look.'

'Pah, nobody would fall for that. Can't we just say straight off that we have found gold?' Christina responded.

'And then we can spray some pheromones and fake gold from Buttericks in the love tunnels. That would make them happy and amenable straight away,' Anna-Greta giggled.

'We don't need to complicate things. I do actually have a really exciting idea,' said Martha and she wrung her hands again. 'But it will, of course, demand a considerable effort from us . . .'

49

The charm course had got off to a flying start. At first there had been very few who signed up for it, but then Christina had the brilliant idea that they should film and produce a 'makeover' programme for those participants who so wished. A film that showed them before and after. Soon the course was fully booked up. Even Rake had become curious and wanted to take part – because, after all, his self-esteem had had a bit of a knock at the Grand Hotel. But Christina said that it was hardly a good idea for the teacher to go on his own course.

On the first day, the course participants were divided into groups, and Christina – as previously agreed – took care of the ladies. She had put on her make-up carefully and smartened herself up with high heels, tight slacks and a matching jumper. In addition, she had glittering earrings and a necklace. Her 1930s-style hairdo (she had heard that this was the height of fashion today) was so elegant that any hairdresser would have been envious. She looked absolutely stunning, and the seven ladies on the course were speechless. Goodness, could a pensioner look as good as that!?

All the participants were over sixty, except for one younger lady, who must have come to the wrong course, and two rather shabby-looking fifty-five-year-olds, who looked older than their years, but who had ended up on the course regardless. The majority of them were just your average Swede, the exceptions being two weird types who were more like characters in a cartoon strip. But, as Rake and Christina had agreed, everybody would be welcome to join the course and the more people they could help, the better.

When the ladies had taken their seats in the classroom, Christina gave them a friendly smile, walked daintily up to the podium and threw out her arms.

'Hello everybody, and welcome!' she said, and swept back her hair in a feminine gesture. (She did the gesture three times so that they would all understand and get the point.) Then, briefly, she described the course syllabus, while looking at the expectant and practically dressed group sitting before her. Finally, she handed out the formal programme.

'As you might know, there is a surplus of bachelors here in the countryside. Many stylish men live on their own on their farms and long for a woman. That, my dear friends, is something we shall change now. Because you – yes, I mean *you* – can make things happen after this course!'

The ladies, with or without spare tyres, with or without make-up, and with or without a moustache, looked at one another and immediately seemed very hopeful.

'But how do you go about it?' one plump woman wondered. She had worn out many bathroom scales over the years.

'We are going to go through it all on the course,' said Christina. 'We'll give you lots of tips about health and nutrition and one should start every day with a walk using walking poles. We will feel stronger, be in better condition, and we will also shed a kilo or two. Then we shall make a visit to my wardrobe where I shall show you some clothes and tell you why I bought a particular item. We shall also learn about using make-up, how to behave in company and the right opening phrases to use when we speak to somebody – and a few other tips about this and that. You will study yourself on film, and it won't be long before you notice a change.'

'What about the menfolk? Surely it isn't just us who should have to please them?' said a woman with a hairnet and some hairs on her chin that needed plucking.

'Oh no. The men receive special teaching from our experienced male teacher. This is going to work nicely, just wait and see.'

A contented murmur filled the room and Christina felt encouraged. She clapped her hands to get their attention.

'Right, then, we can make a start. I have set up a camera in the schoolyard so that you can film yourselves. You will be able to see what you look like, your posture and how you move. Next, we will look at the films together and comment on them. Everybody can have their say, as long as you are nice to each other. Afterwards, I will show you how famous film stars move and then we will compare –' Christina stopped.

A deathly silence had fallen on the room while the ladies reflected upon this. Goodness gracious! Were they going to be filmed? Oh dear, oh dear, how could they manage that?

'All right then, let's go out to the schoolyard and make a start.'

She gathered her group together and took them outside, and it was Rake's turn to enter the classroom. Like Christina, he welcomed them all, described the content of the course and started to share his best advice: what they should look like, how they should dress, and how they could charm those around them. To his surprise, he met with some objections.

'Why would you be more attractive with a scarf around your neck?' one of the participants asked.

'Why can't you drink beer and eat crisps in front of the telly? What else can you do when you come home after work?' another wondered. This gentleman sounded quite simply aggressive. He was a former practitioner of martial arts and had such well-developed muscles that Rake didn't dare challenge him, fearing a punch in the face.

'Well, uhm – err – yes, you could have a beer at the weekend, but not every day. And not too many. Because otherwise you'll end up overweight.' He made his advice more palatable. 'Nowadays, too, you can get good non-alcoholic beer.'

'Non-alcoholic? Pah, you can stuff that up your . . .' muttered a well-built man in his seventies who looked like he had just come up out of a coal mine and had not had a shower afterwards. This was followed by silence, and Rake understood that he was in a minefield here. So, instead, he started to talk about hygiene, perfumes for men and suitable attire. Admittedly, some of the participants were properly dressed, but several didn't seem to have changed their jackets and trousers for decades.

'My jacket is from 1952 and it will last a few years yet,' the man from the coal mine assured them.

'My trousers are so comfortable – why should I change them?' asked another man, who had such saggy trousers that if he had been a stage magician he would easily have been able to conceal a rabbit down each leg. But it got even worse when Rake started to talk about perfumes for gentlemen.

'Soon you'll be telling us to spray perfume on the horses too,' exclaimed a farmer from Burträsk, who looked very dissatisfied.

'And the cocks will go around smelling of Chanel,' another said with a smirk.

It didn't get any better when Rake raised the question of health foods and suggested that the course participants cut down on their consumption of beer and bacon butties, and instead eat more fruit and greens. And then, when he – without any consideration whatsoever – started to talk about the health benefits of using walking poles, there was almost a furore.

'Haven't you got a proper gym here? I mean with bars, treadmill exercisers, cross-trainers and rowing machines? Stuff for real men – I'm not bloody well going to go around with a toothpick!' exclaimed the martial arts strongman.

Then Rake suggested they should have a break, and he hurried off to find Christina for some timely advice. Holding a course was much harder than he had thought it would be. But as they had signed up for a charm course, why were they so unwilling to listen to advice?

'It's going to be harder for you, than me. A man who knows best is hard to get through to. You will have to use cunning!'

Meanwhile, the martial artist was looking for a weightlifting bar in a storeroom, and he had got the others to go along with him. The men immediately started weightlifting, and as the participants were in poor physical shape and over sixty, it wasn't long before various infirmities showed themselves. One person sprained his wrist, another suffered severe muscle strain and on top of that two pairs of trousers – which were already worn to a shine – split.

By this time, Rake had begun to realize that he would have to tread carefully. These guys were tough blokes and he would have to adapt his teaching to the fact. Quickly, he switched to teaching about how you should treat women. When he started talking about that, they became more interested, thank God. Now feeling inspired, Rake went through his entire arsenal of flirting tricks and methods, and told them about how well they had worked, while the course participants keenly jotted down notes – including Brains, who had crept in and was sitting right at the back.

While Rake stood before the group and talked about women, they all looked very pleased – all, that was, except for a bloke with a moustache who made Rake feel uneasy. The man, whose idol must have been Errol Flynn or some similar long-forgotten 1930s actor, listened but didn't say anything. He just stared at Rake. As a teacher of a charm course, you had to be prepared to meet with some strange responses, but Rake felt uncomfortable. The man kept staring, and this was beginning to give Rake the creeps. And then it struck him: he had seen that bloke before.

50

On Monday, Tuesday and Wednesday, the ladies and gentlemen trained separately to become their new improved versions, and on Thursday morning, they looked at how far they had got. On the films that had been recorded on the course, they all saw what incredible progress they had made, and their self-esteem was boosted. On Thursday afternoon it was finally time to join the two groups together. Christina and Rake arranged an afternoon tea with croissants, and the course participants could practise having the nicest conversations they were capable of. At first, they all felt a bit lost, but soon they felt more at ease.

On the last day of the course, everybody had smartened themselves up considerably, and there was hardly a trace to be seen of the originally shy, self-conscious and clumsy course participants. Quite the opposite. Polite, friendly and worldly, they glided into Christina and Rake's end-of-course party, where the male and female senior pupils confidently used their newly acquired social skills. Some actually flirted for real, and 'Errol Flynn' Löwander put on quite a show in front of Elizabeth, an attractive woman in her fifties who had recently moved into the district. She seemed jolly and positive, and he had soon asked for her telephone number and suggested that they should get together after the course. Since she was so pretty, he also asked her if he could take some selfies, and then she smiled amicably, said it was OK, and asked him to send her the photos too.

'Isn't this meant to be a course for pensioners?' Martha asked, with a suspicious glance at Elizabeth and the other younger lady on the course, but, immediately, Rake and Brains explained that you always gained from being flexible.

Anna-Greta, for her part, wanted to make a contribution of her own, so when the course participants entered the decorated gymnastics hall with its soft romantic lighting, she approached Rake.

'What do you think? Shall I spray some pheromones on them?' she wondered, happy to do her bit since she had felt a bit superfluous during the entire course week, and wanted to help.

'No, bloody hell, no! We've got to stick to real-life situations.'

But Anna-Greta, who nowadays didn't always do as she was told, secretly sprayed some passion hormones in the gym and the hall, and stood some distance away to see the result. Nothing remarkable happened, and it wasn't until four loudly purring cats slipped inside the school building that she realized she had mistakenly used pheromones for cats instead of the Horny Little Devil.

In the evening, Christina and Anna-Greta served dainty little sandwiches and champagne, while Rake went around and chatted. But when he mingled among the pupils, it struck him that the Errol Flynn character no longer had a moustache. The Flynn lookalike had evidently realized what would serve him best, and had done something about his appearance. Smiling, he stood there with his urbane manner, holding a champagne glass and conversing with the jolly and pretty Elisabeth again. He smiled, laughed, joked and put his hand on the lady's arm – skin contact, which Rake had talked about – and not her bottom (which Christina had warned about) and seemed to be enjoying himself. But he must suddenly have felt that somebody was observing him, because, the next second, he turned around and stared at Rake. His gaze was hard and suspicious, and when he pulled out his mobile, pointed it at Rake, and started to film him, Rake wanted to rush forward and stamp on it. But he must look unperturbed, because now he had realized who the man was. He was one of the police officers that Anna-Greta had waved down by mistake at the traffic checkpoint. But why was he here? It was highly unlikely that he wanted to become a charmer . . . it felt more like he was just nosing around.

When the evening's end-of-course party was over, everyone had received their diploma and had been invited to sign up for the school's future courses, Rake hurried along to Martha.

'The police have got wind of us!'

Martha's eyelids fluttered slightly, but otherwise she showed no reaction.

'You mean Kurt Löwander?' she said with false nonchalance, but he could hear that her voice was strained. 'Yes, I noticed him; he was the man who interrogated me in Skogsås. But, as far as I know, he hasn't got anything new on us. No, I don't think it is going to cause any trouble.' She smiled and put her arm around his shoulders.

And at that moment he felt relieved that she was there,

even though he had understood that she too was scared. For sure, Martha could be difficult sometimes, but, whatever happened, he felt in some way safe with her around. Because she always had solutions and never gave up.

The day after the big party, Kurt Löwander sat in the police station in front of his computer. He had downloaded the images from his phone and could hardly wait. Of course, for a long time, he had suspected that Rake was one of the members of the League of Pensioners, but now he might have proof. Because with his new photos he could see exactly how Rake moved. At Kungsholmen police station they had worked with Blomberg's CCTV images and they had become much sharper, but Löwander had also got help from a real computer nerd who had downloaded the latest image-processing program from the US. And that had resulted in even sharper pictures than the police in Stockholm had managed. Löwander beamed with anticipation. The teenagers at the school were a real hit, especially those pupils with special talents. He leaned forward. If he viewed the images from Blomberg's flash drive and the new video recordings side by side on the computer screen, he ought to be able to see if it was the same person. What if they matched? Then it wouldn't be long before he would have Rake and the rest of the League of Pensioners put behind bars.

51

The morning sun lit up the kitchen and Martha went up to the window and drew the curtains. They had all had their first cup of coffee, a bowl of porridge and a cheese sandwich. Their joints did, of course, feel as if they were inflexible, but their brain cells were beginning to wake up. The embers in the kitchen range warmed them, and there was a lovely smell from the oven where Martha was baking biscuits. Anna-Greta opened the oven, saw that the biscuits were about be burnt, and took out the hot baking plate. Then she fetched the coffee jug and put it on the kitchen table with the biscuits. There was virtually no movement from those present. Everyone was in low spirits.

'Do you really think the police have got wind of us?' Anna-Greta wondered, and turned to Rake.

'He was so weird, that Errol-Flynn lookalike. And he filmed me, the bastard . . .'

'It's one thing to have us under surveillance, and quite another to catch us,' Martha reassured them.

'We've been far too active, that's what it is,' Brains said worriedly. 'We've been visible all over the place. Much better to lie low.'

'If they come for us, then I think we should have a plan ready. You should always be one step ahead. We can move. We've done that before,' said Martha.

'Oh not again! Are we really going to destroy everything we've built up?' Rake suddenly looked very tired.

'Of course, it would be a pity, but if it was necessary, then –' Martha insisted.

'Just not to Norway, in that case.'

'Don't say that. Nowadays so many Swedes move there that we would vanish in the crowd. Interpol wouldn't have a chance.'

'We could lie low there a while if things get too hot here, and move back here, or to Stockholm, later,' Brains suggested and winked at Martha, a clear signal that she had his support. With that, Martha regained her courage and thought that she could again mention her 'kidnap plans'. Or their future 'Politician Homestay', as she intended naming the operation so as not to frighten her friends.

'We still have a lot to do,' she began. 'It is a question of the future of our country.'

'Aha, I thought you were going to say the world,' said Rake.

'I have checked the coming programme for the Riksdag. The receptionist who answered the phone said that some ministers and members of parliament would be taking part in a conference on the environment and climate to be held in the conference centre in Fallberg.'

'But that's not so very far from here,' Anna-Greta pointed out. 'Only a few hours' drive.'

'Precisely,' said Martha. 'That's where we will have our chance. We'll entice the politicians into coming here, as simple as that.'

'And then nothing will be the same,' Rake sighed.

'Exactly! And that is the whole purpose. We shall get those in power to learn the consequences of their decisions.'

With those words, the rest of the gang woke up, and for the next hour they forgot all about the police and, instead, discussed what they should do with a bunch of politicians who needed to be converted, or, at the very least, to learn something. One daring idea after the other was bandied around, and finally they agreed on a plan in several stages. When they had finished, Martha thought that she had never before seen her gang of pensioners so ready for action as they were now. They were all fired up and you could almost see the sparks, just as if she had said they were going to rob the Swedish gold reserve. And Martha and Brains immediately started the preparations.

When the two retired upstairs late that evening, they took with them a large flip chart and different coloured felt-tip pens. They had driven to Fallberg earlier in the day and done their research, and at the conference centre had managed to get a copy of the politicians' programme. Just as at any other conference, the elected representatives would listen to lectures, have coffee breaks, lunch and dinner and also have access to the spa and sauna. It all seemed well planned and pleasant, so, to entice them away, you would have to think up something really tempting – something that the owners of the eminent conference centre couldn't offer their guests. Martha took Brains's hand in hers, and caressed it.

'You are so inventive, Brains. What do you think we can entice them with?'

'I would go for a wilderness safari with a really good dinner in front of the camp fire.'

'But how do we arrange elk, roe deer, wild boar and such-like for the safari?'

'Do you remember that red-headed boy, Jonas, who likes best of all to be out in nature? Perhaps he and some of my pupils can help? The ones who come from here ought to know a thing or two about wild animals. We can find elk and roe deer, and, with a bit of luck, even a bear. And besides, there are whistle pipe hunter's decoys.'

'What do you mean?'

'Well, there are special whistle pipes for roe deer, for example. You blow in them and rutting roebucks will come out of the forest to have a good time.'

'Why not invent a whistle pipe like that for people too?' Martha giggled.

'I'd never do that; what if you were to get hold of one?' said Brains, and he gave her a hug.

Martha and Brains sat up until very late that evening and sketched out a suitable programme. It felt just as nice and cosy as in the days when they robbed banks; that was back when they had come so close to each other that eventually they became engaged, even though Martha had so far firmly refused to get married. Now they were again planning together, and before they went to bed, they had drawn up a plan for an outing with camp fires, wilderness dinner and lots of sightings of exciting animals on the programme, including the odd surprise, of course.

'This sounds so nice that nobody will suspect our hidden agenda,' said Martha, looking very satisfied.

'Agreed. And of the sixty or so conference participants, at least twenty ought to swallow the bait. Just think, then we would get a significant share of Sweden's politicians whom we can control . . .'

'Quite something, don't you think? Martha asked.

Brains was just about to agree, when suddenly he was overcome with doubt.

'But Martha, dear, I've been thinking about something. What if there is a national crisis and we have all these members of parliament and mayors with us here in Hemmavid – then what would happen? We're not going to do anything stupid, are we?'

'No, not at all. We will just have some politicians on a homestay for the best of reasons. How else can we get them to listen?'

'But if something goes wrong, shouldn't we have a plan B, too?'

'Of course, but we'll sort that out later,' said Martha, who was beginning to feel tired after a long day and was getting a bit groggy in her head. Instead, she put her arms around his neck in a very feminine way and distracted him. And forgot all about the question of a plan B.

Chief Inspector Kurt Löwander had succeeded in improving the image quality of the CCTV recordings from Stockholm too, and, full of expectation, he sat in front of his computer and stared at the screen. Now he had the video of how Rake had stood, walked and moved during the course days and he put them beside the CCTV film from Blomberg's flash drive. So now he would have the answer. He clicked on the two icons and leaned forward. In silence, he followed the film sequences in parallel and the result delighted him. In the end he couldn't contain himself.

'Jackpot!' he roared when he saw that Rake's body language matched one of the suspected figures moving outside the Nationalmuseum and Handelsbanken prior to the robberies. And not only that, he thought he recognized the tall lady, the one with the thunderous laugh. It must have been that lady who could be seen on the CCTV images outside the Stockholm auction house. Those people he had met in Hemmavid could thus be no other than the members of the League of Pensioners. He didn't need to see any more. With a smile on his lips, he picked up his mobile and called the police station in Kungsholmen.

52

At last they were on their way! Martha couldn't have wished for a better day for an outing, yet she was nervous. Deep in thought, she looked out of the coach windows. The first leaves had started to fall and the trees glowed in all their magnificence. The sun shone and they were surrounded by the beauty of nature, which radiated so intensely and overwhelmingly as it only does out in the countryside. Now the politicians would get to see that you could live a full life amid this beauty. And that more people could live in the countryside. But at the same time, they would get to learn quite a lot more. And have the surprise of their lives . . .

The minibus bumped along on the poorly maintained roads between Fallberg and Hemmavid, and the fourteen politicians (including one government minister) bounced involuntarily up and down in their seats as a result. Except for the one major highway there weren't many road connections here in the countryside, and now the Stockholmers and all the others were forced to experience what it felt like when the politicians had stopped funding road maintenance. Martha giggled at the thought that perhaps she should have offered them kidney belts, but since roads like this were a part of everyday life for people in small country towns and the countryside, well, those in power ought to experience it too. And they ought to be happy that it wasn't raining or there was a snowstorm. Then the roads were a lot worse.

In Fallberg, the owner of the conference centre had at first turned down their proposed Wilderness Project, but when Martha promised him 20 per cent of the earnings, he immediately became interested. Martha had told him of her long experience of organizing excursions, and that she now – as the senior agent – represented the new travel agency Wilderness Safari with Surprises. He had invited her into the hotel's fancy conference centre and once there she praised not only the hotel and the delightful conference hall but also the exciting wilderness project. In a never-ending stream of words, she described the fantastic excursion to Hemmavid which included food, camp fires, and thrilling meetings with wild animals. She then handed out some glossy brochures that Christina had put together.

'A few hours' excursion in the wilderness ought to benefit you too, Peter!' she said and smiled suavely (she had learned that you should use first names when you negotiate). 'The conference participants would not return until late in the evening and would thus have to stay an additional night in your hotel, or perhaps even the whole weekend,' she ended her case. With that, the hotel owner was putty in her hands, he smiled meekly and agreed to everything she said.

On the Internet, Anna-Greta had also backed up Martha and published the new travel agency's attractive homepage where she had created lots of excellent references which looked highly credible. No wilderness safari had ever before got so many stars and thumbs-up in customer reviews . . . so when the excursion was finally advertised, all the places were booked up straight away.

Martha looked at the politicians who were being uncomfortably jolted up and down in the coach, and hoped that they would remember how important it was to have proper road maintenance. Anyhow, they would soon be served with a welcome drink and a lovely dinner of roast elk, lingonberries and local vegetables as consolation. Irma had promised to organize all of that, and she would also be helped by the teacher in charge of the school kitchen. This would be followed by a unique wilderness safari which all the members of the League of Pensioners had been involved in planning. They would entice as many foxes, elk and wild boar as they could, and also tell of ancient hunting methods and the history of the district. They would, in Christina's words, present a programme with bite. But for it to be complete, she had proposed that they ought also to recite a poem about hunting from a poetry collection published in 1838. This met with very little enthusiasm, so instead she suggested the last verse of Herman Sätherberg's 'Spring Song', which she read out to them in a deep and emotional vibrato.

Nobody said a word, and Martha needed some time to put on a straight face.

'It is so nice when you read poems and songs for us, Christina dear. But perhaps that isn't what politicians want when they are out on a wilderness safari,' she said in the most courteous manner she could, after which the others cleared their throats and agreed with her.

'We must have something which hits harder,' Rake explained.

'Oh yes, we will!' said Martha, feeling almost guilty when

she thought about everything she had planned. Because in her opinion people didn't usually understand this and that until they had experienced it themselves. And now this was the real thing. As Christina pointedly said, they must apply the pedagogical method of learning the hard way.

Now, at last, they were on their way. Martha thought for a moment that they could start singing together in the coach, but then she realized that it would be much better if she kept quiet so that the politicians were not disturbed and could look out of the window and enjoy the beautiful nature. So, while she had the microphone turned off, they passed dark forests, lakes with their mirror-like surfaces, red-painted farm buildings and traditional wooden fences and meadows where cows and horses grazed. That ought to make an impression, Martha thought, as it was important that the politicians gained a positive picture of the countryside. Not until then would they understand that it was worth investing in.

When Martha felt that everybody had seen what they ought to see, she thought it was time to confront them with the new modern reality. She nodded to the coach driver and pointed to a side road.

'Right, this is where we turn off.'

The driver turned into the smaller road towards the abandoned areas near Hemmavid where you could see the decay in what once had been a flourishing district. In silence, they passed empty farmhouses, abandoned farm fields and clear-cut forest, a landscape that had become wild and inhospitable. There was a certain feeling of uneasiness in the coach, and Martha turned the microphone on again.

'Unfortunately quite a lot of villages and farms have been forced to close down,' she said, pointing out of the coach window. 'It is completely different in Norway. They have a policy which benefits the countryside. The Norwegians are much more skilful than us.'

She'd said this as a provocation. They wouldn't like being told that Norway was better . . . she became quiet, so that the politicians would have time to reflect. Finally, a young politician from Stockholm held up his hand and Martha turned the microphone on again.

'Do you have wolves here?' he wondered.

'Not nowadays,' answered Martha, who realized that the Stockholmer hadn't fathomed anything.

'Well, do you have bears, then?' came from a man sitting on the seat right at the front, an older politician from Norrköping.

'We're going to visit a bear's den, and if we creep up carefully, we might catch sight of the bear,' Martha lied in an attempt to be agreeable. At the same time, she realized that she must be clearer. She raised her voice: 'As you can see, large parts of Sweden are being closed down. This is because it is no longer possible to support yourself here in the countryside.'

'Really, is that so?' said the man from Norrköping with a look of surprise on his face.

The road surface became even more uneven and now they passed closed-down dairies and shops, empty villages and plantations of fir trees on old, abandoned corn fields. They also drove past derelict houses, and desolate, water-filled open mines. It became noticeably silent in the bus, and even though it was normally difficult for Martha to keep her mouth shut, she refrained from saying anything. Silence can sometimes be more effective than talk. Indeed, Martha didn't utter another word until they arrived at Hemmavid. Then when the coach rolled into the village she tapped the microphone a few times, turned up the sound and loudly proclaimed:

'A hearty welcome! We have now almost arrived at our destination. There we will have dinner and there will be lots of surprises. I hope you are going to enjoy yourselves!'

'Surprises?' wondered the politician from Norrköping.

'Yes, that is what is so exciting,' said Martha, smiling.

343

53

The very moment that Chief Inspector Kurt Löwander sprayed himself with his mild men's perfume, Dolce, he regretted it. Setting off to arrest five criminals on the national wanted list, he shouldn't smell of cedarwood and cardamom; no, rather he should secrete an aura of testosterone which commanded respect. But his other men's perfume, Eros Masculine, wasn't particularly suitable either – what if he was stalked by three female criminals aged seventy plus . . .

Because they certainly weren't youngsters, the members of the League of Pensioners; no, they were more in the granny age bracket. But now, at any rate, after months of hard work, he had at last managed to trace them. He had the proof.

He put on his light-blue shirt with the word *POLICE* on the breast pocket, his dark-blue tie, flame-proof trousers and the stylish, dark uniform jacket. Those crafty villains had been on the wanted list for a long time and had so far succeeded in fooling everybody. But not him. His stubbornness had led to results and now it was he, Chief Inspector Kurt Löwander, who would arrest them! With his head erect, he went down the stairs, put on his uniform cap and overcoat and went out to his car. In just a few hours, everybody in the League of Pensioners would be under lock and key.

His Volvo estate started straight away and he accelerated towards Skogsås. His hands on the steering wheel were damp and his body tense. Chief Inspector Gert Aronsson was finally on his way from Stockholm. What a long time it had taken to convince him! He had continually made excuses and had said that he had more important things to deal with; there were Russian bank accounts and financial swindles, and lots of other stuff on Blomberg's flash drive. Löwander had told him about the mysterious traffic checkpoints with the oldies involved, and the similarities between the CCTV images from Stockholm and the video sequences he had made himself. But Aronsson was completely engrossed in his Russian line of inquiry and if it hadn't been for journalist Ingmar Sjöberg, who was forever pestering the police, then those Stockholm officers wouldn't have got anywhere at all.

'We'll get these oldies,' Aronsson had said, 'you must be patient, Kurt. We don't need to put a lot of work into catching them. It's just a matter of time before they make a blunder so that we can lock them up.'

But Löwander hadn't settled for that, and then along came that freelance journalist like a gift from above. But Aronsson's attitude was tiresome.

'So you want us to devote time to this? I hope there won't be any gang shoot-outs!' he joked in Kungsholmen. 'But, what the hell, I suppose we can pay for one day in the countryside. And when we have arrested them, we can load them up onto their wheeled walkers and we can wheel them into the police van.'

Then he had burst out laughing at his own joke. What a clown! He hadn't realized that this was the chance they needed. The League felt safe in Hemmavid and didn't suspect anything. So the police could just pick them up. But, belatedly, he and Aronsson had managed to agree to meet in Skogsås to discuss what to do. They would have to act quickly. Before the oldies began to suspect that the police were getting close.

At exactly 5.30 p.m., he parked his car outside Skogsås cafeteria and went in. They weren't going to meet until 6 p.m., but he liked to be early for appointments so that he could mentally prepare himself in peace and quiet. And he would rather wait here than sit at home with Bettan, listening to her nattering. He ordered a cappuccino and sat down at a round table with a chequered tablecloth. His marriage had been dead a long time and he was worried about his retirement. What would he do then? Get divorced or go to a marriage councillor? Oh well, he could deal with that later, just now what mattered most was the League of Pensioners. The police were on their way. And within a matter of hours the league would be caught!

He was just about to fish out his mobile and check whether he had any messages, when the door opened. At first, he thought it was the police officers from Kungsholmen, but then he saw it was Elisabeth, the nice, jolly woman he had taken selfies with on the course. He got up with a smile. Now it wouldn't be boring to wait . . .

Chief Inspector Kurt Löwander's wife, Bettan, had drunk coffee, eaten two coconut cakes and solved the weekly crossword puzzle in *Land* magazine. She yawned and was just about to make another cup of coffee when she heard the

346

telephone ring. She stood there and looked around. Where had she left it? By the kitchen sink, of course, but the ring signal was coming from the bathroom . . . then it must be Kurt's. She got up, opened the bathroom door and localized the sound to the laundry basket. She dug around among the dirty laundry and found his mobile. He must have been very stressed; he was normally so careful. She glanced at the display. Who had rung him? What if it was a lover? Now she had an opportunity to check. But what was the code for the phone?

She searched on the desk where he had his computer, lifted everything and then ploughed through the desk drawers. Nothing. But she wouldn't give up so easily. During the last week she had phoned him several times at work, but had not got hold of him. When finally she'd rung the police switch-board, she had been told that he had gone home long ago. And she had noticed his transformation too. He now dressed with care and elegance, and used a milder and more discreet perfume for men. But what she had reacted most to was the shaving off of his moustache. There was no doubt, he was hiding something . . .

She searched through the other rooms too, without result. Then she stopped and tried to think logically. Kurt was a bit lazy. If he had written down the codes, then he would have them somewhere close to his computer. So she went back to his study again. His desk was ugly and old fashioned, and she ought to have thrown it out long ago. But, yes, that was right – she had seen a film once where the hero stuck important notes under the desktop. She moved his office chair, got down onto her knees and crept under the massive oak table. And

54

The coach driver passed Hemmavid's closed-down health clinic and village shop before he turned in towards the common where a burning camp fire could be seen through the coach windows. He drove slowly past the picnic spot with its benches and tables, and continued to the far end of the car park next to the edge of the forest. Then he turned off the engine and opened the coach door. Martha stood by the exit, and smiled a welcome.

'Take care on the step. The hospital was closed down and we don't have a health clinic. If anything happens, it means a long journey,' she said, then left a short pause so that the information would sink in. She stepped to one side and let the guests pass. Then she saw that Petra, one of the politicians, was very pregnant. Oh well, that didn't really matter, the outing would only last a few hours.

When the fourteen somewhat battered guests got down out of the bus, they were met by the smiling participants from the charm course. They had all combed their hair and were properly coiffured, dressed smartly and they smiled welcomingly. They engaged in polite and friendly conversation and served dainty wilderness sandwiches to the guests together

349

with something to drink, while Rake stood in the background and kept an eye on them to ensure that they all behaved properly. When the guests had filled their *kåsa* cups – traditional carved wooden drinking cups – Martha addressed them again.

'I hope you enjoy yourselves. Now we shall drink and eat a little, and afterwards we shall continue with our wilderness safari,' she said, raising her *kåsa* and toasting the guests.

Then the politicians mingled and greatly enjoyed themselves with the participants from the charm course, who were now decidedly skilful socialites who listened and seemed interested, while at the same time handing out compliments. They charmed all they could, and never before had these regional politicians and members of parliament met with such friendly attention. It was not long before they were all in a very good mood.

'My friends, please take your seats at the table!' Martha announced when the wind carried the smell of cooking their way, and everybody had started to eye the long table. There, further in among the trees, stood a massive table that Brains and his pupils had built. The long table constructed from thick wooden planks was covered by a large sail cloth – which Rake had contributed – which was decorated with wild flowers and green pine twigs. Beside every place were beer tankards, plates and cutlery, and there were also copies of the book *Survival in the Wild – A Practical Handbook* – something that Christina thought reinforced the wilderness feeling. (But when she had said that she wanted to recite a poem about elk, she had been voted down.)

The seating at the table consisted of massive timber benches which Martha had decorated with soft sheepskin rugs and matching cushions. It all looked very inviting.

When everyone had sat down, the participants of the charm course served beer, mead, privately distilled akvavit or lingonberry juice, after which Anna-Greta served freshly caught perch with baked potatoes and grilled vegetables. There was a smell of smoke, pine needles and forest, and a barbecue aroma came from the camp fire. They soon got talking and laughing. Dusk was approaching and they were enjoying themselves all the more. Nobody noticed when Rake crept quietly away.

He had promised Martha that he would arrange the appearance of some of the forest's wild animals at the evening's event, but when he left the feast table, he felt stressed. How was he going to manage it? He had, of course, boasted that he was as good a huntsman as he was a seaman, but that was empty talk and nothing more than fancy male vanity. Admittedly, he wasn't afraid of cows like Brains, but that was about it. He bitterly regretted his promise. A wilderness safari! Wouldn't it have been better to have given the politicians a free ticket to Kolmården animal park or to Skansen zoo in Stockholm?

When the dinner was coming to an end, it was time to present the evening's programme. Martha got up, opened her arms wide and tapped her glass – and it wasn't until she heard the *dut-dut* sound that she remembered that the *kåsa* was made of wood. Embarrassed, she put the cup aside and instead announced:

'Now, of course, everyone here wants to see wild animals . . .'

'Yes, indeed; bears, wolves and a tiiiiger too!' called out the old politician from Norrköping, who had drunk rather too much wilderness punch. His straight, blond hair stuck to his sweaty forehead, and he looked decidedly the worse for wear. Martha gave him a tired look and went on.

'So we have placed some wilderness hides close to the paths where the wild animals usually pass. Every hide is camouflaged with leaves and branches, and very difficult to discover. You can go inside and sit there quietly and keep a lookout for the animals.'

The gang of politicians applauded and thought it sounded exciting, while Martha silently thanked Brains, who had arranged this. Together with Rake and some of their pupils, they had purchased the hides and placed them close to the forest paths. They were good, stable hides with small entrances and double lookout hatches. He had also put a pocket torch and a compass inside each one so that these office types wouldn't get lost in the forest. There was a soft rug to sit on, and a woollen shawl, if they felt cold.

'And take your mobile phones with you so that you can take photographs,' said Martha and she smiled when she thought about how quickly they would use up their batteries. Brains had actually set up a jamming transmitter which could block the mobile net, to be on the safe side. No unwanted phone calls could be allowed to mess up their plans. 'And finally,' she went on, 'don't forget to have your mobiles in silent mode. You don't want to scare the animals, do you?'

'And from now on, you must be quiet too,' Anna-Greta added in her characteristic thunderous voice, which amid all the excitement had increased in strength and would have frightened off tigers as well as elephants – if only there had been any.

That was the sign for them to be on their way, and, guided by Christina and Anna-Greta, they were taken, one by one, to their vantage points. When they had crept inside the hides and had made themselves comfortable, Anna-Greta reminded them yet again in a loud voice about how important it was to be silent, after which the politicians were left to their fate with the promise that they would be fetched a little later in the evening – in good time for their journey back to Fallberg.

As soon as Christina and Anna-Greta were finished, they sought out Rake and told him that it was now his turn.

'Yes, right you are,' he muttered and adjusted his dark outdoor overalls. Then he went off into the forest with Jonas Bratt, the slightly overweight pupil from year eight who knew a lot about nature. The boy was wearing a camouflage-coloured overall and had sturdy brown boots. His unruly red hair stuck out under his cap. The day before, he and Rake had discussed tactics and planned what they would do. Jonas had valuable knowledge of the district and Rake trusted him. Besides, the boy was jolly and full of positive energy, and would be good company. Jonas always had lots of ideas, and it was he who had kitted out the Crime Scene all on his own, creating a scenario which almost gave Siva Diva a heart attack. If the animals were to cause any problems, he would certainly be able to deal with them.

When Rake and Jonas had gone into the forest, Jonas pulled out his roe-deer pipe. To be on the safe side, he had taken call-pipes for foxes, wild boar, roe bucks and elk bulls, but, first of all, the politicians would get to see the graceful roe deer.

'OK, now you can start blowing.' Rake nodded and Jonas

blew hard into the pipe. After he had done this a few times, three roe deer appeared at the edge of the grove, and they felt more confident. Rake signalled that they should continue, and they quietly crept deeper into the forest until they reached a higher spot. They settled down beside the huge roots of a fallen tree and sat in silence for ten minutes before it was Rake's turn to entice elk. He had searched on the Internet and found various mating calls for rutting elk that he had practised, and now he stood up carefully and silently. Concentrating deeply, he cupped his hands around his mouth and bent his head backwards.

'Ööae, åout, äääääh,' he roared, hoping that he sounded like a wailing elk cow.

Nothing happened, nothing at all.

'Äojy, äojt,' he tried again.

'You must call against the wind,' Jonas signalled to him.

'Ah, yes of course,' muttered Rake, who had completely forgotten that detail. He tried again.

'Ööae, åout, äääääht, åout, åout, äääääht.'

This didn't meet with any response either. Then he pulled out a little tube of liquid that he had found via the Internet, and he prodded Jonas in the ribs.

'Synthetic elk urine from a rutting elk cow . . . this is really top-notch stuff! This is going to work, just wait and see!' he whispered and then slowly started to descend from their elevated position, closely followed by his companion. And while they crept silently along the animal path, he splashed the liquid here and there.

'What won't we do for the king of the forest!' he mimed, and hoped that the politicians would get to see some of

354

Hemmavid's magnificent elks. When Rake and Jonas reached the part of the path where the politicians were hiding, they each pulled out an electronic call whistle which they placed on the ground. Now they could use the remote control to entice foxes and elk to the path, without having to be close themselves. Because they had yet another task to see to. Earlier that day, Jonas and some other pupils had gathered some branches into a large pile. This would be a perfect place for wild boar to seek shelter, and now they would have to check whether they had succeeded in attracting any black boars which might be hiding themselves there. Irma had actually pointed out that there weren't any wild boar this far north, but considering how fast they were breeding, you never knew. When they were almost there, Jonas suddenly stopped.

'Fuck, the dog. We're going to need the dog after all. Wait here while I fetch him; I'll soon be back,' he whispered and vanished quickly into the darkness.

Jonas had indeed talked about his dog earlier, but then he'd said that they would probably manage without him. Perhaps Rake's rutting roars hadn't been good enough. So while Jonas nipped off home to fetch the family's tracking dog Eskil, Rake waited patiently in the forest, afraid of the wild, afraid of all the unknown animals out there in the dark. Bears could be aggressive, he had heard, and you didn't want to meet such a beast on your own. Especially unarmed. As he had rather nervously pointed out to Martha, they must be careful. It would be very awkward if the Swedish Riksdag were to lose some members of parliament because of them!

Meanwhile, some distance away, it was now time for Brains to act. The idea was that the politicians should get the most positive and exciting picture as possible of the countryside, but at the same time experience the disadvantages that had arisen as a result of them having made so many clumsy decisions. So, while these elected politicians were huddling in their hides, Martha gave the signal for the next move. She leaned towards Brains and whispered in his ear.

'It's your turn now. We must now apply the pedagogical method of learning the hard way.'

'Or, in plain speaking, you want me to cause havoc . . .'

'It's not as bad as that, my dear. Good luck!' she said, and gave him a warm, supportive hug. 'You know what it's like. Do you remember the 1970s? Then people said: "There won't be any discussion about the environment stats until the shit lands on the directors' hats". But we say this instead: "Not until Stockholmers by a power cut are hit, will they realize how deep they are in the shit".'

'Are those Christina's words?' Brains wondered.

Martha nodded, and kissed him on the cheek. 'Off you go now!'

He nodded, inhaled deeply, filling his lungs, and waddled off to the workshop where the evening's challenge awaited. Some of his favourite pupils, Sixten with his crew cut, and his mates Lasse and Sophie, had experimented with different types of drones in the workshop, and during the summer had managed to construct a whopper that could carry as much as five kilos. The drone, which they had called Spiderman, could take a load to a specific destination, release it and then return to base. That would suit perfectly. The teenagers themselves ought really to have piloted their Spiderman, but since Brains didn't want to involve them in the dubious activities of the

League of Pensioners, he had practised piloting the drone himself. Because he was going to make damned sure that he was in full control and would not be at the mercy of the wind, as had happened with those Thai lanterns.

On his way to the workshop, he went into the tool shed and fetched a steel-framed funnel fish trap which he carried out into the yard. Then he went to fetch Spiderman, fastened the fish trap on a hook under the drone, and checked that he could open and close the trap with his remote control. It all worked perfectly. He looked up into the sky. A new moon, excellent, not too much light if the police were on the lookout for criminals. He straightened his back and with his strong, veined fingers gripped the joystick. He reminded himself a final time of everything he had learned, adjusted the fish trap, put the drone in a lift-off position and pressed start. Spiderman began to make a growling sound and then lifted up into the sky and zoomed off.

55

Back in Kurt Löwander's home, Bettan was now regretting what she had done. She was ashamed, because like so many others she thought it was a dirty trick to look at somebody else's mobile phone. But as it was her husband's phone, it might be something important . . . yes, she had found innumerable excuses while she tested the various codes and passwords on the Post-it sticker. When the first three codes didn't work on the mobile, she tested them on his computer, and found that one of them did indeed work there. The fourth was for the mobile.

Now there was no stopping her, and without any qualms she clicked her way into his list of contacts. Oh my God, so many female names! And this was meant to be work? No way – he was going behind her back! What about the photos? She quickly scrolled past the nature photos, a series of pictures of elderly ladies and gentlemen and some blurred black-and-white pictures of two elderly men at a bar. On a video sequence, one of them walked back and forth holding a glass of beer and the same bloke was also on a film sequence walking across a schoolyard. What on earth was Kurt saving these for? She scrolled on and suddenly stiffened. Pictures of ladies, quite a lot of them too! And, goodness, he had even taken selfies with the prettiest of them all. Bettan checked the time marker on the photo and discovered that the pictures had been taken on the same day that he had said he was out working with his colleagues. So he was lying! Perhaps he had more secrets in his computer?

She started that up again, and systematically scanned through his files. There were documents and other job stuff, work schedules and similarly boring things. It all seemed innocent – but the folder that he called 'Important things', what was in that? She opened it and found a link to Tinder, a dating site! And several pictures of pretty girls! Tears came to Bettan's eyes. What a bastard! He had been married to her for thirty-five years, and was dating behind her back!

Kurt Löwander had drunk his cappuccino and had a nice time with Elisabeth for about half an hour when he started to glance at his watch. The Stockholm police were taking their time. They ought to be here by now. He was just about to phone them, when Elisabeth mentioned the evening's wilderness safari. She was on her way there to help with the evening.

'Aren't you going to be there?' she asked.

'Err no, unfortunately. I would have liked to have come along, but I've got some work to do.'

'Pity, but I must rush now, otherwise I'll be late,' she said with her charming smile. 'But it was nice to see you!'

Kurt Löwander blushed with pleasure and was about to say why he couldn't take part, but just managed to stop himself in time.

'Incidentally, what are you working on? You've got your

police uniform on. You didn't wear it on the course,' said Elisabeth.

And then it slipped out, although he had promised himself not to say anything. But he did want to make an impression on her.

'It's actually secret. We police officers don't usually say very much.'

'Aah,' she exclaimed in an admiring voice, which he was rather a sucker for.

'Well, you see . . . I'm busy with something,' he confided in her, not without pride in his voice. 'My colleagues from Stockholm and I, we're on to something big, you see. I can tell you later.'

There, at least, he had the sense to stop himself. He hadn't revealed anything, thank God. He looked out through the window, but the road outside was quiet and empty. He looked at his watch again. Could they have met with problems on their way here? Best to phone them. He felt in his pocket for his mobile, but stopped halfway. Damn and blast, he had left it at home. And he was going to show the latest photos to his colleagues. Would he have time to drive home and fetch his phone? No, the policemen could be here any minute. He'd better ask Bettan to bring it here!

Elisabeth nodded when he asked if he could borrow her phone, and quickly he keyed in his home number. He heard a few rings before realizing that he had phoned his own mobile. Usch! He clicked off, and was just about to phone Bettan's number, when he heard an engine and saw a police van turn into the car park.

'Oops, now I must go too, but I hope we'll see each other

360

again soon,' he said, and handed her back her phone, quickly thanking her for the pleasant company and mumbling something about important work.

Elisabeth watched in surprise as he left, paid and then went to the door. On her way out, she saw him next to the police van. Puzzled, she unlocked her Toyota, got in and fastened the safety belt. In her rear-view mirror she saw him on his way back into the cafeteria together with two police officers. Was he going in again? What on earth was he up to?

She returned to Hemmavid and stopped at the farm shop to buy something to eat. She got some fruit, bread and a wrap and looked for something to drink. A Carlsberg would be nice. Next to the shelf with various different beers, she caught sight of Christina, the elegant lady who had been one of the teachers on the course. She had several cans of beer in her basket.

'They are thirsty there in the forest!' she said smiling when she saw Elisabeth's look. 'Men do so like a cold beer.'

'Yes indeed. And I could do with one myself.'

'A pity you couldn't join us for the welcome drink. We have had such a good time. Only you and Löwander were missing. And about Löwander, I wonder whether he is ill.'

'No, he seems to be very busy. I bumped into him in Skogsås. He was in uniform and was going to meet some colleagues from Stockholm. I didn't know he was a policeman.'

'There is a lot one doesn't know about other people,' Christina muttered.

'Do you want to buy anything else?' Roland was about to close the shop.

'Err, no,' said Christina unusually quickly, closely followed by Elisabeth, who had also finished her shopping. They paid, thanked him for his help and wished him a pleasant evening. He closed the cash till and got up.

'Thank you, the same to you. Since you had that charm course everyone has been so nice and polite. It's been a pure delight. Take Löwander, for example. Before he used to be the most boorish policeman in the district, but now he is as pleasant and charming as can be.'

'On the course, he didn't say anything about being a policeman. I wonder why not?' said Elisabeth.

'If you're a police officer, you're a bit secretive and don't say so much. But he has been unusually often in Hemmavid lately. Normally, the police are rarely here at all. But now, I don't know . . . perhaps they are preparing a sting.'

Christina felt a growing uneasiness.

'But surely nothing has happened here? I mean, we don't have to be worried about criminals here, do we?' she asked.

'No, I don't think so. But you can never be certain,' said Roland Svensson, pulling down the blinds to indicate that he was closing. 'It's like they say, in the calmest of waters . . .'

56

For a drone, Spiderman was uncommonly silent and also fast. Despite the fish trap, Brains could manoeuvre the aerial vehicle surprisingly well, and when he steered it towards the power lines, all his inhibitions vanished. The countryside is like culture, he thought, so important for mankind and something that politicians talk so well of – but there is never any money from the Government. So, now, payback time!

Indeed, the further Brains flew his Spiderman, the more angry he became, and by the time he reached the power lines he was really furious. Martha had talked so much about the power grid this and that – why not do something that would really impress her? Why bother knocking out small, local electricity cables? That would only be a little fart in the universe. No, he would do what Martha deep inside really wanted to do. Teach the Stockholmers a lesson! He turned the drone northwards and continued at full speed towards the 220 kV transmission line. Once there, he hovered, aimed carefully and released the steel-framed fish trap directly above it. It crackled and sparkled in a violent flash of light. Then everything went dark.

'That's it, then, now the authorities must react,' Brains

muttered, pleased with himself, while at the same time deeply surprised at his own boldness. But then he thought about Martha again. After the earlier power cut, she had understood how effective an act of sabotage could be. And now he had arranged it. He had dared to do it, and what a smash it was too! Now she must surely be satisfied?

He was immediately in a really good mood, and in his excited state he piloted the drone away from the lines. Without losing his concentration he flew Spiderman just above the treetops and safely back to the house again. When he flew in over the roof tops, he checked carefully to make sure nobody could see him, before landing softly in the yard and turning off the engine. Quickly he dismantled the drone and carried it into the workshop.

The hours in the forest had passed unusually quickly and, so far, it had been a really eventful evening. Rake walked down the path, proud of having managed his part of the wilderness project. Together with Jonas, he had made sure that the politicians had met with experiences on an unimagined scale – although there had been more animals than he had intended. Some of it had been planned, and some of it had sort of happened, in passing. Such as that complication with the call pipes. As an older pensioner, it wasn't always so easy to remember everything.

When Jonas had finished blowing his roe-deer whistle pipe, he had wanted to switch to another one, and then Rake had given him the box with the rest of the pipes. Jonas spent a long time deciding which to use, and when he had taken out the call pipe for foxes, Rake had completely forgotten the little box in the forest. And, as ill fortune would have it, the box was then found by Kalle. Kalle with the utility moped, who was notorious for being curious . . .

With eager fingers, he opened the box, saw the call pipes and immediately wanted to try them out. Excited, he tested one pipe after the other, and simply didn't want to stop blowing. As the motley mating calls echoed over the forest, wild animals began to move in. First came a love-sick elk, followed by a flirtatious fox. Then one yearning animal after the other rushed past along the animal path, emitting various types of grunts and roars. The politicians couldn't believe their eyes.

Martha, who had gone into the forest to see how the politicians were getting on, came to a sudden halt. An elk bull galloped past in front of her to an imminent intimate rendez-vous, followed by a boisterous fox, two badgers and a passionately howling wolverine. And as if that wasn't enough, suddenly an enormous crash could be heard, and out of Rake's heap of branches there rushed a wild boar. And this far north!?

Martha quickly sought refuge behind a large oak tree when the boar ran past, while a variety of calls and mating sounds were mixed with the barking of dogs and warning calls from up in the trees. Indeed, it was as if the entire forest had come to life. For a long time, she watched the spectacle, while noticing that one photoflash after the other came from inside the hides. Now the politicians would certainly have something to talk about when they returned home, she thought, pleased, and hoped that the outing would be something that the guests remembered. But more important than that, soon their batteries would have run down completely.

Martha checked that there weren't any late-arrival wild

animals anywhere near, turned on her head torch and went off to the common to fetch Anna-Greta and Christina. Once she got there, she discovered that all of Hemmavid lay in darkness. Excellent! Operation Blackout had succeeded.

'Martha, there you are!'

Christina came towards her and looked a complete wreck. Her hair was ruffled, her face all sweaty and she was totally out of breath.

'The police,' she panted. 'They're after us.'

'Again? Are you really sure?'

'Elisabeth, the woman from the course, you know, she had seen them in Skogsås. Kurt Löwander met some policemen there who, evidently, had come from Stockholm.'

'Löwander? Pah, he has nothing on us.'

'But what if we end up in prison?'

'No way. The entire district is blacked out. The power cut will keep the police authorities busy a long time,' said Martha with a smile, and thought about Brains. You could always rely on him, and this time he had really done his bit for king and country.

'The police, oh dear me, what are we going to do?' Christina stuttered miserably.

'Don't worry, if something goes wrong, I have a plan B,' said Martha, hiding the fact that, deep inside, she too was very worried. Because some police officers had evidently come all the way from Stockholm to this distant region, and that didn't sound good. You didn't come here unless you had a specific reason . . .

'Plan B? But Brains said that you didn't have one,' said Christina, her voice sounding even more pitiful.

'But that was the other day. Now I have had time to think.'

With those words, Christina calmed down and after she fetched Anna-Greta they all went into the forest again to collect the politicians for the evening's final ceremony.

Thank God they had their head torches, because now everything lay in darkness, including all of Hemmavid, which was entirely blacked-out. But it felt good, nevertheless, because with the power cut the police would have their hands full and would hardly have time to chase old folks in the forest. So, in among the trees, she and her friends ought to feel safe. And one thing was clear: Martha had put considerable effort into saving the countryside, and that meant she couldn't give up now. Instead, she must round off the evening in a nice and tidy way. To get the politicians where she wanted them.

57

Gert Aronsson from Kungsholmen police station immediately took command and informed Löwander that he, Aronsson, was now in charge of the proceedings against the League of Pensioners. What? Löwander stood still. Would the Stockholm police take charge of the operation? He was the one who had traced the wanted oldies. If anybody was going to nick that cunning league, then it was he, Kurt Löwander, and no one else. He had done all the work, was from the area and had all the information. And the Stockholmers had simply assumed that *they* would be leading the operation. Like a colonial power!

'So you have strong evidence, I understand,' said Aronsson with his sleazy, arrogant voice, when he steered the police van now approaching Hemmavid at high speed. The van jolted uncomfortably on the bad roads, and Löwander swore to himself in the back seat. He would rather have used his own car, which had better suspension, but he had been obliged to park it in Skogsås – because, as Aronsson had said, if we're going to carry out a joint operation, then it's best if we stick together during the raid.

'Oh yes, I have evidence so we can nick them,' Löwander answered.

'Out hunting pensioners, yes, what a carry-on. Watch out, oldies, we're on our way!' said Aronsson with a laugh and Löwander felt his frustration grow. The man had such an arrogant and superior tone. Weren't the Stockholm police taking this seriously? They had done in the beginning, but then they'd just dropped the case and concentrated on Blomberg's Russian bank accounts. If it hadn't been for his own surveillance work, the League of Pensioners would have been able to continue with their dreadful robberies.

But now, this was it! At the café he had convinced the police officers that in just a few hours they would be able to bring them in. And then the League of Pensioners would at last be caught. Yes, he had welcomed his colleagues and treated them to coffee and Danish pastries and had hoped to have his contribution recognized and be treated with respect. But they had treated him like air! Above all, they teased him for having forgotten his mobile phone. And he had to admit that he had messed up – but that was only human, wasn't it?

'Do you think your evidence will be enough?' Aronsson wondered.

'Evidence? Yes, for sure. I have had them under surveillance a long time, and we also have the images from Blomberg's flash drive. I've worked on them quite a lot,' Löwander answered.

'The flash drive? OK, but there isn't much in the way of evidence there, if you ask me,' said Aronsson in his broad Stockholm dialect. 'We need more.'

'As I said earlier, when you've seen my new material, everything will fall into place.'

'All right, then, you'll have to show us,' said Aronsson and there was no mistaking the lack of conviction in his voice.

Löwander swore to himself. Was Aronsson's arrogant attitude towards him only because he was a police officer in a country town? Besides, the man was scornful about the League of Pensioners, almost as if he was ashamed of locking up older criminals. But they were certainly involved in the theft at the auction house, and several other crimes. The Stockholm police ought to be grateful. But now, evidently, they had more import-ant things to do. At the café, Aronsson had mainly talked about Russia and money laundering and shady Russian bank accounts. And it almost seemed as if he was grumpy for having to spend a whole day on this. Whereas Löwander himself, while working on the case, had actually come to feel some respect for the League of Pensioners. They were, of course, criminals, but their robberies were smart, and, so far, they had managed to trick the police and investigators throughout Sweden. It would be quite an achievement if the police could nick them!

'Jesus, what bloody awful roads you have here! More than enough to bring on a kidney-stone attack!' Aronsson went on, and his Stockholm colleague, Brynolf Jönsson, swore out loud too. The police van lurched, hit loose stones and banged against potholes so that they all had to hang on. Löwander said a silent prayer, and hoped that the search for the gang of pensioners would not end up in a car chase. Because if that happened, you would need bums of hardened steel. He had only just had that thought when the van hit a larger stone and Aronsson lost control.

'Fuck!' could be heard, followed by the familiar wobbling from a punctured tyre. The van skidded first one way, then the other; there was a scraping sound from underneath, and then it came to a halt.

'Damn, worse than bloody mogul skiing!' Aronsson roared.

'Fuck, fuck, fuck,' his colleague Jönsson added.

But Löwander sat there, silent. Because just at that moment the communication radio started to crackle and the police station in Skogsås came on line.

'There's been a power cut and there's a fire in a transformer station. Probably sabotage. Can you come immediately? We need back-up.'

Martha bumped into Brains when she was on her way to the hides where the politicians were sitting. He had his head torch turned on, looked happy and put his hand into hers.

'Mission accomplished, satisfactory result,' he said with a wink. 'Total blackout.'

'Perfect timing, because the police are after us.'

'Oh Jesus, not again!'

'Yepp, I think so. We must be ready, in any case. Thank God for the power cut. And that you did it big style. The police will be fully occupied with that.'

'I was so dreadfully angry, you see, at the way they treat us here out in the countryside,' said Brains. 'So, yes, it was one hell of a bang!'

There was a twinkle in his eyes, and he looked so proud that Martha simply had to lean forward and give him a big hug.

'Brains, my dear, you are so brave, you really are!'

'Well, Martha . . . from villain to countryside activist! Nobody can say that I'm not flexible.'

*

371

When Martha and her friends arrived at the hides, they were met with beaming faces by all. The politicians had seen so many different wild animals that they were now in the best of spirits. Somewhat dazed, they crept out of their hiding places.

'Wow, that was really something, I must say,' exclaimed the veteran politician from Norrköping who had succeeded in photographing an elk and a timid lynx with his mobile.

'And to think that there are so many different animals here – to be honest, I thought that some of them could only be found in the Skansen zoo,' said another, who thought he had seen roe deer, elk and a wolf. Martha, who realized that the 'wolf' must have been Eskil the tracker dog, kept quiet. The most important thing was that the participants were satisfied.

'By the way, why is it so dark? Has there been a power cut down in the village?' wondered a politician from Lund.

'It happens sometimes, but we are used to it,' said Martha. 'If you are worried, you can borrow my head torch.'

But then the guy flung out both his arms and said that he himself had very good night vision.

Chatting amicably, they walked to the forest glade where the League of Pensioners had planned the concluding ceremony. They had chosen the place with considerable care because in the vicinity of Hemmavid there were some old foundries and prehistoric hunters' pit traps which illustrated the ancient history of the district, and which would give the visit an extra dimension. Earlier in the day, Christina and Anna-Greta had prepared the setting, so that when the group arrived, the solar lamps were turned on, the podium of tree trunks set up, and, beside the old pit trap, there were flaming torches. Christina and Anna-Greta had been inspired by various entertainment programmes on TV, and above all had been fascinated by the scenario around the Robinson reality game show and its atmospheric island council.

'If they can do it, then so can we; a few burning torches will work wonders,' Christina had said, and Anna-Greta had thought so too.

When the politicians had gathered together, Martha ascended the podium of tree trunks and in the flickering glow of the torchlight started to tell them about the prehistoric methods of trapping animals. She pointed to the old pit trap next to them.

'This is from the Stone Age, and as you see, that is how they hunted here in those days. Indeed, for tens of thousands of years, people have gone hunting here, while today we have been able to enjoy the wilderness without having to kill any animals at all.'

'Yes, right; you have to be climate-smart and eat veggies because lettuce doesn't fart,' the man from Norrköping could be heard muttering. His colleagues found him rather embarrassing.

'You have seen game and taken pictures of them without needing to hunt them for real. Which is fantastic, isn't it?' Martha went on. 'Feel free to take photos of the pit trap if you want, but first I would like to hand out a little surprise.'

Christina came forward out of the dark, and handed over a bag with fourteen mushroom-picking knives and a bundle of fancy diplomas on handmade paper with the names of the participants inscribed. Martha smiled.

'It has been really great fun being your guide here today when you have been able to join us in nature. And so that you will remember Hemmavid, we want you each to have a pleasant memento.'

She then called up the participants one by one, and handed out the present and Christina's diploma. The diploma was a beautiful watercolour with elk and roe deer that Christina had painted, and an appreciative murmur was heard all round. Then the participants took selfies holding their diplomas, which they just about managed, because they hardly had any battery power left in their mobiles. Finally, Brains gave each of them a piece of paper, a pen and a board to write on.

'Would you be so kind as to write down what you thought of our little outing? Yes, see it as a course evaluation,' he said.

'But hang on a moment. We must take a group photo first. You mustn't leave before that,' Martha called out, and at this given signal Christina and Anna-Greta each set up a paraffin lamp on either side of the pit trap, and handed a camera tripod to Martha.

'Yes, of course we must take a group photo,' the politician from Norrköping exclaimed, slurring his words. 'I'm going to stick that up on the wall.'

'Righto,' said Martha, adjusting the tripod and pointing the camera towards the politicians. 'Could you please bunch up a little bit?'

The politicians nodded and moved closer together.

'Good, very good,' Martha called out enthusiastically. 'And those among you not so tall, could you stand at the front, and everybody check that you aren't in the way of those standing behind you?'

Martha waited while some of them swapped places, and those who stood on the edge moved further in towards the middle.

'This is going to be really nice,' she went on. 'But just a bit closer, I can't fit you all in. Could you take a couple of steps backwards?' And she gesticulated with her arms as she had seen proper photographers to. 'Excellent, this will be perfect!'

Then she waved the pregnant Petra to come over, gave her a flash unit and asked her to help with positioning the lighting. But this was just a manoeuvre. Because, the next second, a sound was heard from the forest and Martha quickly turned round.

'Oh!' she exclaimed, turning back to the front and waving her hands. 'Back, back, wild boar!'

And like an obedient grey mass, the gang of politicians moved those extra few steps backwards – all that were necessary for Martha's plan to work. A moment later, she and her friends could see a sprawl of arms and feet when the lot of them – except Petra, of course – tumbled backwards and disappeared into the pit trap. The very next moment, Rake came out of the forest with a huge smile on his lips.

'It worked!' he whispered.

Martha gave him a colluding wink, made sure her face didn't reveal anything, and went up to the pit.

'Oh my goodness, dear, oh dear, what a misfortune! You haven't hurt yourselves, have you?'

Mutterings and groans could be heard, but nobody seemed to be hurt.

The rest of the League of Pensioners went up to the pit and looked down. Yes, it was evident that Brains had done his job. The politicians had landed softly and fairly comfortably on all the fir-tree twigs – albeit all in a heap. But the pit had been sufficiently soft and padded so that they wouldn't get hurt, and it was deep enough so that they couldn't get out. So they were stuck there, helpless. Martha turned to Brains and said in a low voice:

'They just need to get their breath back, and then we'll get going.'

He nodded and Martha leaned over the edge of the pit.

'Dear me, dear oh dear, you poor things!' she lamented again, holding her hands in front of her face in a dramatic gesture, while at the same time finding it difficult to keep a straight face – it did look extremely comical with all the politicians who usually sat behind their desks and who had now got stuck in a pit . . . 'Yes, oh dear, what a to-do! But don't worry, we shall fetch help immediately! And, meanwhile, we will have to entertain ourselves as best we can.'

58

'Entertain ourselves as best we can?' A hard-to-decipher muttering could be heard from down in the pit.

'We could play hide-and-seek!' the clown from Lund called out.

'Or why not Stations, without chairs?' another of them suggested.

'While you are waiting for help, you could make yourselves comfortable. Play games, or talk with each other. While we go and fetch ladders, that is,' Anna-Greta suggested.

'Yes, or why not fill in that course assessment questionnaire now, so that we save time. You have pen and paper,' Martha went on.

Now Brains went up to the pit and pointed the solar lamps down at them. They had already been turned on for several hours and weren't as bright as they had been.

'I hope you can see sufficiently well to write, otherwise –'

'Can't you simply phone for help and make sure we get out of here?' the man from Lund cut him off.

'Yes, ring the fire brigade!' the Norrköping man added.

'The fire brigade? Sorry. That has been closed down.'

'But the one in Skogsås, then?'

'Yes, but it's difficult to phone them from here. We don't have mobile coverage.'

'But send someone to Hemmavid, then, damn it! You've got a bloody landline, surely?' shouted the politician from Norrköping.

'Unfortunately, no,' said Brains.

'And we don't have any Internet either. It's as bad as that,' Martha informed them, although it was only partially true, because it did work in some parts of the village.

An astounded 'What!?' was heard from down in the pit.

'Ah, so you have to go to the bank when you pay your bills, then?' concluded a female politician from Stockholm who usually looked after the family finances.

'No, the bank branch has closed down.'

Now it was completely silent down in the pit, and Martha was pleased to note that in a remarkably short time she had been able to inform them as to the lack of facilities in the countryside. The pedagogical method of learning the hard way . . . but she wasn't done yet. And if this was going to work, she must keep the politicians in a good mood.

She sent Christina and Anna-Greta to fetch the baskets of sweets and other goodies, and they soon came back with a wilderness punch bowl, beer glasses, crisps and nuts – and some Jungle Roars. They lowered the goodies down into the pit on a string, and encouraged the gang down there to help themselves. Then Anna-Greta addressed them.

'Unfortunately, this is all we have. We couldn't buy anything in the shop. The cash tills don't work without electricity.'

'But drive to Skogsås then!' came a grumpy voice down on the bed of twigs.

'Yes, but we can't fill up with petrol here, and we must

leave enough petrol in the coach for you to get home this evening,' said Christina.

'But the wilderness punch bowl, that's rather tasty, isn't it?' Anna-Greta tried to console them, and toasted everybody to keep their spirits up. Then she and Christina each sang a song to cheer the politicians up a bit, a lively waltz they had composed themselves called 'Life is full of pitfalls'. And then they toasted again. When the punch and the nuts had started to have an effect, and the atmosphere got better, it was easier for Anna-Greta to deliver the next announcement.

'Unfortunately, we have bad news. The electric grid has malfunctioned so we can't get the fire brigade to come straight away. There have been an awful lot of emergency calls and they are tied up everywhere.'

'So we will have to wait a while for the ladders,' Christina added.

'But I've sent people out to look for ladders, so we shall get you out as soon as possible. Besides, we've got some more light on its way. We do have Kalle with his utility moped.'

Martha had put her foot down about one thing, that when they actually had all these politicians on the spot, it was important also to show them what was possible. And Kalle, with his utility moped, was a perfect example of a young entrepreneur who would be very successful if only the politicians would help with some development funds. So, when the torches and the paraffin lamps had stopped burning, and the solar lamps had faded, Brains went to fetch his pupil. The rest of the gang remained standing around the pit and engaged in friendly conversation, until Anna-Greta suddenly decided that more must be done.

'We must have a word,' she said, and signed to her friends to follow her away from the pit so that they wouldn't be heard. When they had sat down on some stones and tree trunks, she cleared her voice and said in a firm tone: 'We are far too nice and polite! Now that we have caught a gang of politicians in a pit, then they should not be able to slip away, no indeed not.' And since she was speaking unusually quietly, Martha realized that she meant this seriously.

'Yes, but everything is going well. They have been able to learn a bit about what it is like in the countryside today; what more can we do?' she asked.

'We must be even tougher, teach them a proper lesson. We won't let them out of the pit until they give us legally binding promises,' Anna-Greta hissed, clenching her fist at the dark night sky. 'No electricity, no petrol or trains, hardly any buses, no shops, no health care, no dispensing chemists, and closed-down bank branches. How is this country actually being governed?' she went on, inhaling so deeply that her breaths almost sounded louder than her voice. 'And you know what I think is the worst of all?'

Now Martha was getting really worried. 'No, what would that be?'

'The dispensing chemists hardly stock any medicines now-adays, they sell mainly skincare products and make-up. We are all going to die, the lot of us, if the politicians don't shape up and start making demands.'

'Now, now, Anna-Greta, they still sell some medicines, surely?' Martha tried to console her.

'Martha, most of their medicines are out of stock, and lip

380

gloss won't help if you've got an irregular heart rhythm. That's a fact!'

They all looked at their friend in astonishment. They hadn't heard her be as determined as this for a long time.

'But the politicians down in the pit, what are your ideas there?' whispered Christina.

'They must promise that the countryside is put on the political agenda before the end of the year. They must propose concrete plans and fund them. OK? So now we give them a list of our demands for necessary measures. A document that all of them must sign.'

'Ah, yes, then it would be legally binding,' said Martha, and she looked appreciatively at her friend. Anna-Greta was superb when it came to the economy, and she seemed to know about legal things too.

'But how on earth are we going to get them to sign?' Christina wondered.

'Pah, easy as pie. We simply say that it is a quiz. Then if anybody protests, it won't matter. Oral agreements are not worth anything. What counts legally, is what is written down on paper. I wasn't born yesterday!' said Anna-Greta proudly, and even though she was speaking very quietly, you could still hear a slight neighing sound.

'That's very smart, you're a genius Anna-Greta!' Martha exclaimed and hugged her. And they would have liked to cheer and toast – and sing a celebratory song in harmony too. But unfortunately they would have to wait. You should never count your chickens before they are hatched.

59

Kurt Löwander swore like a trooper. Now that he had finally got the Stockholm police to come up here, and they were going to nick the League of Pensioners, the van had got a puncture. And as if that wasn't enough, the wretched vehicle had been knocked about so much on the bad roads – and it was a low-slung van, not a SUV, so the chassis had evidently smashed into something or other; they didn't know what. So, even though they had managed to change the wheel in the light of some head torches, it was difficult to start the van. When finally they got the engine started, it stopped almost immediately. They could drive along at a snail's pace, but not much more. They didn't know why, and unfortunately none of them had much of a clue about engines. And as if that wasn't enough, the emergency control centre had asked them to intervene. The power cut had caused chaos and they needed all the help they could get.

But Löwander protested. 'Not a chance! Our van has broken down. Contact somebody else!' he hissed, and turned off the communication radio, irritated.

Aronsson's overweight colleague poked his head between the seats at the front, and said: 'Well, seeing as we can't nick those oldies straight away, we might as well go to your place and have a snack. And we could have a look at your evidence on your computer, Kurt.'

Löwander was no fool; he had indignantly noted what had come first. The Stockholm police wanted to start with a snack, and then – perhaps if there was time over – they would look at his evidence. What shitheads! But of course he only had himself to blame; he had forgotten his mobile. And now he would have to show himself ready to cooperate.

'Good idea! OK, we'll go to my place,' he said, and they proceeded to drive as fast as the engine trouble would allow.

It was with mixed feelings that, a couple of hours later, Kurt Löwander, entered the two-storey house outside Skogsås. The van's engine had stopped several times and his colleagues were tired and somewhat the worse for wear after the uncomfortable journey. Löwander, too, was worn out and shouldn't really have noticed the atmosphere in his house. But, as soon as he opened the door, he felt something was wrong. Bettan said a brief hello, but her countenance was neither warm nor welcoming. She just looked extremely serious. He glanced around. On the kitchen table was a plate of half-eaten food, and in the living room there was a paraffin lamp and some candles. A fire was burning in the open fireplace: there was still no electricity.

'We had some problems on the way, so I thought I'd invite my colleagues here for a snack and some coffee,' he explained.

'Right,' she said and turned her back on him. She wasn't usually so unfavourably disposed towards him, not even when he put whites and coloureds in the same wash with unfortunate results. So, to appease her, he hurried down into the cellar and fetched two paraffin lanterns, scented candles and

383

a primus stove. Then he lit the lanterns and candles and got the primus stove going.

'I'll make the coffee, and we can sit on the balcony. You'll come and join us, darling?' he tried, in a jolly voice.

'Coffee with you? No, Kurt, but you can all drink coffee.'

She got a cardamom cake and a tin of biscuits from the pantry, and while he brewed the coffee, she got cups and saucers out and put them on the balcony table. Then she walked past her hubby with a flash drive in her hand.

'Have you seen this?' She smiled with cold eyes, and before he could say anything, she answered herself: 'There was a memory stick on the desk, so I filled it with our old holiday snaps and the photos of the children. Family picture that is. That's good, isn't it?'

Kurt Löwander froze. Had Bettan started to mess about with his things too? He couldn't stand her growing jealousy. But he controlled himself, showed Aronsson and Jönsson where they could sit, and once they were comfortable, he poured out the coffee. Bettan came out with the plate of cakes, and put that on the table.

'The power cut caused a problem, so regrettably we had to wait before we could make our arrests,' Löwander explained, making an effort to sound friendly.

'Yes, you seem to have been kept busy at work,' she said in a strange tone. She got up and went to fetch his mobile and computer. 'But you forgot this.'

'Thank you, darling, yes; I was in a bit of a rush this morning.'

Aronsson and Jönsson each took a piece of cake and furtively looked at Bettan.

'A shame about the mobile. Elisabeth phoned,' she went on.

Elisabeth? Kurt Löwander stared, not understanding. Then he twigged: Bettan must mean Elisabeth from the course. He had borrowed her phone when he'd tried to phone home. And he had, of course, phoned his own mobile by mistake. But how could Bettan know who had made a call to his telephone? She must somehow have got into his mobile . . . Löwander felt a growing unease and started to sweat. Quickly he steered the conversation to the subject of the computer instead.

'Great that you brought my laptop with you. I shall be showing some important pictures to my colleagues here.'

'Yes, you do that. Are you thinking of the girlie pictures?'

The ground started to shudder. Fuck, she had got inside his computer too! Löwander was at a loss. How on earth could he wangle his way out of this? Then he thought of something.

'You know, Bettan dear, that material is confidential, so you'd better forget that you've seen it. We are working on an important investigation about trafficking.'

'So that's why you're dating girls on Tinder? Nice contacts you've got there.'

'No, I mean, you mustn't think – we're busy with an important investigation and it is really tragic because, well . . .'

'Nothing is like the bothersome things we meet with in life,' she said, 'but I'm happy to help you to forget. Indeed, even to be rid of the problem.'

Before he had a chance to react, she had lifted up the computer and thrown it over the balcony railings. And, yes, he didn't even manage to get up before she had grabbed his

60

By now it was ten o'clock in the evening and the unfortunate politicians were still stuck down in the pit trap. Anna-Greta did all she could to entertain them, while Martha regularly went up to the edge of the pit and said how sorry she was that they hadn't managed to get help yet, but that assistance was due to arrive any moment. But after a while, Martha noticed that the pit guests were now decidedly restless, and she went and fetched Brains. It was now time for the evening's quiz and for that they must have the utility moped.

'Time for Kalle. We need more light.'

'Yes, we do indeed. Now the politicians shall see the light,' said Brains and he disappeared into the dark behind them. Shortly afterwards the clattering sound of a moped could be heard and the treetops were lit up.

'This is Kalle, one of my pupils. He has invented a utility moped with powerful solar-cell batteries. When there's a power cut, he can come to our assistance,' Brains proudly explained when he presented the boy by the edge of the pit. 'Now you'll have some light, so you can see down there,' he said, and together with Kalle, he directed the spotlight so that the bottom of the pit was fully illuminated.

'There is a lot one can do in the countryside, and there would be even more if we could just get some funds for development,' Martha pointed out. 'This utility moped also works as a complete power bank.'

'Soon it will be possible to charge ten mobiles with it,' said Kalle enthusiastically. 'And I've got a whole lot of other ideas too.'

'Perhaps you could invent some steps,' muttered the Norrköping man, who wanted to get out as soon as possible; he wasn't so popular down in the pit on the bed of fir twigs. In the semi-darkness down there, easily tempted, he had started to put his hands on the female politicians, which he shouldn't have done. One of them hissed defiantly and elbowed him in the belly so that he saw stars; another one kicked him in the crotch so that he sank to his knees; and a third put her hand down his trousers and twisted the propeller so that it almost got into a knot. And all because he had been a bit affectionate. No, indeed, he didn't want to stay down in the pit a second longer.

'Now we have some light for the concluding quiz. So, paper and pen at the ready!' said Anna-Greta, looking down at the somewhat bruised group.

An affirmative mumble was heard from down below, except from the Norrköping man, who wasn't fit to partake and had some wounds to lick.

'Right you are, then; I thought that you could make a wish list of things that you would like to alter here in the country-side if you, yourselves, had the power to do so. In other words, what would you do if you had a free hand? Do you get it?'

The politicians discussed this for a few minutes down on the fir twigs. The murmuring now seemed a bit livelier.

'So I have chosen a few subjects which might interest you,' Anna-Greta went on. We'll do it like this: I'll give you some examples and you can write down what you think of them. You can write it down as a sort of promise. Yes, it would be best if you wrote, for example: *"I promise to . . ."* – do you get it? Then it will be more realistic.'

A weird quiz, some of them thought, because in a quiz you usually got to choose between various multiple choices, and you put an X by your answer, but by now most of them were so tired that they hadn't the energy to protest. Besides, they didn't have anything else to amuse themselves with. So they nodded and said yes without really understanding.

'Right, question number one. We can start with a topical issue,' Anna-Greta continued. 'There has been a power cut and we don't have any electricity. How would you solve the problem politically? You can write it on one line.'

Anna-Greta was then silent as she let them write. When the scraping of the pencils ceased, she went on.

'Bank branch offices have been closed down. What would you do about that? You can't use more than fifteen words in your answer.'

The politicians (one government minister, several municipal mayors and members of parliament) immediately thought that this was a really interesting quiz, because it was about topical issues. So, they happily answered, enthusiastically cheered on by the Mary Poppins figure up there. Without further reflecting on what the quiz might be good for, they wrote down their answers to questions about postal deliveries, bus transport, road maintenance and whether the big companies ought to pay tax in the district where they got their electricity, iron ore and timber – or somewhere else. Anna-Greta kept firing questions at them, and soon they had also given answers on what they would do about closed-down petrol stations and health clinics, and what they thought about illegal lorry transports and the large-scale clear-felling of the forests. The politicians were even asked about the foreign mineral prospectors. The involuntary guests down in the pit trap continued to write, but just as Anna-Greta was about to ask the very last question, a grumpy voice was heard from down in the twigs.

'Haven't you got any more amusing questions? This is more like work!' the Norrköping man muttered, tired and feeling that he had been totally ostracized in the pit. The women were still angry with him, and he had a hangover.

'We can end this straight away if you want. But just don't forget to sign your answers. We shall draw lots among the three best answers, and give a large elk joint to the winner.'

There was more scraping of the pencils, after which Martha lowered a bucket and let it be filled with the A4 sheets full of answers and signed by each and every one. Soon the bucket was full, and when Martha pulled it up, she saw the politicians' neat signatures under their promises. Oh my, oh my! Anna-Greta had achieved great things!

'Good luck to you all, then,' Anna-Greta called out, waving to them down in the pit. 'We're busy collecting ladders, as fast as we can. Because in the countryside we help one another.'

'We're not bloody well sitting here another fucking minute!' shouted the Norrköping man, and Martha reacted immediately. It would be best to put the dampers on that dissatisfaction straight away, she thought, and immediately announced the big elk-joint lottery. While Sweden's politicians were waiting for rescue from down there on the fir twigs, Martha drew lots for a lovely big elk joint. But first she discreetly checked that everybody had behaved themselves and filled in the quiz, because that was the material she needed for the future. She quickly glanced at the answers and her face lit up. The politicians – including the pregnant Petra, who was there by the side of the pit – had unknowingly committed themselves judicially with their written answers and their signatures. Martha was overjoyed. Now she had them in the palm of her hand. If they didn't fulfil their promises, she would simply contact the newspapers.

She turned to Brains, who was waiting in the background. 'That's it, then,' said Martha. 'Mission accomplished, now we can get them out.'

And since Brains had already asked Kalle to bring some ladders on his moped, everything suddenly moved very quickly. Together, they took two strong aluminium ladders, which they lowered into the pit, where eager hands helped to steady them.

'You're so handy!' Martha exclaimed cockily and welcomed the politicians back up.

One after the other they managed to climb up out of the pit, and when they were all up on ground level, Martha led them along the path. They walked together behind Kalle on his moped which lit up the path in the dark. It took a while, but eventually they all safely reached the common where the driver waited in the coach. He had been listening to the radio.

'According to the police, the power cut will last until tomorrow,' he informed them. 'Dreadful with sabotage like that.'

'Unless it was fallen trees,' Martha said innocently. Then she turned to the evening's wilderness guests. 'I hope that you've had a nice day, even though it might have gone on a bit longer than you had expected. I wish you a pleasant journey back to the hotel, and don't forget your diploma.'

The Norrköping man, who had felt so miserable earlier, was now in a good mood again since he had won the elk joint on the quiz which he thought was on account of his intelligent answers. But it was, of course, Martha who had juggled with the lottery. Because, in her opinion, the most important thing was to keep the politicians in a good mood so that they would work hard for the countryside.

The government minister, the town mayors and the eleven members of parliament thanked their hosts for the outing, picked the twigs off their clothes, combed the fir needles out of their hair and then – on rather unsteady legs – got into the coach and sat down. The wilderness safari had indeed been a lot more adventurous than they had expected, but they all agreed that they had experienced something very special. Or, as the MP from Lund put it, 'It's the unusual things you remember, and it will be a long time before we forget this.'

'Excellent,' said Martha. 'Is there any new experience that you will be taking with you?'

'We thought that it was like it used to be in the countryside, but it isn't,' he said, and the others nodded in agreement.

'In that case, I hope you will do something about it. And you promised to do so in the quiz,' said Martha, looking deceptively friendly. And if you don't, she thought silently, well, I've bloody well got your promises on legally binding documents!

Martha and the League of Pensioners waved their guests goodbye, and traipsed home to their house very pleased with what they had achieved. What they didn't know was that just as the coach was about to turn out of Hemmavid in the direction of Fallberg, Petra Wall, MP, grabbed hold of her seat and shouted out:

'My waters have broken!'

And then there wasn't much choice: the politicians had to put up with a long detour, while the driver tried to find the closest hospital, which was 260 kilometres away.

The unfortunate politicians didn't get back to their hotel until early the following morning. They hadn't only seen the wild animals in the forest, but also a baby boy, born on the floor of the bus.

When the fourteen politicians were back at work, they were all in agreement: it was high time to do something positive for the countryside.

Epilogue

The League of Pensioners sang as loudly as they could and there was a lovely atmosphere in the minibus. They had escaped from the police and had every reason to celebrate. But then Martha started up the Norwegian national anthem, and that was too much for Rake, who put his hands over his ears in the back seat and felt sorry for himself. Not that as well! He had been outvoted at the latest morning meeting when the others had decided to move to Norway. And now it was too late to do anything about it. In a fully loaded minibus with a trailer and false number plates, the whole league were on their way to cross the border – to a nation which allowed its countryside to live, and took better care of its citizens.

They had had little choice but to move, because the police had succeeded in tracking them to Hemmavid. And even though the police hadn't managed to arrest them, it had become too dangerous to stay on. But Norway, of all places!

'Sing along now, Rake; don't just sit there moping,' was heard from Christina, who was rocking the *David and Venus* statue in her arms. 'You have such a lovely tenor voice, and *Ja, vi elsker detta landet*' is really beautiful!'

The beautiful Norwegian national anthem was sung in

another round in the minibus, while Rake groaned. After which Martha hushed the singing and gave him a sympathetic look in the rear-view mirror.

'Norway is a great shipping nation, my dear, and we can stay here for a while, until everything has calmed down. In the meantime, we can settle down outside Oslo or Stavanger, close to the sea, if you want, so that you can see lots of ships.'

Rake stopped moaning. What was there really to complain about? The police hadn't succeeded in nicking them, and they could actually have quite a nice time in Norway. Via the Internet, they had managed to sell the Russian diamond earrings to a Thai billionaire who had paid eighty million kronor and had also offered to pay an extra million for the sculpture – which made Christina as proud as could be. But she refused to sell it, because the memory of what it had been involved in was worth much more than a million, in her mind.

With the money from Thailand, they had started a development fund for young entrepreneurs in Hemmavid. And that was very timely, because Brains's and Rake's pupils had become so clever that they had been able to take over the workshop as well as the sailing school.

Besides, Irma's school wasn't going to close; it would flourish with its broader teaching for specially gifted teenagers. Irma had taken over the Gerry Gang's house and Rake's plants and vegetables, and now the school was going so well that politicians from all over the country were phoning to book study visits. Things were actually looking very promising for Hemmavid, and Martha was happy. The countryside recipe from the League of Pensioners (or, rather, from Norway) was now being spread.

The League of Pensioners, too, hoped for a bright future. They would sell the Carl Larsson painting for a very high price in New York, and have that as the starting capital in their new home town – while Martin Borge would have to settle with Christina's painting instead at his stud farm.

In Norway, Brains was going to open a new workshop, Anna-Greta looked forward to meeting the tall, stylish Norwegian men who could match her in height, and Christina planned to open a library. Rake, for his part, wanted to start building model ships and Martha was busy doing research on the best way to steal Norwegian oil. In short, almost all of them were in the process of adapting to their new life situation.

On Roland Svensson's farm in Hemmavid, they were in high spirits. Because Sequin had given birth to a foal, and not only that – the foal was like Sharp Eye. Or, as Roland had texted Martha: *What a horse! He is going to be a real money spinner. And when he has finished competing, I shall sell him for thirty or forty million, and the profit shall go to Hemmavid . . . I say, like you and your friends, that we have to invest in the countryside!*

And when the League of Pensioners got that report, they raised their champagne glasses and started to sing 'The Champagne Gallop' – as they always did after a successful coup. Because now Sequin's foal would race his way to more money for the countryside than anything the League of Pensioners would ever have been able to get in an ordinary bank robbery.

Acknowledgements

To write is a lonely profession, but while writing *The Little Old Lady Strikes Back* I am very grateful to a lovely group of people who has helped and supported me.

Great thanks to my publisher Teresa Knochenhauer and my editor Liselott Wennborg Ramberg at Forum, Stockholm who have worked and helped me with the manuscript. I would also like to give my warmest thanks to Gunnar Ingelman, Lena Sanfridsson and Ingrid Lindgren for reading the chapters and giving advice and making sensible observations while I have been working with the book. I am also grateful to Mikael Ruttkay Hylin, Berit and Anders Wästfelt, Magnus Nyberg and Anna Rask who have read and given me valuable comments.

A special thanks to Rod Bradbury for translating the works into English and Marian Reid for fine-tuning the translation. To Wayne Brookes, my English editor at Pan Macmillan, Kate Tolley, Rebecca Needes, Daisy Bates and the wider team at Pan Macmillan who worked on this book, thank you for all your work bringing the story to a new audience.

In addition I am grateful to Barbro von Schönberg, Annete Sporrong, Maria Paz Acchiardo, Fredrik Ingelman-Sundberg, Isabella Ingelman-Sundberg and Kerstin Fägerblad for encouragement, support and rewarding comments.

THE LITTLE OLD LADY WHO BROKE ALL THE RULES

CATHARINA INGELMAN-SUNDBERG

Seventy-nine-year-old Martha Andersson dreams of escaping her care home and robbing a bank.

She has no intention of spending the rest of her days in an armchair and is determined to fund her way to a much more exciting lifestyle. Along with her four oldest friends – otherwise known as the League of Pensioners – Martha decides to rebel against all of the regulations imposed upon them. Together, they cause uproar: protesting against early bedtimes and plasticky meals.

As the elderly friends become more daring, they hatch a cunning plan to break out of the dreary care home and land themselves in a far more attractive Stockholm establishment. With the aid of their Zimmer frames, they resolve to stand up for old-aged pensioners everywhere. And that's when the adventure really takes off . . .

The Little Old Lady Who Broke All the Rules is an incredibly quirky, humorous and warm-hearted story about growing old disgracefully – and breaking all the rules along the way!

'A good-natured, humorous crime caper'

Independent on Sunday

THE LITTLE OLD LADY WHO STRUCK LUCKY AGAIN!

CATHARINA INGELMAN-SUNDBERG

The little old lady is back! This time, Martha Andersson and her friends – the League of Pensioners – have left behind their dreary care home in Stockholm and are enjoying the bright lights of Las Vegas.

This is their opportunity for a new lease of life and they plan to make the most of it. But before long, they are up to their old tricks. And with ingenious tactics, a pair of false teeth and a wheelchair each, they plot to outwit the security system at one of the casinos. As their antics become more and more daring, Martha and her friends head back to Sweden to continue their money-making schemes. However, they aren't the only ones planning on stealing bucket loads of cash and soon find themselves pitted against a gang of dangerous criminals.

Can the group of elderly friends work together to outsmart the younger robbers and get away with their biggest heist yet? Or will this job be a step too far for the League of Pensioners?

THE LITTLE OLD LADY BEHAVING BADLY

CATHARINA INGELMAN-SUNDBERG

The third hilarious installment in the much-loved series: *The Little Old Lady Behaving Badly*.

Nothing can stop The League of Pensioners, a wily gang of blue-rinsed rebels. They have a plan and to realize it they are going to need money, lots of money.

Martha and her friends set out to catch some of the biggest financial fish in the sea. In their hunt for the big bucks, the gang plan to cheat billionaires out of their luxury yachts in the south of France's sun-bleached Saint-Tropez.

But with the police hot on their heels, will this group of unassuming conspirators be able to cover their tracks?